THE CAPTAIN'S DAUGHTER

ALSO BY MEG MITCHELL MOORE

The Admissions
The Arrivals
So Far Away

· THE ·

CAPTAIN'S DAUGHTER

A NOVEL

Meg Mitchell Moore

DOUBLEDAY

NEW YORK LONDON TORONTO

SYDNEY AUCKLAND

All rights reserved. Published in the United States by Doubleday, a division of Penguin Random House LLC, New York, and distributed in Canada by Random House of Canada, a division of Penguin Random House Canada Limited, Toronto.

www.doubleday.com

DOUBLEDAY and the portrayal of an anchor with a dolphin are registered trademarks of Penguin Random House LLC.

Jacket photograph © Dan and Alexandra/Offset
Jacket design by John Fontana

LIBRARY OF CONGRESS CATALOGING-IN-PUBLICATION DATA
Names: Moore, Meg Mitchell, author.
Title: The captain's daughter : a novel / Meg Mitchell Moore.
Description: First Edition. | New York : Doubleday, [2017]
Identifiers: LCCN 2016051410 | ISBN 9780385541251 (hardback) |
ISBN 9780385541268 (ebook)
Subjects: | BISAC: FICTION / Contemporary Women. |
FICTION / Family Life. | FICTION / Coming of Age.
Classification: LCC PS3613.O5653 C37 2017 | DDC 813/.6—dc23
LC record available at https://lccn.loc.gov/2016051410

MANUFACTURED IN THE UNITED STATES OF AMERICA

1 2 3 4 5 6 7 8 9 10

First Edition

For Frank Moore, 1947–2016

And for Shannon Mitchell, another captain's daughter

THE CAPTAIN'S DAUGHTER

PART ONE

June

1

Eliza

"No," Sheila Rackley was saying, "that's *not* how it happened at all, you have to listen to this, it was way worse . . ."

Just then one of Sheila's children, whose hair was red, whose skin was a pinky brown with freckles, and whose eyelashes were pale, just like his mother's, appeared before the group of women. He cleared his throat like a senator about to introduce a bill, and said, with great ceremony, "Jackie is being mean to me, Mommy."

An expression of annoyance briefly crossed Sheila's face; its passage was so fast that Eliza Barnes wasn't sure if she'd imagined it or not. It was June, the last day of school, and already hot. They were at the club. Someone had ordered a round of Bloody Marys, which were sweating as much as the women themselves, though the women did it more delicately. Even the celery in Eliza's drink seemed to have given up, allowing itself to slip in an undignified manner into the tomato juice. Sheila held up a hand to the women and said, "To be *continued*," before turning to her son and stage-whispering, "Edward, you did absolutely the right thing, telling me politely instead of screaming, it's just that Mommy was in the middle of a story—"

"Is that someone's phone?" asked Jodi Sanders.

"I don't care," said Catherine Cooper. "If it's mine, I'm letting it ring and ring. It's summer vacation! I'm off duty."

"Actually," said Eliza. "You're sort of *on* duty, now that it's summer vacation, wouldn't you say?"

"I've got two words for you, Eliza," said Jodi. "Summer. Nanny."

"Hear, hear," said Sheila. Her Bloody Mary was gone; she flagged the pale wren of a girl who was serving that day and asked her for another. "Kristi Osgood is home from McGill."

"I already hired her," said Deirdre Palmer.

"Figures," said Sheila. "You need her for your one perfect, well-behaved Sofia."

"She does!" said Eliza. "You have no idea how much work this EANY gala is for Deirdre." East Africa Needs You, Deirdre's pet project. Deirdre and Eliza went way back—all the way to a breast-feeding class they took at the hospital soon after Sofia and Zoe were born. Sofia and Eliza's oldest daughter, Zoe, had no choice but to be best friends, really; their friendship had such auspicious, intimate beginnings.

"Eenie, meenie, miney, moe," said Sheila, one hand on her son's shoulder. "Anyway. To continue what I was saying. What was I saying?"

"*Mom,*" said Eddie. "I mean *really mean,* let me just tell you what—"

Sheila emitted a small frustrated huff, made a sun visor out of her hand, and peered at her son. After a quarter of a minute she stood and led him firmly to a secluded spot farther from the pool where she crouched in front of him and gesticulated wildly. Eliza could see Eddie nodding, then shaking his head, then nodding again, before turning away and trudging back toward the knot of kids by the pool, a doleful sag to his skinny shoulders.

Eliza scanned the pool area for Zoe and her other daughter, Evie; Sofia and Zoe were reluctantly and temporarily allowing Evie's ten-year-old earth to orbit their thirteen-year-old sun.

Whenever Eliza pointed out that she herself would have given her eyesight or at least three of her toes for a sister when *she* was growing up, Zoe let her eyes drift into an almost-roll that she always caught at the last second. Because she knew that Eliza's loss of her own mother when she was so very young (only twelve! Younger than Zoe was now!) had induced in Eliza a pain that had faded over time but had never gone away, that still—often—came out of nowhere to strike at her wrathfully and unforgivingly, like a rheumatoid arthritis flare-up.

Eliza had not had the vocabulary at the time to define the effects of her mother's death. But she understood, then and now, on a deep and primordial level that every day after the event would become a search for the thing she'd lost.

As a result: lots of therefores.

· Therefore, Eliza would be the best mother possible, because she
   was alive to be so.
· Therefore, she would appreciate each and every day, no matter
   what it brought.
· Therefore, she would take exquisite care of herself: omega-3s,
   mammograms, the occasional green juice.
· Therefore, she would kiss her daughters good night and tell
   them she loved them even on days that they infuriated her or
   left their dirty clothes on the bathroom floor and hair balls in
   the shower drain. *All of which they did.*

Eliza lifted her face to the sun and let the voices of the women around
her fade into the background. Jodi was asking, "Whose phone *is* that?"
Sheila was ranting, "Honestly, if they spend all summer bickering I'm
going to hire *two separate nannies* and spend the whole summer *by
myself* in Hyannis," and Catherine was saying something about how
Henry was incensed about the increase in docking fees at the club this
year and how some people were starting to look elsewhere; didn't the
superior beings who ran the club know that they couldn't just do that
without *any warning?*—some people did not have *unlimited funds* with
which to dock their boats. Not that it was a problem for the Coopers, of
course, but what if it was a problem for others?

Eliza breathed in, breathed out. Sun on her face on a June day. Drinks
in the early afternoon, carrying with them a sensation of illicitness that
made them taste even better, like the women were all teenagers, getting
away with something while their parents had their heads turned the other
way. Cosseted offspring splashing gleefully about in the safe confines of
the yacht club pool, slathered in expensive sunscreen, clad in swimsuits
that ranged from adorable (Evie, rocking a mini Boden one-piece with
age-appropriate polka dots) to borderline tasteless (Jackie Rackley, also
thirteen, in a bikini that looked ready for Copacabana). Who would have
thought that this, any of this, was what the future held for a lobsterman's
daughter?

Eliza didn't want to open her eyes, because if she did, if she caught the
glance of Jodi or Catherine or Sheila, one of them might whisper aloud
what Eliza was sure they all thought of her secretly. *Interloper,* they'd say.
You don't belong here.

That was something she'd been feeling lately a lot more than usual, and for that she blamed Phineas Tarbox. A ridiculous name, *Phineas Tarbox*. An actual Boston Brahmin, the real deal. His office was on Commonwealth Avenue in Boston's Back Bay, not far from Judith's home. Judith was Eliza's mother-in-law. In fact, Phineas had been recommended by Judith, *of course*, like many things in their lives were. Judith was the unseen conductor of their orchestra, always calmly moving her baton.

It was after their visit to Phineas Tarbox that Eliza felt something dark, almost sinister, creep into her marriage. An unwelcome guest. It wasn't just that Rob was busy and distracted with a big work project, often too tired at the end of the day to do anything but fall into bed, although that was true, or that the girls gobbled up time and energy from both of them, which was also true, and expected. It was something more. It was that sometimes she looked at him, this man she'd been married to for so many years, this man whose body was so familiar to her that she'd recognize even the crease of his elbow if shown a photograph of only that, and she saw a stranger.

"*Eliza!*" said Sheila. "Wake up, that's *your* phone that's been ringing this whole time."

"What? *Oh.* Oh geez, sorry." Eliza scanned the pool again, located Evie, who was following Zoe around like a pup tracking its mother, and dug in her mammoth pool bag for her phone. A Maine area code. Only her father called her from Maine, and this wasn't his number on the caller ID.

"Hello?"

"Eliza?"

"This is Eliza." The voice on the other end was familiar in a way that seemed thrice removed from her ordinary life.

"Liza, it's Russell."

Something somersaulted—one of her organs. Could organs somersault? Many years ago, Eliza had completed two years of medical school at Boston University, so she knew that they couldn't. Not that you really needed the medical training to know that.

"Russell Perkins?" She had to get up from her lounge chair and walk away to shield herself from the other women, who had fallen silent, sensing from Eliza's tone, both voice and skin, that *something dramatic* was about to happen. Or, maybe, had already happened.

"That's the one," said Russell Perkins, Eliza Barnes's first love, her knight in shining armor, the Bruce Springsteen to her Mary. Zillions of memories flooded her: a pickup truck, a barn in winter, half of her clothes off, new desire. A nearly deserted island in summer, the inside of a car, a room in Bangor. She was sixteen again, seventeen, eighteen, all in a matter of seconds.

She glanced back at the women, who had returned to their conversation but were stealing occasional tastefully curious glances at Eliza, glances that said both *We are here for you if you need us* and *Are we missing something good?*

"Listen, Liza, you might want to get yourself up to Little Harbor just as quick as you can."

Ohmygod, thought Eliza. Her legs almost gave out and she had to lean against the fence that enclosed the pool. It was happening. Her dad was gone. He'd been pulled overboard by a trap. He'd had a heart attack, or a stroke, or a fight that went wrong. He'd rolled his truck over on the way home from the bar. It was bound to happen, each of those evil creatures was waiting in the wings to lay their pronged teeth into Charlie Sargent's skin. Hazards of the job, of the lifestyle, the pay grade.

All those years they spent together, just the two of them, leaning on each other. All those chicken cutlet dinners she'd prepared, and now he was gone. She was officially an orphan.

Could you be a thirty-seven-year-old orphan?

"Liza?"

She croaked out something that tried to be a word but didn't make it.

"Your dad hit his head on the boat this morning, the Coast Guard had to go out and bring him back in. Val took him to the emergency room, his arm was hurt too."

"He called the Coast Guard?" Her dad would never call the Coast Guard, not unless it was a *very serious emergency.* She italicized the words in her mind because that's the way her dad always said them to her. *You take care of things yourself unless it's a very serious emergency, Eliza.*

"He won't let anyone help him. He'd never tell you himself that he needs you, so I'm telling you. He needs you."

Eliza recalculated. She wasn't a thirty-seven-year-old orphan. She wasn't an orphan at all. But her dad needed her. She turned back toward the lounge chairs. She could see that Sheila Rackley was finally completing her story and that it had been a doozy. Deirdre had her hand over her mouth, and her narrow, bronzed shoulders were shaking with laughter. Even Catherine Cooper, who was a tough audience, was smiling.

"Liza?" said Russell, and her stomach twisted again in that unsettling way. Nobody else called her Liza.

"Okay," she said. She cleared her throat. She turned toward the pool and saw Zoe standing at the edge of the diving board. She felt the same urge she always felt, to call out *Don't jump!* because bad things could happen on diving boards and she wanted to protect her children from every possible danger. She fought the same impulse each time she watched them buckle themselves into the backseat of a friend's car and wave at her nonchalantly. *Don't go!* she always wanted to say. *Stay here with me, where you'll be safe!* The world was full of untold menaces.

Zoe executed a perfect swan dive, which had been honed by hours of practice and the assistance of a *personal dive coach.* Eliza knew that was ridiculous. Yet because of the coaching the dive was gorgeous. Eliza kept her eyes on the water until Zoe's head popped up (because you never knew) and felt the odd combination of pride and wonderment she often felt watching her daughters. It was almost envy, although she'd never say that out loud, because that was embarrassing. The things they knew how to do, the professional instruction they'd received in their young lives! Skiing, tennis, sailing—pastimes that had been so far off Eliza's radar when she was a child that she had thought only kids in movies engaged in them.

"Okay," she said again. "Okay, I'll get up there as soon as I can. I just have to figure out a couple of things, make some arrangements for Zoe and Evie. For my daughters."

When Eliza was Zoe's age all she knew how to do was row a skiff from the wharf to her dad's boat, the *Joanie B,* named after Eliza's mother, and how to use the gauge to measure the lobsters, and how to V-notch the pregnant females. She could also crack a lobster like nobody's business, pull every scrap of meat out, wasting not even a fraction of an ounce. Not exactly a useful skill set in Barton, although once, admittedly, at a midsummer yacht club clambake she'd had one too many gin and tonics and had made the rounds with her double-jaw lobster crackers, allowing herself to be timed by Deirdre's husband, Brock. (In her defense, the gin and tonics at the club were very strong.)

"Okay? Thank you for calling, Russell. Thank you, really." Her organs did that strange gymnastics again.

Last she knew of Russell he'd moved up to Bangor and was training to go into sales. Life insurance, or something equally necessary and staid. Life insurance! Russell Perkins, one of the best lobstermen Little Harbor had ever seen. It was *outrageous*. Must be that that hadn't stuck, that he'd come back. The good ones always came back. They couldn't really figure out any other way to live—they didn't want to.

Eliza stood motionless, holding the phone. She wasn't sure what to do next, call the children over to her, or go back to her bag, to start getting her things organized, or call Rob, who she knew was in the middle of a meeting with his client, the indomitable Mrs. Cabot.

Eliza was for a moment quite paralyzed. Fresh Bloody Marys had arrived at the table, and Deirdre brought one to Eliza, first putting it into her hand, and then closing Eliza's fingers around the plastic cup. "You look like you saw a ghost," said Deirdre.

"I did, sort of," whispered Eliza. "Thank you, Deirdre." Her father, who never needed anyone, needed her. Russell Perkins, who never called her, had called her. If she left in an hour she'd be in Little Harbor before sunset. Cue the Springsteen. *There were ghosts in the eyes of all the boys you sent away.* Eliza tipped the cup back; she downed the whole drink in three gulps.

2

LITTLE HARBOR, MAINE

Eliza

Zoe had called Eliza twice when she was going through New Hampshire, where cell phone use while driving was not allowed. Then Zoe had texted her twice but Eliza had been disciplined and had not looked at her phone, thinking of a very effective campaign she'd recently seen in the supermarket that featured a driving texter failing to see two elderly people crossing the road.

The third time Zoe called Eliza was passing through Ellsworth. Three teens from Ellsworth had died on this road when Eliza was in high school—for the longest time there had been three wooden crosses there, adorned with flowers, teddy bears, bright strings of beads. Now Eliza slowed significantly on the curves, centering her car—Rob's car; she'd left hers behind for kid-related reasons—exactly between the yellow lines and the edge of the road.

Once she had passed the danger zone outside of Ellsworth she called Zoe back. She listened to her for a while and then said, "Oh, sweetie."

Jackie Rackley had started doing extremely enviable things with certain friends and posting the photos on Instagram and then tagging other girls who *weren't* included. Just to hit them over the head with their unincludedness. (Zoe had had to explain this to Eliza twice.)

"All this happened in the last four hours? I'm perplexed. We were just with Jackie this afternoon." Maybe, thought Eliza, most friendships had an element of treachery to them—grown-ups were just better at hiding it.

"No," said Zoe. "The pictures were taken at different times. She's just posting them now."

"It's okay to be upset," said Eliza carefully. She had read that you were supposed to validate your kids' shifting emotions as they were growing, so they would continue to confide in you.

"I'm not *upset,*" said Zoe. "I'm *mad.* She's being a jerk." If this had been Evie it would have been a waterworks show, but Zoe wasn't crying. She never cried. She snarled. She snorted. She seethed. Sometimes she raged. But she didn't cry. Even as a young child she'd borne insults and injury stoically, blinking hard and going internal. This was probably unhealthy, but Eliza didn't know how to change it. You couldn't force someone to cry, could you?

Even so. If Eliza could have, she would have turned the car around, driven back to Barton, parked in the Rackleys' driveway, rung the doorbell, and unleashed a bucketful of venom on Jackie. For many obvious reasons, that wasn't practical. But also. You had to be so careful with teenagers. Your children wanted you to save them. Or they didn't want you involved at all. They wanted you to tell everyone. Or they'd die if you told anyone.

Because she was nearing Little Harbor, Eliza opted for a practical, efficient approach: "Do you want me to talk to her mother?"

"No! No, do *not* do that. You have to promise me you won't do that."

"I won't," said Eliza. "I promise. But you really can't waste any mental energy on it. You're a smart girl, you don't need friends who would do something like that."

"She's *not* my friend," Zoe snarled.

"Exactly!" said Eliza. "You know who your real friends are, and they don't treat you this way."

"That's not the problem."

"So what's the problem?"

"The problem is that now everyone who follows me can see that *I* wasn't included. And *I* can see that I wasn't included. That's the problem. It sucks."

When Zoe was born and had finally stopped screaming like a fisher cat (she hadn't had a problem crying that day) long enough for Eliza to breast-feed for the first time, the careworn nurse had said, "Here's your daughter." *Ah,* thought Eliza. *Lovely.* And then the nurse had said, "I've got four of them. Good luck!" Eliza had looked at her newborn little girl and thought, *Maybe you needed the luck, Nurse Whoever-You-Are, but I have good sense on my side.* Then, after some sustained effort, Zoe had latched on for her very first meal. She'd been so small and fragile (she'd been born almost four weeks early), Eliza had felt like she was holding a collection of raw eggs.

Eliza wanted to knock the teeth out of the world that had turned that trusting, slurping little thing into a girl left out of someone's stupid Instagram post.

"Zoe, sweetie? I'll call you soon. For now, go do something! Get your mind off of it. I promise Jackie Rackley isn't worth an ounce of your any-thing."

"What should I do?"

"Ride your bike!"

"You always say that. Riding your bike is your solution to everything."

Eliza did always say that; she loved bike riding. "That's because fresh air and exercise clear your head."

"Fine," said Zoe. "I'll ride my bike."

"Wear your helmet," said Eliza, and at the exact same time Zoe said, "I know. Wear my helmet."

"I'll call you soon, little bunny. I love you."

"I'm not a little bunny," said Zoe. And then, maybe reluctantly but then again maybe not: "I love you too."

Eliza hung up the phone the exact second she crested the last hill and the harbor opened up before her. She gasped the same way she always did. It was so beautiful, it really did take her breath away, the craggy shoreline, the stands of pine, the gray-blue water. To the right, she knew, just out of view, was the wharf, and off to the side, all of the lobster boats rocking on their moorings. If they were in for the night. Would they be in? She checked the clock on the dashboard: six thirty, yes, they'd all be in. She opened her window and took a deep, cleansing breath. Even the air felt different here: unadulterated and pure, like air from biblical times.

She pulled over, for just a minute, and got out of the car. When Eliza had first brought Rob to Little Harbor she'd stopped the car here and made him get out just like this and she'd said, "Breathe. *Breathe.*" Rob had breathed, and then he'd looked at Eliza like she was a teacher and he was a student afraid of getting the answer wrong, and then he'd said, *"Yes!"* although she never really knew if he was pretending or not. Not that she'd blame him if he were: Rob was from away, and there were certain things you just didn't know if you were from away. Such as: what the sky looks like when the boats go steaming out at dawn, a bright white ball just above the waterline, and around it a yellow glow like a halo, the sky going from black to gray to orange in just a blink.

You didn't know the way the town feels before the first set of the season, the whole place lit up from within. That Christmas Eve shiver, when you're waiting to see what's going to get brought to you. You didn't know what a boat looks like setting out with a full load of traps stacked six high and six across; you didn't know what it was like to see a little boy of seven or eight, sitting on top of a pile of his daddy's traps, grinning like there was no tomorrow, wondering how long it would be before he'd grow into a big strong man too. You didn't know the way you can look at a man who's been out on the water his whole life and see nearly every trap he's hauled and every line he's tossed over just in the set of his eyes, the pleats in his face.

Of course, growing up here she couldn't escape fast enough. If it had been possible to put wings on her shoes and fly up and out she would have done it. What were the chances that the motherless daughter of a lobsterman would get into an Ivy League school, would actually figure out how to *go*? She'd not only beaten the odds, she'd downright obliterated them. She'd had to take out student loans from here to eternity, but she'd done it: she'd gone.

At Brown, in her freshman composition course, Eliza had described her hometown as "a tight knot on the edge of the Atlantic—an angry little knuckle." *Beautiful!* the teaching assistant had scribbled in the margins. *So vivid!* "An angry little knuckle," indeed. What a pretentious college freshman she'd been. Luckily she'd abandoned the writing when she'd decided to go to medical school. Although she'd always thought she might have liked law school too.

She thought of Phineas Tarbox and shuddered.

Next to Eliza on the car's seat was her Givenchy bag, and inside the bag was a letter her mother had written to her as she lay dying. She'd left it with Val with strict instructions to give it to Eliza on her sixteenth birthday. Val had been Eliza's mother's best friend: a BFF before BFFs existed. You might have thought them an unlikely pair: Val, native to the bone, and Joanie, a Main Line Philadelphia transplant who'd washed up on Little Harbor's shores and never left. But it had worked.

When Eliza was home, Joanie's letter lived in her nightstand drawer. But anytime she left the house for more than a night she took it with her. It was single-spaced, written on yellow legal paper, and the handwriting was terrible, but that didn't stop Eliza from reading it over and over again.

Not that she needed to read it anymore; she'd long ago memorized every single word. In it, Joanie laid out four lessons. She'd meant to lay out ten (Val told Eliza) but she'd died somewhere between four and five. Sometimes when her heart ached and she felt lost Eliza wondered what the other lessons were.

My dearest, dearest Eliza, began the letter.

The first thing I need to tell you is that cancer sucks. Everyone knows that. But I didn't really know it, not for real, not until it came for me. I never took it seriously, I thought it was a disease for other people.

The cancer itself sucks, and so does that awful heartbroken look in your dad's eyes that he tries to hide but can't, and the brave expression on Val's face, and the well-meaning hospice volunteer who speaks to me in a way that makes me want to haul off and punch her.

If only I had the energy.

I am thirty-one years old, Eliza, and you are twelve, and I won't be here when you turn thirteen and that, as they say, is the long and the short of it.

Thirty-one! I thought I would live twice as long, maybe even three times as long, and the fact that I won't is just so incredibly surprising to me. Like it can't be right. There must be some mistake! I want to call out every time I see a nurse, a doctor, anyone. Excuse me, ma'am? Sir? You have the wrong person, I'm only thirty-one and my daughter is only twelve. And she needs me.

But people die all the time, young and old, short and tall, black and white, parents of infants and toddlers and preteens and teenagers and adults. It's the circle of life, it's all perfectly natural.

I just never knew the circle would be so very small in my case.

I have to write this letter in little bits and pieces, Eliza, because I tire so easily. So don't hold it against me if it reads as somewhat disjointed. I myself am disjointed now, and I expect I will be until the end. Whenever that may be.

I don't want Val to give you this letter right away, my darling Eliza. I'm going to ask her to wait until you're sixteen. Sixteen seems like the right age. You'll have a lot of questions you'll need answered when you're sixteen.

When you die, Eliza, which I know you will do many many many happy years in the future, I strongly advise you to choose a different path. Heart attack. Stroke. Something quick. Slipping away blissfully in the night at the age of ninety-four. There are so many better options than this endless, useless, goddamn painful suffering, which takes so long and at the same time goes by so, so quickly.

There. I've finished complaining. I want you to remember me as strong and beautiful, not as ugly and suffering and whiny. Being beautiful has always been important to me, maybe more important than it should have been. (That, my mother, your grandmother, would say, is how I got myself in trouble in the first place. Never mind that what she considered "trouble" is what I considered "my life.")

If I have to die young (thirty-one! I can't stop repeating the age, as if repeating it will make whoever is in charge Up There reconsider), then I would like to die in a much prettier way, not wasted down like this, not with mouth sores and throat sores with my beautiful hair shorn close to my head.

Shorn! What a deliciously descriptive, awful word.

Do you know, Eliza, when I was a student at The Baldwin School (Lower Merion Township, Pennsylvania, a place you have never been and I suppose now you will never go) I won the prestigious Baldwin Creative Writing Award? Diane Douglas thought she had it all tied up, but in fact she did not.

I never liked Diane Douglas.

I was meant for wonderful things, that's what my senior English teacher, Ms. Collier, she of the stylishly cropped gray hair and nonchalant printed scarves, always told me. I was meant to go off and write Something Important. The Great American Novel, maybe, or a small but meaningful book of poetry.

Do you know what I've written, Eliza? Shopping lists. Recipes. Thank-you notes (you can't escape your upbringing, no matter how you try). A couple of letters home that went unanswered. Which breaks my heart for you, because I would love to leave you with more family than you have.

That's it, until now. Now I am writing my magnum opus, my masterpiece. My letter to you.

In her father's driveway, Eliza saw the familiar blue pickup and Val's ancient, rusty Civic. That car had been brand-new when Eliza was a senior in high school, two thousand years ago. Frugal didn't even begin to describe the way Val was about cars.

Val ran one of the two restaurants in town—one of three, now, if you counted the new café, The Cup. Four, if you included The Wheelhouse, which was really just a bar. Although a lot of the locals turned their noses up at The Cup, Eliza was *not* planning on turning hers. She could tell from her father's descriptions ("fancy-pants coffee," "avocado smoothies," "bread with little seeds and things stuck in it") that she would embrace the menu at The Cup with guilty, open arms.

After Joanie died, Val stepped into the role of Eliza's proxy mother—she never got married, never had her own kids. And Joanie's parents never forgave Joanie for embracing a life so different from the one she'd been groomed for; they shifted their focus entirely to the three children who had remained loyal and near. So it was Val who bought Eliza her first box of tampons, her first real bra, her one and only prom dress. It was Val who helped get together the application to Brown, and Val who came to every one of Eliza's cross-country meets when Charlie was hauling. It was Val's house Eliza went to after school each day the first dreadful year after Joanie died, when Eliza couldn't bear to go to her own empty house. And it was Val who'd taken Eliza on that awful trip to Bangor in that car, all those years ago. Eliza felt a little spasm of something terrible when she thought about that.

She parked behind her dad's pickup and had no sooner gotten out of the car than Val appeared, wrapping Eliza in a giant hug. Val smelled like maple syrup and cinnamon (the pancakes at Val's were *to die for*— Evie always got two servings and ate them both); she smelled like the ocean and vanilla. She smelled like home. It was unnerving how much Val made Eliza think of what she'd lost and at the same time about what she'd gotten instead.

"I'm so glad you're here. I need to run home to feed Sternman, but I didn't want to leave your dad." Sternman was Val's stout old Lab. "He doesn't know you're coming," said Val. "After you called me I decided not to tell him, thought he could use a surprise." She looked at Eliza with an expression that Eliza couldn't quite read, and then she said, "Oh, Eliza. I'll come in with you for a minute."

Eliza wasn't sure what she was expecting when she walked into her childhood living room, where her dad was dozing in his old leather recliner, circa 1982, a rare gift to himself after a good season. Val entered before Eliza and went to stand protectively behind Charlie. She touched Charlie gently on the shoulder of his good arm and said, "See who's here!" Charlie opened his eyes and looked around with a startled expression that reminded Eliza of a bewildered old dog who'd been flung out of sleep. She felt a ball of dread begin to form in her stomach.

Eliza knew about the sprained arm, so she wasn't surprised by the sling; she knew about the gash on the head, so she wasn't surprised by the bit of shaved scalp and the line of stitches above Charlie's temple. She knew that head wounds bled like crazy and often looked worse than they were. But something else wasn't right. Charlie had just visited Barton in March, only three months before, and he'd been his regular old self then. He'd even gone into Evie's fourth-grade class with a lobster trap and a V-notch to show the kids. (Every iteration of both kids' classes had seen this routine numerous times, but they never tired of it.)

Now he looked frail—not at all like the big strong ox who had hoisted her up on his shoulders so she could work the hydraulic hauler for the first time; not like the man who'd won the trap race three years running at the Lobster Festival; not like the man whose big hand had taken hers at her mother's funeral and had crouched down and whispered, "We're gonna be okay, me and you." Charlie Sargent was sixty-four years old now, but after one fall on the deck of his boat he looked one hundred and ninety.

"Hey, Dad," she said. She bent and kissed him very carefully on the cheek, avoiding the stitched-up area on his head, avoiding the sling. "It's so good to see you. Russell had me worried there for a minute, but you look fine to me. Right as rain." She could hear the falseness in her words rolling around her throat in the same way that the Bloody Marys from earlier in the day were rolling around in her stomach. She never said things like "right as rain." (Who did, really, besides Mary Poppins?)

She sat down on the edge of the worn-to-bits sofa. She'd wanted to buy Charlie a new one the previous year but he wouldn't have it. She'd wanted to do lots of things for him at all different times and he wouldn't have most of them. He said things like, "What I have'll do just fine" and "You and Rob don't need to spend your money on me." She couldn't get him to understand that in Rob's world you didn't spend money and then find it was gone—it was practically a renewable resource, like sunlight.

"He's going to be just fine," said Val, but there was a catch in her voice that made Eliza look more carefully at her. Val handed Charlie a cup of water and shook two Advils out of a bottle that was sitting on the side table and said, "Here, Charlie, it's been four hours." To Eliza she said, "For the pain." If Eliza didn't know better she'd think they were an old married couple. Charlie took the cup unsteadily. She leaned forward to help him lift the cup to his lips, but he regained the balance in his arm and did it on his own.

"I'll be just fine," repeated Charlie, when he'd swallowed the pills and handed the cup back to Val. "Might have to take a couple more days off of hauling, that's all." He smiled and looked a little bit more like himself.

"A couple more?" said Eliza. "I think it's going to take longer than that!"

Charlie cast about for a way to change the subject: he asked about the girls, and about Rob. Then he said, "I keep telling Val that she's going to have to get a cappuccino maker down to Val's, to keep up with the competition over at The Cup."

Val made a soft hissing sound and said, "Believe me, that place is no competition to me. And I don't know of any fisherman who wants his coffee served up with a boatload of foamed milk, a sprinkle of cinnamon on top. No sir. Do you, Charlie?"

"No," said Charlie. He leaned his head back and closed his eyes. "No, I don't guess that I do."

Val woke up each day even earlier than the fishermen, since she was the one who served most of them their breakfasts. By this time in the evening she always showed her fatigue. All the lobstermen (and two women, though they usually got called lobstermen too, that was the way they wanted it) were too; it was a funny life, up before dawn, in bed not too long after sunset, sometimes before.

But now Val looked more than tired. She looked like her body had been taken apart and then put back together haphazardly, with some of the pieces not tightened all the way. And if Eliza had to put Val's expression into a single word, she might say that Val looked scared. Val, who wasn't scared of anything.

She thought of her phone ringing at the club, Russell telling her she'd better come home, the ten seconds when she'd thought her father was gone.

Wait, was that *today,* the Bloody Marys at the club? It seemed like another world suddenly, to Eliza, like someone else's life.

3

Mary

Mary Brown wiped table four with the cloth. The cloth was bamboo and reusable, although she sometimes forgot the reusable part and had had to dig one out of the garbage more than once under the slightly kind, slightly judgmental eyes of Andi and Daphne, the café's co-owners. Mary thought that it wouldn't kill them every now and then to wave a hand and say, "Don't worry, Mary, it's only a silly cloth!" but they never did; they just let her keep on digging. That was the only part of Mary's job she didn't love.

Sometimes when she made mistakes like that she sang a little song to herself: *Mary Brown, get out of town, Mary Brown, go upside down.* It helped get her mind off the embarrassment. Mary embarrassed extremely easily. That was her cross to bear (an expression she inherited from her mother, as in: *Single motherhood, that is my cross to bear*).

One of Mary's other crosses to bear was the fact that her name was the absolute plainest thing anybody could dream of. And yet at the same time so very easy to make fun of. Bloody Mary. Virgin Mary. Mary, Queen of Snots. Trevor Spaulding, awful boy, had come up with that last one in the fifth grade.

Mary's own mother was named Vivienne, which was, in her own words, a name that turned out to be way too extravagant for the life she'd ended up in. A mother at eighteen, married at nineteen, divorced at twenty. Now she worked in a salon in Ellsworth called A Cut Above where she highlighted hair and waxed eyebrows. Mary's mother had made lots of mistakes (in general, not with the hair and the eyebrows) and she liked to remind Mary about it. "Don't screw up like I did, Mary." "It's not worth it, Mary." "Five minutes of pleasure for a lifetime of pain, Mary."

And then, realizing that she was talking to *her own daughter,* the result of the five minutes of pleasure, she tried to walk it back. "That's not what I meant, Mary. I just meant: stay in school."

No wonder Mary was so easily embarrassed.

"Table three needs a wipe-down!" sang Daphne from the other side of the café. "When you get to it."

"Of course," said Mary agreeably. She liked wiping down the tables—she found it very soothing and satisfactory. You could see where the work began and where it ended. Unlike most things.

Daphne and Andi were lesbians, and they were married. To each other. (Mary had to clarify the married part *more than once* for her mother, who tagged Daphne and Andi's sexual preference at the end of their name like a suffix, always with Andi's name first: Andi and Daphne, the Lesbians.)

Mary didn't care a nickel about what people did together in bed—she was really very open-minded. Not exactly adventurous (her boyfriend, Josh, said) but definitely open-minded. Even so, sometimes she did have to fight back a giggle when Daphne and Andi used the word *wife* to describe each other, only because of how proudly they said it, how they lifted their chins a fraction of an inch as though saying, *Go on, challenge us, we dare you. We have a marriage certificate and we file our tax returns jointly.*

Honestly, Mary didn't really know much about tax returns (she was seventeen), but Daphne and Andi talked about them like they were a very important marker of a real relationship.

"Earth to Mary!" said Andi now. Sometimes Andi snuck up on Mary like a ghost, startling her right out of her thoughts. Mary's thoughts had a nervy habit of wandering. This had often been a problem at school, except in math. She didn't even have to pay attention to the teaching in math, not really, she just looked at the work after and it made a sort of automatic sense; the numbers floated right where they were supposed to be. Her spelling, on the other hand, was atrocious.

Last year's math teacher, Ms. Berry, had pulled Mary aside and asked her if she knew what an *aptitude* for math she had and if she understood how *critical* girls with good math skills were going to be to America's ability to keep up with other countries.

"Just think about it, Mary," Ms. Berry had said, two weeks before graduation.

Mary thought about it. But by then Mary already knew what her future held, and it wasn't more math classes.

Her cell phone in her apron pocket buzzed and she stole a look at it.

Josh: **WHEN R U COMING?**

"Customers, Mary, all hands on deck!" said Andi.

Mary put the phone back in her pocket and glanced out the window of the café—there were only two customers approaching, it was hardly an *all hands on deck* situation, but Andi and Daphne had relocated to Little Harbor from New York City and they liked to use nautical phrases whenever they could. Not that the fishermen Mary knew ever actually said *all hands on deck*. And Mary knew a lot of fishermen.

"I'm on it!" Mary called out. She took her place behind the counter, depositing the bamboo towel correctly in the to-be-washed bin, and waited for the door to open. "I am at your service," she told Daphne. Under cover of the counter she slid her phone out and texted Josh back **SOON, BABY.** She felt a little thump of anticipation when the bell on the door jangled. The sound reminded her of Christmas, those first couple of minutes after you open your eyes and you think, *Anything could happen today!*

Vivienne said Mary was more optimistic than she had a right to be.

Mary loved waiting on customers. She loved the way the café made her feel: competent and valuable, in a way that nobody and nothing else made her feel.

"You wouldn't last a minute in New York City," Daphne always told Mary. "You're way too trusting and sweet. And I mean that as a compliment." The way she said it, though? Somehow Mary didn't take it as a compliment. She'd never been to New York City.

In the summer the café was open until eight; they served dinner salads and "small plates," mostly to summer people just off their sailboats, and they had just gotten a beer and wine license, which, to hear Andi tell it, had been like *pulling fucking teeth.* Sometimes Andi didn't have the nicest language.

"*Small* plates?" said Vivienne scornfully when she'd come in at the beginning of the summer to get a look at the place. When Vivienne was growing up in Little Harbor the lot where the café was now had been a dying gas station. "Smaller than what?"

Vivienne refused to call Daphne and Andi's place a café, she insisted on saying *coffee shop,* even though it was right there on the sign, same font but smaller letters as the name of the place. *The Cup,* it said, *a café for all.*

"A coffee shop for some," Vivienne called it, because she said that only the summer people went there. (True.) And then she laughed in that way she had, that made her sound older than she was. Smoker's laugh. Another mistake. "Don't ever start, Mary, once you get in the habit it's impossible to stop." If she ever saw Mary with a cigarette, she said, she would smack her from here to next week. That was just an expression, of course.

The Cup served two different kinds of white wine, two kinds of red, one champagne ("Technically," said Andi, "it's not champagne, it's not from France, so it's *sparkling wine,* but call it what you want"), and a light beer and a dark beer, both from the Atlantic Brewing Company in Bar Harbor. Local. The summer people loved local beer. They loved local everything, local marmalade and chutney from Nellie's in Blue Hill, fair trade organic coffee beans from Wicked Joe in Topsham, lobsters pulled from traps right in Little Harbor and sold straight off the boat at the co-op. They liked local until the summer ended and the days got shorter and the wind got colder and they high-tailed it back to Boston or New York or Philadelphia or their winter ski condos in Colorado or Park City, Utah.

One of the customers coming in now was Russell Perkins. Mary wasn't sure she'd ever seen Russell Perkins in The Cup—he went to Val's. Obviously. The Cup wasn't open early enough for the lobstermen. ("Not our target market," said Andi, shrugging.) But here he was, dressed in regular clothes, not fishing gear. Mary squinted at him and tried to be offended by his presence. Was he walking in like he owned the place, sort of?

This question was out of an attempted loyalty to Josh, who despised Russell Perkins. Russell was one of those guys who always dropped his traps in the right place, always sensed the movement of the lobsters before they knew where they were going themselves, always caught more than everyone else. Well, more than Josh, anyway, who had bad luck dropping his traps. "Not that I'm keeping track," said Josh. Though of course he was. Mary got nervous when Josh had a bad day out on the water. He was like a little boy on the edge of a big tantrum, his face screwed up with confusion and pain. Sometimes it felt like a full-time job, making him feel better. Sometimes it felt impossible: it felt like the kind of job she didn't want to spend her life doing.

But despite her efforts, Mary found Russell sort of charming. Okay, very charming, extremely charming. Look at him now, smiling at her, in a way that wouldn't let her not smile back. He was so handsome. For an older man. ("*Never* date an older man," was Vivienne's advice. Another mistake. They were only after *one thing*.) Too late for that: Josh was twenty-four.

Russell was with a woman Mary didn't recognize. A summer person? The woman was wearing white shorts and a silky-looking tank top that said *I have money*. She had super-long legs, lots of freckles, and masses of dark curly hair that Mary (who was, after all, her mother's daughter) could tell was tamed by an experienced hairstylist and probably some very expensive product. Her bag was baby-blue leather; it looked soft as butter and had a little gold tag with a word Mary couldn't read. She was stunning, actually. What was Russell Perkins doing coming into The Cup with a stunning summer person?

"Hey, Mary," said Russell, and Mary said, "Hey, Russell."

The summer person looked up at the menu and squinted in a way that made little lines pop out at the corners of her eyes. Now that the woman was closer Mary could read the word on her bag: *Givenchy*. "I can't believe it," she said to Russell. She was standing close to him; their arms were touching. "You can get a cappuccino in Little Harbor! Knock me over with a feather. Val told me, but I didn't believe her. She's freaking out, though she won't admit it." The woman reached into her blue butter bag and pulled out a long brown wallet with a bright gold zipper. "My treat, get whatever you want. Are we doing coffee or beers?" She smiled at Mary in a friendly way, and then said, "You look so familiar to me. Why is that?"

"That's Vivienne's girl, Mary," said Russell. "Looks just exactly like her mama." He winked at Mary and Mary tried even harder to dislike him but she couldn't help it: she smiled. To the woman Russell said, "Better make it drinks, I'm up at four tomorrow, no coffee for me."

"Vivienne?" The woman closed her eyes and put one finger on her chin like she was drawing a memory out of it.

"Vivienne Brown, a year behind us." Russell rocked back on his heels and stretched his hands in front of him and cracked his knuckles.

"Oh!" said the woman. "Right. Vivienne. Of course. I remember her, *such* a pretty girl. You *do* look just like her, wow." Her voice was deep and musical and seemed to travel all over the place in just that one sentence. She put her hand on Russell's arm. Mary had never seen this woman before, but there was something so natural about the gesture that made Mary experience a flash of something. Envy? She supposed this was what people meant when they talked about chemistry.

Mary's phone buzzed again, another text. **HURRY UP IM LONLY.** It was only six thirty. They were still open for another hour and a half and then there was cleanup to do. She wouldn't get to Josh's until almost eight thirty. He went to bed before ten to be up at four to haul, just like Russell, just like all the lobstermen. Josh wanted her to quit her job at The Cup, get something with hours that matched his better. "See if Val's hiring," he said. "Work the breakfast shift, it'll be perfect." Mary didn't want to work the breakfast shift, didn't want to get up at four, didn't want to spend all of her time around a bunch of stinky lobstermen, didn't want to give up Andi and Daphne and her *own personal* apron with a screen print of a coffee cup with steam coming off the top. So she had told Josh she'd asked and Val didn't need anyone. (A red flag: that she needed to lie.)

"We have decaf," said Mary now, in her best customer service voice. Andi, who was counting bags of beans, nodded her approval.

"Drinks," said the woman firmly. "Beer, Russell? What kind? Do you mind if I have something else, I can't drink beer anymore, it gives me such a bloated belly, let's see, wine, or . . . ooooh, you have champagne? Do you close soon? Eight? Okay, good, I need to get back to my dad anyway, we'll be quick, promise." She smiled even more brightly and said, "I'll pound my champagne."

"Not necessary, Eliza. What would your dad say?" Russell laughed.

Eliza. Okay, now it was coming together. Eliza Sargent, Charlie Sargent's daughter. Charlie Sargent had been taken in by the Coast Guard yesterday, Josh told her all about it the night before in that weirdly happy voice that he used when he talked about other people's misfortunes. This was a red flag, though a small one. Mary was trying to ignore the small red flags, considering the situation.

Charlie Sargent came into The Cup sometimes in the early evening and bought a few of the lobster cookies. The cookies were shaped like lobsters, not made out of them. He always winked at Mary when he paid and said, "Don't tell Val." He must be okay enough, if Eliza Sargent was here at The Cup, standing close to Russell Perkins.

Mary hadn't told anybody about her secret, not even Josh. She would tell him soon. Maybe not tonight, maybe tomorrow.

The ringing of a cell phone interrupted her thoughts and Charlie Sargent's daughter reached into her bag and pulled out a phone. "Sorry," she said in Russell's direction, before she answered, saying, "Hi, honey. Sweetie—Evie? Evie, I can't quite understand you . . . Evie, you have to stop crying if you want me to be able to understand you."

There was such kindness and love in Eliza Sargent's voice that Mary felt, ridiculously, tears rise to her eyes. She was so emotional lately, she cried over the stupidest things. Just the other day that blond woman with the ringlets getting kicked off *The Bachelor*, that got her going.

Eliza moved away from the counter, so Mary could no longer see her expression. After a couple of minutes she returned to Russell's side, slipping the phone back into her bag. She rolled her eyes in an exaggerated way that indicated she didn't mean any harm by it and said to Russell, "My second call from a crying girl in just over twenty-four hours. Evie got to the end of *Bridge to Terabithia*. I don't blame her, I felt the same way, when I read it."

Russell said, "Never read it." He winked at Mary again. Funny how winks could be creepy from some people and perfectly acceptable from others. Russell's were acceptable, even enchanting.

"Did you order?" asked Eliza. "I'll have a glass of Cabernet after all, not champagne. I know, it seems crazy, it's summertime, we should all be drinking white or rosé. So sue me." She shrugged like someone who didn't expect to get sued at all.

A rich woman with a blue butter bag, a woman who moved through the world so easily—though she was technically a local, this was every summer person Mary Brown had been brought up to dislike. ("Thinks she walks on water," Vivienne would say, even though, if Eliza Sargent showed up at the salon, she'd treat her like royalty, give her one of those hand massages while her color set, expect a twenty percent tip.)

But Mary didn't dislike this woman, as much as she wanted to. In fact, it was the opposite. This, she realized, was exactly the kind of person, exactly the kind of *mother*, Mary Brown wanted to be.

4

Rob

Rob was gazing into the depths of the refrigerator. A midrange Viking. He'd wanted to get the professional version, which cost north of ten grand, but Eliza had put her foot down, hard. She said she'd be embarrassed to have a professional-grade refrigerator when she wasn't a professional chef, when she wasn't a professional anything. "You're my professional favorite person," said Rob, but she wouldn't bend. She was embarrassed even to have the midrange, she would have been more than happy with a Frigidaire, but that time Rob had put *his* foot down.

"Are you cooking dinner?" Zoe asked suspiciously. She was so sneaky and quiet, like a cat. Rob turned. Zoe looked so *tall*. Had she grown since yesterday? Since this morning?

"Yes!" Rob said confidently. "I am going to make a frittata."

Normally, if Eliza went out of town, she'd prep a couple of meals for them, but of course the thing with her dad had been sudden and there'd been no time. Besides, Rob could cook for his children! He wasn't completely useless in the kitchen. He'd designed enough kitchens; he should be able to maneuver around one without too much trouble.

"Do you know how?"

"Zoe," he said sternly. "Of course I know how to make a frittata."

"You do?"

Not really.

"Yes," said Rob. "Now, why don't you go out in the garden and see if anything is growing yet." Eliza planted a killer garden every year.

"Like what?"

"Tomatoes."

Zoe looked at him. "I'm pretty sure it's too early for tomatoes. Don't those come in, like, August?"

"Go look anyway," he said. "Just in case."

While she was gone he nipped into the downstairs bathroom and quickly googled *frittata recipes* on his phone, committing the steps as much to memory as was possible. It seemed easy enough.

Zoe came in holding a bunch of freshly harvested rhubarb and held it out to him. "Um," said Rob, "I'm not sure rhubarb would go in a frittata."

Zoe shrugged and put the stalks on a counter. "That's what was growing."

"I thought you watched all of those cooking shows," he said. "Didn't you look for something that made sense, frittata-wise?"

"That's Evie," said Zoe.

"That's me what?" asked Evie, entering from who-knows-where. She was wearing a pair of too-small shoes from the dress-up box and a dress that once upon a time had been Eliza's. It came down to Evie's ankles.

"It's you who watches the cooking shows."

Evie nodded. "I mostly watch *MasterChef Junior*."

"Can you go find me something to put in this frittata, in that case?"

"Sure." Evie was always up for anything.

"Maybe lose the heels first?"

"Okay." She kicked off the shoes like a bridesmaid about to cut loose to "Twist and Shout" at the end of the reception and headed out the slider that led to the deck. She came back a few minutes later with a handful of basil, a bunch of parsley, and a few fava beans. "Better," said Rob, and Zoe rolled her eyes. Rob could work with this. He'd use the herbs in the frittata and serve the fava beans on the side, if he had time to google how to cook fava beans.

It was hard, being a mom.

The frittata was too dark on the bottom and slightly underdone on top but both girls had the grace not to mention it. The fava beans were a loss: he overcooked them into mush and shuttled them into the disposal when nobody was looking.

"When is Mom coming back?" asked Zoe, taking a long pull of her milk. Chocolate, the girls had made it themselves. He knew they were taking advantage of him but he let it slide. It was just for a couple of days.

"Soon," said Rob. "Day after tomorrow, I think."

"You have a funny look on your face," said Evie.

"I do? Sorry. Just thinking about work."

Evie nodded knowingly. "Cabot Lodge, right?"

"That's right. Cabot Lodge." Cabot Lodge was a gargantuan project, a second home for Christine and Jonathan Cabot, dear friends of Rob's mother. It was the biggest (in truth, the only) project Rob had taken on since hanging out his own shingle after leaving the architecture firm of his mentor, Mo Francis, the previous year. And Christine Cabot, future proprietor of Cabot Lodge, was driving him out of his mind.

Cabot Lodge was going up in Naples, Maine, on the shores of Long Lake, which was far enough from Rob's typical work area in Massachusetts to be sufficiently maddening. He didn't have access to his usual guys; Mrs. Cabot had hired a general contractor who was unknown to him and who was also sort of scary. Mark Ruggman.

"It's funny," said Evie, taking a large bite of the improperly cooked frittata. "Ever since you stopped working for Mo Francis, you're here more. But you're *here* less." She made little air quotes over the word *here* and raised an eyebrow at him.

Rob coughed. The girl was perceptive. He said, "That's very astute of you, Evie."

Evie nodded and said, "I don't know what that word means. And also, Zoe's on her phone."

Rob saw that Zoe's iPhone was tucked discreetly into the folds of her napkin and she was looking down at her lap and tapping away at it.

"Zoe! Put that away," said Rob. Zoe kept tapping at the screen until Rob said, *"Zoe!"* again and she said, "Sorry," rolled her eyes, and put the phone on the island. Then she said, "Jackie Rackley is *so annoying* on Instagram."

"Can I get Instagram?" asked Evie.

"No," said Rob and Zoe together.

At bedtime, Evie said, "Oh! I forgot. You're supposed to check me for lice. A girl in my class had it at the end of the year. I forgot to tell Mommy, we were all supposed to get checked."

"They don't check you at school?"

"It was the last day. They just told us to get checked at home."

He looked at her head. Evie had Eliza's hair: massively thick and dark and curly. A battalion of lice could hide in there, remaining undetected for days, weeks, months, multiplying, dividing.

He took a deep breath and peered at her part. "Looks good," he said after a moment.

"That's not how Mommy does it," she said. "She takes this lice comb and she really gets in there . . ."

He took a comb from Evie's nightstand and moved it around a little bit on her scalp. You couldn't comb through those curls without a lot of prior planning.

"That's not a lice comb."

"What's the difference?"

Evie sighed patiently and said, "Believe me, there's a big difference. Call Deirdre. She knows how to do it."

"I don't need to call Deirdre!"

Deirdre was the closest of Eliza's friends. She was, like all of the Barton women, fit, tan, and busy busy busy. The women of Barton traveled in a great perfume-misted herd and were always planning things that did not include their husbands. What did women talk about, over all those drinks at the club, those girls' weekends, the occasional spa day in Boston? What secrets did they spill about the men in their lives? Frankly, it made Rob nervous to think about it.

Eliza, who did not trust everyone, said Deirdre had a solid heart under the tan and the Pilates muscles. Deirdre had one child, Sofia ("the European spelling, no *ph*"), and a husband named Brock, with whom Rob occasionally went out sailing and sometimes for a drink after.

Deirdre was putting on a gigantic gala at the end of the summer to benefit African children, which mystified Eliza. ("Why not find a cause closer to home?") Rob had grown up among aggressive fund-raisers, competitive do-gooders, cutthroat gala creators. He got it.

Despite all of this, Rob had had a strange feeling about Deirdre ever since last year's holiday party at the Colemans'. There was something about that night he couldn't put his finger on. Actually there was a lot about that night Rob couldn't put his finger on—Rob and everyone else in town. Jennifer Coleman had discovered a new cocktail, the Angel's Delight, and it had gone down easier than a penguin on an ice slide.

No, he didn't need to call Deirdre. Eliza would be home soon; he could manage. "I can find the lice in my own family, thank you very much," he told Evie. He made a few more casual swipes through her hair and said, "All clear."

"Are you sure?" Evie looked up at him, her small brow furrowed. "That didn't feel very thorough."

"Positive."

Evie sighed and got up from her bed and turned to face Rob. She was wearing a long white summer nightgown of the type favored by maiden aunts in old movies; she looked, standing there in the middle of her bedroom, like the Ghost of Christmas Adorable.

She pursed her cute little lips together and asked, "Is Grandpa hurt badly?"

"No, not too badly. He bumped his head on his boat. Not a big deal. He had to get a few stitches." Eliza's father was an honest-to-God lobsterman, the real deal, with orange overalls and a genuine Down East accent. He used hilarious, inscrutable expressions like "all stove up," for sick or injured or broken, and "being awful spleeny," for complaining a lot.

"So Mommy'll be home soon?"

"Yes. Mommy will be home soon." Rob folded down her sheet and comforter and gestured to the bed. Evie climbed in, and Rob pulled the sheet and comforter to her chin, the way she liked it, even in the summer.

"If she's not, will you make another frittata?"

He felt cheered: here was an endorsement of his dubious cooking skills. "I will if you'll pick some more of that kick-ass basil."

Evie made a disapproving face. "That's a bad word."

"Basil?"

She shook her head and smiled. "No. Kick-ass."

"Watch your language," he said sternly. She smiled wider. Evie's smile could knock a hurricane right off its track. Rob said, "You're right. Sorry. That *fantastic* basil."

"Okay. I will." Evie nodded and laid her head on her pillow. Sometimes she still slept as she had as a toddler; every now and then Rob looked in on her and she was on her stomach with her little bottom sticking up in the air, like it was floating on a cloud. When he saw that he wanted to freeze-frame her entire life.

"Can you do me a favor, Evie?" he whispered.

"What?" Her voice was already sleepy.

"Can you avoid becoming a teenager?"

"Okay," she whispered. "I'll try."

Downstairs, after he'd poured himself two fingers of Scotch, Rob opened the door that led to the garage. His car was gone, and Eliza's Pilot was in its usual spot. That made sense, of course; her car was the family car, and should remain with the family. But he felt a small spasm of loss at the sight of the empty garage space. He loved his car. He loved his boat too, a Hinckley Sou'wester 52, a fortieth-birthday gift from his mother.

You weren't supposed to love material things so ardently, but when he was standing on the deck of *A Family Affair,* with everything exactly where he wanted it, each knob, each instrument, each rope, Robert Barnes II couldn't help but think that a Hinckley Sou'wester 52 didn't seem completely material. There was something about it that bumped against the celestial.

Once he closed the garage door an unnamed bleakness descended on Rob like a duvet. He didn't like having Eliza gone. He missed her! And he didn't like the fact that they'd left the Phineas Tarbox situation unresolved. He wasn't accustomed to having anything unresolved between them.

One or two days, though: that was nothing. Just a blink, and she'd be back.

5

LITTLE HARBOR, MAINE

Eliza

"Hey, Dad," Eliza called from the kitchen. "Your fridge was empty, what've you been eating?"

She stepped into the living room. Her father was in his recliner. The remote rested in his hand, though the screen was quiet and dark and his eyes were closed. When he opened them his face took on the discomfited expression of a person caught in the act of something shameful. He rubbed at his eyes in a way that reminded her of Evie.

"Oh, sorry," whispered Eliza. "I didn't know you had dozed off. I was just saying, thank goodness I went shopping, you have nothing here. You're like Old Father Hubbard." She spoke with a levity she didn't feel.

Eliza reached for the hair elastic around her wrist—the de facto jewelry of the busy mother—and wrapped it around a makeshift bun before she began to unload the groceries. She'd gone to Ellsworth, to the new Hannaford, which, in her childhood, was a grim and stalwart Dave's

Shop 'n' Save. (Who was this mysterious Dave? She never knew.) Now, at the Hannaford, you could buy kombucha and quinoa and hemp seed; you could buy organic strawberries and mangoes, natural cures for urinary tract infections, gluten-free bagels. Although Eliza had bought none of these things: the first rule of cooking, she knew, was to know your audience. She bought two bags of white rice, a box of cornflakes, two packages of chicken cutlets, coffee, milk, bananas, a dozen eggs.

She took the desiccated sponge from its perch on the edge of the sink, wet it, squirted soap onto it, and went at the fridge's grimy shelves.

"I don't like to waste groceries. I eat at Val's most days."

"Val's isn't open for dinner. What do you eat for dinner?"

He shifted. "I manage."

"You go to the new place, The Cup?"

He snorted. "Right. Yuh, that's exactly what I do, I go over to The Cup and pay fifteen dollars for a sandwich."

"They're not *fifteen dollars*. And, anyway, I have it on good authority that you like the lobster cookies they sell there."

"Who told you that?"

"Nobody. Little bird."

"The coffees are five."

"Not *five*, Dad." Just that morning, admittedly, Eliza had paid four twenty-five for a large cappuccino. (Worth it.) The same girl, Vivienne's daughter, had made it for her. She was sweet, too, taking great care with the frothing of the milk. She even made a lobster claw design with the foam in the top of the cup.

Eliza's phone, which she'd set on the coffee table, announced a text message. Evie, from her iPad Mini. **I FOUND OUR NEXT DOG.** There was a link that brought Eliza to a photo. Since they'd put Fred, their beloved golden retriever, down the year before, Evie had been on the hunt for a dog to rescue. She tended to be attracted to the scrappiest of the scrappy, the neediest of the needy. Eliza took comfort in the knowledge that this exhibited Evie's rock-solid heart and charitable leanings, but some of the dogs really forced a person to be generous with the word *pet*. The current offering was named Maisy. She was a sorry sight, with patches of fur missing from her back and shoulders, and a desperate look in her eyes. A tip of one ear appeared to be absent. Eliza texted back, **I DON'T THINK SO HONEY,** and set to work on the chicken cutlets.

Eliza broke an egg, mixed it with water, and dipped the cutlets first in the egg and then in some crushed cornflakes. She never made chicken cutlets at home. It simply wouldn't occur to her to introduce this very basic component of her childhood cuisine to her own children. Zoe didn't like cornflakes, and Evie disapproved of the way chickens were treated; she'd accept a free-range egg, but that was her limit. Making them now, though, especially in this kitchen, was soothing and familiar. For the longest time this was the only meal Eliza knew how to make for her father. Sometimes she'd add a very simple green salad, sometimes a bowl of buttered noodles.

At the kitchen table, which was so small her knees and her father's knees bumped up against each other, Eliza tried to keep the conversation moving. She caught Charlie up on the Barnes family summer: Evie's theater camp, Zoe's science camp, Rob's plans to take his outrageously expensive boat *A Family Affair* on an extended cruise to the Caribbean the next spring if he could find a couple of buddies to go with him. She was fully aware of what a privileged idiot she sounded like, but when she wasn't talking, the silence encroached.

She described Rob's first project on his own after leaving Mo Francis's firm. "We thought he'd be home all the time!" she said. "But he's working more." She told her dad about Cabot Lodge, and about how Mrs. Cabot had decided that she didn't like the plans Rob had drawn up *based on her specifications* and had him start all over.

"Rich people," said Charlie, shaking his head.

"Right?" said Eliza agreeably. "They are *such* a conundrum."

Charlie gave her a look.

"I know," said Eliza. "I know."

When Eliza was growing up, the richest people she knew were the McPhersons, who had a gorgeous house on the Point, and who came up every summer from Philadelphia.

"Remember the McPhersons?" she asked Charlie now. "That lobster bake?"

"I do," he said. "Hell of a time."

"Do they still have that house?"

"I believe they do. Only sandy beachfront in the town."

Eliza remembered a Saturday, midsummer, a fog draping itself around the Point like a blanket. She was thirteen, slightly sunburned, her hair untamed, the pain and grief after her mother died still floating along the surface like a lily pad. Charlie was hired to be cook and entertainer both; he and Eliza had been there all afternoon, while Charlie dug the hole, laid the rocks, built the fire, tended it for hours. Then, when the fire was ready, he moved the rocks to the side with a shovel. He had a pile of seaweed ready to place over the pit, and pieces of tarp he would lay over the pans once they were on the pit. "Much easier," he told Eliza, sweating over the shovel, "to cook the whole damn thing in the kitchen. But they want it authentic, so authentic is what they get."

Then the guests started to arrive, tripping down the wide expanse of grass to the sand. The ladies left their shoes on the ground. Their toenails were painted bright red or pink, and they wore sundresses. They all wore perfume. They all carried glasses of champagne. For the men: darker cocktails in what Eliza didn't know then were highball glasses.

"She wanted me to call her Dottie," said Eliza now. "But I wouldn't."

"This is Charlie Sargent," said Mrs. McPherson to her guests. "If you haven't met him other years. My own personal lobsterman." Eliza waited for Charlie to look to Eliza, to roll his eyes in her direction, so they could exchange a look that said, *Can you believe this woman?* But his smile got bigger and he didn't roll his eyes, and he said, "And this is my assistant, Eliza." She could hear the way he was dialing up his accent.

"Awww," said the women, looking at Eliza, who scratched a mosquito bite and looked back at the women. "Isn't she *sweet*." And one of them said, "I'd *kill* for that hair."

When it was time to put the food on the pit Charlie made a big show of picking through the tub of lobsters he'd brought.

"I got some quarters, I got some halfs," he said. "This one, Mrs. Wheeler, I caught special for you. This one's a chicken, smaller than the others. I know you have a tiny appetite." He winked at Mrs. Wheeler, who giggled. He was laying it on thick, Eliza could see that, and they were eating it up like a square of blueberry cake.

When it came time to crack the lobsters everybody sat on big plaid blankets in the sand. They wore bibs, like overgrown children, and had hand wipes set up beside them. Charlie perched on a little stool he used for tending the fire, and held up a lobster as an example. He twisted off the tail, broke it open, pushed out the meat. "All in one piece, that's how you want it—that's it, Mr. Frank." Then the claws. "Bend backwards on the claw, Mrs. Carrington, backwards, that's it. Always backwards." He showed them how to use the crackers, how to get the claw meat out all in one piece. When someone struggled he walked around and kneeled beside him or her, taking the claw or the tail out of the person's hands. They dipped the lobster in the bowls of butter, ate the corn, ate the potatoes, devoured the blueberry crisp. Eliza moved closer to her father, and though she was offered food she ate none. Instead she watched the women, the way they tipped their heads back when they laughed, the way they had of putting a hand on the forearm of the person they were talking to.

When Eliza needed the bathroom, Mrs. McPherson ("Really, sweetheart, it's *Dottie*, I insist, Mrs. McPherson is my *mother-in-law*!") directed her to the half bath off the kitchen, but when Eliza got there she tried the knob and discovered that the door was locked. She was about to knock when she heard odd noises coming from under the door—groans, gasps. Sex noises. Carrie Simmons had told her about sex noises, but because Eliza was a young thirteen without the benefit of the internet or frequent trips to the movies she hadn't heard those noises before. She found a different bathroom, an upstairs one, and returned to the party.

Then the sun set and darkness fell, and, in the sky, a full moon rose.

"I arranged that for you too, Mrs. McPherson," Charlie said, nodding. "I brought you the moon and all." And the party guests, to a person, laughed. They loved Charlie Sargent, they loved Dottie McPherson's own personal lobsterman! They loved summer in Maine.

At the end of the night, Mrs. McPherson handed Charlie an envelope. She was flushed now, chortling and warm. She hugged Eliza. She hugged Charlie, holding him too close for too long. She said, "You, Charlie Sargent, are a treasure. It simply wouldn't be summer in Maine without you."

During the drive home Eliza was silent until Charlie pressed her. When she couldn't hold it in any longer, she spat out, "Why do you let them do that?"

"Do what?"

"Put you onstage like that. Aren't you embarrassed?"

"Embarrassed? What do I have to be embarrassed about?"

"It's all so fake." She thought about the sex noises. "They're so *fake*. Like rich people don't know how to crack a lobster by now, they've been doing it every summer for years. And you—"

"And I what?"

"You play along, play up your accent. For them."

There was a quick flicker of hurt in his eyes; she caught it when they passed one of the main street's only streetlights. "Doesn't bother me, Eliza," Charlie said. "If it doesn't bother me I don't see any reason why it should bother you."

The next morning, while her father was still asleep—it was a rare morning for him to sleep in, a Sunday in summer, when you couldn't haul anyway—Eliza opened the envelope: ten one-hundred-dollar bills, crisp in their envelope. The envelope said *Ellsworth Savings and Loan* on it in red. The bills were all facing the same way. Ben Franklin with his odd hairstyle, his hooded eyes, over and over again she looked at him, all ten of him. How many days of hauling did that equal, a few hours on the beach at the McPhersons', the big show with the lobster crackers?

Later that afternoon there was a shopping trip, all the way to the mall in Bangor: a new dress for Eliza, a new pair of shoes, a shirt, and a new lunch box for Charlie because he said his old one was falling right about to pieces. A stop on the way home for burgers and root beer floats at Jordan's, which Eliza and Charlie ate sitting side by side on the rickety picnic bench, watching the summer traffic go by, not saying much.

"Dottie McPherson had a stroke a year or two back," Charlie said now, bringing Eliza back to the present. "Not sure she makes it up every year, but her kids do." Eliza still remembered Mrs. McPherson's bosom, her perfume, the half bathroom, the noises.

She took a bite of cutlet. They were delicious, if she did say so herself. She might have to bring these into her Barton repertoire after all, no matter the concerns Evie had about the chickens. Surely she could find cutlets from free-range chickens if she looked hard enough.

Her father had eaten only a couple of bites. "Dad. They checked you out for a concussion, didn't they?" She closed her eyes and tried to recall everything she'd learned about concussions in med school. All that came to her was the irrelevant and nonmedical instruction to feed a fever and starve a cold.

He shrugged. "I think so."

"Does your head hurt now?"

"Little bit. Not much."

She squinted at him. Charlie never admitted to being in any kind of pain. She nodded at the sling. "When do you think they'll let you get back to it?"

Charlie cleared his throat. "Don't know. Soon, I hope. My traps must be full to bursting."

"Well, when's your next appointment?"

"Don't have one," he said. He smiled his famous crooked smile.

"That smile made my heart stop the first time I saw it," her mother told her once. Eliza knew the story, of course: her mother sitting on the wharf with Val, watching the boats come in, love at first sight, etc., etc. She herself knew what it was like to sit there, waiting, heart slamming against her ribs, the heat rising from her skin like it had a life of its own. Eliza was not sure she believed in love at first sight, though she did, of course, believe in love. She believed in love so deeply that she felt her heart do a double twist now, thinking about Rob, her girls.

But, boy, love got complicated. She thought about Phineas Tarbox; she thought about sitting at The Cup with Russell, and about all the things that were still unsaid, so many years later. What she had felt the night before with Russell, she didn't know if it was desire or simply the memory of desire. Or maybe the distinction was unimportant: maybe the two were one and the same, interchangeable.

"Dad, you have to go back, get the stitches out, get the arm looked at."

"Can't you take out the stitches? It'd be cheaper."

"I'm not a doctor. I'm not a nurse. I'm not supposed to be doing that stuff!"

"You're nicer, though. Than the ones that are. You come close enough for me." He grinned.

Charlie Sargent could charm the shell off a lobster, Eliza's mother used to say. Joanie was very proud of that description: she'd made it up herself.

"A follow-up visit should be covered," she told her father. Last she knew her father was paying monthly for basic insurance with a sizable deductible.

He stopped grinning.

"What? Dad? What is it?"

"I'm not insured now."

"What?"

"The premiums were so frickin' expensive, and then with the deductible it wasn't worth it . . ."

"Dad. You can't do that, you can't be uninsured." A little globule of panic bubbled up inside Eliza's throat. The year before she'd wanted to buy him more and better insurance but he wouldn't let her.

"I never get sick," he said. "Healthy as a horse." He returned the fork, still full, to his plate and placed the flat of his hand over his chest as if to indicate the robustness of what lay beneath.

"I know, but. *Dad*. You can't not have health insurance. Rob and I can help you with that, you know we want to."

Charlie set his mouth in a thin straight line. As if for show he cut a large piece of meat and brought it in one valiant motion to his lips. "Don't need help, Eliza."

"But."

He chewed and swallowed slowly and deliberately and then he said, "You know you're always welcome here, Eliza, but I'm sure your family needs you more than I do, so you can go on back home when you're ready."

"Are you kicking me out?"

He laughed. "Course not. I'm just giving you permission to kick yourself out."

"No," she said stubbornly. "I'm not leaving until we make you a follow-up appointment."

"Eliza, I'm fine. It was a knock on the head and a bump on the arm. Never should have called the Coast Guard, that made it seem worse than it was. Soon enough I'll be out on the boat and you won't have to worry about me." But there was something behind Charlie's eyes, something fleeting and dodging, and his gaze didn't meet hers.

Her phone dinged again. The Barnes family had a strict no-screens-at-dinner rule but since she was far away she allowed herself a peek, in case she was missing a fire or an earthquake or a playdate invitation that required immediate response. Evie, again. **HOW ABOUT THIS ONE.** This time she'd included a photo directly in the text, a skinny, semi-bearded, vexed-looking terrier mix who looked like he'd left some of his hair at whatever home had given him up. Exactly Evie's style. **HE'S 9 AND HIS NAME IS COLUMBO**, said the next text. **HE'S AT A SHELTER IN CONNECTICUT.**

Eliza, who was in no mood for sugarcoating, texted back **9 IS TOO OLD HE WOULDN'T BE WITH US LONG ENOUGH** and returned her attention to her father. There was a spiderlike blood vessel on the side of his face that she didn't remember from his last visit to Barton in March. All that time in the outdoors, years and years and years of it, of course it could do a number on your skin. A bruise bloomed around the stitches, and the skin around his neck was sagging. Her father, who had always been the strongest, most invincible man she knew, looked suddenly weak and ravaged.

"You go on back home, Eliza, I'll be right as anything this time tomorrow."

She chewed on that for a minute. Something didn't feel right. "When you look me in the eyes, Dad, and tell me that you are one hundred percent fine if I go back home, I'll go. And not until then."

Her father's gaze slid away from her. She took in the unadorned sink, the dish rack with the single sad little coffee cup in it, and she felt her heart cracking.

"That settles it," said Eliza. She recalculated the rest of her week. She could ask Deirdre (read: Deirdre's summer nanny) to help out with the girls if necessary. Rob just had the one project, and his hours were more flexible now that he wasn't commuting into Boston for work. "I'm staying, Dad, just for a few days, until you're all the way back on your feet. Right after dinner, I'll call Rob."

6

LITTLE HARBOR, MAINE

Mary

Josh was beery and cheery, two empties on the table, one in his hand, lying on the old plaid couch.

Mary could blame part of her tardiness on Andi, who decided to take the espresso machine all the way apart for its weekly cleaning right before closing time. But then Mary also had to blame herself, for offering to lend a hand. She helped pour a mix of water and vinegar into the machine and let it run. She helped disassemble the frothing wand and clean that. She helped remove the brew head and clean *that*. She did all of these things despite the fact that Andi kept telling her she could clock out, and despite the fact that she knew Josh was waiting for her.

"I'm okay," she told Andi. "I'm good." While the wand soaked in warm water, she wiped the entire machine down, rubbing away any spots or streaks until she could see her reflection (which looked tired, and worried). Every so often she glanced at the clock over the espresso machine. The clock hands kept moving forward, the way clock hands do, and every time another minute went by she felt a small sickening burst in her stomach. Still, she cleaned on. She ran the vinegar water through the machine once, twice, three times. When her cell phone buzzed in her apron pocket she ignored it.

Andi and Daphne used to call Josh Mary's "young man," like they were elderly grandparents unaccustomed to the ways of today's youth, though Mary knew for a fact that Daphne was thirty-six, the same age as Vivienne, and Andi was forty-one. Sometimes to tease her Daphne called Andi "old lady"; these were the only times Mary saw Andi get irritated with Daphne. Once Mary had heard her say under her breath, "Jesus Christ, Daph, it's five goddamn years, let it go."

Then once Josh had lingered too long in the café at closing, waiting for Mary, and Andi had talked to him for a couple of minutes, and after that something had shifted: they stopped the jokiness, and every now and then Mary caught one or the other of them giving her a look that lived between parental and something more.

Mary put her phone down on the table and bent and kissed Josh. She'd stopped at home to put on the yellow dress that she loved and that Vivienne hated: "Makes you look like a prairie girl." She felt feminine and pretty; she even added a *Hunger Games*–style wraparound braid that Vivienne had taught her to do. Vivienne was always threatening to have Mary come in so the girls could "do something" with Mary's hair.

Josh tasted like Miller Lite. He gestured toward the full cans on the table and said, "Have one, babe." She touched her belly and said, "No thanks, maybe later."

On the screen was *Fast N' Loud*, Josh's favorite car-restoring show. He had to pay extra for the Discovery channel on cable to watch it. There were months when that was a stretch, the extra twelve dollars on the cable bill, but he never considered giving it up. Sometimes Mary paid for part of the bill from the envelope of cash she got from The Cup. She half hoped that Josh would turn the money down but he never did. Maybe she was just as much to blame, for offering. Also, it seemed only fair to help foot the bill, she reasoned, since she and Josh watched a lot of television together.

Mary's math teacher, Ms. Berry, had by April of senior year noticed that

Mary was slipping in her grades and forgetting to turn in homework. She asked Mary to stay late one day to talk about it; she even suggested that she might want to call in Mary's mother for a conference—she smiled and used air quotes and called it a "one-on-one," like that made it more fun, intimate and girly, like a slumber party. But Mary, who knew Vivienne would rather pull off her own eyelash extensions than come in to talk to a math teacher, mumbled something about a really bad cold that had dragged on through the spring. And then she slipped even further under the radar until school came to a close.

It was easy, in a school like theirs, in a life like hers, to disappear. People did it all the time. In fact, it was the people who didn't slip who stood out.

It was funny, because Mary knew almost nothing about Ms. Berry, except for the fact that she hailed from New Hampshire, lived in nearby Franklin, and owned a German shepherd named William, but sometimes when she thought about disappointing her Mary got a rocky feeling deep in her belly.

It was the same feeling that she remembered having as a nine-year-old when she'd lost one of her brand-new birthstone earrings at the state fair in Presque Isle. "Well, that's that," Vivienne had said. "Guess you didn't have them screwed in tight enough." The stomach-dropping permanence of the loss: Mary would recognize it for the rest of her life.

"Aw, come on, darling," Josh wheedled, pointing to the Miller Lite.

He liked it when she drank with him; he liked that it loosened her up. Mary liked it too, if she was being honest. Sober, she was like a balloon tethered to the ground with a series of durable ropes, trying but unable to wrench herself free. After a beer or two, it was as though an invisible hand reached out from nowhere and cut the ropes, and off she floated, into the sky, darting among the clouds, away from herself.

"Maybe later," she said, though she was not going to have a beer, not today.

His expression became a little less cheery. So she pretended great interest in the television: "What are they working on today?" Actually, though, she had no interest in cars.

"Check this out, babe," Josh said, nodding at the television screen.

Josh's dream was to own a '69 Chevy Camaro in blue with two white stripes down the front that he could cruise around town in. He wanted to enter it in the Down East Auto Show in Ellsworth, lined up with the others, hood popped, engine on display. "You can practically *eat* off those engines, they're so clean!" he had said once.

Mary slid Josh's legs over to make room for herself on the couch, then put his legs on top of the yellow dress. He hadn't mentioned the dress. Maybe Vivienne was right: maybe it wasn't a good dress on her. Maybe she did look like a prairie girl. She ventured, "Mmm, you smell clean."

"Had all the time in the world to shower, babe, you were so late." Josh smiled again but this time there was something less nice behind the smile: more beery, less cheery. Sometimes Josh's face changed really quickly like that. Was it normal, for that to happen? Mary didn't think so, but she didn't really have anyone she could ask. She didn't have a best girlfriend the way teenagers in the movies or on TV shows did. She used to. She used to have Alyssa Michaud, before that whole stupid mess with Tyler Wasson.

Virgin Mary, Tyler Wasson had called her after the big disaster, and then he'd gotten all of those assholes on the basketball team to call her that too. Mary's eyes burned, thinking about it.

When Josh, who was new to town, asked Mary to go to the movies with him, Mary figured he thought she was older than she was, even though not very many people mistook her for older. But then it turned out that he knew exactly how old she was, knew she was still in high school. One date led to two and then three and Mary, who had never been on an *actual date* before, and who thought (at first) that Josh was funny and charming, was smitten. When she thought about that asshole Tyler Wasson she practically put her virginity on a platter and said, "Here you go!"

Not that Josh had asked, specifically, in so many words.

As it turned out, she was grateful for the company. All through the winter, through the end of stupid senior year, Mary had somewhere to go after school, on weekends, she had someone who was expecting her, someone who cared where she was and when she was coming back. What was the occasional black mood, the occasional unpredictable silence, compared to that? What did it matter that the dates happened only in the beginning and now he just wanted her to come over and watch TV after work? She had someone, and someone had her.

Now Mary took a deep breath and let it out super slowly and said, "I brought you something, from the café. Cookies!" And she put the lobster cookies on the secondhand coffee table.

Josh glanced at them briefly and said, "Great," with zero enthusiasm. Mary should have given them to Vivienne—she had a sweet tooth. Apparently that was Mary's fault too; Vivienne barely ate a dessert in her life until she got pregnant with Mary. "Girls ruin your figure," she said gloomily, chomping on Twizzlers, though Vivienne wore a size two and was by all accounts still considered a knockout.

"It's true," said Daphne *and* Andi, who claimed to have very different types. "Your mother is indisputably gorgeous." As a footnote they added, a stitch too quickly, "And you are too. You look just like her." But Vivienne was the brighter version, an outdoor floodlight to Mary's low-wattage indoor bulb.

"They're still pretty fresh," she said to Josh, about the cookies. A sticker on the bag said Standard Baking Co., Portland. Just yesterday Eliza Sargent, Charlie Sargent's daughter, had bought a package of them to bring home to her kids and one for her dad. Mary had taken extra care with Eliza's coffee; she was just learning to make designs with the cappuccino foam. Summer people loved that stuff, and even though Eliza was not technically a summer person she didn't seem like a townie either.

"Oh, *look*!" Eliza had said, squinting at the cup. "It's a . . . what's that, a lobster claw? Fantastic."

It was supposed to be a flower but Mary didn't want to embarrass either of them by saying so.

"Okay." Josh's eyes were back on the flat-screen.

Well, this pissed Mary off a little bit. She smoothed the skirt of her yellow dress and said, "Josh. I *brought* you something. I brought you a present. You could at least *acknowledge* it."

His eyes flicked back at her. "I did," he said. "I said thanks."

He hadn't said thanks. Mary tried to let it go, but at the same time a bunch of warning bells were all going off one after another in her brain, and the red flags were waving like crazy. If this was how Josh reacted to a little gift, well . . . what about something way bigger?

She opened the package of lobster cookies and stole a glance at Josh to see if he noticed or cared. Neither. Mary's stomach was so funny lately, sometimes she ate nothing at all and sometimes she just wanted to stuff her face with grease and salt. Was *this* normal?

Mary gave herself a quick little internal lecture about acting like an adult. In August she'd be eighteen; by next year at this time she'd be a mother. Or not. Who cared if he hadn't thanked her for the cookies?

She hadn't paid for them, why was she making such a big deal out of it? She had to watch those juvenile reactions, those silly hurt feelings. Those were high school feelings, or even younger, and she wasn't young anymore.

She dislodged herself from under Josh's legs, walked around behind the couch, and squeezed his shoulders.

"Something wrong?" she asked, leaning close.

"Shit haul today, that's all," he muttered.

"Again, baby? I'm sorry."

It had been a shit haul the day before, too. Come to think of it, a shit haul for a couple of weeks now. Not for everyone in the harbor, but for Josh. "Things will pick up by the end of July," she said. "They always do." She made a little sympathetic noise.

"That's an old-school Stingray," said Josh, to the flat-screen.

This meant nothing to Mary, but she nodded along as though it did. She felt nervous; she was running out of time to get Josh in a better mood. She came back around and sat next to him on the couch. She lifted his hand and traced the veins and muscles with her forefinger. Strong hands, like any fisherman. "Old-school for sure," she affirmed.

This was *not* how the night was supposed to go.

"Corvette," he said. "Been sitting in that garage for more than thirty years."

To Mary every car on Josh's show looked just like every other car on Josh's show. This one was a dull and ugly brown with an unexceptional shape to it. An older woman who looked kind and had her hair pulled back into a headband was standing next to her grown son. They wanted to restore the car in honor of their dead husband/father. Well, that was sweet, but even so. Mary was not going to let her heartstrings get tugged on just then. She had other things on her mind.

"Hey, babe?"

Josh grunted and leaned closer to the TV.

"You want to do something, tonight, something besides this? I came over here after work, I put on this dress, I thought maybe we could—"

Josh whistled.

Not at her, though, at the show. *This wasn't how it was supposed to go.* Mary smoothed the skirt of her yellow dress again. Come to think of it, yellow was not a good color on her, washed her right out. On the screen somebody was going on about fuel injections. "A hundred grand, fully restored," Josh said. "Holy shit. What I wouldn't do with a hundred grand."

Josh hadn't even heard her—she might as well not be in the room with him at all. He whistled again and said, "A *hundred* grand. Just sitting in their garage like that."

"Josh!" she said, and she knew right away that that wasn't the tone of voice she should have used. "I'm trying to *talk* to *you!*" Her voice going up on the *you*.

Josh said, "Jesus goddamn Christ, Mary, I'm trying to watch this goddamn *show!*"

Warning bells, all over her body.

On the television the guy in the leather jacket with the slicked-back salt-and-pepper hair was saying, "Fuel lines, brake lines, water lines, anything that's rubber is going to have to be replaced."

A little flame rose up from Mary's gut, and she said, slowly and carefully, like she was reading out loud a paper in English class, "I'm leaving, Josh." She got up.

"Don't," he said.

"I'm leaving," she said.

"Mary, don't, I'm sorry, okay? Jesus, but I was just trying to watch the show." He pointed the remote at the television and the screen went dark. "Okay? See? Happy now? I shut it off."

She didn't like the look in his eyes. But she sat, and at first when he put his arm around her she thought, *Okay, good, it's going to be okay and soon I can tell him,* and the warning bells momentarily stopped.

He would turn into the person she wanted him to be. She just had to wait a little longer.

7

Rob

It was Taco Night at the Palmer house. Brock was out of town in who-knows-where. (Brock, who did something lucrative in the mystifying world of debt consolidation, was always out of town.) Rob was more than welcome to stay and eat with the girls, Deirdre said. She had a gargantuan taco bar spread the length of her extensive kitchen island, nearly a dozen small white bowls filled with various fixings: scallions, cilantro, olives, pico de gallo, shredded cheese. And so on. "There's plenty!" she said. "Stay!"

But Rob had left some paperwork for Cabot Lodge on the boat—a misguided attempt a few days earlier, before Eliza left, to get some quiet work time in, some perspective. He was going to take the launch from the club and pick up the papers and be back in time to collect the girls from Deirdre's, get them home, and kiss them good night.

On the way to the club from the Palmers', he called Eliza's cell phone twice. She didn't answer either time. He blamed the service up there in Little Harbor. She'd been gone fifty-one hours and he'd talked to her only once, long enough to learn that her dad had hit his head and sprained his arm. It didn't seem like a big deal, but she wanted to stay a few more days to make sure all was well. As long as Rob could hold down the fort.

Could Rob hold down the fort? Of course he could—that was one of the supposed results of leaving the architecture firm of his longtime mentor, Mo Francis, to go into business on his own. More time at home, less time commuting back and forth to Boston. ("You're here more," Evie, the miniature grown-up, had told him. "But you're *here* less.")

"Of course," he'd told Eliza. "Of course I can hold down the fort. You be with your dad." Eliza's dad was a gruff, taciturn specimen of a man, but Evie and Zoe and Eliza went absolutely crazy for him. Rob did his best with Charlie Sargent, just as he knew Eliza did *her* best with Rob's often-present, sometimes-abrasive, usually tipsy mother, Judith. Judith and Eliza, to put it gently, sometimes clashed.

Rob pulled into the club's entrance and the guy in the booth waved him through. Eliza always slowed down significantly to let the booth guy get a good look at her when she drove to the club. She practically pulled out three different forms of identification and offered her fingerprints, a bank statement, and a description of what she'd had for breakfast. She hadn't grown up going to yacht clubs—she had a semisecret fear that somebody was going to throw her out, even though, of course, they were members in good standing and had been forever. Rob had learned, all these years into his marriage to Eliza, to approach her relationship to money the way a bounty hunter might approach a criminal: on tiptoe, in the dark, without a warrant.

In fact, knowing how Eliza felt about their accepting so much from Judith was one of the reasons he'd decided to have the talk with his mom about the money. But he didn't want to think about that right now.

Rob passed into the parking lot that served the clubhouse and the tennis courts and continued on toward the dock. He could see her out there, *A Family Affair*, all fifty-two gorgeous feet of her. They said in the yachting world that there was nothing quite like a Hinckley, and, by golly, they were right. Though speculation in Barton was rampant over the price—was it two and a quarter million? Two point five? Surely not *three* million?—Rob did not know the figure himself. Nor did he really want to.

The kid running the launch was young, three shades of cocky, good-looking in the way that was familiar to Rob from his prep-school days. Broad shoulders, good hair, deep-but-not-Miami-deep summer tan. A thoroughbred. One of the Marshall twins, Rob couldn't say which. The twin said, "You're not taking her out this close to sunset, alone, are you, sir?"

"Nope, just want to visit." He never took the boat out alone; he'd promised Eliza. Also he didn't want to leave the girls with Deirdre for too long—he really wanted to get those papers and get back to work.

He climbed aboard the launch, and the Marshall twin started the motor.

"Nice evening," attempted the Marshall twin after a few moments of silence.

"Sure is," said Rob. Then looked and saw that it was true. The sky was azure and the moon was very faintly outlined, as if politely awaiting its chance to come out.

He shelved his thoughts about Cabot Lodge and felt for his lucky coin in his pocket. Sometime after Rob's father, Robert Barnes I, moved to Thailand to live with a beautiful, smooth-skinned, young woman named Malai, he sent Rob a ten-baht coin, featuring King Bhumibol Adulyadej on one side and the Temple of Dawn on the other. This was long ago, when his father's absence was still new, the wound raw and bleeding, and Rob took the arrival of the coin in the afternoon mail—the envelope tattooed with foreign stamps—as a sign that his father would be coming back soon. He put the coin in the pocket of his school pants on that very first day, making a promise to himself that he'd keep it with him until his father returned.

Obviously, Rob was wrong about the coin's significance. His father wasn't coming back, not then, not ever. And yet it became a habit, moving the coin from his pocket to his dresser each night, returning it to his pocket in the morning, feeling the raised, bespectacled face of King Bhumibol Adulyadej. He'd clung to that coin when Eliza went into early labor with Zoe, when he shot a 79 on the Old Course at St. Andrews, the day he told Mo Francis he was starting out on his own—and every day in between. He'd no sooner leave the house without that coin than he'd leave the house without underwear.

The Marshall twin pulled the launch alongside *A Family Affair,* idled, looked to the sky, and squinted. "This boat is fucking awesome, man," he said. He dropped the cockiness, tapped down the barrier of cool, and became a little kid in front of the biggest toy in the world. "Best boat in the harbor."

"I know," said Rob. He didn't even attempt modesty, because the Marshall kid was exactly right. Sometimes bigger boats came through. But not better, no sir. Not better.

"Fifteen minutes?"

"Yup," said Rob. "Right. Fifteen minutes. Just want to check on a couple of things, grab something I left."

He climbed aboard *A Family Affair* and walked reverently fore and aft along the boat's side decks, running his hands along the custom-made stainless hardware, the hand-varnished dorade boxes, the dodger grab rails covered with supple elk hide. He bent to feel the elegantly shaped teak toe rails. Belowdecks, not one, not two, but *three* cabins, every corner rounded, every detail perfected, down to the dovetail drawers, the custom-built dish rack, the teak flush-mounted knife stand.

Rob collected the papers and tried hard not to think about the thing with his mother and the money. He tried not to think about the fact that Eliza's high school boyfriend lived in Little Harbor too. He tried not to think about the "casual drink" Eliza had had with the boyfriend when she'd first arrived. He tried not to think about the way she'd worked that into their only conversation, scrupulously careful to make it sound like no big deal.

Don't be an asshole, Rob. Probably it *was* no big deal. Russell Perkins was just an ex, and everybody had exes! He had Kitty Sutherland, whom he'd dated the first two years of college, before he met Eliza. Headbanded, Kennedy-like, blond-bobbed Kitty Sutherland, who, even in the most grungy of the grunge days in Providence, never exchanged her ballet flats for Doc Martens, her tailored pants for oversized men's jeans with flannel shirts.

But Kitty Sutherland meant nothing to him anymore. Could Eliza say the same about Russell Perkins? There was something about those men who worked with their hands, who pulled their livings right out of the sea, like some sort of mythical creatures, that made Rob feel hopelessly inadequate. There was a fear, always tickling the back of his mind, that one day he'd lose Eliza to the world she came from. And he couldn't lose Eliza. She was the light in the darkness, the bird singing in the trees, and every other cliché he could come up with. If he ever lost her, he wouldn't be able to go on.

8

LITTLE HARBOR, MAINE

Eliza

Today's shelter dog was a corgi and Great Pyrenees mix named Elijah. Eliza, packing to go home, squinted at the photograph in Evie's text and wondered how on earth those two breeds were able to mate. Actually, she wouldn't mind seeing it, if only to verify that it was possible. It seemed like the beginning of a dirty joke: *A corgi and a Great Pyr walk into a bar* . . .

She texted back, **WE CAN'T GET A DOG WHOSE NAME IS SO CLOSE TO MINE**, and immediately came the reply: **WE CAN CHANGE THE NAME**.

Whoever had thought it was a good idea for young children to be able to text from iPads deserved a swift kick in the pants. Eliza loved Evie to the moon and back, of course, but there were times when it was *perfectly fine* to be out of touch. In her opinion. How were these kids going to grow up with even a half an ounce of self-sufficiency when they had grown-ups at their constant disposal? She texted back, **NOPE!** Then she added the blowing-a-kiss emoji (Evie could be sensitive, and an emoji could make all the difference) and turned off her phone. She could always blame Little Harbor's spotty cell service.

Of course, there were plenty of parents who wanted to be in close touch with their children 24/7. "It's ridiculous," Sheila Rackley had said about Jackie a few weeks ago, all fake-complainy. "She texts me *all the time.*" You could tell, though, that she was proud of the fact, like she and Jackie were both members of the same popular high school clique.

Her father had gone down to check something on his boat.

"How're you going to get yourself out there?" Eliza had asked suspiciously, indicating his hurt arm.

"I'll have one of the kids row me out. I want to ask around anyway, see who can help me out. Don't want to stay too long off the water."

Eliza had studied her father over the past few days as carefully as she could manage without his shrugging her off. He looked tired, and he was sleeping more than usual, but he'd been through a shock, that was to be expected. Eliza had examined the wound on Charlie's head, which was healing nicely. The sling was the bigger problem: of course he couldn't haul with the use of only one arm. Although with enough help, the right kind of help, he could at least ride on the *Joanie B*—he could maybe even drive it, one-handed, and direct somebody else to check his traps. With a sternman and one other guy, he could probably manage. Not that Charlie Sargent was big into asking for help. But he was worried about his traps, left untended for this many days, so he'd take hauling with help over not hauling with no help.

"You promise me you're just checking the boat, you're not going to go sneaking off into open water, are you?" she'd said.

"Never had any reason to lie to you before, Eliza, not going to start now."

She tried not to harp on the fact that he didn't meet her eyes when he said that.

If she left by one o'clock she'd be home before dinner. If Charlie found the right kind of help he'd go out to haul in the morning. By the time she woke at home he would already have risen in the predawn darkness and had his usual cup of coffee and fried egg sandwich at Val's and started the motor of the *Joanie B* and headed out under a gorgeous summer sunrise. He'd turn to his sternman and say something about how Bobby Cutler had better start hauling like a man if he wanted to pay off that new boat before his son got old enough to take over, and life would start to return to normal.

And Eliza would be slumbering in her own bed next to her own husband with her children just down the hall in their respective rooms. School had been out nearly a week! Let the summer commence. Trips to the beach. A day sail on *A Family Affair.* Evie's theater camp performance. And, of course, Deirdre's charity gala, East Africa Needs You. *Eenie meenie miney moe,* Sheila had said, and Deirdre hadn't laughed. Of course not. She was taking this all very seriously, *as well she should,* but Eliza couldn't help but think that if they took all the money and effort that went into the gala and just sent it right to Africa . . . well, wouldn't it have a bigger impact?

But Deirdre's heart was in the right place, and Eliza's fund-raising experience was nonexistent.

She unzipped her bag and started to pack the pile of clothes she'd carried down from upstairs. It was amazing how many of her things were scattered around her father's small house. Not only amazing, it was totally rude and inappropriate. She would have chastised the girls if they'd left such a mess in someone else's house. She supposed she had reverted to her own untidy teen years, being back in her childhood home.

Maybe Charlie would be glad to see her go, be happy to get back to his orderly and unadorned life: the single coffee cup, the simple dinners, the quiet. Later in the summer, when the camps were over, when Charlie's arm was one hundred percent healed, she'd bring the girls up for a visit. They loved going out on the *Joanie B,* loved helping Charlie pull the traps; they howled with laughter when he told stories about their mother doing the same, day after day, summer after summer, with the *atrociously smelly herring* (Zoe) and the *super-funny orange overalls, did you really wear those, Mom?* (Evie, and yes, she did). For the girls, hauling traps was a tourist activity, a quaint, temporary glimpse into a bygone world, like riding the Viking boat in Epcot's Norway.

She collected her cell phone chargers (two? Why had she brought two?), her multivitamins and probiotics, her toothpaste, the novel she'd made zero progress in reading, the *Us Weekly* with Taylor Swift on the cover that she'd had no trouble getting all the way through. But she couldn't find the notepad on which she wrote her ever-expanding to-do list (Eliza was modern in many ways but a staunch traditionalist in the list-making department), and that was sending her into a little bit of a panic. She lived and died by her list.

She was on her hands and knees, looking under the sofa, when she heard a knock at the door, and then Val came in. "Hey," she said. "I heard you were heading back home, Eliza."

"Where'd you hear that?" Nothing under the sofa; Eliza stood and sighed. If Val was here the restaurant must be closed. Time was slipping away; she'd be later than she planned getting on the road.

"It's a pretty small town," said Val. "I hear most things. What are you looking for?" Eliza was almost always happy to see Val, but the loss of the notepad was really vexing her—she *hated* losing things.

"I just can't find my notepad—I wrote down all of these things Zoe needs for science camp when I was talking to her last night. It's driving me batty." She felt a childish need to blame Val about the notepad even though, obviously, it was Eliza who had misplaced it. "It was weird things, like worms and snails and yogurt containers and something about a blood-testing kit . . ."

She moved to the kitchen; Val followed her, making clucking noises that were soothing in their own way but that didn't make the list any more found. "Your mother was the same way, you know, about losing things. Couldn't stand it." Eliza's survey of the kitchen was interrupted by a familiar sensation in her belly; this happened when somebody brought up her mother out of the blue like that, especially someone who, like Val, had known Joanie intimately. It was a feeling so strong it came with its own sound: *thwomp,* or *fromp,* a sound that reminded her even this many years later of the magnitude of her loss. She was torn between saying, *Don't talk about her, it still hurts too much* and *Let's sit down right now and you tell me every single thing I might not know about her.*

"I'll run and check upstairs, maybe it's under your bed," offered Val.

Eliza tore open a kitchen drawer that nearly loosened itself from its runner with the force of her frustration. "It's a notepad, not an earring back! Shouldn't be hard to find."

The all-American junk drawer, which in her father's simple life was not very junky at all: Eliza could see a measuring tape, a screwdriver, a pair of ancient kitchen shears, a coil of rubber bands. And beneath those items, a sheaf of folded papers that she pulled out anyway, partly because she was a confirmed snooper and partly because she was hoping that somehow the notepad had crawled underneath the sheaf of papers, forgotten the time, and fallen asleep.

How extremely odd; her father had somebody else's medical report in the junk drawer in his kitchen . . .

And then there was Val, frozen in the kitchen door, holding Eliza's notepad. On Val's face was an expression that reminded Eliza of her daughters when they were trying and failing to keep a secret. Both of her children were terrible liars, and for that Eliza was grateful.

"Here it is!" said Val with false brightness. "It had slid between the bed and the bedside table. And I also found a bobby pin and two sticks of gum."

Eliza looked more carefully at the paper. It was dated April 12. Patient's name: *Charlie Sargent.* But that couldn't be right—her father would rather sleep on porcupine quills than go to the doctor; it was only at the behest of the Coast Guard that he'd agreed to get his arm and head treated the other day. They'd brought him to the ER themselves because his head had been bleeding and he'd had to get the stitches put in and the sling put on. But back in April?

"Eliza," said Val, dropping the false brightness.

DOB: 3-30-52.

"Eliza," more sharply.

Insurance: *None.*

"*Eliza.*" Val was panicking now. Eliza held one finger up, like she was signaling to the waiter that she needed another minute.

She turned to the next page, which was the results of a CT scan, and which contained these words, which Eliza had to read three times to make sure she'd gotten them right: *Suggestive of occipital glioblastoma multiforme, left lobe.*

Payment: *Out of pocket, MasterCard, Valerie Beals.*

Now the words were swimming in front of Eliza, the letters mixing themselves up in different order, turning on their sides and then righting themselves.

"Wait," said Eliza. She met Val's eyes. She'd looked into those eyes so many times over the years—it had been that voice that had told Eliza her mother was finally gone, that face, as familiar as her own, to which she'd told her *terrible thing* to all those years ago. But now there was something unfamiliar about Val, like invisible ropes were pulling at her, changing the contours of her face into something unrecognizable. "I don't understand. A glioblastoma multiforme is a brain tumor."

She looked down at the paper again. *Immediate follow-up recommended.*

"Listen," said Val. "You listen to me, Eliza."

"A glioblastoma, Val, is an *incurable brain tumor.*"

Already, in her mind, Eliza was maniacally googling *brain cancer treatment options;* she was flipping through the neurology section in one of her old medical school books. She was even singing the ridiculous song about the organs that Evie had learned in the third grade. *My body is working day and night, working and working all the time . . .*

"Eliza, honey. Your father is sick."

My brain controls everything, everything my body does. My lungs are breathing in the air, putting oxygen in my blood . . .

Val sat at the table, motioned Eliza to sit across from her, and folded her hands as if in prayer. "Charlie wasn't feeling right for a while, for a good long time, but of course you know him, he wouldn't admit to it. Even so, he was getting so tired out in the boat, coming in earlier and earlier, catching less and less. This was right after he came back from visiting you in March—right before his birthday. Still wouldn't take a sternman with him. Then in early April there was one time he got a little bit confused, came in off the boat, one of the guys told me he was slurring a little, it seemed for about twenty seconds he didn't know where he was . . ." She paused. "So I didn't give him any choice, I made him an appointment at Maine Coast Memorial, took him in. He had the CT scan, and they didn't like the way that looked, so they ordered an MRI. And that confirmed the diagnosis."

"Why didn't you call *me*, Val?" Eliza's voice broke like a twig. "*I* should have done that." It made her feel like the worst kind of daughter to think that she was downing cocktails at the club or, for God's sake, maybe taking a barre class when her father was sick.

"He wouldn't let me, Eliza. Of course I suggested that. But you never heard a man so determined. He didn't want you to know . . ."

"But he's got to come to Boston, Val. For treatment. He can't stay *here*! That was April, and it's almost July—Val, he's got to see a neurosurgeon. Right away. He needs to see one yesterday." Eliza looked around wildly, as though her father were hiding, diseased and untreated, under the table, and she could drag him out and drive him to a Boston hospital. "He's got to go now, he needs to come back with me *today*. Val, do you have any idea how serious this is. *Glioblastoma*? It's the worst kind of brain tumor you can have, the very worst. The most aggressive kind of brain cancer there is."

"Yuh," Val said fiercely. "Course I do. I heard everything that doctor said to him, Eliza, every word. He didn't want you to know, Eliza. He still doesn't. You know your dad, if he wanted your help he would have called you right up and asked for it. If he wanted you to know, he would have told you himself."

Eliza slumped forward in her chair. "Oh, Val. *Val*. What are we going to do?"

9

NAPLES, MAINE

Rob

Mark Ruggman, the general contractor on Cabot Lodge, was slugging from a gigantic Dunkin' Donuts cup, so Rob didn't dare bring out his Starbucks grande cappuccino—he left it growing cold in the Pilot's cup-holder. Sissy drink. Worse if you took a good sniff and smelled the extra shot of vanilla. But, hey, in the words of Selena Gomez by way of *Breaking Bad*'s Uncle Jack, the heart wants what the heart wants.

"Hey," said Ruggman, when Rob dismounted from the minivan, whose tires had bitten into the soft dirt surrounding the foundation of Cabot Lodge.

"Hey yourself," said Rob. He winced a little at how eager he sounded. (Shouldn't it be the other way around? After all, *he* had hired Ruggman.)

Cabot Lodge, all seven thousand square feet of it, had been framed and Sheetrocked; it had windows, doors, a roof, siding, and you would think, if you didn't know better, that this meant that the bulk of the work was done. (Rob knew better; Rob would bet a bundle of money that Ruggman knew better too.)

Through the stand of pines along the edge of the water, Long Lake looked bright blue and inviting—it looked freshly scrubbed, like the cleaning people had just been there. Far to the left he could see the *Songo River Queen II* loading passengers for its noon voyage. Rob didn't know where the *Songo River Queen I* was; perhaps, like Robert Barnes I, it had decided to move to Thailand years ago with its mistress.

Closer to Cabot Lodge, a lone stand-up paddleboarder glided by, then a trio of kayaks. A single cotton ball of a cloud hung low in the sky, and from a house a few docks down a motorboat whirred to life. It was all very *On Golden Pond*. Very paradisiacal.

"It's coming along here," said Rob approvingly. The day before, Ruggman had let him know that the cabinets were in, and Rob wanted to check them out.

Christine Cabot was hosting Thanksgiving for her extended family. Before the first snowflake fell she wanted the house shipshape for ski season at any one of the many accessible mountains. She wanted to put to use the ski racks she'd requested for the outside of the house, the bunk beds she'd ordered for her dear grandchildren, the crockery in which she planned to serve chili.

When Rob had first met with Christine Cabot he had croaked out something that wasn't exactly a lie but wasn't fully the truth either. Rob had said, "You'll be in by Thanksgiving, no problem." Christine Cabot had beamed at him, showing a perfect mouthful of they-couldn't-all-be-real teeth, and he'd been once again the fatherless student at Buckingham Browne & Nichols, riding a wave of charm and optimism. He'd been the Ivy League undergrad, the willing husband and father, the jolly party guest. *Give them what they want, and they will smile at you.* His Achilles' heel, if ever he had one: the need to please.

"Should we wait for Christine before we go in?" he asked Ruggman.

"She was here." A modicum of satisfaction seemed to pass over Ruggman's face slowly.

"Here? Already?"

"'Bout ninety minutes ago."

"Without me?" Now Rob felt like a boy stranded at a cotillion.

"Apparently." Ruggman leaned over and spit into the dirt. You had to be a certain kind of man to pull off that kind of unapologetic dirt-spitting. Rob was not that kind of man; he never had been.

"And she—she saw the cabinets?"

"Oh, she saw 'em." Another swig of coffee. Ruggman rocked back on his heels and squinted at the lake. The stand-up paddleboarder's progress was impressive.

"Ruggman. Why do I get the feeling that there's something you're not telling me?"

Ruggman cleared his throat. "Thought she would have called you herself. Truth is"—he spit again—"she hates 'em."

"What do you mean she hates them?" Rob made a great show of reattaching the *th* to the word.

Rob knew that this stage of the project could be the hardest part. After the framing came the finishes: the lighting fixtures, floors, trim work, built-ins. And the kitchen fucking cabinets. These, he knew, were the times that tried men's souls.

"Dunno," said Ruggman. "She hates 'em, she wants to start again."

"But that means—"

"I know." Ruggman looked almost sage.

"Possibly delaying move-in," said Rob.

"Your words," said Ruggman. "But, yeah." He polished off the coffee and crumpled the cup in his meaty paw. "Gotta go check on the guys, holler before you leave and let me know where you want to go from here." He eyed Rob's pocket. "Phone's ringing."

"Oh. Didn't hear it. Thanks." Rob answered without looking—he assumed it was Eliza. He moved away from Ruggman, toward the back of the property.

"Robbie?"

Only one person on the planet besides Mrs. Cabot called him Robbie: she of the boundless energy and coiffed hair, charity chairwoman extraordinaire, doting grandmother to his two little princesses, alternately the bane of his existence and the reason for it. His mother. Judith.

"Hey, Mom." A little voice said, *Talk to her about the money. Now, do it now, straighten it out. Tell her you made a mistake.*

"I just got off the phone with Christine."

A miniature elf began knocking against Rob's skull with the back of a hammer, from the inside.

"Is that right?"

"She's frantic."

"*She's* frantic?"

"She's got her whole family coming for the holidays."

"She mentioned that, Mom. I believe she mentioned it more than once."

"And she says the cabinets are *hideous.* She says she has to start over, finding new cabinets."

"Well."

Judith went on: "I haven't heard her this upset since Jonathan Junior dropped out of law school."

Rob sucked in his breath. "Jonathan Junior was a complete cokehead, Mom, that's why he dropped out of law school."

"Robbie!" said Judith.

Last Rob knew Jonathan Junior was at a wilderness treatment facility in Montana; they'd thrown him to the actual wolves.

"Mom. She chose those cabinets, she picked them out. She liked them when she chose them!"

"Well, she doesn't like them now. So you'll help her, right? You'll fix it? The customer is always right. Isn't that what you all say?"

"I think that's what they say in Home Depot."

"Don't be fresh, Robbie."

It was hard to feel chastised and angry and nervous all at the same time, but, as Rob learned at that moment, not impossible.

"Robbie? Are you still there? You know Christine has *several* friends who want to build houses even *bigger than hers* in that same area. Work like that could keep you busy for years. If you are intent on making your own way in the world."

"I know, Mom. That's why I took this job in the first place."

Ruggman called, "Hey! Barnes! We need you over here!" Rob liked being called by his last name. Made him feel salt-of-the-earth.

"Mom, I've got to go. I'm working, Mom—"

"But you'll help her sort it out?"

"Of course I will."

The elf with the hammer: *tap, tap, tappity tap.*

"That's my boy, Robbie. I knew you'd get her in by Thanksgiving."

He looked down. "Mom, Eliza's on the other line, I have to go."

Eliza was crying. More than crying. She was sobbing. He hadn't heard Eliza cry like that since—wait, had he ever heard Eliza cry like that? He couldn't make out what she was saying. The paddleboarder had reached the dock. Ruggman was striding toward him.

"Rob?" asked Eliza, from another world. "Are you there?"

A cloud passed over the sun, and for an instant the world went dim.

"I'm here," he said. "I'm here."

10

LITTLE HARBOR, MAINE

Eliza

This can be fixed. That's what Eliza thought after she got off the phone with Rob, who had listened while she sobbed, and waited until she could speak, and then offered to drop everything and drive up to Little Harbor that minute. That didn't make any sense, they both knew that, but she loved that he offered.

Everything could be fixed, with enough determination. Eliza was a firm believer in that; she was always repeating those words to her daughters. Torn math sheet? No worries, we'll download another from the teacher's website! Colored outside the lines on the social studies poster? Scribble over the blue part with a white crayon, *there,* good as new. Broken car?

Heart? Dreams? All repairable. *This can be fixed.* She repeated it on her way to the wharf, over and over again, like a mantra.

Was it money that was holding Charlie back from talking to her? Well, she had money, *they* had money. Rob's mother had gobs and gobs of money, more than she knew what to do with. You couldn't buy yourself a new brain. But you could buy yourself the best doctor in Boston, you could buy yourself *options*. She just needed her father to come in off his boat so she could talk to him. She picked her pace up to a jog, then a run. When she arrived at the wharf she was breathing aggressively.

Oh, *damn.* She was hoping to be alone, but the girl from the coffee shop was there, the sweet girl who made the uncertain designs in the cappuccinos. Mary. She turned when she heard Eliza approaching and her face had such an open expression that Eliza felt terrible for wishing her away.

"Hey," said Eliza. "Hope you don't mind if I join you." She tried to make her voice sound normal and sociable, not at all like someone who'd just learned devastating news. She didn't even know yet what she would say to her father; she hadn't worked that part out yet.

"Sure," said Mary. She did something interesting with her body where she didn't really move but appeared somehow to make extra space for Eliza beside her.

"It's Mary, isn't it? From the café?"

"Right." Mary smiled shyly at Eliza.

"Eliza."

"I know. I remember."

"Are you waiting for someone?"

"Yeah," said Mary. "My boyfriend. He's . . ." She cleared her throat.

"He's a fisherman?" Eliza supplied.

"Yes."

"What's he doing coming back now? It's only—" Eliza checked her watch. "Two thirty."

"Yeah. Sometimes he, I don't know. Sometimes he doesn't go out all day. If he had a bad day the day before. He gets sort of, I don't know, upset." Mary laughed, but it was that uncertain girl-laugh that Eliza sometimes heard from Zoe and her friends. That laugh made Eliza feel both incensed at and tender toward young girls. She wanted to say, "Don't laugh if you don't think it's funny, you don't owe this world anything!"

and at the same time she wanted to say, "Come here, sweetie, let me give you a hug, it's going to be okay."

She turned and studied Mary: she was really very pretty, with pale blond hair and gorgeous skin. But she didn't hold herself like a girl who thought she was pretty. Eliza had given up on the gorgeous skin after so many years on lobster boats; there was no amount of high-end products that could undo her freckles. Now, when she went out on sailboats at home, she slathered herself with sunscreen, though to hear the dermatologists tell it the damage had been done long ago. It was all a lost cause.

Eliza could see the *Joanie B* out on its mooring, and she could even see her father moving cautiously around on it, and she tried to ignore the way her brain kept repeating the words *He's sick he's sick he's sick* over and over.

After a while she said, "Sometimes I think about how many people have sat here waiting for these boats to come in. Through the ages. You know? It's such a funny thing, a town like this. I mean, growing up here it seemed totally normal that this was what most of the men did for a living, disappearing in a boat and then coming back at the end of the day. And then I went out in the world and I saw that most people don't do that, most people go off in cars and go to offices and move money around or design buildings or manage international businesses . . ." She trailed off. *Tumor tumor tumor,* went the little voice in her head.

"I never thought about it that way," said Mary.

"Why would you?" asked Eliza. "This is your world. Am I babbling? Sorry if I am. I do that, I babble when I'm trying to keep my mind off something."

"That's okay," said Mary. "I don't mind."

Cancer cancer cancer.

"My mother used to wait here for my father. In fact, she met him right here. She was a summer girl, and she fell in love, and that was that. She never left. She always told me it was like a fairy tale."

"That's beautiful," breathed Mary. She smiled.

"She died when I was twelve."

"I'm sorry."

"*I'm* sorry. I didn't mean to come right out with that. It's just—I guess I'm just feeling maudlin."

Glioblastomas were almost universally fatal.

To change the subject, to keep the terrible words from marching back and forth across her mind, Eliza said, "You have really pretty hair, you know. I bet you get out of the shower and it just dries like that, so smooth and flat."

The occipital lobe was at the back of the brain, where you would cup somebody's head to help them sip from a cup of water if they were sick. If they were dying.

Mary looked startled, like she hadn't ever really thought about it. "I guess so."

"Lucky."

"My mother says my hair is a disaster. No body to it."

"That's crazy," said Eliza. "No offense to your mother. But *my* hair is a disaster. Can't do a thing with it except stick it back and hope for the best."

That, in fact, was the subject of Lesson Number One in the letter Joanie had left for Eliza: hair.

Your hair will make you crazy but it will make others envious, and the second thing will make up for some (but not all) of the first. I had the same hair before it was ravaged by chemo. I hope you remember me with it more than you remember me without it.

I am beyond tears, Eliza. I've leaked them all out. My body is drying up beneath me: my lips, my skin, my organs.

Sometimes you bring me a bowl of ice chips, my darling, and they are like nectar to me.

Here's what you do with your hair, Eliza. Nothing. When you were young I used to braid it for you. I used to take a fine-toothed comb and part it straight down the center and create order out of the chaos. When you turned eleven you didn't want the braids anymore (my heart broke a little at that) and then you were truly at a loss. You are just now getting a handle on it. I suggest the following. Don't try to tame it. Trims twice a year. (I'll have Val take you, Charlie won't be up to the task.) Always air-dry; never blow-dry. Never cut layers; never allow anyone else to cut layers. If you're going out somewhere and you want to look especially beautiful, pile it on top of your head. Use Conair Secure Hold bobby pins in black, always buy in pack of 90. No hairspray. Let a few curls fall around your face. They will swoon.

"Oh *no*," said Mary. "*Your* hair is beautiful, all those curls. I'd give anything."

"You're sweet to say that," said Eliza, even though the terrible words were still marching.

A glioblastoma, on a scan, showed up white and glowing against the gray of the brain.

Mary laughed more sincerely. Now Eliza was glad that Mary was there, taking her mind off the awfulness a little bit. "But I guess we always want what we can't have. Human nature."

After a few beats Mary, looking not at Eliza but down at the navy-blue water, kicked her legs against the wharf and asked, "Are you glad you left? Like, for good?"

Eliza didn't even have to think about that. "Oh boy, I'm *so glad* I left."

Mary looked stricken, and Eliza added quickly, "I wasn't always! It was hard, leaving. It really was." At Brown, freshman year, first semester especially, she had been completely lost. Providence, though not a big city in anyone's idea of big cities, seemed gigantic to Eliza. Her roommate, a sophisticated beauty named Francesca Spencer from Manhattan, was so private-school polished and chic that next to her Eliza felt like she'd grown up in a hamster cage. She worried constantly about Charlie, rattling around the little house alone. She was so strapped with college expenses that she never had any money; a sandwich from the Hole in the Wall on Thayer Street was a grand extravagance.

She got over each of those points in time, but, in fairness, she had called Russell once from the pay phone in the student union and begged him to come get her.

He had refused.

He hadn't forgiven her. Not then. She wasn't even sure if he'd forgiven her by now.

Mary still looked troubled, so Eliza went on. "And there's a lot to be said for growing up in a place where everybody knows everybody—"

She stopped, because she could see Mary's shoulders start to quiver just a bit, and then to shake in earnest, and then she was crying for real. Eliza said wretchedly, "Oh my gosh! I'm so sorry! I didn't mean—"

Mary waved at her, as if to indicate that the crying jag was unrelated to Eliza, and gulped out, "No, it's not . . . it isn't . . ." before her crying began anew.

Eliza was momentarily at a loss, and then it occurred to her that to put aside one's own worries for a moment to help somebody else with theirs was always the right move.

"Mary? You don't have to talk to me, you barely know me, but you can. I'm a pretty good listener."

Mary made a great heaving sound that seemed like a marriage between a cry and a swallow.

"Do you have someone to talk to, even if it's not me?" Eliza moved closer to Mary and put her arm around her. Maybe she was out of bounds, but she was around enough teenage girls to know that you did not leave one alone and crying unless she specifically requested to be left alone. You always tried first. She waited: Mary didn't request to be left alone. If anything, she leaned in toward Eliza, and she could have been Evie or Zoe, distraught over a recess slight or the party invitation that never came.

"It's okay, Mary," Eliza said firmly, even though she didn't think anything was okay. Nothing was okay. That silly little song again: *My brain controls everything, everything my body does.*

She thought about all the daughters and wives and sisters and lovers who had ever waited on this wharf for someone to come in off the water. *He's sick he's sick he's sick.* She thought about how sometimes the people you were waiting for didn't come back at all. She felt her own eyes begin to fill, and she had to blink the tears back and take a deep breath. Beside her Mary's crying had slowed and she said, "I'm sorry, I don't know what . . ."

"No," said Eliza. "You don't need to apologize for a thing. Okay?"

Mary didn't answer.

"Okay, Mary?"

"Okay."

"I'm going home for a few days to see my family and then I'll be back up for—well, because I have to do some stuff for my dad. But here, give me your cell phone. I'm going to punch in my number, just in case you need an ear."

Mary hesitated.

"It's not optional." Eliza tried to look stern, the way she looked when her children started to walk away from the dinner table without clearing their plates.

"Okay." Mary pulled her phone from her pocket and presented it to Eliza without looking at it. Before she found the contacts Eliza saw a text that said **HEY BABE SORRY ABOUT B4.**

She glanced at Mary, who was looking out at the water again. She entered herself as a contact along with her phone number and, what the heck, her email address. You never knew. By the time she looked up again she could see a skiff coming toward them, Charlie as passenger, an unfamiliar man rowing.

"Here comes my dad," said Eliza, and her heart started thumping to the beat of *tumor tumor tumor.* "I can't tell who that is rowing him in—"

"I can," said Mary. "That's my boyfriend, that's Josh."

They both stood up and waved.

In the moment before the skiff reached the wharf Eliza did something that surprised her. Later, she couldn't have said what on earth possessed her to take the conversation in this direction. She turned to Mary and said, "You know what my mother used to tell me?"

"What?"

"She used to say, 'When in doubt, choose brave.' "

Mary considered this. "I like that," she said.

"It sounds corny," admitted Eliza. It really did, now that she'd spoken the words aloud, it sounded like something Zoe would roll her eyes at. Although truthfully the words had sustained her again and again throughout her life. "But it's amazing how many different circumstances it suits."

"Maybe," said Mary.

Eliza took a deep breath and watched as the skiff grew closer and closer and she steeled herself for what was to come.

11

LITTLE HARBOR, MAINE

Mary

The lady at the clinic reception desk had brown eyes, dairy-cow eyes, and a soft bosom—her boobs were practically napping on the desk in front of her—that made Mary want to sink into her arms and stay for a week and a half. Mary's throat was dry and scratchy, and when she opened her mouth to say her name she realized she hadn't spoken to anyone since Vivienne left for work in the morning. She hadn't eaten anything, either, and her stomach complained about that. Loudly.

"Okay," said the woman. "Let's get you sorted out, then. Better get comfortable, there's a bunch of forms the first visit. If you have an insurance card, I'll go ahead and make a copy."

Mary lowered her eyes and whispered, "I don't."

"Okay," said the woman, extra cheerfully. "No problem, insurance isn't required for treatment here."

It was your basic form: name, address, date of birth, previous health conditions, etc., etc. Date of last period. Reason for today's visit. Ugh ugh ugh. *Pregnant,* Mary wrote miserably, but she didn't allow her eyes to fill. In not too long she was going to be a mother. She couldn't allow herself to go to pieces over a simple little form. *Pull it together, Mary.*

The dairy-cow woman at the desk told Mary that a counselor would call her any minute, so Mary picked up a magazine and pretended to read it until she heard her name. When she did, she followed the counselor down a long hallway and through a doorway and into a room with white walls and two chairs. This woman looked nothing like a dairy cow; she was small, smaller than Mary, with brown hair cut close to her head (*too short, too boyish,* Vivienne would say), no makeup, no breasts. "I'm *Sa*-rah," said the woman, leaning on the first syllable. "I'm a medical assistant and a counselor here, and I'm going to start by asking you some questions, and then you'll see our nurse practitioner, Patricia. K?"

"Okay," said Mary. She sat in the chair *Sa*-rah motioned her to and pressed her knees together so they wouldn't quiver.

Sarah looked at the forms, cocked her head, and said, "We'll have you take a pregnancy test in just a minute. Even if you've taken five at home, even if you've taken fifty. We still do our own."

"Okay," said Mary.

Sarah asked the questions the way she seemed to do everything else: quickly, with no movement wasted. She reminded Mary of Vivienne's friend Sam, who worked in the ICU at Maine Coast Memorial. Sam was Mary's favorite of Vivienne's friends.

These were the questions.

"Are you in a committed relationship?"

"Do you feel safe in your relationship?"

"Was the sex consensual?"

"Do you feel safe at home?"

"Are you *at all* worried that you might have contracted an STD?"

"Are you having any pain?"

These were the answers.

Yes, yes, yes, yes, no, no.

Mary was blushing madly by the end, she was blushing like a freak, but Sarah could have been talking about the weather, she was so casual about the whole thing, and if she noticed the blushing she didn't say a word about it. Mary put a hand to her cheek to try to cool it and Sarah didn't seem to notice that either.

When she was done with the questions Sarah sent Mary into a nearby bathroom with a cup and instructions. "To collect your urine," she said, like it was a hobby, like collecting stamps or exotic rocks. Before filling the cup, Mary let her eyes roam around the bathroom: there were all sorts of posters, and business-card-sized information about hotlines, and full-sized pamphlets. *There's more to life, use protection,* said one. *Half of all STDs are in people under the age of* 25, said another. *Silence hides violence,* with a woman's mouth covered by a man's hand. *You are not alone.* A third—*ugh*—showed a pregnant woman with bruises all over her arms. Mary looked at the posters, and what flashed before her was the odd hooded look Josh's eyes sometimes took on when he got impatient with her.

But these posters were talking about *violence,* hitting and pushing and hurting, actual hurting. Violence, not impatience. These posters had nothing to do with her, with Josh. She wasn't these women. She didn't need a card. When she was done she placed the cup in the little window, as Sarah had instructed her to do.

Mary was relieved to learn that she didn't have to take off her clothes for an exam, that the nurse practitioner would just talk to her once they had the results of the test. The nurse practitioner, Patricia, was older and taller than Sarah and had the slim body and leathery skin of a passionate hiker or a long-distance runner. She shook Mary's hand and smiled, and when she smiled deep creases formed around her eyes. She said, very carefully, like the words were infants who required special care, "We have the results of your test. It's just as you thought, Mary, you're pregnant. About eight weeks, based on the date of your last period."

Even though Mary knew this already she realized that she'd been hoping for the test to prove her wrong. She thought, unexpectedly, of Ms. Berry writing a complicated problem on the board and looking to Mary to solve it.

"Now," said Patricia, "I'm sure you've been thinking about your options . . ."

She waited and looked at Mary until Mary nodded.

"And if you've made up your mind one way or the other we don't have to spend too much time talking about all of them." She waited again.

"I haven't," whispered Mary. "I haven't made up my mind."

"Not a problem," said Patricia easily. She opened a drawer and selected papers from three different piles. "We have information here on abortion, adoption, and carrying to term and raising the baby yourself. I'll give you all of these when you leave."

She laid the papers on the counter and looked again at Mary. Mary cleared her throat and said, "For, um." She couldn't get the word out, she kept tripping on it. "For an *abortion*." Patricia waited. "How, um. How long . . ." *Get it together, Mary,* she told herself sternly. She cleared her throat again and thought of Andi and Daphne and how kindly they spoke to her, and how they used to tease her about Josh being her *beau,* making it all sound so innocent and fun, like something out of a movie about American high schools. She felt like she'd disappointed them, of all people, by getting into this situation. She said, "When would I need to? Decide by."

"We do not perform abortions here," said Patricia kindly, and Mary thought what a funny word *perform* was in this context. Like this whole thing was a play or a YouTube video. Entertainment. "We can give you information on the procedure, but if you want to go that route you'd need to go to a clinic in Bangor. We can give you contact information for that clinic. The laws in the state of Maine dictate that abortions can be performed up until twenty-two weeks. *But* there is a limit to how far individual doctors and clinics are willing to go. In Bangor the latest is thirteen weeks and six days. After fourteen weeks you'd need to go to a Planned Parenthood clinic or down to Massachusetts."

"Thirteen weeks and six days," repeated Mary softly. It was such a specific number of days.

"That gives you some time from now," said Patricia. "You would need to make an appointment earlier, of course. And if you're certain about it, the earlier the better, it makes things easier all around." She squinted at Mary, and Mary wondered how many times a day or a week she said things like that. "If you're not certain, of course you want to make sure you are. We encourage patients who aren't certain to at least call the clinic in Bangor and to make an appointment to get more specific information."

Except for that time she'd waited for him at the wharf, Mary had lately been avoiding Josh. She had it in her mind that after this appointment things would somehow change, that she'd be able to tell him, or that the need to tell him would magically have disappeared. When he showed up at the café, Mary ducked into the bathroom and asked Daphne to tell him she wasn't working that day. If he came to her house she planned to turn off all of the lights and lock the door and hide under the covers. But Josh hardly ever came to her house.

"Lover's spat?" Daphne inquired. "Oh, too bad. I'm sure you'll get over it. These things happen."

"Daph and I used to fight like cats and dogs," said Andi cheerfully. "Now we're older, who has the energy?"

Mary laughed the way she thought they wanted her to laugh and pushed the broom vigorously into the corner of the café, where muffin crumbs congregated.

Now Mary took a deep, shuddering breath that felt like it traveled all the way down to her toes. Did the baby inside her feel that breath? Did he or she sense where Mary was at that very moment, what she was talking about?

"What about my mom? Does she need to sign a form or something?"

"Doesn't have to be your mom," said Patricia. "A trusted adult needs to be involved in the decision for someone under eighteen. That can be a grandparent or someone else. And if you have no trusted adult in your life there are licensed staff at the clinics who can fill that role."

Mary thought again of Andi and Daphne; she thought of Ms. Berry. She even thought of the phone number Eliza Sargent had tapped into her cell phone at the wharf. She couldn't, in a million years, imagine asking any of these warm and wonderful women to help her undo her pregnancy. *Undo.* It sounded so easy and technical, put that way. *Delete.*

Mary tried to read from Patricia's tone of voice what she thought Mary should do. Surely she had some opinion! But her voice was easy and neutral, just like Sarah's had been. She was giving nothing away.

"Now. If you're considering carrying the pregnancy to full term, Mary, we have information on here on proper prenatal care, including vitamins, healthy food, and so on. We don't offer prenatal care at this clinic, but we can give you a list of doctors who do. Getting your baby off to a healthy start now is essential. If you're smoking, if you're drinking, if you're using drugs, any of these actions can be extremely harmful to the fetus."

"Okay," said Mary obediently. "I'm not."

At the front desk, Mary was relieved to learn that the clinic charged for visits on a sliding scale; for those without insurance and no ability to pay there was no charge, just a voluntary donation. Mary dug in her wallet for a five-dollar bill, which seemed inadequate—less than a movie!—but the woman took it with a smile. The people at this clinic seemed to be the least judgy people on the planet. Mary was almost sorry to leave.

Now she had the pamphlets (*literature*, the bosomy lady at the desk called it—another funny word, in Mary's opinion); she had a packet of prenatal vitamins; she had a list of care practices in Ellsworth and Bangor; and she had a gnawing sensation in the center of her body that could have been hunger or panic but more likely was the certainty of her future settling in like an anchor.

The only, only thing that sounded good to Mary after that was a root beer float, so she pulled into Jordan's on Route One on the way home. When she was younger and her father still took his weekend fathering duties seriously, he used to bring her here to sit at one of the wooden picnic tables with a grilled cheese and a vanilla soft-serve. Thinking of grilled cheese now made her stomach turn over.

She realized her mistake as soon as she turned the ignition off and saw Alyssa Michaud climbing out of her father's steel-gray Jeep Cherokee. A little-known fact about Alyssa was that she had failed her driver's test *three times*—twice for inadequate parallel parking and once for driving on the wrong side of the road at the very beginning of the test. ("I *thought* it still counted as the *parking lot.*")

Mary knew this because she and Alyssa had once been best friends; in fact, they'd been best friends all the way through junior year, when Tyler Wasson had dumped Mary in favor of Alyssa. He later dumped Alyssa too. After that, Alyssa got serious about college and Mary got serious about Josh.

So it was a miracle that Alyssa Michaud was even driving, but anyway. Here she was, in the Jordan's parking lot, catching Mary's glance and heading her way.

Alyssa was wearing a baseball cap with—of course—BATES written across it in maroon. Alyssa was the top in their (tiny) graduating class and was going to college in Lewiston, where she was going to walk from one brick building to another and (according to the catalog in Alyssa's bedroom that Mary had seen, before everything went down) spend a lot of time lying on beds of colorful leaves with stacks of books by her side. Alyssa's father owned a Jeep dealership in Ellsworth, and when she was a junior her parents had paid for a college counselor to walk her through the application process, and now, here she was, in a Bates cap, wearing white short-shorts and platform flip-flops. It was hard not to resent her for all of those things.

Mary had lived in Maine her whole life and she couldn't remember a single time she'd lain on a bed of colorful leaves. By the time the leaves fell, the ground was always damp and cold and you wouldn't want to lie around on it. But, to be fair, maybe the weather was different in Lewiston.

"Hey!" said Alyssa. "Long time no see, stranger." Her face, to Mary's surprise, looked genuinely happy.

Mary glanced behind her to make sure her *literature* wasn't visible from the car window. In a place like this, her news would be practically broadcast across the very high frequency radio—the VHF—before she even got home if Alyssa found out about it. She blocked the car with her body just in case.

"Hey," said Mary. She worked up a smile and threw it at Alyssa, waited to see if it stuck. Alyssa's hair looked shampoo-commercial bright and shiny, and her T-shirt was so thin and tight you could see her belly button and her toned ab muscles. Mary felt a powerful spasm of envy.

"Whatcha doing over here?"

"Nothing," said Mary. "Just getting some stuff done, day off. Thought I'd get a root beer float."

"I *love* the root beer floats here," said Alyssa firmly. "They're the best. I might get one too. Or maybe a clam roll."

At the mention of clam rolls Mary's stomach again rocked dangerously. How could she be so hungry and so nauseous at the same time?

Alyssa jerked her head toward Route One and said, "I'm actually on my way back to the nail salon. This gel color lasted, like, a minute. I'm going to scream at them." For evidence she held up her hands.

"You should," said Mary, although she actually thought that Alyssa should not, and also that she probably would not. She peered at Alyssa's nails; the only thing she could see wrong was a tiny bare spot on one pinky.

"I haven't seen you in forever," Alyssa said, kicking at the parking lot's asphalt with a flip-flop.

"Yeah," said Mary. She stared hard at the giant representation of a soft-serve ice-cream cone that had stood on the roof of the restaurant since long before Mary had had her first root beer float. "I've been busy. Working."

Alyssa squinted and blew a strand of hair up toward the rim of the cap. "Good for you," she said. "I should have gotten a job this summer, I've just been going to the beach." She looked with manufactured dismay at her tanned legs.

"Screw 'em," Vivienne had said, after Tyler dumped Mary for Alyssa. Mary had taken the unusual step of crying in Vivienne's arms, that's how badly she'd been hurt by the betrayal. She wasn't ready to have sex with Tyler, that was part of the problem, and apparently Alyssa was. Vivienne had never liked Alyssa; she thought she "put on airs" because her dad owned that dealership in Ellsworth and her mother had some mysterious secret store of money. "That little bitch was always too big for her britches," Vivienne had said, stroking Mary's hair with uncharacteristic tenderness, not even mentioning that she could use a conditioning treatment. Mary remembered wincing at the word choice, but she also remembered that it felt good to have her mother on her side.

"You'll find someone else," Vivienne had gone on. "You should come out with me and the girls after work. We'll show you a good time, show you how it's done."

"Um," Mary had said. "Maybe?" Vivienne was young to be the mother of somebody Mary's age, for sure, but she wasn't Mary's *age;* she was still her *mother,* and Mary couldn't envision a scenario where she'd want Vivienne or "the girls" to "show her how it's done."

It didn't occur to Mary for a long time, not until after the summer had taken all of its tragic—and just very occasionally comic—twists and turns, that maybe Vivienne could have suggested to Mary a different kind of immediate future, maybe one without a boy *or* a man in it.

Mary started to move with little shuffling steps toward the counter. It was only eleven but already a line was forming: lots of older tourists (RV types) in L.L. Bean shirts, a few unfamiliar teenage girls in spaghetti-strap tanks. Mary was trying to work her mouth around a farewell that would show Alyssa that there were no hard feelings anymore, that she wished her well in college, but before she could make the words fit together a great wave of food odor—not just clams, but fries and shrimp and scallops and the ubiquitous lobster roll—swelled forward and hit her with a force as powerful and surprising as a punch. Then everything in front of her separated into rainbow-colored pixels and Alyssa moved to the very edges of her vision as Mary hit the ground.

12

Eliza

Eliza had spent hours trying to get her dad to come to Barton with her, with no luck, and by the time she'd given up she hadn't wanted to start home after all. The roads leading out of Little Harbor were so long and winding and lonely, and Eliza was a terrible night driver—she always had been.

She'd gotten up with the sun to drive home instead; she'd left so early that The Cup wasn't open. Val's was open. Privately Eliza was not a fan of Val's coffee.

During the drive to Barton, Eliza thought again about the meeting with Phineas Tarbox, which had come about after their previous attorney had retired and moved to Florida. Years ago, their previous attorney had walked them through the creation of their wills, their estate planning, all the minutiae of living in an adult, responsible world. Then, when he notified them that he was leaving the business, Rob had been anxious to get their affairs settled elsewhere.

Affairs settled? thought Eliza. *Are you planning on dying, Rob?*

"I'll just feel better," Rob said. "When everything is taken care of."

Better than what, Rob? Eliza had wanted to ask, but hadn't.

It had begun as sort of a nice evening. Phineas had only the last slot in his day free, a five o'clock appointment, and they planned to go for tapas and sangria after.

"We are pathetic!" said Eliza. "Our Date Night is a trip to talk about wills." But she was looking forward to the tapas and the sangria.

They'd sat with Phineas Tarbox, who turned out to be a jocular, suntanned man with large hands and minty breath, and gone over all of the paperwork submitted by the previous attorney's office. And, yes, Eliza's eyes did glaze over a little bit with all of the details, and, yes, she did spend some time studying the law school diploma on the wall (Yale) to verify that his name *really was Phineas Tarbox*.

It was.

Then, suddenly, Phineas Tarbox was frowning.

"There's just one thing," he said. He flipped through the papers. "I don't see that you've appointed guardians for your children." He frowned harder, and the suggestion of a crease appeared between his brows. Only the suggestion, though—he probably got Botox. Men did, these days, rich men.

"I thought we did that," said Rob. He glanced at Eliza.

Eliza shifted uneasily. "I'm not sure. Did we?"

Phineas shuffled the papers some more. "You didn't. I don't see it here—no, no, you haven't. It's not here anywhere. So that's something we'll want to take care of right away." He looked up, flashed a courteous smile. "It's not uncommon, people begin the process before they have children, maybe, and then they forget to complete it, and then they turn around and their kids are—"

"Thirteen and ten," said Eliza.

"Right," said Phineas. "Exactly. As long as you're ready to pull the trigger—*just an expression, of course!*—we can draw up the papers right now, and you can sign them here, and then you can go on your merry way."

"Great," said Rob. "We can pull the trigger anytime. The guardian will be my mother, Judith Barnes." He said this very firmly.

"Hang on," said Eliza.

"I adore Judith," said Phineas. His smile was odd enough (almost coquettish) to make Eliza wonder if something besides paperwork had passed between Phineas and Judith. "I simply adore her," Phineas added. Eliza could smell the mint on his breath.

"Many do," said Rob.

Phineas made some notes on a Post-it. Eliza stage-whispered to Rob, "We've never discussed this." She couldn't believe how *easily* he'd answered the question. How *presumptuously.* Like the script had been written, and he was just reading from it. She turned to Phineas and said, "I'm sorry. But I don't think we're prepared to—I mean, we haven't . . ."

Phineas looked from Rob to Eliza and back to Rob again. He tented his fingers and nodded kindly. He smiled so that the little crinkles around his mouth deepened into rich-person wrinkles, the kind created on ski slopes and sailboats and nurtured by the Monaco sunshine. This probably happened all the time, in his office, in his line of work, this sort of confusion. Didn't it? Did it?

Rob said, "Eliza."

"We're not going to *die,* Rob," said Eliza. "I mean, both of us? What are the odds?"

"Probably not," said Rob. "But people die. Parents die sometimes." *Don't I know it,* thought Eliza. "We need to be prepared."

Judith, the guardian of her children! Judith was a functioning alcoholic with lots of wonderful shoes, a tiny waist, and pots of money. She might give the girls a place to live, but she wouldn't give them a home, study their flash cards with them, make them eat kale. Eliza's stomach twisted. Behind her she heard the whir of pages sliding out of a printer— the sound of her fate being sealed.

"You do need to be prepared," interjected Phineas, clearing his throat. "Believe me, the right decision now can save a heck of a lot of trouble down the road, in the event of something unforeseen. I've seen some doozies in my time." He walked to the printer and picked up the papers. He tapped them on the edge of his desk to line the edges up perfectly.

"I'm sure you have," said Eliza. "But even so, I'm not ready to sign."

Phineas Tarbox cleared his throat again. Did he have some sort of problem? Allergies? It *was* April: the height of the pollen season. He said brightly, "Why don't you take the documents home with you? And return them when you're ready."

It was agreed.

After, they did go for the tapas, but something dark and nameless had slithered among the *gambas al ajillo* and the *patatas bravas.*

The sangria, however, was delicious.

Partway through the meal, Rob put down his fork and said, "Should we talk about the elephant in the room?"

"There's no elephant," said Eliza. Not true. Obviously.

Rob waited. Eliza took another gulp of sangria and said, "Okay. Fine."

"Okay fine *what*? Say what you're thinking, Eliza."

People loved to hear about the way Eliza and Rob had met, the icy street in Providence, Eliza holding the sandwich, sliding into him. What did they call it in romantic comedies? A "meet cute." Silly name. That wasn't the whole story, that was just to make it into a neat, packaged tale, the kind people liked to hear at cocktail parties. The whole story was that Eliza had been watching Rob for weeks, months even. She'd watched him with Kitty Sutherland. And she'd said to herself, *That one*. And one day she'd followed him, and she'd bought a sandwich she couldn't afford, and she'd thought carefully about what to do next.

It was true about the sliding into him; the street was really very slippery, and it was a hill. She hadn't meant to slide, but gravity and weather had gotten the best of her. The rest, as they said, was history.

"I'm not comfortable with the choice of your mother."

She looked down, but even so she could feel Rob's gaze on hers. She knew what he'd be doing, blinking in that innocent, bewildered way he did anytime the world surprised him by not going his way. Bumps in the road always came as such a *personal shock* to Rob because he didn't encounter many. "But why? We don't have anyone else."

She was still looking down when she said, "Of course we have someone else. We have my father. He's the other option."

"Oh, Eliza. I mean a realistic option." The *tortilla espanola* arrived, then the *calamares en su tinta*. The platter with the garlic shrimp sizzled. Eliza drank more sangria.

"Let's talk about it another time," said Rob.

"Okay," said Eliza. The garlic from the shrimp sat sticky in her throat. The sangria was making her feel tipsy, but it was the hot and uncomfortable sort of tipsy, not the merry sort. "Another time."

After that, Rob had put the folded sheaf of papers on the kitchen desk, where Eliza took care of the bills and signed permission slips and noted doctor's appointments on a big wall calendar. Normally Eliza was meticulous about the kitchen desk, but the papers sat and sat; they sat like the final guests at a cocktail party who remained even as the hosts cleared the glasses from around them.

Of course she and Rob weren't going to die *at the same time.* She should just sign the papers, compromise, the way married people did, the way reasonable people did.

But she couldn't do it. She didn't feel reasonable. She felt that signing the documents was akin to signing over her children completely to Judith's world, to Rob's world. Nothing would be left of Eliza's world, nothing at all! She wanted to cry and stamp her feet like a child. If the unthinkable happened, and the girls went to Judith, all vestiges of Eliza, of Little Harbor, of the boats and the wharf and the traps, of the little house Eliza had grown up in, of Charlie's strong hands and weathered face, would be gone, swallowed up in a wave of endless ease and privilege.

Eliza and Rob weren't going to die, not at the same time, of course not.

But they might. Phineas was right: they had to prepare for all eventualities.

First Rob took the casual approach: "Hey, could you sign those papers when you get a chance?" Then he tried the harried approach, via text: **GOT VM FROM PHINEAS WE NEED TO GET THE DOCS OVER TO HIM.** He tried the stern approach, the goofy approach, the cajoling approach, the friendly, no-nonsense approach. Once he left the papers on her pillow, like they were chocolates at a fine hotel and he was in charge of the turndown service. She moved them from one place to another and then finally shifted them to Rob's third-floor office, out of sight, out of mind, unsigned.

Except they weren't out of mind. They were on Eliza's mind constantly—more, she'd wager, than they would have been if she'd just signed them. And the worst part about it was that Rob was right. He was right! Judith was the obvious choice, really the only choice. She loved the girls in her own weird, gin-soaked way. Charlie hadn't been a realistic candidate before—it would be ridiculous to expect the girls to grow up in a lobstering village, and even if Charlie was financially compensated by their estate he wasn't going to move to Massachusetts and stop hauling traps. Now that he was terminally ill, he obviously wasn't a candidate at all.

And yet! Even now, even so many months after their initial meeting, even in the shadow of her father's diagnosis, her mind kept going back to Phineas Tarbox's office and the easy way Rob had answered for both of them, the way he'd just assumed. What he hadn't said (because he hadn't needed to) was, *Your family isn't good enough for our kids. But mine is.*

Her resentment over all of this was buried deep, like the pea under the princess's mattress. And, like the princess, Eliza could feel it each time she shifted in the night.

Or maybe it wasn't a pea, maybe it was something small like a pea but sharper, like a razor. You could rip a seam with something like that. And then what? Once the seam was ripped, everything spilled out.

————

Eliza had been gone from Barton a week, but by the time she got home it felt like much longer. It was like living in a time warp, being back in Little Harbor. During her absence the peonies in the yard of the Cavanaughs' house across the street had come into full bloom. Mrs. Cavanaugh was out in her clogs, holding a pair of clippers and studying the garden. It didn't seem right—in fact, it seemed downright inconsiderate of the peonies—that her dad had a brain tumor, the very worst kind of brain tumor you could have, and the peonies were blooming so exuberantly. How dare they. She remembered a similar feeling from when her mother died; just two days later, Eliza was expected to go to school and do math and science, and it was all so unbelievable, that the numbers still added up the way they were supposed to, and her lungs and heart still did their jobs of breathing and pumping, and she still had to go to the bathroom and drink water when she was thirsty: all of these normal, pedestrian activities, with such a glaring void in the world.

Charlie had been angry with Eliza for snooping in the drawer; he was angry with Val for telling Eliza about his tumor. No, he didn't want to talk about it. No, he didn't want to go see a doctor in Boston; he wouldn't go home with Eliza to Barton. He wasn't leaving his traps untended. No, he didn't want to go out to dinner in Ellsworth or to The Lobster Trap in town. He wanted to watch television and go to bed, and he'd say goodbye now, Eliza, because he was getting up too early in the morning and he knew she'd be gone before he got back.

"You can't haul," Eliza had said. "With your arm!"

"Got some help," he'd said. "I got it figured out, Eliza, you don't need to worry about it."

Eliza had wanted to ask Russell to help, but Russell had his own traps to haul. He shouldn't take on Charlie's too. Although he would if Eliza asked him.

When Eliza was sixteen, Val used to tell her, *A flame like that is going to burn itself out.*

And it did, of course. Eventually.

Eliza waved at Mrs. Cavanaugh and pulled into her own driveway, then let herself in the front door.

"Hello?" she said. "*Hello?* I'm home. Where is everybody?"

Evie would be at theater camp, but Zoe should be home, and certainly *Rob* should be home, tucked up in his home office, working on Cabot Lodge. Unless he'd gone up to Naples again. Would he go to Naples without telling her? She didn't think he would. She put her overnight bag in the foyer and climbed the stairs to the third floor. Rob's office was a disaster. It looked like an army of industrious rodents had visited during the night, scattering plans and books and papers all around. She saw that on Rob's drafting table were not one, not two, but *three* coffee cups, each partially filled, with the contents beginning to congeal.

Eliza closed her eyes and thought about how long Rob had listened to her when she told him about Charlie. She thought about how he had offered to drop everything and drive up. She opened her eyes. The coffee cups were still there. She closed the door.

Zoe's bed was neatly made, with her ancient stuffed elephant, Marvin, sitting on top of the pile of pillows. Evie's bed had the top sheet bunched up and hanging out the bottom, but at least she'd tried. Eliza and Rob's bed was not made at all. Eliza closed that door too. She'd get to it later; she'd get to all of it later. She was suddenly exhausted and had to fight the urge to crawl into the unmade bed and go to sleep. When she heard the front door open she flew down the stairs, just as Deirdre, Sofia, and Zoe were coming in.

"Mom!" said Zoe, and her face lit up like a Christmas tree. She was a little too cool for a full hug in front of others, so she offered Eliza her specialty: a half hug, half lean. That was okay. Eliza knew the love was under there somewhere, maybe hidden inside those stupendous legs. You couldn't take your eyes off teenage girls, you really couldn't: their legs just got longer and longer and longer. But you couldn't *say* that to them because they just rolled their eyes and made you feel old and short-legged and thick. "You're home!" said Zoe. "For good, right? You'll see the fireworks with us."

Deirdre was sporting a navy-blue halter dress, which showed off her toned shoulders, and matching navy espadrilles. She smelled like a garden after a spring rain shower, and she looked like a walking ad for probiotics, glowing with good health and the appropriate amount of gut bacteria. Eliza had on a pair of grimy shorts that she'd worn twice without washing, and an old Lobster Festival T-shirt she'd found in her childhood dresser drawer. She hadn't meant to stay so long in Little Harbor when she'd packed, and she hadn't especially wanted to do battle with her father's geriatric washing machine.

———

Lesson Number Two from her mother's letter:

Floss, Eliza! I have good teeth. Your father has good teeth. Your teeth have come in pretty close to perfect. This is a gift, not a right. Take care of it.

———

"I'm home!" said Eliza. "I'll see the fireworks with you." Zoe smelled exactly like herself, like hair that had been washed too often and too vigorously. She smelled like overly fragrant lotion from Bath & Body Works, and a little bit like Belgian waffles. She smelled glorious. "I'm *home,*" said Eliza.

"Rob had to drive to Boston," said Deirdre. "Something about meeting with Mrs. Cabot, an emergency. Super early, he should be on his way back. He didn't want to bother you. Kristi has the day off from nannying, so I brought Evie to camp, and then I took these two"—she indicated Sofia and Zoe—"out to breakfast at Big Joe's. And here we are."

"Big Joe's!" said Eliza. "Lucky." That explained Zoe's Belgian waffle cologne.

She tried not to be bothered that Rob and Evie were both gone. Of course Rob had to work. And of course Evie had to go to camp! Soon they'd be holding auditions for the end-of-session performance of *Charlotte's Web.*

When Sofia and Zoe left the room, Deirdre said, "He said—well, he didn't tell me any details. But he said something is going on with your dad. I figured you could use a hand."

When Deirdre said things like *I figured you could use a hand,* sometimes Eliza heard *Clearly you can't handle things yourself.* It made her feel inadequate, even though that's probably not how Deirdre meant it. Deirdre never seemed to feel inadequate. Of course she didn't! She was living in the exact same kind of world she'd grown up in. Deirdre's parents were both alive and well in Darien, Connecticut, residing in the four-bedroom, three-bath center-hall colonial where Deirdre and her younger sister, Bethany, had grown up. Her parents golfed together four mornings a week and traveled internationally twice a year. Brock's parents had retired to Clearwater, Florida, and Deirdre and Brock took Sofia to see them every April vacation. Deirdre and Brock were fully pedigreed. They were purebreds.

Rob was also a purebred, and Rob's girlfriend before Eliza had been a purebred too. Kitty Sutherland. Eliza was a mutt. Brown hadn't even been Rob's first-choice school—he'd wanted to go to Princeton and hadn't been accepted. Brown had been more of a safety, he'd told her once. She never really got over his saying that. She could never get Rob to understand what a big deal it had been for someone from her tiny rural high school to get into an Ivy. *It had literally never happened before.* He would never truly comprehend how she'd had to claw her way there, and then scrabble to keep herself afloat once she arrived.

Deirdre said, "Sooo . . ." And Eliza understood that this was the place where she could bring Deirdre into the kitchen and tell her about Charlie, but the thought of doing that filled her with a bone-deep fatigue.

Just then they heard the mudroom door open and Rob called out, "Helllooooo!"

"I've got to run," said Deirdre. She called up the stairs, "Sof?"

"Leave her here," said Eliza. Rob's phone rang, and he called from the mudroom, "I'm going to grab this, I'll be quick!"

"Are you sure?" asked Deirdre, about leaving Sofia.

"Of course."

"Oh my God, *thank you,*" said Deirdre. In Barton you were supposed to go out of your way to thank someone who did you a favor, even if it wasn't one you'd asked for, so that in turn they could over-thank *you* when you returned the favor or performed a favor of a similar value. It had taken Eliza a little time to learn these rules, but she was pretty sure she had them down now. "I've got a hundred and thirty things to do for the gala. And with Kristi off today . . ."

"Go," said Eliza. "It'll be my pleasure to have her here."

While Rob finished his phone call, Eliza went at a few sticky spots on the island with the rough side of the sponge, and then she pulled out the spray bottle and gave the whole place a good wipe-down.

"Let me do that," said Rob, off the phone now, wrapping his arms around her. "I thought I left it clean."

"I got it," answered Eliza. "I have to tell you the whole story, and if I stop moving I'll start crying." She'd only had a chance for the short version on the phone with Rob. Besides, there were a lot of unidentifiable sticky spots on the counter.

Rob leaned back uncomplainingly when the spray bottle came near him, and he made surprised and sympathetic little noises at all the astonishing parts, and he didn't try to jump in and finish Eliza's sentences the way some people did. It felt good to talk and have someone listen, and when she had finished talking, Eliza said out loud what she'd already known was true: "If he won't come down here I have to go back, right after the Fourth. I'd bring the kids with me, but there's not a lot of room, and I don't want to upset them, and they've got their activities going on down here. . . . But I can't leave my dad alone with this. He won't do anything on his own, I know he won't. I have to go back."

"Of course," said Rob. "You go."

"But the girls."

"I'm here."

"You have Mrs. Cabot."

"Mrs. Cabot can wait."

"No she can't. Can she?"

"No," admitted Rob. "Mrs. Cabot doesn't know how to wait." They both stared at the counter, and then Rob said, "Deirdre can help!"

"She has the gala. She's really busy."

"But she has a full-time nanny. And one child."

"True," said Eliza, thinking. "But *we* didn't hire Kristi to take care of *our* kids."

"We could hire our own nanny."

"Don't be ridiculous."

"What about my mom?"

Eliza rolled her eyes. "She'll probably get them drunk." It was *such a cliché,* having a boozy, rich mother-in-law, Eliza realized this; it was a subplot to so many sitcoms, but the fact that it was a cliché didn't make it any less true.

Rob laughed. "I bet she won't. Not too drunk, anyway."

If anyone asked Eliza about her relationship with her mother-in-law her answer was always, *It's complicated.*

(As a wedding gift, Judith had paid off the eighty thousand dollars remaining on Eliza's student loans.)

The first time Rob had brought Eliza home to the Back Bay town-house where he'd grown up, Judith had mentioned Rob's ex-girlfriend Kitty Sutherland twice, and even though Rob had blown an imaginary referee whistle and said, "*Mom!* Unnecessary roughness!" she'd told one more story, something about Rob and Kitty and a trip to Nantucket, just hilarious. Kitty's heel broke on one of the cobblestones, ha ha ha ha ha, they almost missed their dinner reservation . . .

If Jackie O. and Gidget had a baby, that baby would grow up to look like Kitty Sutherland.

On that same visit, Eliza, who had been dispatched to the guest room, had lain under a heavy quilt, in sheets so soft they felt like butter. This was before she knew the phrase *thread count.* She'd stared at a black-and-white photograph of a sailboat leaning into the wind. This was before she knew the phrase *coming about.* The next morning, Judith had called Eliza into the living room, where she and Rob were already standing in front of the picture window.

"The first snowfall!" Judith had said, turning triumphantly to Eliza, as though she had Mother Nature herself on her payroll. Like she was giving them a gift.

So, thought Eliza, pushing her hair away from her face, trying to tame its unruliness. *So. This is wealth.*

It's complicated.

Lobster boats didn't *come about,* by the way. They just turned.

"Why don't we ask her?" Rob prodded now. "She's always saying she wants to be more involved in the girls' lives." Eliza thought about Phineas Tarbox and sat down on one of the stools. Rob got up and stood behind her, rubbing the knots in her neck. He always knew just where they were without her having to tell him.

"It's complicated," said Eliza.

"Doesn't have to be."

"Owwwww," said Eliza.

"Am I hurting you?"

"Yes."

"I'm sorry!" He whipped his hands away.

"No, don't you dare stop."

It was so disorienting, going from *that* world to *this* in a few short hours. It felt like the voyage should have taken light-years. "Okay," she said. "Let's ask Judith."

PART TWO

July

13

Mary

This is going to be a good night, thought Mary. Vivienne was working late at the salon (it was a Thursday) and Josh was coming to pick her up and take her to a movie in Ellsworth. She had stopped avoiding him, and look what had happened! A real date. She was excited. Maybe, before the movie or after it, she'd tell him about the baby. She had the words lined up and ready to go: *Baby. Pregnant. Us.*

She was waiting by the front door—the movie was at seven, and they were supposed to eat beforehand. Josh was supposed to come at five. It was okay that he was a little late. She'd built some extra time into the plan. Maybe it had taken a while getting back after hauling, turning in the catch at the co-op, settling up.

It was five minutes after five, and then it was five fifteen, and then five twenty.

Doesn't matter, she told herself. *We can eat quickly.*

Five twenty-five.

She went outside to sit on the front steps of the house. She picked at a mosquito bite on her knee and looked at the sky: still bright, with a band of clouds that looked like it had been pushed by hand over to the farthest edges. The smells of the harbor reached her, bumping along on the early-evening breeze. She picked at her fingernails and checked her phone.

Five thirty. *We don't have to eat. We can go right to the movie.*

Finally: Josh. She got up, ready to get immediately into the car. But Josh got out before she had a chance to get in.

"Let's go right away," Mary said.

"Your mom's not home, is she?"

"No." Mary looked at her wrist where a watch would have been if she'd

had one. "We were going to eat, remember? The movie starts at seven."
She tried to keep her voice easy and friendly. She had prepared the words
once again. *Baby. Pregnant.* She just wasn't sure when to let them out.
Not now, obviously: Josh looked agitated, and they were rushed. Her
stomach churned with a brewing disappointment.

"I have to put something inside," said Josh. "Real quick. Just for a little
while." He was holding a crumpled-up brown bag, the kind you brought
your lunch in to elementary school if you didn't have a lunch box. "Somewhere in your room, okay?"

"What is it?"

"Nothing. Just something I can't keep at home right now, it's not a big
deal."

"Let me see it."

"Come on, baby, it's not a big deal." There was a flash of something
across his face. "Let me just go put it in your room."

He was already past her, and into the house.

"Is it a gun?"

"No."

"Drugs?"

"Sort of."

"What do you mean, sort of?" She followed him into the house. He
was already in her bedroom, looking around. She took the bag to open it,
and Josh snatched it out of her hands, rolling the top down more tightly.

"Totally legal. Prescription."

She blinked and squinted at him. "Whose prescription?"

"Don't worry about it, it's under control."

"Josh."

"It's nothing," he said. "Just a painkiller, no big deal, not heroin or
anything. I just can't keep it at home."

"Why not?"

"There's a few hundred dollars' worth in here, a little more, even. Just
keep it safe, until I ask for it. That's it, that's all you have to do."

She considered this. How hard would that be, really? To put a lunch
bag in her closet and forget it was there. But still.

"Why don't you keep it at your house?"

"Too risky."

"But . . ."

She took a deep, uncertain breath. She wanted to say, *I don't want that bag near me. I don't want anything bad near me. Because of the baby.* But instead she just thought it.

"It'll just be a bag, sitting there, doing nothing. Just a little salt and sugar. What could happen?"

Salt and sugar? thought Mary. *What the . . . ?*

"Come on, babe. Don't make everything a big deal." He smiled at her, and she saw a flash of the old Josh, the charming one, and something inside of her relented. She didn't want to make everything a big deal, she really didn't. There were enough things that were a big deal. She opened the closet door. She watched as he found a place for the bag in the back right corner of the closet, behind an old pair of Nikes. He had to get down on his hands and knees to do it, he had to really stuff himself into the closet. She watched as he covered the sneakers with a T-shirt from the previous year's Lobster Festival.

Then the flash of charm changed to something more sinister as Josh pulled himself back out of the closet, and Mary felt like ice cubes were moving up and down her spine. Then Josh said, "You know I would never do anything to hurt you, right, baby?" and smiled again.

And then his hand was open, palm flat, on her back, pushing her forward, out the door.

"I know," said Mary hesitantly. She felt like an idiot, because she hadn't known Josh had anything to do with drugs, taking or selling. How had she not known that? There were probably all sorts of signs that she hadn't picked up on, but she didn't even know what signs she could have looked for. Needle marks, chapped nostrils, what? Stupid, naive, plain, pregnant Mary Brown.

A little salt and sugar. What did that even mean?

"It's just this one time. Once the fishing picks up I won't need this anymore, I swear. It's just been shit so far this summer, you know it has. It's not my fault."

She said, "Just this once?" Maybe it was true; maybe he didn't *use* any drugs, maybe he just had to get himself out of the slump. But nobody else in town seemed to be in a slump. It was *shit so far this summer* just for Josh, apparently. Red flag.

"On my honor." He let go of her back and held up his right hand like he was taking an oath.

———

Later, after the movie, after Josh had dropped Mary off, after Vivienne had gone to bed, Mary looked in the brown bag, which held another bag, this one clear plastic, secured with a black twist tie. Inside the plastic bag were dozens and dozens of orange pills. She untied the twist tie, took a pill, and laid it flat on the palm of her hand. The pill had an *M* on one side, the number 60 on the other. She took up her phone and searched: *Salt and sugar. Street names. Drugs.*

Google delivered her results, with a picture to match. Morphine. She felt sick to her stomach. She'd had only popcorn for dinner, maybe that was why. They'd barely made it to the movie.

But she knew that it wasn't the popcorn. Was morphine even a street drug? How little she knew, about drugs, about everything!

From somewhere off in a great distance came that old familiar sound: warning bells, ringing like there was no tomorrow.

14

BARTON, MASSACHUSETTS

Eliza

Eliza was chopping vegetables for a salad while Judith enjoyed her own private happy hour at the kitchen island. Eliza had to go back up to Little Harbor the day after next, but for now she was home, preparing a picnic to take on *A Family Affair* for the holiday the following day. She was making grilled pork tenderloin and roasted vegetable salad with walnut pesto made from the basil in her herb garden. The idea was that Judith would come with them on the boat and that the next day Eliza would go over some details of the girls' schedules with her before heading back up to Little Harbor. This would leave Rob free to concentrate on Cabot Lodge.

Immediately after they'd made their plan came the sense of dislocation.

There it was again, the sinister intrusion of Phineas Tarbox, with his tented fingers, his minty breath, his kind, knowing smile. Just sign the papers, Eliza. What are you waiting for?

"Where are the girls?"

Judith had just come from getting her eyebrows threaded. Sixty-five years old, and getting her eyebrows threaded! Did it never end, this quest for beauty? Eliza, for one, was hoping to stop trying by the time she was sixty-five. She was hoping to sit around watching all the television she had missed while her children were small and eating mini Kit Kats purloined from her grandkids' Halloween bags and speaking with brutal honesty about everything she came across. Brutal honesty was expected of women in their sixties; it was part of their dubious charm, and that was one of the few ways Eliza would unequivocally look to Judith's example.

"They're around," said Eliza. She felt the tiniest trace of irritation creep into her voice. Would it kill Judith to get up from the stool and offer to help? Would it kill her ever to say, *You're doing a good job, Eliza!* Eliza knew that nobody could ever replace her own mother, but still. It might be nice if Judith tried to step into the role every now and then. Of course she'd be helping once Eliza returned to Maine, but really, did she have to take herself so blatantly off the clock when Eliza was home?

"You know, Eliza! I forgot to tell you this. I know someone who is summering in Little Harbor! Can you believe it? Gail Byron. No relation to Lord." Judith laughed at her own joke. "She's staying in a *gigantic* place, thirty bathrooms or something. Do you know it?"

"I think I know of it," said Eliza politely. "But I don't think it really has thirty bathrooms."

"Well. Gail Byron has always been known to exaggerate. Perhaps you'll run into her, though?"

"I'm sure I won't," said Eliza. Different social circles, for sure.

When Eliza became a grandmother she wanted to do for her grandchildren all of the things her own mother had never had a chance to do for Evie and Zoe, like dress them in glittery outfits and take them to see *The Nutcracker* in Boston at Christmas, buying them a whipped-cream-topped hot chocolate afterward.

"Look, here's Evie!" said Judith lustily. She hopped off the stool and displayed her cheek to Evie. Evie hesitated, looked doubtful, and eventually produced an approximation of an air kiss.

What if Eliza had *grandsons,* though? She shuddered at the thought of it. She wouldn't know what to do with boys, she'd never even changed a boy's diaper. It seemed so complicated, having to tuck the little penis away before it sprayed all over you. And most boys would never want to go to *The Nutcracker* with Nana, of course. She hoped her grandchildren called her Nana. She would rail against anything else, particularly Granny. *Granny* implied a kerchief, osteoporosis, a walking cane. Judith had chosen to be called *Grandmother*. Of course.

Eliza moved on to the carrots and smiled at Evie. She was trying to appreciate every ounce of Evie's prepubescence, because now that Zoe was in the throes of puberty Eliza realized what was coming. She hadn't known enough to appreciate it when Zoe was ten, her body still seal-slick and with an adorable bit of pudge around her midsection. Evie stood next to Eliza, and Eliza placed a carrot round on Evie's tongue the way she imagined Catholic priests did with the wafers at Communion. She'd always wanted to try Communion, but apparently Catholics weren't open to feeding newcomers; you couldn't just sidle up and partake. Rob and Judith weren't Catholic either. They were elbows-off-the-table Protestants. Eliza's college roommate Francesca had told her that the wafer tasted just like a bit of rice cracker, no big deal. Definitely light on the calories, Francesca had said. Francesca had later been discovered to have an eating disorder.

Evie chomped on the carrot. Evie had always been really good at eating all of her vegetables. Both girls had. Now Zoe was veering away from the vegetables; she wanted to drink four-dollar Starbucks concoctions and eat Cheez-Its all the livelong day.

"What's up, sweetie?" she asked Evie. It was so, so good to be home, in her own kitchen, making a salad for a sailboat picnic, like it was just a regular day, like nothing was going on. Like her father wasn't dying. Maybe there would even be sex tonight!

Once, long ago, Eliza had told Deirdre that her sex life with Rob was "robust." She'd been tipsy on margaritas; if she hadn't been, she never would have used such a *ridiculous* word. She'd laughed right after she'd said it, to cover her embarrassment, and she'd assumed Deirdre was laughing with her, but once Eliza stopped laughing she instantly saw a hooded, indefinable look cross Deirdre's face—was it interest? Disgust? *Envy?*—and she'd swiftly changed the subject.

It was true, though, if a weird choice of words. But something shifted that year, when Rob was mired in Cabot Lodge, and it shifted again after the meeting with Phineas Tarbox. If Eliza had to put it into words she would have said that Phineas Tarbox had climbed into bed with them, settled himself between them.

She tilted her ear toward Evie like an attentive mother in a television commercial might do.

And Evie said, "Are you going to put Grandpa to sleep?"

Eliza stopped chopping cucumbers. "Evie! Don't be ridiculous. Of course not. Why don't you jump in the pool or go ride your scooter around the block? It's a beautiful summer evening." In fact, it was sort of overcast and uncomfortably humid.

But Evie, bless her heart, wouldn't put the subject to bed. She cocked her head at Eliza—she looked astonishingly adult when she did this, like a PTO president assessing a report from the treasurer and finding it wanting—and said, "Well, maybe you should."

"*Evie!*"

"Out of the mouths of babes," murmured Judith. She sat up straighter and looked interested.

Eliza squatted down until her eyes were at the same level as Evie's eyes. She said very, very firmly, "Evie. Please understand. Nobody is putting anybody to sleep. Grandpa has cancer, yes, but he's going to get treated for it, and he's going to get better." *Liar, liar, pants on fire.* "Maybe he'll even come here, to see some doctors in Boston! Wouldn't that be fun, to have Grandpa staying with us for a little bit?"

Judith coughed and rattled her ice cubes harder.

"You put Fred to sleep," said Evie stoutly. Fred had been thirteen and suffering from severe arthritis, and Eliza had stood beside him in the vet's office, cradling his head when the light went out of his eyes.

"*I* did not put Fred to sleep." Eliza took a deep, cleansing breath, the way she'd learned to do at barre class. She never felt cleansed after the breaths, but other people seemed to believe in it, so she kept trying. "The vet put Fred to sleep. Because Fred was a dog. And he was suffering. Don't you remember?"

"No," said Evie.

"Of *course* you remember. His hind legs didn't work any longer. And he wasn't eating. He was uncomfortable. He was in pain, Evie, and it would have been cruel of us to let him be in pain when we could have done something to help him."

"But . . ." Evie chewed on her lower lip; it was a habit that hung somewhere between adorable and unsanitary, since she was always opening up cuts that took eons to heal. "I heard you telling Daddy. You said his head hurts a lot, and that sometimes he sees two of something when there should be only one."

Eliza blinked. "Also, like we talked about back then, dogs don't think of the past and the future the way humans do. They live in the present, only in the present, so when they're sick, being sick becomes their whole world."

"Very Zen of them," said Judith. The ice cubes ticked against each other as she moved toward the bar to pour herself another drink.

———

Lesson Number Three from Eliza's mother:

Read. Read! You'll want to read the books about girls with no mother. Anne of Green Gables. The Great Gilly Hopkins. Pippi Longstocking. Bambi! Some of these stories may seem far too young for you by the time Val gives you this letter but I want you to read them anyway. I want you to see that these creatures survive. I want you to understand that having a mother is not as essential as we've all been led to believe it is. I hate to think that you can live without me, Eliza, but even more than that I hate to think that you can't.

———

Would it kill Judith to maybe grab a walnut to chop? *Something?* If Rob had married his college girlfriend Kitty Sutherland would Judith have offered to help with the cooking? Would Kitty Sutherland be making walnut pesto salad with roasted vegetables, or would she have her Fourth of July party catered?

She would have it catered. No question.

"Mom?" said Evie.

Teachable moment, thought Eliza. *Keep going.* She looked deep into Evie's gigantic brown eyes and said, "When we put dogs to sleep, Evie, we're relieving them of the pain they're feeling *at that moment.* They don't have the same concept of time that we have. They don't have the same memories that we do. We don't do that to people."

"In some states, they do," said Judith. "Oregon and so forth."

"Judith," said Eliza. "Not helpful."

"But Fred always remembered where we kept the dog treats and the tennis balls. So he had a memory."

She had Eliza there. Now Eliza was the one chewing her lip.

"Right. But it's not the same."

"How do you know?"

"Well," said Eliza helplessly. "People have—studied it."

"What people?" Evie had opened her eyes so wide that it looked like the rest of her features might fall into them.

"Scientists. Scientists have studied it. Dog scientists."

"But how do they *know*? How a dog thinks?"

"I'm not sure, exactly. They do tests and things. Very scientific tests."

Evie looked skeptical, as well she should. Eliza had no idea how anyone knew anything about a dog's experience. "They know," she said smoothly. "I promise you. They know."

Evie allowed her eyes to scan the kitchen. Then she said, "Grandpa can't do his job anymore, with the lobster traps."

Deep breath. Just before coming home, Eliza had watched Charlie bump his hip into a small side table that had been in the living room since time began. It was a visual field cut from the tumor that made it happen, she knew that, even if her dad didn't; the tumor was in the left lobe, so he'd experience the visual cut on the right side of both eyes. He'd hit the hip hard, she'd heard the *thwack* of bone against wood, and she'd waited, the way you did with a child, to see if he was going to cry or not. He hadn't acknowledged anything. It must have hurt, though.

"Yes. Yes, that's right, he can't work right now. That doesn't mean he won't again."

Of course he wouldn't work again. Soon he wouldn't even be able to drive his truck safely, never mind his boat—he might not be able to see if someone pulled out in front of him.

"But he's not a dog, sweetie, he's not living only in the present. He's going to get medicine and see a new doc—"

"But he's uncomfortable, right?" Evie interrupted, and selected another carrot round.

"Sometimes he's uncomfortable."

"Is he uncomfortable more than he's comfortable?"

Even if Charlie got treated, and even if the tumor shrank from the treatments, it would come back; it would spread like the tentacles of a sea creature until it had invaded not just his left occipital lobe but everywhere. They did, in the brain, with this kind of cancer. *They always did.*

Eliza straightened her legs and leaned her hands on the edge of the countertop. She could no longer see the vegetables clearly; her eyes were filling up. She cleared her throat and said, "Have you ever considered being an attorney, Evie?"

Evie sniffed suspiciously. "What's an attorney?"

Eliza regained the knife, picked up a red pepper, and wiped her eyes with her arm. "A lawyer. Somebody who argues cases in court, before a judge and a jury."

"Oh," said Evie, offhandedly. "No, no, I don't think I want to be that. I want to be an actress. Or maybe a dog scientist. I didn't know that was a thing until now."

Another carrot, and she sauntered off.

"I think . . . ," said Eliza weakly. "I think I might just have a glass of whatever you're having, Judith. If you don't mind pouring me one."

15

LITTLE HARBOR, MAINE

Mary

Mary had entered her dates into a website that told her all about her baby's development. At nine weeks, it was the size of a grape, with tiny earlobes and nostrils. *A grape!* So tiny. Although of course grapes could be many different sizes. She chose a medium one to put in her mind's eye.

The salon was closed on the Fourth of July. But the day before had been very busy, everybody squeezing in their waxes and highlights before the holiday, and Vivienne was looking forward to sleeping in, getting her "beauty rest." She'd asked Mary to be quiet when she left the house to go to The Cup, which would close early to observe the holiday but was still open from seven to five. The Fourth was a big sailing day for people out on the Point and was expected to be a good day for business. People started drinking early, and when they drank early they got hungry early. Or they requested Andi's special picnic baskets to take out on their boats. Or they needed a midday pick-me-up latte to make it all the way to the fireworks. Or all of the above.

Later, after dark, some of the guys would set off fireworks from a lobster boat out in the harbor. Everybody would watch, residents and summer people alike. Aside from the Lobster Festival in August and Trap Day in April it was the closest the town came to a big event.

Mary was in the far corner, wiping off table twelve, when she heard Andi say, "Hi, Vivienne!" in a surprised and cheerful voice. "Looking beautiful, darling." Mary looked at the clock; it was only eight forty-five. Not good. Vivienne was supposed to be sleeping. Mary pretended she hadn't heard Andi and kept her head down, wiping, though there was nothing to wipe anymore.

It didn't take Vivienne long to find her near table twelve—the café wasn't very big, and there was nowhere to hide. "Your friend woke me up," Vivienne said. She pulled out a chair and slouched into it. She *did* look like she'd just woken up: no makeup, hair in a messy bun—the at-home Vivienne, not the salon Vivienne. Not even close to the salon Vivienne. Actually, the at-home Vivienne was in some ways prettier than the salon Vivienne, though Mary would never dare say that, because that was not something the salon Vivienne wanted to hear.

"My friend?" Mary was genuinely perplexed. Did she have any friends?

"Alyssa Michaud, the little twat who stole your boyfriend."

Mary winced. "It wasn't—oh, never mind." Tyler Wasson was so far in the rearview mirror it really didn't matter what Vivienne thought about that.

Vivienne unleashed the bun, shook her hair out, and then re-bunned it all. This happened so quickly that Mary wasn't sure if she'd imagined it. "Said she'd been trying to call you but you never called her back. Said she was *worried* about you." Vivienne went super light on the pronouns when she was tired or annoyed.

"Huh." Mary feigned confusion and threw a glance toward the counter to see if anyone could save her. "That's weird. I wonder why she'd be worried. I never even see her anymore. She's going to college soon and—"

The door swung open and three customers entered: now she could feel Andi and Daphne send her signals but Vivienne said, "Sit," so Mary sat. Andi and Daphne, for whatever reason, liked Vivienne enough ("a real character!") that Mary hoped they'd forgive her the transgression of taking a seat at table twelve when she should be behind the counter. She'd work extra hard the rest of the day to make up for it. She'd clean the bathroom, even though it wasn't her turn. Andi and Daphne were very fair about the bathroom cleaning, they'd drawn up a schedule and taped it next to the mirror, and they all rotated days, though if Mary was being honest she'd have to say that Daphne always missed the water spots on the faucet and Andi sometimes forgot to empty the wastebasket bin.

After the *incident* outside Jordan's, Mary had ignored Alyssa's four texts and two voice mails. They all said variations on the same thing: **OMG. I NEED TO KNOW THAT YOU'RE OK, MARE. THAT WAS SO WEIRD, HOW U JUST PASSSED OUT LIKE THAT. ARE YOU SURE YOU'RE OK? CALL ME, OK?**

Mare. That had been what Alyssa had called her in *sixth grade.*

Finally, to stop the messages, she had texted back, **I'M OK THANKS.** She was, she was okay! She was fine, it was a fluke, having to do with being too hungry and too warm and too pregnant (she didn't tell anyone the last part). That's what she'd said to the semicircle of friendly and concerned faces that were surrounding her when she came to. "No, please don't call an ambulance, really, *please,* I'm fine. I just need a little something to eat . . ." A kind grandmotherly lady with a southern accent had helped her put her head between her knees until she was ready to stand fully, and then she hadn't even had to wait in line or pay for her root beer float. "On the house," said the guy who brought it over. She'd picked gravel out of her hair for the rest of the day, but she was fine.

"Well, I know *why!*" said Vivienne now. "She said she's been trying to get in touch with you. She said you passed out cold outside Jordan's, in line for a root beer float or something. Last week! Last week, and you didn't tell me?"

Mary tried to make her face smooth and immobile like a mask.

"Mary? Mary." Vivienne's voice was pleading now. Vivienne never pleaded with her, about anything. "How come you didn't tell me?"

Mary shrugged the tiniest shrug she could manage: an infant shrug.

"I've only passed out once in my life and it was when I was pre—" She stopped, and Mary felt the muscles around her eyes twitch. She felt her features slide into an expression; she was giving herself away. Vivienne cleared her throat and finished the sentence. "It was when I was pregnant, Mary. With you."

Still Mary said nothing, but she knew, she could tell by the change in the atmosphere, that the secret was out. She watched Vivienne's eyes fill; Vivienne batted at them like a mass of hornets was flying around her. "Are you *pregnant*?" Thankfully Vivienne lowered her voice to an almost-appropriate level and everyone else in the café was otherwise engaged. Mary nodded, mute.

Vivienne took a minute before she said anything and Mary had the feeling that things could go one of any number of ways.

"This is such bullshit, Mary," Vivienne said finally.

Or not. There was really only one way it was ever going to go.

"I know."

"This is such goddamn bullshit. I cannot believe that I'm going to be a thirty-six-year-old grandmother."

"You'll be thirty-seven," whispered Mary. "In January."

Vivienne didn't answer that; she folded her arms and would have stared into Mary's eyes except that Mary kept her own eyes lowered.

"Sorry," whispered Mary.

The three customers had taken to-go cups. They were dressed for sailing, with rich-people's caps and belted shorts in tan and navy and white.

Daphne moved toward the table and said, "Everything okay, you two?"

"Yup," said Mary.

"Nope," said Vivienne, and Daphne laughed uncertainly and said, "A couple more minutes and we'll need you back behind the counter, Mary."

"Of course," said Mary pleasantly. She had put back on her mask, the mask of a person who was not having this conversation.

Vivienne batted some more at her eyes and hissed, "*Shit*, Mary, I just got my eyelashes done yesterday, I'm not supposed to cry for twenty-four hours."

"Sorry," said Mary again. She was so very sorry, for so many things.

Vivienne blinked wildly and stared at the ceiling, like she was willing the tears to go back where they came from. "Forget it," she said finally, returning her gaze to Mary. "I did a two-hour process on Trisha from Your Eyes Only last week for nothing but a tip. She can fix up my goddamn eyelashes on Monday." Then, unexpectedly, she reached over and grabbed Mary in an aggressive hug that nearly took the wind out of her. "Oh, Mary, Mary," she said into Mary's hair. "*Mary*. What are we going to do?"

Mary felt a pang of something: guilt, or regret, or sorrow. But she also felt something else. Inevitability. This wasn't like talking about it with total strangers at the clinic who saw dozens of teens a day or a week. This was her *mother.* The fact of Mary's pregnancy was real now, it was out there, and there was no going back now, only forward forward forward in whichever direction she decided to go.

She didn't answer the question; she didn't know the answer. "Want a coffee?" she asked after Vivienne peeled herself away. "Let me make you a cappuccino." She didn't wait for a reply and started toward the counter.

"Boy trouble," she said, in answer to Andi's raised eyebrow over the coffee machine. Let them think it was Vivienne's trouble. Vivienne sure thought all the trouble was hers.

16

Eliza

On the way to the boat on the Fourth of July, Eliza checked Zoe's Instagram feed without letting Zoe see that that's what she was doing. The latest post, a photo of Zoe and Sofia jumping together into the pool at the club, both of their bodies squinched up for a cannonball, had garnered eighty-three likes. Eliza wondered who had taken the photo. Probably Evie; she was a secret whiz with the camera.

The comments on the cannonball photo said things like *omg you two are awesome* and *so gorgeous.* It seemed a little bit over the top for a simple shot, but when Eliza checked the rest of the feed she saw that all of the comments on all of the posts included similar hyperbole. Then she checked the posts Zoe had commented on and found the exact same thing: lots of hearts, lots of *gorgeous* this and *awesome* that over the most mundane of subject matters. She scrolled down more and noticed a comment from @rackleyj02. Jackie used lots of pretty emojis and was super extravagant with the compliments. Little two-faced bitch.

This was like anti-bullying, in a way: instead of putting each other down there was a constant buildup of ego and confidence, confusing in its own way. She sighed. How exhausting it must be, to be young, in this world.

"No electronics on the boat," said Evie not so long after that, standing bossily over Eliza. She was wearing a two-piece stars-and-stripes Ralph Lauren bathing suit that Judith had bought her especially for the Fourth of July. Judith and Ralph Lauren were both patriotic to the core. Judith had brought one for Zoe too, but Zoe refused to wear it for some unidentified thirteen-year-old-girl reason. "I hope she doesn't think she's *fat*," Eliza had said to Rob, but she didn't dare ask Zoe, because what if she put ideas into her head. Zoe currently had the shape and fat content of a straight pin, but of course she couldn't see that.

"I know, sweetie," said Eliza to Evie. "I know. But this is important."

"That's *your* rule, Mom, if I'm not allowed to bring my iPad you shouldn't be allowed to have your phone."

"Just a second, honey, I'm in the middle of something . . ."

When Eliza first got back to Barton, Charlie's health problems had seemed eminently repairable. She had money, she had time, she could fix this! All she needed was some thinking time to figure out how to get him to Boston to see a good doctor, to set up an initial appointment, maybe get him enrolled in a trial. There were always new trials, new treatments. Always.

"*Mom.*"

"No, I know, you're right, Evie, you really are right. I'll put it away. Look! I'm powering it all the way down. I'm putting it down here, not in my pocket. You're right, it's my rule, I should follow it."

It had been Rob's idea to have everyone out on *A Family Affair* for the fireworks, but now that they were here she saw that the muscles around his jaw were flexing and releasing, which meant that he was stressed. She could see why: it was *stressful*, owning something so expensive and then inviting people on it to eat and drink and be merry. Then again, what was the point in owning something like this if you weren't able to enjoy it because you had to be so careful with it? Judith, who had actually paid for the boat, didn't seem to be having any problem enjoying it. There she was, sucking on a gin and tonic, talking animatedly to Deirdre about the top five fund-raising disasters she'd encountered; Deirdre was listening avidly and smiling uneasily. Eliza crossed the deck to where Rob was standing and slipped her hand in his. He smiled.

For sixteen months, while this boat was being built, Rob had slaved over all of the hundreds of decisions that went into the customization. He'd made several trips to Trenton, Maine, where the hull was manufactured, and then to Southwest Harbor, where the whole thing was put together. Who knew there was so much to choose? The navigational electronics. The wood down below. The sail-handling systems, the fabrics for the cushioning. The generator, the hull color, the bottom paint. So very many things, things Eliza didn't even know about.

Fourth of July before her senior year of high school, Eliza and Russell had watched the fireworks while lying down on the deck of his boat, moored in the harbor, passing between them one Bud bottle, then another and another. The Bud bottles were warm but they didn't care; it tasted like nectar. There were very few clothes on either of them by the time the finale came around.

By the same time the next year, Russell wasn't talking to her. She had her bags packed for Brown, one foot in her dorm room.

Rob was chatting with Brock. He squeezed her hand, and Eliza stood for a moment and watched without really taking in the conversation— something about infrared cameras. Rob had a way of listening to people that made them feel like whatever the person was saying was the most important thing Rob had ever heard. He could have run for office with that little-boy sincerity, that gorgeous blond hair. Boy, she'd be a terrible political wife, though. She hated to dress up, she never got her nails done, and her own hair was unruly. The political handlers would probably make her wear it in a bun. Evie and Zoe would look great on camera, though; Zoe would look classy and Evie would have the right amount of mischievous adorableness.

Brock was saying, "I remember sailing with my dad, it would take three people to change those sails by hand back in the day . . ." and Eliza let her mind drift. It was a godsend of a sunset, wide swaths of mauves and oranges mirrored in the harbor's water, a real stunner. This was the sort of sunset people photographed and published in coffee-table books about charming New England towns. The girls had gone below to play a board game—because of Eliza's insistence on a low-tech outing, she had brought along Clue and Life and Sorry!—and she thought about calling them up to see it. Once the sun had vanished altogether the fireworks would start.

But just like that—*pop!*—the most elaborate of the colors began to fade and dip, and little bits of gray snuck in behind the oranges and mauves, and it was almost too late to get the girls up for it. Sunsets, like childhood, were gone in a blink.

"What's the plan for storing her over the winter?" Brock was asking. About the boat, of course. It was always about the boat.

"Going to get her back up to Southwest Harbor," said Rob. "Might sail her up myself, we'll see."

"Hey, well, if you need a hand with that—" Brock cleared his throat, and when Rob didn't answer immediately Brock looked a little embarrassed, like he'd started to take his clothes off in front of someone who might not be interested in sex after all.

"Definitely," said Rob, and Brock looked relieved. "You'll be my first call."

Rob's mention of storing the boat over the winter led Eliza to unseasonable thoughts of Christmas, which made her think about scheduling the Barton family Christmas card photo. They usually took it in August or early September, on the beach. She used to put the girls in matching outfits, but of course she couldn't get away with that now. Eliza loved sending out Christmas cards—she refused to call them holiday cards—and she loved getting them back, too. She still got cards from college friends, med school friends.

Wait a second. *Med school friends.* The little thread of a thought she'd first had when she learned about her father's disease, but that she hadn't had time to study carefully, and then she'd forgotten about altogether, was still there. She pulled at it.

"Holy shit," she said. "Christmas cards, Christmas cards. Zachary Curry." Brock and Rob looked at her, both startled. "Sorry." She slipped her hand out of Rob's grip. "I have to go look something up really quick. I'll just be a minute." The longing for her iPhone was almost a physical desire.

Was Evie, the electronics policewoman, still bent over the Clue board?

"Send the girls up," called Judith. "Can't be long now." And Eliza refrained from suggesting that Judith go and get them herself.

"I'll get them," called Deirdre. She disappeared belowdecks and returned followed by Zoe, Evie, and Sofia. Eliza passed them on the way down.

"Where are you going, Mom?" asked Evie suspiciously.

"Bathroom."

"The head!" called Rob.

"The *head*." Of course Eliza knew that, but there weren't bathrooms on lobster boats, so she didn't use the term too often. If you were a man on a lobster boat you just took care of things over the side of the boat; if you were a woman or a girl you just goddamn held it. Or, if things got really dire, you called on a used bait bucket. Ugh. Those were not the days. She remembered practically dehydrating herself as a teenager so as not to suffer the indignity of the bait bucket.

On *A Family Affair,* of course, the head was practically gilded.

Zachary Curry, Zachary Curry. Her friend from medical school. The year before last she'd tracked him down after reading a mention of him in *The Boston Globe.* She'd put him right on the Christmas card list, where she put everyone, whether they wanted to be there or not.

She found her phone and sat for a moment on one of the plush salon berths surrounding the table, waiting for it to power up. The girls had left the Clue envelope opened in the middle of the table: it had been Colonel Mustard, that sneaky bastard. Library, candlestick. (Gruesome, when you took the time to think about it.) Evie had won. That must have made Zoe irate; no wonder she'd been snarling when the girls came up.

The first thing Eliza noticed when she powered up her phone was a missed call from a Maine area code. No voice mail. Not Russell's, she'd put his in as a contact. Not her dad, not Val. She tried to call the number back, but there was no answer.

Never mind that now, though. Safari. Google. Eliza and Zachary had been partners for the cadaver dissection, long before Eliza stopped out, long before Zachary got one of the three coveted spots in the Johns Hopkins neurological surgery residency programs. She remembered it like it was yesterday: the cadaver's olive-green gallbladder, the toughened skin on the elbows and knees, the smell of the formaldehyde. After the first day with the cadaver, Eliza and Zachary had taken the T to Pizzeria Regina for a large pepperoni pizza and beer, which made a lot more sense at the time than it did in retrospect.

And now Zachary Curry was a neurosurgeon at Dana-Farber. *Tough stuff,* he'd scrawled on his card back to Eliza, *but I hope we're making strides.* That was the thread she'd forgotten to pull at. Quick, Eliza, quick, hurry up, search. Dana-Farber was recruiting for a Phase II clinical trial studying the efficacy of an antigen vaccine to treat glioblastoma multiforme. Zachary Curry would be able to put Eliza in touch with the recruiters for the trial. Zachary Curry could possibly save her father's life.

"I've got it!" Eliza called out to anyone who would listen. "I've got it, I think I figured it out!"

Nobody heard her, because at the exact same moment the fireworks started. *Bang, bang, bang, pow, bang* again, *pop pop pop.*

17

BARTON, MASSACHUSETTS

Deirdre

Deirdre could feel herself gearing up to pick a fight with Brock after the Fourth of July fireworks.

There was no reason for it, none at all. It was a treat to have Brock home for the holiday weekend, because he was so often away. The fireworks had been just as splendid as they always were. They'd watched them from the deck of Rob's boat, moored out in the harbor, along with Eliza and Rob's mother and the three children. It had been crowded and festive, just the way you wanted the Fourth of July to be, and both Deirdre and Eliza had made copious amounts of food, although Eliza's roasted vegetable salad with walnut pesto had put Deirdre's simple Caesar to shame. (Of course.) They'd had a cocktail called a Saffron Cooler, which was an update to the wine spritzers Deirdre remembered her mother and her mother's card-playing friends drinking in Deirdre's youth in Darien, a card table set up on the backyard patio, suntanned faces thin-lipped with concentration.

Yet she'd come home after the fireworks feeling prickly and out of sorts. It had nothing to do with the luxuriousness of *A Family Affair:* Deirdre really and truly didn't care so much about boats, she'd grown up dutifully sailing with her father when her presence was required, she understood the difference between a mainsheet and a jib sheet, but she didn't live and breathe the ocean the way many people did, the way Rob did, the way Brock did. If either of them were to envy Rob's boat, it would be Brock. Brock, who was never impressed by anything, was impressed by Rob's boat. Everybody was. Three *million* was the price tag being thrown about town for the Hinckley, but of course Rob hadn't bought it himself, his mother had.

But it wasn't the boat. It had more to do with . . . well. It had to do with a different kind of envy. It had to do with watching Rob and Eliza, who had sat together, the sun setting behind them, lighting them up like a tableau. There had been that odd little bit where Eliza had been glued to her phone, which was unlike her (even Evie had scolded her), and then she'd disappeared belowdecks for a while, until she'd suddenly shouted, "I've got it! I think I figured it out!" and after that her entire demeanor had changed, and she'd seemed for a little while almost like she was *on* something, jittery and unfocused.

But then, back up on deck, sipping her Saffron Cooler, Eliza had sat next to Rob and they had talked for such a long time. What had they been talking about? Deirdre didn't know. But every now and then Rob would reach out and touch Eliza's unfairly beautiful hair, or Eliza would put her hand on Rob's arm to make a point and then keep it there long after the point had been made. And the prickly feeling had come upon Deirdre, and now it refused to leave.

It was a terrible thing, to envy your best friend. Made Deirdre feel like a monster. And she wasn't a monster! She was a good person, she was just doing her best. Look at all she was trying to do for the EANY kids, look at all she did for her own family.

Standing in the kitchen, Deirdre could see a wobbly version of her reflection in the door on the microwave. She looked tired. An ex-boyfriend, in the process of breaking up with her, had once told Deirdre that she had a good heart but that her angles were too sharp. She even *looked* sharp: sharp nose, sharp elbows, sharp clavicle, sharp cheekbones.

She supposed she could get fillers, like Sheila Rackley, soften things up a bit.

If she got fillers, would Brock give up his occasional sleeping berth in the guest room and return full-time to the marital bed? (Did she *want* Brock to give up the guest room and return full-time to the marital bed?)

Once, when they'd both had one too many margaritas at Don Pepe's, Deirdre and Eliza had got to talking about sex and Eliza had described her and Rob's sex life as "robust." Deirdre had experienced a flash of envy then that was so bright and hot she thought Eliza must have seen it.

Sofia had gone to spend the night at the Barnes's house after the fireworks, and Deirdre supposed that Sofia's absence had contributed to the prickly sensation. She always felt the fact of her one child most strongly when Sofia was gone overnight.

Because the quiet of the house on those nights when Sofia was invited to a sleepover made Deirdre painfully aware of what life would be like when Sofia went off to college and left them for good. Deirdre heard her own footsteps echo in the hallways (a slight exaggeration, fair enough, because of the no-shoes-in-the-house policy) and stood underneath the lintel staring at Sofia's tidy, empty bedroom and wondering what would become of her and Brock, without a child to hold them together.

She'd wanted hordes of children, she'd wanted a whole army. She'd wanted the mess and the chaos and the crazy soccer schedules. One family in their town had five children—five! And not even a set of twins in the bunch. The Bryants. Becca Bryant was always running around like a chicken who couldn't find the time to get its head cut off. She got at least a dozen speeding tickets a year and didn't even care: that was just the price of the life she'd chosen. ("We count it in the budget!" she'd say breathlessly, dropping one kid at the soccer field, ushering three more into the minivan, some of them not even hers, but who was Becca Bryant to notice a small detail like that, for she was busy busy busy.)

But Brock wanted only one. He was first in line at the new vasectomy clinic when it opened.

And that's where the fight started on the Fourth of July.

Brock turned on *SportsCenter* as soon as they got home, checking the baseball scores. Something about the sounds of *SportsCenter* put Deirdre right over the line. She couldn't help but think of those *SportsCenter* voices as the soundtrack to the rest of her life.

"Maybe we could adopt," she said, apropos of nothing.

Brock was a Yankees fan; they'd lost by six to the White Sox, so he was already in a mood. Deirdre moved so that her body partially covered the television screen and Brock shifted correspondingly on the sofa so he could still see.

"Adopt what?"

"A *baby,* Brock. Maybe we could adopt a baby."

"Deirdre, you're in front of the screen, I can't see."

She moved so that she covered even more of the television. She thought of the kids in the EANY materials, the undernourished, potbellied, huge-eyed creatures who numbered in the zillions. They all needed to be fed, every single one of them.

She said, "Maybe we could adopt a baby from Africa. A little African baby." She'd want a little girl, girls had such a harder time of it in the rest of the world, there were terrible things awaiting so many of them. They should bring all the girls here, to *Barton,* where they could go to science camp and visit the dentist twice a year whether they needed it or not and get their eyes checked if they couldn't see the last line on the eye chart. Yes, a little East African girl with a big gummy smile. She'd call her Asha, because that meant "life" and was a word Deirdre and the rest of the citizens of Barton would be able to pronounce without trouble.

"Deirdre, come on. You know we're not doing that." Brock's tone was perturbed, but not angry, not yet.

Although presumably little Asha would come with her own name.

"Why not?"

"Because we're not. It's not a realistic scenario." Brock probably used phrases like *realistic scenario* at work all the time; he probably didn't know that it sounded ridiculous in everyday conversation. "But if you want to fight about it, fine, let's fight about it." Now he was going a little bit beyond perturbed. Brock made a great show of sighing and switching off the TV—he really had to lean around Deirdre now, because she was blocking it almost fully, but somehow he managed to find a hole between her body and the television into which he could point the remote. The *SportsCenter* noises evaporated into silence, and the only sound remaining was Deirdre's elevated breathing. Her eyes felt hot, and she tightened her hands into fists.

Brock said, "We made a decision to have one child."

"*We* did not make a decision, Brock. *You* made a decision."

He sighed again. "That's not how it happened, Deirdre. You were as on board as I was, at the time. You know that's true."

"That's not fair," she said. It wasn't fair, it really wasn't!

The lyrics of one of Sofia's favorites from the previous summer came to her then, unbidden but catchy as hell. *Didn't they tell us don't rush into things? Didn't you flash your green eyes at me?* "Wonderland," by the indomitable Taylor Swift.

"Life is not a Taylor Swift song," she'd told Sofia recently. Wasn't it though, sort of?

Or shouldn't it be?

It's all fun and games 'til somebody loses their mind . . .

It wasn't fair of Brock, he'd caught her off guard when Sofia was tiny. There'd been the diapers and the middle-of-the-night crying and the way every part of her body seemed to be leaking something—tears, milk, blood. She'd been lost in Sofia's confounding, round-the-clock neediness and a bit in her own despair and Brock had gone on a work trip just two weeks after Sofia was born and even though Deirdre's mother had come from Darien to help out it had still been really, really hard and so when Brock said he had made an appointment at the clinic for (his euphemism) "the ol' snip-snip" in two months she didn't know or care enough to argue back.

"Okay," she'd said, too exhausted to pull any additional words out of her mouth besides the irrevocable two: "Snip-snip."

By the time she came out of it and Sofia had resolved into something wonderful the deed was done.

Oh, but it was hopeless. Even if they got a baby tomorrow (unlikely), Deirdre would be three hundred by the time little Asha was eighteen. Deirdre wouldn't know where to get Asha's hair properly braided—they'd have to drive into Boston, or Everett—or how to raise her in a way that respected both the culture she came from and the one into which she'd been placed. Little Asha would be the only person of color in Barton's bright-white school system. Then she'd grow up and leave Deirdre too, just like Sofia was going to, and Deirdre would be left with the very same emptiness she was trying to avoid.

It was impossible, of course, to compress these thoughts and fears into one or two sentences. So instead she said ridiculously, "If Eliza wanted to adopt an African baby, Rob would let her."

Brock said, *"What?"*

"He would. I know he would. And you never want to do anything, Brock. *Anything.*"

"You don't mean that. Do you mean that?" The fact that his tone softened somehow made things worse instead of better: here came a pity party for poor little Deirdre.

"No," she said. "I guess not." Oh, hell. Maybe she was getting her period. Maybe it was early menopause. Maybe she'd simply had too many Saffron Coolers on the deck of that painfully gorgeous boat and hadn't had enough food and needed to go to sleep.

"I'm going to bed," she said.

"Okay," said Brock. "Good idea."

First she'd go upstairs to check Sofia's Instagram feed—that feeble ligature tying her to her daughter.

Once she left the room she heard the television go back on.

Was this how it went, you knew every inch of your daughter, every book read and bowel movement produced and favorite television show watched, and then breath by breath she began to depart, leaving only vestiges, a lone soccer sock behind the hamper, an uncapped toothpaste tube in the bathroom, until eventually she was gone, a ghost sailing toward the ceiling, or (worse) toward a future that contained nothing of you?

"Oh, *Deirdre*," said Eliza once. "It's not all that bad, sweetie, you're making it sound so *dismal*. It's just life! Time passes." Easy for Eliza to say, she still had sweet chubby Evie, who adored her, who almost never scowled, who didn't yet own an iPhone, just an iPad. Evie was a true innocent: she could text only from a wireless zone! And Eliza had Rob, of course. She had *Rob*.

Rob, who had that blond lock of hair that fell impertinently forward. Really, it was ridiculous for a grown man, a man of forty, to have hair like that: so blond, first of all, and thick enough that there were actually *locks* to fall forward.

Brock wore his hair in a defensive crew cut.

There were things in this world that Deirdre didn't trust. Dentists with off-white teeth. Her father-in-law after a martini. Her mother-in-law *before* a martini. Screw-top wine bottles. The backstroke.

But some kind of instinct made her trust Robert Barnes more than she trusted most. She'd follow him to the ends of the earth and back. If only he'd ask. If only he'd ask!

No, life was not a Taylor Swift song, she'd been right to tell Sofia that. Life was more like an Adele song: heartrending, wide-ranging, beautiful, sad, and painful, all at the same time.

18

Eliza

Eliza took Charlie to Val's to have the conversation. They couldn't talk properly in Charlie's house—it would be too easy for Charlie to walk away, start fiddling with his truck or the traps waiting for repair in the backyard, or something. She figured that even one-armed he'd find a way to ignore her.

It was late in the morning and all of the fishermen were out on the water. They didn't pass by the harbor on their way to Val's but she imagined the *Joanie B,* swaying alone on its mooring. They'd need a viable plan, soon, for taking care of Charlie's traps.

Val's was almost empty. The only other customers were sitting on the same side of a bench in one of the booths. Tourists, if ever tourists there were. They were Brooklynish hipsters, the guy with a man bun and the woman with a turquoise T-shirt featuring a cat wearing its own hipster spectacles. Both were looking around with moderately eager expressions; you could tell they were spending the week in Bar Harbor and had Yelped the place, looking for a Genuine Down East Experience. You could tell that even though they were super happy to have found it they were also too hip to reveal the true depths of their excitement.

Both Eliza and Charlie optimistically ordered the Fisherman's Breakfast, Val's specialty—optimistically, because the Fisherman's Breakfast was massive. Eliza could see the hipster couple watching them and then looking back at the menu, pointing. *Oh, for heaven's sake,* thought Eliza. *Go back to Greenpoint and leave us in peace.* She would have made that joke to Charlie, but she was pretty sure he didn't know where or what Greenpoint was, and why should he?

These were the same mugs Val had been serving her coffee in since time began: off-white, chipped in places, sturdy on the bottom, thick handles. And the counter stools were also the same. In Barton they would be called *retro* and the Coopers or the Rackleys would use them to outfit a basement bar. Here they were just old stools.

"Okay, Dad," said Eliza. "Sit down. We're going to talk about this right now."

They were already sitting, both of them, but the exhortation had been part of Eliza's rehearsed speech and she forgot to revise based on current circumstances. A small misstep, but nothing she couldn't recover from, and Charlie was too kind or too stubborn to point it out. She pulled out a small black notebook where she'd written down her plan of attack. She'd started creating it on the Fourth of July, belowdecks.

"Here we go, Dad. You're not going to believe what I figured out when I was home—"

Charlie sipped his coffee and watched her, saying nothing.

"Wow, Eliza, what did you figure out when you were home?" said Eliza. She used that voice she used when her children were ignoring her and she said to them what she wished they were saying to her. Her children loved when she did that. No they didn't, not at all, a lot of eye rolling always ensued. Even Evie was learning how to roll her eyes.

Charlie remained impassive. His shoulders were slumped forward and he was using one hand on the table to steady himself. She could see in the way his cheeks sagged the effort this little breakfast outing of hers was taking him. And yet he'd said, okay, sure, let's go to Val's.

She could almost see the tumor growing, invading the surrounding tissue, expanding, expanding, expanding. How big would it be now? The skull was so rigid, that goddamn tumor was pressing against it all the time. They had to shrink it *right away.*

That had been one of Evie's first full phrases, she was only two, toddling around, still in a diaper, saying, "More apple juice *right away,* Mommy." Or: "Need to watch *Doc McStuffins right away.*"

Val took the hipsters' orders and disappeared into the kitchen. "So I'll just go ahead and tell you," Eliza said. "It starts with a coincidence." Charlie blinked and gave a slight nod and drank some coffee.

Eliza told him about Zachary Curry, and about the clinical trial. She told him about the enrollment process.

Charlie cleared his throat, put down his coffee cup, and said, "No, Eliza."

"Even if you're not selected for this trial, Dad, they can do the chemo from there, or radiation, however they decide to treat. I'd just really like to see you at a hospital with a research focus. It makes such a difference in a field where things are changing all the time. Some of these new therapies are genetically targeted, and that's what you want to have at your dis—"

"Eliza."

A tone in his voice stopped her. She'd been looking down at her notes while she talked, but now she looked up.

"I said no. I'm not interested in going to Boston."

"Listen, Dad, they're the cream of the crop down there. I know it seems like a haul, but you're not going alone. Obviously. I got us an appointment next week. I'll take you down. All you have to do is *listen*. Just listen to the recommendations, and we'll take it from there."

"No. Not interested, Eliza."

"Or don't even listen! Just sit there, plug your ears, I don't care, and I'll listen. I'll listen! All you have to do is be there. Bring your brain, and be there."

One of the hipsters dropped a spoon, and it clattered to the floor. Val appeared, filled the hipsters' coffee cups, brought a new spoon, looked significantly at Eliza and Charlie.

"Eliza. You're not the only one that can look things up, you know. I went to the library and did some of my own research. I know what's coming. I know all about it."

He'd gone to the *library*! Little Harbor's tiny library was open three hours a day, three days a week. Less in the winter, if you could believe it. Eliza imagined Charlie bellying up to the single computer, typing his own terminal disease into the search bar. The image made her want to cry. What would have come up for Charlie, of course, would be the very same information Eliza herself had found: a poor prognosis, an exhausting treatment plan that, if pursued, would leave him ravaged, buying himself maybe a few extra months, maybe a year, maybe more, but at what cost?

"I'm not interested," he said, "in suffering like your mother did."

"You're not suffering yet, Dad! You look great."

This, obviously, was not accurate. Charlie didn't look great at all. In all of Eliza's thirty-seven years Charlie had never looked worse, or weaker, or more hopeless. Eliza knew that it wasn't so much about the pain with this sort of tumor—the brain doesn't have pain receptors, that was part of Year One Neuroscience—but his visual field cuts would get larger and larger, his fatigue would get worse and worse, his appetite would all but disappear, and that was just the beginning.

He said, "Yuh."

"*Dad!* You're giving up, before you've even tried anything. We have to at least meet with a doctor in Boston. We have to do as much as we can."

Val delivered them an obscene amount of food that neither one of them was going to touch. Eliza's stomach rolled over once, twice, three times. The Fisherman's Breakfast comprised two eggs any style, a giant pancake, two pieces of French toast, and two pieces of bacon. Charlie made no move toward his fork. Eliza gamely took up the maple syrup and squirted some on the pancake and the top piece of French toast.

"Is this about the insurance?" she asked. "Because you know Rob and I can cover it, whatever it costs—"

He watched her for a moment and then said, "It's got nothing to do with insurance."

"But you don't give up. You're tougher than this. I know you are." Charlie Sargent was tough with a capital *T*. Ten years earlier, when a few guys from a nearby harbor were cutting traps in Little Harbor's waters, Charlie had tracked the guys down and knocked them from here to Southwest Harbor, all by himself, no backup. If they'd come back he would have done it again, whatever it took. But they never came back.

Just two years ago, when there was talk of heroin coming in over the water from Canada, Charlie and some of the other fishermen had said, *Not in our harbor, asshole,* found the guy responsible, and paid him a middle-of-the-night visit that they never talked about. The guy went packing.

Charlie had put his beautiful wife in the ground. When they threw the first shovelful of dirt on Joanie's grave and Eliza couldn't even see through the tears—she was crying with those giant, gulping sobs, crying so hard Val handed her tissue after tissue after tissue and she'd soaked through all of them—Charlie had gripped Eliza's free hand and looked stoically ahead, blinking hard but never crying.

He was tough!

When Eliza was seventeen, Charlie threw his back out one night and hauled the next day as though nothing was wrong. He came home that evening—regular time, no earlier than usual—pale and shaking. Later his sternman told another captain that Charlie had vomited twice over the gunwale from the pain, but every single one of his traps in that day's rotation was properly tended and rebaited and sent back down, and then he went back out and did it all again the next day.

Charlie Sargent was the toughest of the tough.

"You're tough enough to beat this thing," she added. Then she cringed, hearing herself say that: it was such a nonmedical, vague, and ultimately ineffective way to approach the situation. And also it wasn't true. Tough didn't really have a part to play in this scenario. Glioblastomas were universally fatal, no matter who you were.

And even so, *even knowing all of this,* there was still that part of her that said, *Fight, Dad.* That said, *Don't give up.* That said, *You might be the one to beat the odds, why not, why shouldn't it be you?* That was the daughter part of her, not the medical part of her, of course. The medical part of her knew better. But the daughter part had a louder voice.

"I know they can't take out the tumor, Eliza. They told me that already, in Ellsworth. You know what they also told me? That if they tried, there's a good chance I'd end up blind."

"Not necessarily," she said, although she knew it was true; since the tumor was in the occipital area of the brain, blindness was a very likely outcome of surgery.

"You ever met a blind lobsterman?"

"Dad—"

"Did you?"

"Maybe not," she said.

"Course you haven't. 'Cause there ain't any."

"But there's chemo, radiation, clinical trials. What are your other *options,* Dad? Are you just going to sit around and let this happen to you?" She tried not to let her voice rise to a hysterical level, but it was hard.

Charlie talked over her and waved his fork for emphasis.

"I don't need to go to some upscale doctor in Boston to find out this thing is going to kill me. I know that already. Something bad happens, some emergency, I can drive myself to Ellsworth and see a doctor there."

"You can't drive if you have double vision. You can't drive if all of the straight lines have gone wavy on you! Or if you can't see out of the right side of both of your eyes."

Charlie considered that. "Fair enough. Val'll drive me."

"You are *so exasperating,* Dad!"

He shrugged and cut into his pancake and said, "I've been called worse. I expect I'll be called worse again before I die. Now you listen to me, Eliza, and you listen good. I watched your mother fight through cancer. I watched her waste away right in front of my eyes. I watched her lips crack and her hair fall out and her appetite leave her. I watched her until she didn't recognize me and she didn't recognize you and she didn't know what the hell she was doing anymore on God's green earth. I don't want to put you through watching me fight. I don't want to put myself through the fighting, neither. I don't."

That's when she lost it—never mind the Brooklynites, never mind Val, never mind the pimpled teenager who washed dishes for Val, never mind any of it. The tears came and she let them slide down her face like rain down a window. She didn't care. She wiped a big glob of snot with a napkin that already had maple syrup on it and she didn't care about that either. She cried like a little girl and between sobs she said, "I can't lose you too. It's not fair, Dad. It's not fair. I need you. It's not fair. I'll be all alone."

Charlie put down his fork and reached for her hand and covered it with his own bigger, calloused one, and he said, "You don't need me anymore."

"Yes I do! I *do!*"

"You've got your own family, Rob and the girls."

"I do need you. You've got grandkids. They love you. They need you. We can't lose you."

"You're losing me anyway, Eliza."

"Stop it, Dad. Don't say that. You're not allowed to say that."

"It's true, honey. And I'd rather not have my body all stove up by a bunch of doctors down in Boston into the bargain. Just take it how I'm saying it. Take me at my word."

Charlie Sargent's word was solid gold, everyone knew that. He asked anyone in town to take him at his word and they'd do it without a second thought and normally Eliza would too, but this time she couldn't. She wouldn't! Eliza stared hard at the cat wearing spectacles on the Brooklyn T-shirt. "No," she said. "I won't. I won't let you just give up. I don't accept that. I'm sorry, but I don't. I'm not leaving here without you."

Charlie picked his fork back up and filled it with food that never made it to his mouth. "Well, then," he said, "I guess you're not leaving."

19

LITTLE HARBOR, MAINE

Eliza

"Hey, Eliza. You up for hauling with me tomorrow?" That had been Russell, on the phone.

She'd thought that he'd been joking. Hilarious. Tell me another. She'd said, "I'm sure that would be entertaining for you, Russell, but my dad has an appointment to get his stitches removed, so I'm afraid I'm not available."

"I know about the appointment. Val can take him, I already asked her. I need a sternman for tomorrow, just for tomorrow."

"Why do you know about my dad's—oh, never mind." Small-town life. Not that Barton wasn't small, it was, but next to Little Harbor it was a bustling, full-blown metropolis. "You don't need a sternman," she said. "You have a sternman. You have Gavin Tracey." Gavin Tracey had been hauling with Russell all summer.

Russell coughed and said, "My sternman's useless." Zoe had told Eliza a few months ago that when a healthy person coughed or cleared his throat before speaking he or she was probably lying. It was a signpost. This was one of the fascinating and sometimes useful pieces of information Zoe had picked up from obsessively watching *Brain Games* on the National Geographic Channel.

"That's the first I ever heard of a Tracey being useless," Eliza said. The Traceys were hardworking and loyal; most of them came out of the womb holding a V-notch.

Not literally, of course.

On the phone she heard a familiar sound that she knew was Russell sucking air in through the gap between his front teeth. He'd never gotten the space fixed. Children in Little Harbor did not get their teeth fixed or their palates expanded or their eyes checked or their reading deficits tutored as a matter of course the way they did in Barton. She herself had a slightly crooked eyetooth and still, in the odd moment, alone in front of a mirror, considered (and then always quickly abandoned the idea of) adult braces.

"All right. He's not useless, but he needs the day off tomorrow and the lobsters are really friggin' crawling. I can't keep up. I'm stuck."

"You're *stuck*? There's nobody else in the whole town you can ask to haul with you, Russell?" By this point Eliza was arguing more for show than anything else. A big chunk of her wanted to know if she still had it in her.

"Okay, okay, Eliza. Are you going to make me say it?"

"I think I am."

"I want to haul Charlie's traps while we're out there. Someone should. Some of the guys offered but he wouldn't let anyone."

Eliza knew it was killing Charlie to leave his traps untended, so she let Russell continue. Technically, they needed permission from Marine Patrol to haul someone's traps.

"I thought if you came with me he'd be okay with it. Anyway, we won't tell him until it's all done, until we give him the money, and he's not going to get mad at *you*."

"Okay," Eliza said, a little frisson of excitement bubbling up despite herself. "Fine. I'll haul with you. What time are you going to pick me up, around seven thirty?"

"Yuh."

"Really?" He was taking it easy on her. Nice.

"Hell no, Eliza, of course not. Day's practically over by seven thirty. Why don't you go ahead and set your alarm for four. Unless you need to do your hair first."

"Go to hell, Russell." Do her *hair*.

"Pick you up at four thirty."

"*Fine.*"

Now they were, improbably but also inevitably, on the way to Russell's boat, a forty-seven-foot fiberglass beauty named *Legacy*. Eliza was wearing the clothes Russell had brought her: a pair of boots that were slightly too big, overalls that fit dismayingly well. She actually looked the part. White cotton gloves, because that's what the full-timers wore. It was the part-timers who wore the blue rubber gloves; the full-timers always had the tanks of hot water to warm their hands in when it was really cold. You got a real ribbing on the VHF if you wore the blue gloves. "You washing dishes over there?" she remembered her dad saying to someone more than once. "You just get your nails done and don't want to mess them up?"

Lobsterman humor was a *very specific* kind of humor.

The sun was rising spectacularly, pinks and oranges that later would turn to a clear and cloudless blue. That was the best part of summer hauling: the sunrises. In the fall it was the way the mist hung over the harbor, and in the winter, well, it was when the day was done.

Russell's skiff had an outboard motor; Charlie still rowed his with oars, he was as old school as it got. Lots of the fishermen's houses in Little Harbor had an old-fashioned skiff in the front yard, given over as a plaything when it got too old to serve its original purpose. Kids would fool around in them, practicing hauling traps, pretending to be their daddies.

"Think you could still row a skiff if you had to, Eliza?" Russell asked, pulling the rope on his outboard.

"Sure I could." She'd always had great balance with the oars, it was one of the many skills from her childhood that had absolutely no bearing on her present life.

On *Legacy,* Russell started the engine. The key was in the ignition already—they all were, same as they were in all of the pickup trucks parked at the wharf, and you'd no sooner touch another fisherman's truck or boat without permission than you'd dump a tankful of keepers back into the ocean. He busied himself with his electronics and his compass, switching on the GPS, consulting the radar.

The water was dark and inscrutable as always but the surface was smooth like glass: no chop. That was good. Eliza wasn't ready for chop, but she wasn't about to admit that to Russell, in the same way that she wasn't about to admit that part of her was nervous to be out on the water, scared to make a mistake. This wasn't a friendly afternoon sail on *A Family Affair* with Rob doing most of the work.

Russell uncovered the bait box and Eliza said, "Holy cow, I forgot how much this bait *stinks,*" and made a big show of gagging in case that caused Russell to change his mind, bring her safely back to shore, and let her get on with her day.

"You get used to the smell," said Russell. "You probably remember that."

He put the baskets in place and filled them with circulating salt water. She figured Gavin Tracey did some of this stuff usually—she might get fired for incompetence, she was just standing there like a total landlubber. But she didn't know Russell's boat the way she knew her father's and didn't really remember what to do and she didn't want to make a mistake and cause Russell extra work. For all the joking, she knew that the good fishermen took their work seriously and wanted everything done the way they wanted it done, no exceptions.

Once a guy had borrowed her dad's skiff and tied it back up with a different knot than the one he'd found it tied up with and, man, hadn't her dad gone apeshit on that guy, didn't talk to him for half the year at least.

"I guess," she said, about the bait, but she wasn't sure. The herring were bigger and creepier than she recalled. They reminded her in an unsettling way of Evie's pet goldfish. And they really did smell deadly. Also, it was discomfiting to have so many wide dead eyes staring at you, like they were keeping a ghastly secret that they might, at any minute, decide to share with you.

Once the engine was warmed up, Russell opened the boat to cruising speed and said, "I'm not going to put you through a real offshore trip today. Don't think you could handle it."

He didn't look at her when he said that, but she could see a smile playing at his lips.

"Bullshit. Nice try. You don't go offshore this time of year anyway." Nobody did. The best time for offshore fishing was October through December. Everybody knew that.

"Fair enough," he said. They passed the channel marker and not too far away Eliza could see Grindstone lighthouse, automated now but still functional, thirty-nine feet high, flashing every eight seconds, as steady and reliable as anything in Eliza's life had ever been.

"We'll do my traps first, then we'll head over to Charlie's." He was yelling more than he was talking, to be heard over the noise of the motor, and she just nodded because it was easier than trying to yell back.

Russell's buoys were red and white and bright yellow, same as they'd been when he first got his license, before they'd graduated from high school. Eliza had painted many of those buoys with him, in his father's shop, over that long winter during their senior year, dozens and dozens of them, the dark coming on so early in the beginning of January that they needed their headlights to drive home from school.

It was really odd now to think about the fact that she had had time to sit around painting lobster buoys while she was finishing up high school, while she was getting accepted to *Brown*, of all places. Her children would never, not in a million years, have time to paint lobster buoys, not when they had tennis and swimming and sundry after-school activities and pounds of homework every night.

She remembered how relaxing it had been, though, how simple and satisfying, almost *therapeutic,* just the two of them, crowded near the electric heater in the otherwise unheated shop, scraping and painting, scraping and painting, electric heat coming from their bodies too. She felt warm, thinking about it, about their bodies, eager and young, attached to each other more often than not, and for a minute she had to keep herself from standing too close to Russell. *Another life,* she reminded herself. *A lifetime ago.*

"Shedders are starting to come on," said Russell. "Heard it on the VHF day before yesterday. You want to keep an eye out for them when you're banding."

"That's good," said Eliza. "I will." Lobsters that had shed their old shells, moving out of their cramped living quarters, were shedders; they gained weight and length when they shed, so their appearance made for more keepers in the batch. But they were fragile, with their soft jelly bodies, and you had to take care with them. "You want me to double-band them if I see them?"

"Yep," said Russell.

Russell had brought a Thermos of coffee for each of them, and he handed one to Eliza. If she didn't look at or smell the herring, if she concentrated on the blue-black water and the stunning sky, if she ignored the fact that her hand was shaking with cold and it was hard to keep the coffee from splashing out, she could almost pretend she was on a scenic cruise.

Soon enough they'd arrived at the buoys and Russell pulled up alongside the first one and cut the motor.

"Ready?"

"Ready." Russell reached over the starboard side with his gaff and his hook, grabbed the pot warp, then pulled the line from the water to run it through the hauling block and into the hydraulic hauler. The line coiled itself on the deck below the hauler. The line strained, and they both looked respectfully into the inscrutable dark water until the trap broke the surface. Eliza was at first so mesmerized by the waiting that she forgot she was there to do a job until Russell said, "Grab it, Liza," mildly aggravated, and Eliza broke the trap.

"Nothing," he said. Sometimes you had to pry a crab off the trap's walls, but this trap was empty.

The second trap in the string had four keepers, and the third had two lobsters that looked promising until Eliza flipped them over and saw that the undersides of both were berried with eggs. "Check 'em," said Russell. In Maine you had to V-notch an egg-carrying female to mark her as a breeder; once she was V-notched you couldn't trap her even if you caught her at a time when she had no eggs. These were notched already.

Russell's jawline tightened. "Let's rebait."

She grabbed a bait bag, saying nothing.

"Watch yourself," said Russell, and Eliza obeyed, making sure her feet were clear of the line.

"Ready to go again?" Russell asked, and he started the motor to go out to the next set of buoys.

"Yep," she said. "Ready as I'll ever be."

Same motion, over and over and over: pull the traps over the rail, check, empty. Measure the lobsters, toss back the small ones, mark the ones with eggs and toss those back, toss back the big ones, band the ones that were left. Take care with the shedders.

Rebait, lower it back down, same thing again and again. Sometimes they would pass another boat, or another boat them: the man or woman on the other boat would lift a hand, and Russell would lift one in return.

The day wore on. Eliza realized too late that she'd forgotten sunscreen. In the predawn darkness, dark enough that they had needed the lights on the bow, she hadn't thought about it. She was going to fry. Russell found her an extra cap, and she put it on. The cap said MAINE in big black letters and below it were the words EST 1820. Total tourist wear; she didn't know why Russell had it on his boat, but she was glad he did.

Time passed. Another trap over the gunwale. She was getting tired. As it turned out, barre class and gentle three-mile runs by the water in Barton were ineffectual training for honest manual labor. She'd been stronger the summer she was fifteen, hauling with Charlie on the *Joanie B.* She'd been sinewy, with visible muscles in her forearms and a fisherman's tan that started three inches below her shoulder. Not that that was a good look, necessarily, but when you were fishing six days a week you didn't think too much about how you looked.

She emptied the trap, prying a crab off the side and tossing it over. She rebaited. Her back hurt. And she had to go to the bathroom. She should have gone easier on the coffee. How many traps did Russell have, anyway? She knew most of the fishermen fished in a three- or four-day rotation, but it felt to her like they were checking every single trap he'd ever owned.

She wouldn't admit it, though, no sir. She wouldn't cry uncle, whatever happened. She tried to channel the medical school Eliza, who'd once stayed up for thirty-six hours and then had nailed her pharmacology exam, highest grade in the class.

"One more string and we'll head over to Charlie's," said Russell finally, and Eliza tried not to let the relief show on her scorched face.

Charlie's buoys were red and black and bright blue, and when Russell cut the motor near the first one she felt the strangest sense of disorientation, like she was walking on her hands, underwater, in a dream. She started to sway a little bit, confused. Russell had to come up and catch her by the elbow so she didn't tip over.

"You okay?" he asked.

She shook her head. No. Yes. No. "Sure," she said. "Just got a little dizzy." Then it wasn't her dad's buoys making her dizzy, it was Russell's proximity, his touch, the long-familiar weight of his fingers on her arm, all of it as unexpected and potentially devastating as the shock of an electric eel, because of the accompanying memories it brought up. Russell's was the same body it had always been, long, lean, muscle piled on muscle layered over bone. Unselfconsciously strong. Different from Rob's body. Russell had dark hair and dark eyes; Rob was fair with light eyes; it was almost like she'd sought out Russell's opposite in every possible way.

Another life, she told herself again.

Russell made her sit down in the captain's chair for a minute and drink some water from a bottle he pulled from his cooler. She squinted out at Charlie's buoys bobbing in the water until she felt better and then together they hauled Charlie's traps just the way they'd hauled Russell's.

Eliza hesitated after they'd emptied the first trap.

"Whatcha doing?" asked Russell while she stood there dumbly, balancing the trap on the gunwale. "You waiting for a personal invitation to put some bait in that trap?"

"I thought we might pull them," she muttered.

"*Pull* them? In July? You think Charlie would want us to pull his traps in *July*?"

"No, but." The unspoken question was this: *Is he ever going to get out here to haul these traps himself?*

"Season's just getting started. The best fishing's still ahead of us. Rebait."

She did what Russell said and he started the motor and moved the *Legacy* to another string.

"Geezum, these are full to bursting," Russell said at the next string. "Unbelievable. I should leave my traps out that long, see what happens." The lobsters were crawling all over each other, filling up most of the traps, and there was always a crab or two or a pregnant female or a lobster that was too big or too small, but you couldn't argue with the fact that this was one hell of a catch. "Well," said Russell. "Charlie Sargent did always know where to set his traps. I'll give him that, the old bastard."

Eliza nodded and swallowed hard and different parts of her wanted to scream, *Touch me again, on the arm, anywhere!* And then after thinking about it, *Don't get too close!*

Did any part of Russell's memory fire up with that touch on her arm? She couldn't tell.

After they emptied each trap and measured each bunch, Russell put Charlie's keepers into his backup holding tank to keep them separate from his own. Eliza knew he'd keep them separate when they got to the co-op to turn in the catch, too, and she knew he'd give Charlie what his lobsters had fetched and maybe even some on top of that, and he wouldn't subtract for bait even though he was using double what he'd normally use by baiting double the number of traps for the day, because that's how Russell was.

After that she let the motion and the physical work and the monotony take over her whole body. And although she was ravenous she wasn't going to say anything until Russell did because it had occurred to her maybe an hour before that she hadn't brought any food for herself. Rookie mistake. She'd starve before she'd admit to it!

She thought about the ladies of Barton, who were always trying to lose the last six pounds of baby weight or vacation weight or holiday weight. She would give them this, the Lobsterman's Diet, hours of manual labor on an empty stomach under a punishing July sun.

Finally, *finally,* Russell cut the engine, reached again inside the cooler, and handed her a sandwich wrapped in wax paper. Eliza was so hungry she almost ate the paper along with the sandwich.

"I don't normally feed my sternman," Russell said. "But I made an exception for you."

"Take it out of my pay," she said, unwrapping the sandwich.

"Ham and cheese," he said. "Just for you, Liza."

"Like hell it is," she said, trying not to let her heart jump at the way he said her name. Lobstermen didn't allow pig of any kind on their boats; it was a long-held superstition. She peered inside the bread. Turkey.

Here was Eliza Sargent Barnes, eating bread (*white* bread!) and lunch meat. She was inadequately sunscreened, and she smelled like herring, but despite all of that (or because of it) she was about as content as she remembered being in a long time. She wasn't thinking about her dad's tumor, or how the family would manage without her if she stayed up here longer, or about Rob and Cabot Lodge, or about whether Judith had served Zoe a cocktail yet. Or about Phineas Tarbox. The sun was high in the sky and it was glancing off the water and there wasn't a hint of fog around: it was that rare perfect day, the kind of day they made postcards out of, the kind of day tourists who had never worked on the water imagined every day was like when they said things like, "I think when I retire I'll buy myself a nice little lobster boat."

While they ate, Russell said, "Charlie might have to hire you to take his boat out when things pick up, until his arm is better."

She appreciated the fact that Russell was pretending Charlie's main problem was in his arm.

"Right," she said. "I'm sure I'd be his first call."

"You're doing okay, Eliza, you're doing okay after all. Don't sell yourself short." She smiled and took another bite of her sandwich. If Russell had pulled a vat of Kool-Aid and a bag of Doritos and a box of ultra-hydrogenated packaged donuts out of the cooler she would have been happy to eat those too. Russell said, "I figure another hour or so and we'll be done, you okay with that?"

Russell had been consulting his equipment, checking the weather, listening in on the VHF all along. Occasionally he chimed in, ribbing one of the guys, making a comment about the catch or the weather.

"Sure," said Eliza. She wasn't sure if she could make it another hour but she also wasn't sure she wanted to stop. "An hour sounds good."

After lunch they hauled another of her dad's strings and then a few more after that, and when it was time to start up and head back to the harbor Russell moved the gear and nothing happened; the boat didn't move.

Russell said, "Shit," under his breath.

"What is it?"

"Nothing."

"Why aren't we moving?"

She could see a muscle tightening in Russell's neck, and there was a certain look on his face. She knew that look—her dad took on the same look every so often: when his aftercooler got clogged up and he had to run the boat dirty; if the heat exchanger went; if he had to come up with a few grand to take the *Joanie B* to the machine shop and pay a mechanic to take the engine apart. Boat repairs could ruin your season.

"Russell? What's going on?"

Russell moved the bait box that sat over the hatch. He opened the hatch, then climbed down. She peered into the hatch and saw that he was pouring from an oil can into the reverse gear.

"Is the reverse gear broken?"

Russell climbed out of the hatch. The neck muscle twitched again, and Russell sighed. "Not broken," he said. "Just wore out."

Eliza eyed the oil can. "How often do you put oil in it?"

"Don't worry about it."

"Every day?"

"Eliza. It's not your problem. Don't worry about it." Now the gear responded, the motor started, and they were off.

Over the noise of the motor, Eliza shouted, "It's not safe to run your boat with a broken reverse gear, Russell." She felt bossy saying that, but it was true.

"I know that, Eliza. It's not broken. It's wore out."

She thought, *worn,* chastised herself for thinking that, and said, "But it might break soon."

"Might."

"So . . ."

"I just don't happen to have fifteen grand to get it fixed right now, okay, Eliza? I'll probably have to wait until the end of the season." If he said anything after that, the wind and the motor took the words.

Fifteen grand? Eliza was taken aback. A lot of money. She said, "Maybe I—" Then she stopped: could she offer Russell fifteen grand to fix his reverse gear? Of course not. Would he take it? No question, he wouldn't. So she stopped, and she let the ocean spray swallow the words she hadn't said, and she waited.

Russell throttled down as they got close to the harbor and turned back to her and said, "Guy came to me a couple of days ago, said he had just bought ten traps and was looking for advice on where to set 'em."

"Yeah?" said Eliza. "Who was that?" She retrieved a dropped herring from the deck and tossed it into the bait box. A few seagulls circled, waiting for action. Off in the distance she could see another boat approaching.

"Guy from out of town, think he was from down your way. A southerner."

She snorted. "Yeah." Only in Little Harbor would someone from Massachusetts be considered a "southerner." "So what'd you tell him?"

"I gave him the best advice I have for someone like that."

They neared the co-op, where they would turn in the lobsters and fuel up and pick up the next day's bait.

"Which is?"

"Which is. Sell the traps, use the money to buy some lobsters."

She should have known it—that was one of the oldest punch lines in the book, a joke as old as the lobsters themselves.

"Holy cow," she said. "All this time I've been gone, nobody's thought of any new jokes?"

"Nope," said Russell. "No need to, when the old ones'll do." He took a deep breath and smiled, and Eliza smiled back.

20

LITTLE HARBOR, MAINE

Eliza

It was after they'd turned in the catch and tied up the boat and taken the skiff to the wharf that Eliza realized she'd forgotten her phone at her father's house that morning. She hadn't noticed it earlier because even if she'd had it she would have been too nervous to take it out on the boat. Eliza was notorious for inflicting water damage on her electronics and the electronics of those around her. She purchased every extra protection plan Apple had to offer.

Now, though, she noticed the phone's absence. She hadn't talked to the girls all day, she hadn't checked in with Rob, she hadn't seen which pathetic stray dogs Evie had fallen in love with or what Zoe was up to on social media or what Eliza's own four hundred and sixty-two Facebook friends had been doing on this faultless summer day. They were probably swimming and sailing and mentioning casually that their children were growing up to either rule or change the world; on Facebook, Eliza's friends were often certain that their offspring were going to do one or the other. Statistically speaking, though, well, most of them weren't, were they?

(Privately Eliza thought Evie might beat the statistics, but she would never declare that via social media. Much better to let it all come out as a surprise in a decade or two.)

She borrowed Russell's phone to call Rob. She dialed the number while Russell went off to talk to some of the other fishermen. She'd forgotten about that, that easy camaraderie of men and women just off the water, the way they talked about the day's catch and the weather that had just blown through and the weather that was coming up next. It was different from how she and the other women of Barton were around each other. Or maybe it wasn't different at all, maybe it was the exact same sort of relationship, just in a different context.

She saw Josh, the boyfriend of Mary from the café, skirting the outside of Russell's circle without joining in. Something unsettling about that guy, something shady about his body language. And also. He looked too old for Mary, what was he, twenty-five, twenty-eight? If Eliza had known Mary well enough, if she had had less on her own plate, she would have sat her down and said, "Run, Mary, run!"

Maybe she'd do it anyway.

Rob answered after the second ring, even though Russell's number wasn't associated with a contact on Rob's phone. As a general rule, Eliza ignored numbers that weren't associated with a contact on her own phone, but that just showed you that Rob was more trusting about the world than she was.

"Hey!" she said. "It's me, don't be fooled by the number, I left my phone back at the house."

"Hey," said Rob. His voice was strained. "I left you about a hundred messages today."

"I didn't get them. Like I said, I left my phone back at the house."

"Left it and went where?" His words sounded like someone had taken a pair of scissors to them and snipped.

"*Whoa*, Rob."

"Sorry." He didn't sound sorry. "But we needed you today. We've been trying to call, the girls have been sending messages, we even tried your dad's house, no answer, you had us all scared to death—"

"My dad had a doctor's appointment. Val took him. That's why there was no answer, he had to get his stitches removed." This conversation was not distantly related to the conversation she'd been anticipating. She said, "What's going on, why do you sound like that? Did something happen?"

"Of course it did."

"What? Rob, *what*?" Oh dear God, her children, something had happened to her children! Her heart thumped and careened. All day she'd spent out on a lobster boat, avoiding the lines that could trip you up and the hydraulic hauler that could cut the tips of your fingers clean off (it had happened!), thinking about high school, when the real danger was back in Barton.

"Nothing specific, but, I mean, it's been a whole day, a hundred things have happened, a hundred different things, and we all tried to get in touch with you and none of us could. Christine Cabot is driving me out of my *fucking* mind and I can't concentrate with the girls in and out, and Zoe wanted a ride somewhere and when I couldn't take her because I was on the phone with Ruggman, and I can *never* get Ruggman on the phone, she completely flipped out—"

Rob never swore. Well, sometimes he swore, but when he did he used temperate, harmless swears, like *bastard* and *damn it:* gentlemanly swears. Sometimes he apologized after: it was adorable. He never pulled out the big, bold swears. In fact, Eliza felt that she'd had to rein in her own tendencies over the years, tendencies born of hour upon hour upon hour spent in a workingman's world. Normally she would have made a joke out of Rob's swearing just now, but she was starting to get peeved. A hundred things happened *every* day, and Eliza was there for most of them. When Rob worked for Mo Francis he was gone thousands of hours a week, and he was commuting back and forth to Boston every single day, and he was at the beck and call of not only Mo but all of Mo's clients, and guess who took care of the hundred things every single day?

Welcome to motherhood, she wanted to say.

"Come on, Rob, don't scare me like that. I was hauling traps today, that's all, and I didn't bring my phone with me." She was about to continue, to tell him all about what it had been like to be back on the water, about how hard she'd worked and how good she'd felt and how rotten the herring had smelled but how she'd stuck her hands right in the bait box anyway. Before she got a chance he spoke again, more sharply.

"What do you mean you were hauling traps? I thought your dad's arm was in a sling. I thought he couldn't work! You just said he had to get his stitches out."

"His arm *is* in a sling. I didn't go with my dad. I went with Russell."

A long, pregnant pause.

"Huh."

"What's *that* mean?" She saw Russell slap one of the men on the back by way of goodbye and walk back toward her. More boats were coming in now, the harbor was almost full, and there was a line of skiffs tied up at the wharf. It was a gorgeous sight that set Eliza's heart rocking. They were hours from sunset but pretty much everyone out there had put in a legitimate twelve-hour day. Eliza's back muscles were beginning to ache, and her legs quivered. Even her forearms hurt, especially her forearms! She opened the passenger side of the truck and leaned against the seat. Somebody else stopped Russell to talk, a guy about her dad's age. The truck directly in her view had a bumper sticker that said FUCK THE WHALES AND SAVE THE FISHERMEN. Lovely. It would be fun to try to explain that one to Evie, shepherdess to the vulnerable mammals of the world.

"Whose phone is this? Is this Russell's phone?"

She didn't answer.

"Eliza?"

"Yes. This is Russell's phone."

"Okay."

"Okay?" Was Rob giving her permission? "Okay, what?"

"Okay, nothing. Okay, that makes sense."

Was Rob *jealous* of Russell? That would be like Eliza being jealous of Kitty Sutherland. Would Eliza be jealous if Rob spent the day hauling traps with Kitty Sutherland? That image was enough to make her nearly laugh out loud: Kitty Sutherland hauling traps, wearing a Lilly Pulitzer headband and pedal pushers and rosy-pink nail polish that matched her rosy-pink lipstick. Kitty Sutherland getting her hands dirty in anything other than Canyon Ranch mud bath.

Actually, the image of Rob hauling traps was pretty funny too. He would absolutely get a sunburn, he had *such* Aryan skin.

No, Eliza would not be jealous if Rob hauled traps with Kitty Sutherland.

But then again, Rob and Kitty didn't have the same history together that Eliza and Russell had. They didn't, for example, have the Thing They Would Never Talk About.

She studied the craggy shoreline and the curve of water that led out of the harbor. There was still a boat moving in from the distance, kingly, postcard perfect.

"I'm sorry, Eliza, but I thought you were going back up there for your dad, and now you're riding around on lobster boats with your ex-boyfriend. I'm just a little confused about what exactly you're doing there."

She closed her eyes and tried to think of the nicest things she could about Rob.

She thought of the way her heart still cartwheeled when they kissed, and how sex with him was more than sex, it was an anchor to the world. She thought of the way it felt to lay her head on his chest at the end of the day. She thought of how his hands had looked holding five-pound Zoe for the first time. She thought of the way at a party he always searched the room for her if she was talking to someone else. She thought of the way he was so patient teaching Evie how to serve a tennis ball—Evie's serve had been *awful* when she'd started playing tennis and now it was killer. When Eliza got sick, he brought her apple juice, which was the only kind of juice she liked, and he brought it in a tall glass with crushed ice and a bendy straw, which was the only way she drank it.

Rob said, "Eliza? Are you there?"

Deep breath. There were so many more things. He was always very kind to ladies of the seventy-five-plus set at the club. He managed to combine a sort of Lord Grantham from *Downton Abbey* charm with a dash of appropriate and refined flirting; he made the ladies think fondly of their first beaus, of dancing to Glenn Miller and drinking Singapore Slings.

"You know what I'm doing here," she said.

"I thought I did, but now I'm not so sure. It's been, what, five days since your dad told you he's not coming to Boston for treatment? And now you're hauling lobster traps?"

Eliza fingered a little tear in the pickup's seat. "The reason I was hauling, Rob, is because I was *helping*. My dad needed help, because he can't haul his traps right now, and they'd been sitting out there for days. So I helped haul them and reset them."

"I see."

"Do you? I'm not sure you do. You've never lived in a place like this, you don't understand how it works."

"I understand the concept of people helping people out, Eliza, I'm not the Bubble Boy."

Except for the bubble of money that you've always lived inside, thought Eliza.

Rob went on. "What it sounds like to me is that you've spent, what, a bunch of days in Little Harbor since the girls got out of school, and I *know* your dad is sick, and I know that's awful, Eliza, and we all want to help you help him, but I wonder if you're latching on to something else."

"What something else is that?"

Russell, seeing Eliza was still on the phone, stepped away again.

"Come on, Eliza."

"What?"

"The idea that the life you're playing at is more appealing than the one you actually live."

"Rob, I'm not *playing!*"

But he was still talking, he talked right over her. "If that life was so appealing, Eliza, you never would have tried so hard to get out of the place you came from."

"What do you mean? Away from people who work with their hands?"

"Give me a break, Eliza. No, of course not. I mean, come on. *I* work with my hands."

She was an elastic, and she was stretching and stretching and she was overcome by the idea that deep down she was still the same scrappy lobsterman's daughter, listening to the men curse around her, salty water, salty language, that she'd never fit into Rob's life, she was a square peg trying to wrench herself into a round hole, always had been.

And then the elastic broke. And she said the worst thing she could think of. She said, "No you don't, Rob. You don't work with your hands." She paused, for effect, but also to see if she might stop herself. She didn't. "You just draw the pictures so other people can build what *you* draw with *their* hands."

And that was the last thing she had the chance to say before Rob hung up.

21

BARTON, MASSACHUSETTS

Rob

Rob surveyed the kitchen. Earlier in the day Evie had attempted to make egg salad, and there were eggshells strewn across the counter, little bits of hard-boiled yolk chunks scattered in piles. The kitchen looked like a bunch of chickens had partied hard and then gotten the heck out of dodge without cleaning up after themselves. In his third-floor office, he knew, the Cabot file was in similar disarray. Rob closed his eyes and imagined himself aboard *A Family Affair*, light and variable winds, the ocean wide and inviting. The boat was equipped for serious sailing, a trip down to the Caribbean, but Rob would give anything for just half a day's sail from the yacht club and back. An hour, even. A cruise around the harbor.

Eliza's words floated back to him. *You don't work with your hands. You just draw the pictures so other people can build what* you *draw with their hands.*

He knew, of course, that these problems were trivial in comparison with what Charlie Sargent was facing. And yet.

He pictured Eliza in some borrowed lobstering gear, her hair tied back to keep it out of the wind. He pictured her emptying a trap, throwing it back over the side. He pictured her losing her balance when the boat started up again, leaning into the ex-boyfriend, his strong workman's hand steadying her, Eliza laughing.

His biggest fear, the fear that had plagued him since the first time

Eliza had taken him to Little Harbor, was coming true. Eliza had realized that she belonged there instead of here. That's why she wouldn't sign the Phineas Tarbox papers. He was going to lose her.

You just draw the pictures.

The words stung.

Zoe had left her phone on the kitchen counter when she'd gone upstairs, and Rob picked it up.

Zoe got more texts in ten minutes than Rob got in an entire day. He scrolled through. Most of the texts seemed to be pieces of enormous strings of other texts; they were all plump with emojis and most of them appeared to be requests for one friend to go like another friend's Instagram post.

He didn't hear the footsteps behind him. Zoe was as quiet as a burglar. "Is that my phone?" asked Zoe suspiciously. "Are you looking at my phone?"

Rob gave her the stink eye and said, "I pay the bill, I can look at the phone." What had happened to the patient dad he used to be, the one who had turned Evie's tennis serve from her Achilles' heel into her secret weapon? Where was the guy who had taught Zoe how to tie a cleat knot? Zoe rolled her eyes and let out a small dissatisfied huff. Rob looked down at the phone and said, "Who is Stanley? I didn't know you had a friend named Stanley."

"That's Sofia," said Zoe. "That's just a nickname. We all have them." Rob could see her trying to restrain herself from reaching for the phone.

"What's yours?"

"Bob."

"Interesting." A wave of exhaustion slapped Rob. He didn't understand Zoe's world. He didn't even understand his own world! Was Eliza going to call him back? Was she going to apologize for what she'd said to him? Was he going to apologize to her? How far over the line had he stepped? How far had *she*? His insides felt scraped out, empty. What was it like to know you had a tumor in your brain, that it was just a matter of time until it grew big enough to kill you? What was it like to know your father did?

Zoe said, "Were you talking to Mom?"

"I was," said Rob.

Zoe gazed at him. "Were you two fighting?" Ever since the parents of her friend Hannah Coogan had announced their divorce, Zoe had been ultrasensitive about any possible discord between her parents. This fact made Rob feel tender toward and protective of Zoe.

Then Zoe did something with her face—a lift of the eyebrow, a thing with her mouth that was part grimace and part smile—that made her look exactly like Eliza, and Rob felt himself soften further.

"No," he said gently.

"Oh," Zoe said. "It sounded like you were."

"Conversations sound different when you only hear one side of them."

"Right." Zoe chewed on a thumbnail and said, "When's she coming back?"

"I'm not sure."

"What Grandpa has is really bad, right?"

Rob considered Zoe. When she was born she'd weighed the same as a bag of sugar; he used to gaze at her tiny scrunched-up features and try to imagine what she'd look like as a toddler, a teenager, an adult. *Impossible,* he'd think. *She'll never get that big. She'll never not need us the way she does now.* But she had gotten big. She was old enough for the truth, and yet still he wanted to keep it from her.

"Dad?"

He opened his arms, and Zoe stepped into them. She was tall enough now that he could rest his chin on the top of her head. "Yes," he said. "What Grandpa has is really bad."

He sighed and prepared himself to climb the stairs to the office and to face the Cabot file. As he turned to exit the kitchen, he heard a rattling sound and Evie flew through on her scooter. She was broadly smiling and one of her legs was pumping against the floor. She came to a stop in front of Rob and Zoe and contemplated them.

"You're not allowed to ride that in the house," Zoe said. "Dad, she's not allowed to ride that in the house. Tell her."

Rob said, *"Evie,"* in a tone he hoped exhibited disapproval and authority.

Evie shrugged and circumnavigated the kitchen. On her next go-round she stopped and said, "Can I get Instagram?"

"No," said Rob.

"Never," said Zoe.

"Probably not never," corrected Rob. "But not now."

"Worth a try," said Evie.

22

Eliza

By the time Russell came back to the truck again, Eliza had composed her-self, even though inside she was a rainbow of different emotions: angry, guilty, confused. To his credit, Russell didn't ask her what was wrong or why her face was, well, for lack of a better term, *lobster red,* or anything else about the phone call. He said, "Good solid day of work, Eliza. What do you say we get a beer."

It wasn't really a question, based on the inflection, but Eliza answered it like one.

"I don't know . . . I should go back, check on my dad."

"Val wouldn't leave him if he needed anything, you know that. Call him first, though."

It was true. Val was probably at the house right now, fixing some sup-per for Charlie, or else she'd brought Charlie back to eat with her. Val wouldn't leave Charlie to fend for himself.

"You're right," she said. "Val will take care of him."

Eliza called, just to be sure. The stitches had come out easily, Val said. No pain. Had Charlie, by any chance, made any other appointments while he was there? Consulted with oncology or neurosurgery?

"No, honey," said Val. She sighed. "I tried, course. You know, Eliza, you can lead—"

"Oh, Val," interrupted Eliza. "If you tell me that you can lead a horse to water but you can't make it drink I swear on my father's traps I'm going to lose it."

"Okay, then, Eliza. Listen, your dad's resting, you want me to bring the phone over or let him sleep?"

"Let him sleep," said Eliza. "Thanks, Val."

She ended the call and looked at Russell and shrugged and said, "Let's do it. Let's go get a beer."

There were exactly three places to get a beer in Little Harbor. One was the seafood restaurant, The Lobster Trap, open only in the summer, where the tourists and the summer residents went. *Hoity-toity,* her father called it. Then there was The Cup, where no self-respecting lobsterman was going to end his day. Finally, there was The Wheelhouse, domain of the fishermen. They went to The Wheelhouse.

Russell headed straight for the bar and returned with two bottles, Bud, cold.

"They were out of champagne," said Russell. "So I got you this."

"Oh, give me a break," said Eliza. "Nobody drinks champagne after hauling." Though, in fact, she would have killed for a *very cold* glass. "Let me give you money for mine," she added, reaching for her wallet, which it turned out she didn't have. She'd left it at her father's house that morning, along with her phone. She rummaged around her side of the booth where her sweatshirt was anyway, for show, and muttered a little bit, also for show.

"Don't worry about it," Russell said. "I think I can buy you a beer."

Russell sat across from her in the booth. Those same booths had been there long before Eliza had illegally drunk her first beer at The Wheelhouse at age fifteen. They'd been there when she was ten years old, sent by her mother to fetch her father home on a Saturday night, the way all of the men had to be fetched home at one time or another. Probably the booths had been there since time began.

Russell was so tall that his knees bumped up against hers. Even if she'd wanted to get her knees out of the way she wouldn't have been able to, so she left them where they were, gently pressing into his. That was okay, right? It was just knees. She tried not to think about the winter painting lobster buoys in the barn. To help her not think, she drank a lot of the first beer fast, and felt it go right to her head. Must have been all of that sun on the boat—she'd put her tourist hat on too late.

"I owe you for today anyway," Russell was saying. "One-ninety-five. Not the best day, not the worst."

Eliza stared at him. He'd gotten some sun too, despite his own hat. In Massachusetts you were practically put on trial for child abuse if you let your kid get a sunburn; you were even looked at askance if you let yourself get anything other than a reputable, resort-ready tan exactly three shades darker than your normal skin tone. Here a sunburn was normal, just a fact of life, a part of the workday, a battle scar. "You're kidding, right?"

"Why would I be kidding?"

"You're not going to pay me one hundred and ninety-five dollars."

Russell stretched his legs; he had to tilt his body toward the outside of the booth to do that. She missed his knees, once they were gone, but she didn't know how to get them back. "Sure I am. You work, you get paid. Gavin Tracey doesn't volunteer on the boat, I didn't ask you to volunteer on the boat. I asked you to work."

That's when Eliza made her mistake: she laughed. It wasn't meant to be a bitchy laugh, more like a hey-buddy-stop-your-kidding-around kind of laugh, good-natured and sociable. But it came out all wrong.

Looking back later she saw that's when it all went downhill. She didn't know it immediately. But she should have seen it from the way Russell's features slid together.

"You keep it," she said, trying to recover, trying to sound affable. "Half of what we hauled is going to my dad anyway. And you used your fuel to get to his traps, and your fish to bait them. And I don't—" She stopped herself. Too late, though.

"You don't need it."

Well, bingo! Of course she didn't need it. One hundred and ninety-five dollars! She felt awkward being in this position, but . . . she spent that on a hair appointment, on one shoe out of a pair, on her weekly house-cleaning, and didn't blink. Judith Barnes, who made *significant* monthly deposits into her and Rob's checking account, owned two Birkin bags and was looking at a third. And let's not even get started on the Hinckley. It was true, Eliza Barnes didn't need Russell's one hundred and ninety-five dollars. Russell needed it much more. The price of bait had nearly doubled this year, creeping closer and closer to one hundred dollars a tray. *Fifteen grand* to replace the reverse gear!

She tried coming at it from another angle. "But I'm not even a good sternman. I'm useless. I don't deserve to make whatever Gavin would have made."

Someone had accidentally put a few extra Ss in one of those words before it came out of her mouth: *uselesssss*. Eliza could feel some of her hard edges softening.

Russell narrowed his eyes and tapped his fingers on the table.

"Put my share in the fund to fix your reverse gear," she added.

He unfolded himself and rose from the booth. "Drink up, Eliza, I'm going for two more."

"Mine's empty," she said, and it felt like a dare, the way she hit the bottom of the bottle against the table.

The second beer went down easier than the first, if that was possible, and then Russell returned to the bar. Again Eliza reached for her non-existent wallet and again Russell refused. Two beers turned to three, then to four. At beer three and a half Eliza said, "So, Russell, you seeing anyone?"

"I see people."

"Anyone—special?"

"Jesus, Eliza."

"Sorry! Sorry." Some years ago Russell had married a girl from out of town—Beatrice Prince. That was the name of Russell's last boat, before *Legacy*. Eliza had never met Beatrice Prince, neither person nor boat. (She'd gotten all of her information from Val.) They'd been married three years and then Beatrice Prince had decided the lobstering life wasn't for her; she'd taken off for Bangor or Augusta or wherever it was she'd come from, and she'd taken a bunch of Russell's money with her—the money he'd been saving for a new boat. That's when Russell had left town for a while, tried out the civilian life, found it didn't suit him, come back home, started again, taken out loans, bought *Legacy*. Eliza knew money was a worry, always a worry. "Sorry!" Eliza said once more. "I didn't mean to pry."

"Okay," he said. "But I don't want to talk about it."

Good riddance to bad rubbish, Val had said about Beatrice Prince.

Russell excused himself to use the bathroom and to talk to a couple of men at the bar. Elton Cobb, who ran the co-op. There was Ryan Libby, and there was Jack Cates. There was Michelle Davis, one of the two women in town who owned their own boats. Most people in the bar were varying versions of the men and women she'd known her whole life: hardworking, hard drinking, loyal, independent.

Eliza peered into her beer bottle; it was nearly empty. Holy lobster traps, *four beers,* on an almost-empty stomach. The turkey sandwich had been a long time ago. Eliza had earned her drinking stripes early, but they had faded over time.

The last time Eliza had had more than two drinks had been at the Colemans' holiday party the previous December, where she, and many others, had been brought down by the innocuously named Angel's Delight. Rob had been hungover for at least thirty-six hours after that party. He always got oddly quiet and remorseful when he drank a lot, like a chastened schoolchild, but he was even more so after that night. Eliza, hungover, became short-tempered, hungry for French fries, and irrationally aggravated by clutter. It wasn't the best version of herself.

Currently, though, she was really enjoying the feeling the beers were giving her. They were cushioning her from her absence from home, and from her fight with Rob, and from the pounding terror she felt over her father's health, and, after spending the long day with Russell in close quarters, from the Thing They Would Never Talk About.

A flame like that is going to burn itself out.

She looked around the bar; it was filling up now, all the lobstermen back from the haul, and there was a merry, reckless feeling in the air. In the corner there was a jukebox—a jukebox, in this day and age. How ridiculous. How wonderful. Eliza felt like she'd stepped right into a Springsteen song: workingmen, their girls, their troubles and triumphs.

Flames could burn themselves out, but did they ever flare back up again?

The year before her mother died—Eliza would have been eleven—was the first time her dad let her ride in the back of his truck on Trap Day. The traps were piled five or six high. You had to hang on when the truck hit a bump. When you got to the wharf, you had to load them all on board for the first set. And then you were off: another season begun.

The year after Joanie died Eliza told Charlie, "I don't want to go. I don't want to go to Trap Day. Can I stay home? I want to stay home and read."

"No way," said Charlie.

"Why not?"

"How would that look, Eliza? A daughter of mine, not helping out. You know how it is. No one goes till everyone goes."

And then, at the end of that day, the light low in the sky, a strip of orange racing across the horizon, the last of the boats pulling out, the traps piled so high they made the boats look lopsided, she loved the town all over again.

Now she felt a door in her mind unhinge, and from it tiptoed a thought that she couldn't quite capture. It slithered away from her, herring-slick. When Russell came back maybe she'd try to articulate it. She was facing the door to the bar when it opened and in came Mary from the café.

"Mary!" called Eliza. She waved her over enthusiastically—more enthusiastically, it was true, than she might have without the four beers.

Mary looked around the bar and moved toward Eliza. She wore a cautious expression and her movements were sparse and economical, like she'd spent her bottom dollar on them and couldn't afford to be wasteful.

"Sit down! Have a seat." Eliza gestured toward the space Russell had left. "You're not here to have a beer, are you?"

Mary shook her head and slid into the seat.

"Too young for that anyway, right?"

Mary looked startled. "I'm seventeen," she said. "I'll be eighteen August third. But anyway I don't like beer. Well, sometimes I do. But not now."

"That's a nice birthday. August! Mine's in January, it's completely dreary."

Mary nodded.

"Want a Coke or something?"

"No, I'm good," said Mary. "I'm just—I'm looking for Josh."

"Your boyfriend."

"That's right."

Eliza lowered her voice and, emboldened by the beer, said, "How old is Josh, anyway? If you don't mind my asking." It had been in college when she'd first heard people saying *my asking,* instead of *me asking.* All those years of saying it wrong, she couldn't believe it. She was humiliated.

"He's twenty-four."

Eliza absorbed this; she was torn between feigning indifference and stepping in as a mother figure, saying, *I forbid you to see him. I order you to find a boyfriend your own age immediately.*

Mary smiled uncertainly at Eliza, and Eliza, seized by a desire to be kind, said, "Hey, you know what? My father was older than my mother and they had the greatest love I've ever witnessed." She said that though she still had the image in her mind of Josh skulking outside the circle of men at the wharf, creeping like a fox outside a den of chickens. Mary's smile widened but not so much that it reached her eyes. Then Eliza said, "I haven't seen him. It's crowded over at the bar, though, who knows. He could be there."

Mary nodded again and made no move to get up. She looked tired, and the skin underneath her eyes had a lavender tint to it. Eliza suddenly remembered the Fourth of July missed call and said, "Hey! Did you try to call me? Over the holiday, when I was home?"

Immediately Mary's eyes filled—quickly, like inside there was a tiny tap that someone had just turned on—and Eliza said, "Oh. I'm sorry!"

"No, that's okay, it's just—" Mary swiped at her eyes with the back of her hand and then she folded both hands on the table as if she were at prayer and took a deep breath. The bar noises receded to the background, and Eliza fixed her gaze steadily on Mary. Mary leaned in toward Eliza and said, "I did try to call. I just—I just wanted to talk to someone."

Eliza leaned in too. "You did? Is everything okay?"

"Not really," whispered Mary. "Not at all. I'm just . . . well, I'm sort of . . . no, not sort of, I'm *pregnant*." She choked out the last words like they were a rotten bit of food.

"Oh, sweetie," said Eliza. She half rose from her seat. And immediately, a shadow passed over the table and Mary made a nervous jumping motion and looked up: Josh.

"Thought you were meeting me at the bar," he said to Mary.

"I was, I was looking, I just stopped to say hi."

Eliza wanted to say, *Excuse me, young man, is that how you greet your pregnant girlfriend?* But because she was trying not to pry she stuck out her hand and said, "Eliza."

He accepted it. Wimpy handshake, awful sign, an indication of bad breeding. Eliza had made sure her daughters could shake hands with a vise grip; she'd been taught that way by her father. "Josh," he said.

"Nice to meet you," Eliza said. It was a reflex, even if she didn't mean it.

"Yeah. You too."

Eliza thought, *Yeah?* She said, "You have a good haul today? Russell and I, we had a pretty good haul, for early July. It's starting to pick up, right?"

"Yeah," said Josh. "Yeah, I guess it is."

"Got a couple of shedders."

"Yeah."

"It'll be August before we know it."

Josh shrugged and looked at Mary and said, "Let's go."

Mary gave Eliza a funny look—sort of wry, sort of self-mocking—and rose from the booth.

"Mary—" said Eliza, but she was gone, melting into the crowd.

Now Eliza could capture that slippery thought: now. It was something about young love, brought on by the jukebox and the atmosphere and all of the memories that were unearthing themselves and standing in front of her, asking for attention.

It was this: that your whole life was a quest to recapture the feeling you had the very, very first time you fell in love. She tried not to think about the long-ago night on Turtle Island, the tent, the sleeping bags zipped together, arms and legs and lips and necks and the *heat* they gave off. Oh, man, the heat. A flame like that is going to burn itself out.

When Russell came back she was so lost in that thought—drunkenly, she believed that it explained everything about the human condition— that she didn't notice him until he had regained his seat across from her. She thought maybe she should try to explain her thought to Russell, but when she looked at him she saw his face was pulled tight with irritation.

"Sorry," he said, "to be gone so long. I was just talking to the guys about something."

Eliza smelled gossip, and sat up straighter. This sounded promising. "What? Something good?"

"That guy who was over here, talking to you, Josh—you know him?"

"No, I only just met him."

"They think he's pulling some shit, stealing from traps."

"Really?" In Little Harbor, in any lobstering community, that was one of the gravest offenses that existed. You didn't touch another person's traps without permission, period. And if you did, and if you got caught, Lord help you when the wrath of the vigilante justice system rained down upon you.

"That little shit," she said. It wasn't her usual way to describe someone, but Russell had brought back a fresh beer for each of them and she was feeling agitated and feisty and *local.*

"They said we better watch out for Charlie's traps. He'll know now that they're going untended. That guy's no good."

"Wow."

"Don't say anything to Charlie, though. I don't want him to worry. I'll keep an eye on his traps."

"Okay," she said. "I can help, anytime. And, thank you, Russell."

He shrugged. "Sure."

To change the subject she said, "It's so funny being back here. It feels like I never left."

"But you did." A new note crept into Russell's voice. It almost sounded—well, to call a spade a spade, it sounded *accusatory.* And also a little wounded.

She kept her voice purposefully light, even blithe, and said, "I did."

There was a long pause then and Eliza studied the table in front of her. Across the room someone made a whooping noise and someone else said, *Motherfucker!* You'd get kicked out of the club in Barton for yelling that.

The table was rough and scratched with the history of a million bottles of beer, a thousand fishermen's hands resting where hers were now. Back when you could smoke in public places in Maine and the smoke hung thick and impenetrable around the bar there would have been an ashtray on this table, right next to the napkin dispenser. Eliza had to go to the bathroom and her stomach was roiling from the beer but she didn't want to get up. She was rooted, and she remained rooted until Russell said, "Do you ever think about it?"

"What?"

"You know what."

Oh. Oh, God. They were going to talk about it. They were going to talk about the Thing They Would Never Talk About.

"No."

"You don't?"

"We were *eighteen,* Russell. It was another lifetime. We were babies."

Then Russell was reaching under the table and grasping her hand, and that felt so familiar that her thoughts got tangled with each other. It was too loud in the bar all of a sudden, and the universe was tilting, and it felt like each piece of her colliding worlds was contained in that fraction of a moment. Also, there was no air in the bar. Where had all the air gone?

"I have to go outside," she managed. "I'm sorry, I—" She slid out of the booth and pushed her way through the crowd. She heard footsteps behind her, and then Russell's voice.

"Liza? Eliza, you okay?"

She walked toward Russell's truck, taking deep, shuddering breaths. "Yeah," she said. "Sorry, I couldn't—I just couldn't breathe all of a sudden." She leaned against the truck and looked up at the sky. Night had fallen while they were in The Wheelhouse, and a fingernail of a moon hung just above them. Russell stood next to her, close enough that his hip pressed against her waist. Her thoughts were all mixed up. *Your whole life was a quest to recapture the feeling you had the very, very first time you fell in love.* The fight with Rob, her dad, missing her family but also, weirdly, missing the place where she was at that exact moment. How could you do that, how could you be homesick for a town you'd left life-times ago when you were in that town right then?

She was going to ask Russell that, and so she turned her face toward his, and that's when she saw that he was looking at her in a certain, familiar way, and then he was leaning toward her and she wasn't sure if—

But as it turned out, her stomach, that unpredictable, capricious organ, had its own ideas for the evening.

"I'm going to be sick," she said. "Oh, God—"

Eliza had enough forethought to turn away from the truck and toward the untended, scrubby grass at the edge of the parking lot, where she threw up four beers, a turkey sandwich, two cups of coffee, and a lifetime of confusion and pain.

When she was done, when her humiliation was complete and her insides were empty, Russell, bless his gigantic and forgiving heart, put Eliza gently in the passenger seat of the truck and drove her in an inde-cipherable silence back to her father's house.

23

BARTON, MASSACHUSETTS

Rob

"Go!" Judith said. "Just go, Robbie." She was curled up on the sofa with Zoe on one side of her and Evie on the other. "The girls and I are fine, we're going to have cocktails and watch a *Dance Moms* marathon."

Rob said, "Cocktails?"

"Mom doesn't let Evie watch *Dance Moms*," said Zoe. "She says it's too crass for a nine-year-old."

"Zoe, I'm *ten*."

Judith said, "Anyway, while the cat's away . . ."

Rob repeated, "Cocktails?" and rubbed his temples.

"Virgin coladas," clarified Evie. "Except Judith's isn't a virgin."

"I bet it isn't," said Rob.

The argument with Eliza over the phone last night had left him with an unsettled sensation deep in his stomach. All day he'd known he should apologize, and all day he had failed to make the call. He was mad at Eliza, but at the same time he was sad for her. And the mad and the sad were all wrapped up together. The longer he waited, the harder it was to pick up the phone—even though he knew dwelling on a stupid argument, on a hastily flung offense, was an insult to Charlie's illness.

Besides that, it had been another doozy of a day on the Cabot project. Anytime something went wrong with the Cabot project Rob worried about the thing he'd done with the money, the thing that he couldn't undo.

Until this year, Judith had deposited in Rob and Eliza's bank account a tidy sum that came from her stock dividends. The stock itself would pass to Rob eventually. The dividends alone represented a significant amount—enough to pay for a good percentage of their lifestyle. But then he turned forty. He had his own business, and his business was doing well; the mortgage on the house was small, due to a generous down payment (also funded, admittedly, by Judith). Glowing on the horizon like holiday lights on a tree was a tantalizing string of new work. The Cabot project was under way, and Mrs. Cabot, who was absolutely delighted with the *brilliant* plans from such an *up-and-coming* architect, had many friends who were interested in building second and third homes in the same area. She'd be sure to pass Rob's name along to as many of them as he wanted. Added to all of that, he knew that Eliza had always been mildly sickened by the knowledge that so much of their life was underwritten by Judith. He wanted to prove to her that they didn't need it. He wanted to make himself worthy of her. He wanted to cut the cord.

"We want to support ourselves," Rob told Judith. "On my income alone."

They were in the Avery Bar at the Ritz-Carlton at the time; Judith had tickets to *Pippin* at the Boston Opera House.

Judith put the empty glass down and raised her hand to signal the waiter for another and said, "Let me get this straight. You don't want any more money from me."

"Correct," he said. "I want us to live on my salary alone."

Judith said, "Salary!" and wiped her mouth with a cocktail napkin. To Judith salaries were like the maraschino cherry in a cocktail: a pretty garnish, and also tasty, but not the thing itself. "What does Eliza think of this plan?"

"She supports it," said Rob. "One hundred percent." He added, "She wanted to come today, to talk to you. But Evie had a birthday party to go to."

In point of fact he hadn't exactly told Eliza. He was certain that *if* he told Eliza she would indeed support it one hundred percent. He just didn't want to tell her until it was official, until he'd nailed Cabot Lodge (literally and figuratively) and put at least one more project on the books. He wanted to surprise her.

"I think it's ridiculous, Robbie, to do this. Money begets money, you know. With what your father left me when he decided to stay in Thailand with Malai—"

Left me was a bit of a euphemism for what Rob's father had done with his money, but it seemed unwise to bring that up now. Judith had fought tooth, nail, and everything in between for what she deemed her fair share of the estate of Robert Barnes I. ("For pain and suffering," she'd snarled into the constant phone calls with the attorneys.)

"It might seem ridiculous to you," said Rob. "But I promise it makes sense to me. To *us*. To Eliza and me."

"Just don't come back and tell me you've changed your mind," said Judith. "Because once you've made your decision, you've made your decision."

Judith had a stubborn streak a mile wide and fourteen breadths long. When Rob's father had taken up with Malai, Judith had said she never wanted to talk to him again, and she hadn't, not one single syllable of one single word for more than three decades. By the time Rob was ten his father had as good as dropped off the face of the earth. Rob could have a dozen half-Thai half siblings running around the outskirts of Bangkok and he wouldn't even know it.

Better that way, most agreed, although sometimes, like when the club started organizing the spring father-son golf tournament, Rob felt a pang of sadness so violent it almost sent him to his knees.

"I won't change my mind," he said.

"Good. Because I'm going to take the money I've been giving to you and I'm going to put it in an investment my financial adviser and I have been talking about for a while now."

"So it will be—"

"Inaccessible," Judith said. "Think of it as a long, long-term investment opportunity. I won't be able to get the money back without considerable time and expense on my part. Which I will not be willing to undertake. Because you are certain."

"Got it," he said. "I'm certain."

Now, with his sober daughters curled up next to his tipsy mother, he needed to get out for a while, to sit somewhere quiet—no daughters, no mothers, no Mrs. Cabot, no females at all—where he could think.

You don't work with your hands. That was a cruel thing to say.

But Eliza was never cruel. Sure, she could be grumpy, especially when she didn't get enough sleep or overindulged in fried food or had a hangover, but she wasn't *cruel.*

And if she wasn't cruel, then maybe she was just honest. Maybe, in fact, she was *right.*

He thought he'd stop in for a beer at Don Pepe's, but when his fingers were on the door handle he saw through the glass a bunch of semifamiliar women at the bar, a lot of highlighted blond hair being tossed, and he lost his desire for a shot of tequila and a steak fajita.

The same thing happened at Boardwalk (there was no boardwalk in Barton, but the bar prevailed) and Mainsail: gaggles of women, more dolled up for each other than they ever got for their husbands. Tuesday night in Barton was Ladies' Night Out, an unofficial designation, and one that Rob had forgotten. It was a world without husbands, a world without men. So much for getting away from females: they were everywhere.

Rob settled finally on The Wharf Rat, the only dive bar in Barton. No wharf nearby, and hopefully no rat, but really you never knew. Outside, under the awning, a few twentysomethings were smoking. Rob was peering through the cigarette haze, trying to get a read on the bar's dim interior, when a familiar figure came weaving down the street: Deirdre Palmer, wearing an outlandishly brief shirt that showed off her nutbrown, toned shoulders.

She grew closer and closer and finally, recognizing Rob, leaned toward him. "Hey, hey," she said. "What are you doing out on Ladies' Night?" There was a strong scent of perfume, and something else too—limes? From the margaritas at Don Pepe's, probably.

"Nothing," said Rob. "I mean, I'm just out. I didn't know it was Ladies' Night."

"You going in here?" she said, pointing at the bar. Rob shrugged. "I'll come too," said Deirdre. She took his arm and led him inside, toward two adjoining barstools. It was *not* Ladies' Night at The Wharf Rat. Deirdre was one of only two females in the place, the other being a fiftysomething biker with a tattooed wrist and a navy bandanna tied to her head, so Deirdre's appearance garnered significant attention. She took in this fact nonchalantly and said to Rob, "I've lived in this town fourteen years, and I've never been in this place."

"Me neither," said Rob. The bartender leaned toward them, his eyes resting on Deirdre's shoulders, and Rob said, "Two Buds. Bottles."

"Bud bottles," said Deirdre. "Look at you. You speak Townie."

"I guess I do."

The bartender slammed the beers down on the bar like a challenge, which Deirdre accepted; she downed a third of hers at once. "So. I've been meaning to tell you. I *love* your mother."

Rob absorbed this news along with a healthy gulp of his beer. He wasn't going to let a woman beat him at beer drinking. The Bud was fantastic. It made him feel like he was back in college, that first pour from the keg, the feeling that the night was young and anything could happen: anything. He said, "You *do*? What am I missing?"

"Oh my God," said Deirdre. "*Love.* She's hilarious, she's absolutely hilarious. We talked a lot on the Fourth of July and she agreed to help me with the gala."

"Interesting," said Rob, taken aback. His mother had earned a lot of adjectives in her life, but *hilarious* was not a common one.

"All these details she thought of in one conversation—boy oh boy, I have no idea what I'm doing. I have so much to learn." Deirdre paused and tugged on her top. "She freaking loves Eliza, huh?"

Again Rob was stymied. "She said that?"

Deirdre scratched one of her brown shoulders. "She didn't have to. It's obvious, the way she talks about her. She admires her, the way she came from nothing."

Rob stiffened. "Eliza didn't come from nothing." He thought of Charlie's tiny two-bedroom, the little square of kitchen, the town with the single main street. More than once Eliza had driven him by her high school, a low, unassuming building painted a tired tan color with a single playing field and a chain-link fence separating the whole place from Route One. "She didn't come from *nothing*," he repeated. "She just came from different."

"Oh, don't take that the wrong way," said Deirdre. "You know what I mean. Your mother admires Eliza's smarts, and her guts. She thinks she's a great mom."

"She *is* a great mom." To the bartender: "Keep 'em coming."

"I know," said Deirdre defensively. "That's what I told her."

"She went to *two years* of medical school! And part of the third!"

"I know she did."

"And then when Zoe was born early she thought it was because of the stress . . . so she decided to stop."

"Rob, I know."

Why did it feel like they were arguing, when they were saying the same thing?

"It's called 'stopping out,' you know. When you take a break in medical school. Eliza calls it the euphemism of all euphemisms."

"Got it."

"She could have gone back. She should have gone back! Eliza would have made an amazing doctor. It's killing her, that she has these connections that could get her dad into a clinical trial and he doesn't want anything to do with it."

"I know," said Deirdre. "She told me."

"I mean, what do you do with that? How do you help a guy who doesn't want to be helped?"

Deirdre coughed and said, "It's awful."

"I just wish there was something else I could do—"

Deirdre paused respectfully.

Now that Rob was on this track he was thinking about when Eliza saw a gunshot wound for the first time—the bullet had nicked some poor bastard's scrotum, and one of the guys on Eliza's team passed out, had to be treated himself. Not Eliza! She held her ground, applied pressure, got through it, came home high as a kite over it. She was amazing.

Except for what she'd said the day before: that had really wounded him. *You just draw the pictures so other people can build what* you *draw with their hands.* She didn't say the next part, but she easily could have. *For* men *to make with their hands. Real men.*

"I can't believe your mother bought that boat for you," Deirdre was saying.

"Eliza hates the boat."

That was unfair. Eliza didn't hate the boat. She just thought it was ridiculous that anyone spent that amount of money on one item. Whereas Rob thought, *What is money for if not to use it for Hinckley-level irrefutable beauty? A Family Affair* represented the underlying tension to any of their arguments: a fundamental difference in the way they saw the world.

"That boat is stunning," said Deirdre. "That boat is perfection. Brock thinks so too. It's one thing we've agreed on lately. About the only thing." She sighed and rubbed at her forehead. She looked genuinely sad. "Your mother gave you what is probably the best fortieth-birthday present ever given."

"She did. She really did. But I can't talk about my mom right now. Thinking about her makes me think about Cabot Lodge, and I'm trying to get my mind off Cabot Lodge."

"Ohhhh, right. How's that going?"

"Badly." Big, big gulp of Bud. "I wouldn't be surprised if I lose the job."

Just then his phone, which he had laid on the bar, buzzed, and he glanced at it, in case it was his mother or the girls or Eliza. *You just draw the pictures.*

"Speak of the devil," observed Deirdre, looking at the phone too. "Christine Cabot. Should you get it?"

Rob was already feeling the beer—no, he decided, he should not get it. "No way," he said. His voice sounded blurry. "I'll call her another time."

"Anyway, you're not going to lose the job," said Deirdre. "You're the architect. You've already designed the house. How can you lose the job?"

"It's complicated," Rob said. "But believe me, it can happen." *You draw pictures for other men, for the real men, to build with their hands.* What was Ruggman doing right now? Probably something manly, watching, oh, who knows, manly internet porn, or drinking moonshine or washing his balls or downing a large glass of raw eggs, Rocky style.

"I get it," Deirdre said, nodding, drinking, nodding and drinking, all at once.

"You do?"

"Sure," she said, shrugging. "Everything is complicated." He wondered how her top stayed on when she shrugged; there must be some sort of magical work with elastic or tape, because the shirt didn't move. "People think nothing is complicated, if you live in a nice house and have a boat. But that's bullshit. Things can still be *hard.*" She hiccuped, and Rob saw that she was drunker than he'd realized. Well, sure. She must weigh about three pounds.

"Right," he said. How nice it felt to have someone utter those three simple words: *I. Get. It.*

He reached for a new subject. "When's that tennis camp start?" If Eliza was going to be in Maine for a while longer, pushing through her scheme to help her father, he'd better get a handle on the scheduling end of things.

"I don't know," said Deirdre morosely. She was having a bit of trouble holding her bottle straight; it kept leaning to one side or the other, like a heeling boat.

"Okay," said Rob. "I just want to make sure I have it down before they start. I get mixed up sometimes, the two different schedules—it's confusing, right? All this kid stuff."

He had meant this as a demonstration of camaraderie, mucking through the details of parenting together, but somehow what he said had flipped a switch in Deirdre. She started crying.

"Hey," he said. "Hey, hey." He almost patted her consolingly on the shoulder, but she was wearing so little that he couldn't find a reasonable place to put his hand without looking like he was molesting her. "Hey," he said again. "What is it? Deirdre? What'd I say?"

"Nothing," Deirdre said, wiping savagely at her nose with the feeble cocktail napkin the bartender slid toward her. "It's just that when I was out with the ladies earlier, Shannon Markum announced that she's pregnant. With her *fourth.*"

Rob waited; he still didn't understand the problem. He didn't know who Shannon Markum was. Sometimes it was hard to keep track of the women in Eliza's crowd: most were tall, blond, some shade of tan much of the year, clad similarly in yoga clothes or tennis clothes or sundresses, holding water bottles or Starbucks mugs, driving Tahoes or Expeditions or Suburbans, small blond children spilling out of them, those children also clad in tennis clothes, also toting water bottles and sometimes even their own Starbucks cups.

"Oh, it's nothing," she said. Deirdre hiccuped and then went on. "You know those pajamas kids wear? With the feet?"

That was out of left field. But he did know those pajamas. He said, "The fluffy ones. With ducks or bunnies on them."

"Right." Deirdre pointed her bottle at him and a few drops spilled out onto the bar. "Or, at Christmastime, elves or Santas. Sofia doesn't wear those anymore. Of course she doesn't! She's too big. She's almost as tall as I am. She's a teenager. They would look ridiculous."

Rob brooded over this. "Zoe's too big for those pajamas too," he said. "Evie's borderline." A memory came to him, Zoe on a Christmas morning, so young that Evie wasn't even born yet, asleep in the middle of the Christmas presents, exhausted by all of the fuss and bother.

Now he was depressed. Time was passing. He was aging. Right here at The Wharf Rat, with Deirdre Palmer crying next to him, he was aging. Charlie Sargent was terminally ill, Cabot Lodge was in trouble, nobody in his family wore pajamas with feet. He never should have come out on Ladies' Night: he should have known better. Ladies' Night was a dangerous, dangerous business.

He ordered another round.

He could see now why Eliza valued Deirdre's friendship. She was a good listener, a solid presence.

If only he could get this one thing clear in his mind, this thing from last December. He could, actually, if only he asked. So he did.

"Do you remember the Colemans' holiday party?" It was a clumsy segue, but no matter. It made sense in the depths of his own addled mind.

Deirdre laughed, revealing her extremely white teeth and a silver filling toward the back of her mouth. Old-school fillings; now they were all tooth colored. Not that the mollycoddled children in Barton were allowed to get cavities. "That depends," she said.

"Oh." Rob fiddled with the label on his beer bottle. "Because I was wondering . . . do you remember when we were standing under the mistletoe? Near the half bath off the kitchen with the marble floor?"

"The half bath off the kitchen with the marble floor," said Deirdre. "Always the architect, Rob."

"Do you?"

"I remember. Sort of."

"Well, what I was wondering . . ."

"Yes?" prodded Deirdre.

"I was pretty drunk," Rob said.

The next morning, he'd call Eliza and apologize. She'd said some shitty things on the phone but he'd been the one who'd put her on edge first, getting angry that she'd gone out on a lobster boat. It was only his fear of losing her that made him do that, but still. What kind of husband was he, losing his shit over something like that with Charlie as sick as he was? He should be oozing nothing but understanding and caring. He should be reaching over to Eliza's plate and taking every single worry off of it and moving them all over to his so that the only thing left was her father. And that, starting now, was exactly what he would do.

"Everybody was drunk at that party," said Deirdre. "The Angel's Delights." She smiled. "Brock and I had to take an Uber home!"

"Okay, so my question is, did you—" The memory was hazy, but it was *right there,* if he could just reach his hand out a little further he could grasp it.

"What happened was . . ." Deirdre paused, and the very bar seemed to take a breath.

"Yes?"

"You kissed me."

"I did *not.*"

She shrugged again, and this time one strap of her top slipped a little bit. She pushed it back up. "Okay," she said. "If you insist. But you did." She said that emphatically, almost kindly, like a teacher explaining something to one of the slower students in the class.

"Impossible. That's impossible. I'd never do that. I'm happily married. I'm so in love with Eliza."

"I know you are."

"And if I did something like that—well, I'd remember."

"Okay," Deirdre said again. "But before you say that. Why don't you tell me if this seems familiar." She grasped the buttons of his shirt and pulled him toward her. And kissed him. Full-on, unabashedly kissed him, in The Wharf Rat, in plain sight of the bartender and God and everyone else.

Deirdre stopped kissing Rob and looked him straight in the eye. She seemed alarmingly unapologetic. And also very drunk. The biker let out a low whistle.

Oh boy. Things had taken a turn. Things had *definitely* taken a turn.

Robert Barnes II was out of his element. No question. He was a man sitting in a testosterone-filled bar on Ladies' Night, with a woman who was not his wife, waiting and waiting—almost without breathing, he was waiting so carefully—to see what would happen next.

24

Mary

Andi had given Mary a bunch of smoothie greens that were technically past their sell-by date and now Mary was in her kitchen making them into a salad. "They're perfectly fine," said Andi. "I'd eat them myself, I would, we just have to abide by the date. Per the health board." The greens still had firm stems and bright, healthy leaves.

Mary had planned on a salad with the greens, avocado, and tomato slices, but first she had to clean up the kitchen, which was small and cluttered in the best of circumstances and downright impossible to work in the rest of the time. Vivienne was a famous non-cook; she said it proudly, like some people would say, *I don't smoke* or *I don't shoot heroin.*

To make room for the cutting board on the small square of counter, Mary moved three different piles of mail, a hairbrush, a flatiron, a tube of mascara with the top loose—all Vivienne's—and her own copy of *The Fault in Our Stars,* which she was reading for the sixth time; she could quote certain passages out loud, if anyone asked her. (Nobody ever did.) Mary loved *The Fault in Our Stars.* When the movie had come out two summers ago she'd gone with Tyler to see it, and she'd wept through the entire second half while Tyler had tooth-murdered the leftover popcorn kernels and snorted at all of the best parts. She should have known then.

Mary also loaded Vivienne's breakfast dishes into the dishwasher—Vivienne's breakfast was always the same, two heavily buttered English muffins with instant coffee—and then she started in on a sticky substance on the Formica. It was a Thursday, and Mary had the day off. Vivienne went to work at one on Thursdays because the salon was open until nine.

Someday, Mary thought, she would have her own tiny house, and it would be clean and orderly, with gleaming counters and nice food stored neatly in the cupboard.

Her fetus-tracking website told her that the baby was an inch and a half long, the size of a prune, with little indentations on the legs that were planning to turn into knees and ankles.

She was thinking about that when Vivienne came into the kitchen, dressed for work, her hair wet from a shower. Vivienne plucked the hairbrush from the pile Mary had made on the table and began to work it carefully through her hair, pulling gently when she snagged on a tangle. While she brushed she watched Mary.

"I saw that jerk Tyler Wasson in Ellsworth," Vivienne said, after a while.

"Oh yeah?" said Mary. She was trying to make her voice sound uninterested.

"Yeah. He was with his mom, coming out of Cadillac Mountain Sports."

Mary had liked Tyler Wasson's mom. She felt an unwelcome ping of nostalgia. But she didn't like to think about the girl she'd been then: that girl had been innocent and trusting and zero percent pregnant. She worked off the skin of the avocado the way Daphne had shown her and shuffled the nostalgia to the back of her mind.

Vivienne stopped brushing and said, "I just don't know how you got yourself into this situation, Mare." Mary looked up from the avocado and blinked at her and Vivienne said, "I mean, of course I know *how*, but I'm just not sure *why*."

"It wasn't on purpose," said Mary. She went back to making her salad. She finished the avocado and got to work on the tomato, slicing it the way Daphne had taught her, tucking her fingers under so that she wouldn't cut them off. "Obviously."

"Obviously," repeated Vivienne. "But: here you are."

"Here I am," said Mary.

It was hard to say now, in the bald daylight seeping into the kitchen, what had made her tell Eliza Barnes at the bar.

Eliza had said, "Oh, sweetie," and had looked like she was about to start crying herself. Eliza had sounded the same way she had the time Mary overheard her talking to one of her children on the phone, and for just a moment there Mary had felt safe and cared about. Then she'd smiled in a sad way and half stood, like she was going to hug Mary or something. That was when Josh had come over to the table, and that had been it.

Josh wouldn't tell her what he'd gotten into with some of the guys at The Wheelhouse, and his mood had turned so black so fast. She'd told him she felt sick to her stomach (true) and had gone home right from the bar, and straight to bed.

Everybody had black moods sometimes, right? Didn't they? Did they?

Vivienne picked up the book and said, "What's this?"

"Just a book," said Mary. She'd only had it hanging around the house for three years, did Vivienne notice *anything* about her?

"Any good?"

Mary sighed and said, "It's perfect."

"What's it about?"

"It's a love story. And a tragedy."

Vivienne snorted and said, *"Love,"* like she'd taken a bite of a nail sandwich.

"Someday I'll fall in love," said Mary. "Someday somebody will fall in love with *me.*"

A complicated expression crossed Vivienne's face and for a brief hopeful second Mary thought Vivienne was going to agree but then she just snorted again and brushed her hair even harder. She picked up the mascara and inspected it and said, "Oh, Mary, what are you going to *do?*"

Mary shrugged. She thought about the parents in *The Fault in Our Stars,* who were kind and loving, even in the face of tragic circumstances. Those parents would never say, *What are you going to do* because they would be busy saying, *What are we going to do.*

"What did Josh say?"

"I haven't told him."

"You haven't *told* him? What do you mean?"

Mary arranged it all in a bowl: the greens, the avocado, the tomato, and said, "I mean, I haven't had a chance."

"Mary. You need to."

"I know."

"If you don't tell him, I will. Somebody needs to make sure that he—"

"Don't, Mom. *Don't.*"

"Mary, something like this doesn't go away on its own, he's going to have to help you, you're going to have to go to a clinic . . ."

"I know that."

Vivienne opened the mascara and applied it without the benefit of a mirror. It looked perfect anyway. Of course Vivienne wasn't a mother from a novel. Nobody was: mothers from novels were made up.

After Vivienne left for work Mary brought her salad over to the table and picked up the book.

What if Mary's heart turned into a dried fig, and nobody ever loved her? What if *she* never loved anyone? What then?

25

BARTON, MASSACHUSETTS

Rob

Rob stood in the kitchen, making waffles for the girls. Zoe was nowhere in evidence, but Evie had perched herself on a kitchen stool and was watching his every move. In fact, it was unnerving, the way her eyes were following him. Her eyes were exactly like Eliza's eyes, so it felt to him like it was *Eliza* watching him, *Eliza* peering into the black and sullied depths of his soul.

"Your phone's ringing!" said Evie. She glanced at the screen. "It's Deirdre. Should I get it?"

Rob reached across the island and snatched the phone from Evie's hand. "No!" he said. "No, you should not get it." His heart was thumping like a steelpan, and his pounding head felt like it had its very own heartbeat. "I don't want to talk to anyone."

"Okay," said Evie uncertainly. "Sorry." She flicked her eyes back and forth, back and forth, just like Eliza did when she was hurt.

"Sorry," said Rob. "Sorry, Evie, I didn't sleep well last night, I'm a little tired. I'm just not ready to deal with today's plans yet." If *I didn't sleep well* could serve as a euphemism for *I am aching*, then, true, he hadn't slept well. He couldn't believe he'd gone out drinking with Deirdre. He couldn't believe that he'd let that kiss happen, that he'd done something that would hurt Eliza. Eliza, whose father was dying and who would do anything to help him. Eliza, who had dropped out of medical school to raise their children; who gave a killer shoulder rub; who made a lemon crème brûlée that was to die for; who laughed at ninety-nine percent of his jokes because she actually thought they were funny . . . *Eliza.* "Okay, sweetie? Do you accept my apology?"

She considered him and said, "Yup."

"Good. Thank you." He would deal with Deirdre later.

"I just can't remember," he said aloud to himself, "if you put the oil in the waffle maker *before* or after you heat it up . . ."

"Ask Judith," Evie said.

Rob was pretty certain the closest Judith ever came to a waffle maker was Sunday brunch at the Ritz-Carlton.

"Ask me what?" came Judith's voice, followed closely by Judith herself. It was seven thirty in the morning but Judith was in full makeup, stylish white pants, and a cerulean tank top with a matching cardigan. She looked like she was on her way to a private Caribbean island.

"Ask you how to use the waffle maker!" said Evie. "Daddy's trying."

"I *know* how to use the waffle maker," said Rob. "I'm not trying; I'm doing. Morning, Mom. How are you?"

"I feel incredible," Judith said. "Just wonderful. I took an Ambien, and I clocked ten solid hours. I feel like a new person. Your guest room is like a tomb."

"Great," said Rob.

"In a good way."

"Better."

"I'm guessing *you* were out until all hours," said Judith. "You look awful."

Evie swiped Rob's phone and disappeared from the kitchen. "I'll be back," she said. "For the waffles."

Rob tried to make his voice sound detached, nonchalant, and, above all, very, very monogamous. "Not too late," he said to Judith.

Rob tried not to look at Judith's raised eyebrow. He was an adult! He was allowed to go out if he wanted to! He worked the first set of waffles carefully out of the maker and set one on a plate. "Evie!" he called. "Breakfast!"

Evie returned, put Rob's phone back on the counter, and said, "Mom called."

His heart vaulted. "She did? Why didn't you tell me?" Probably Eliza didn't want to talk to him—probably she'd sensed from afar that he was a despicable, unlovable human being.

Evie knitted her brows together. "You said you didn't want to talk to anyone, so that's what I told her."

"Did she say anything?"

Evie climbed onto a kitchen stool. "She said she's sorry. And she'll call you later."

"Okay," said Rob. With a flourish he produced the maple syrup and poured it over the waffle in the shape of an *E*. The *E* didn't last long, because it soon settled into the grooves of the waffle, but Rob was a great believer in the *It's the thought that counts* philosophy of life.

Evie studied the waffle and smiled. She could see the *E*. "Oh! I forgot one thing. She said the work you do is very important."

"She what?"

"She said the work you do is very important."

"Interesting," said Judith. She was attempting to make herself a coffee. "So where'd you go last night, anyway?"

"I met up with some of the guys—"

"Which guys?" asked Evie.

"Huh?"

"Which guys did you meet up with? Any of my friends' dads?"

"No," he said. "I don't think so, there were a bunch of us. Now eat, before it gets cold."

But Evie persisted. "Well, which guys? I bet I know some of their kids."

"Eat, Evie. Just eat."

Judith fiddled for a while with the cappuccino machine and said, "Heavens, Rob, this is so complicated. You should get the kind with the capsules."

"Mommy says those are wasteful," said Evie. She took a single bite and shook her head, laying down her fork carefully next to her plate, as though she were setting the table for a formal dinner party. "These aren't right," she said. "These don't taste the way they do when Mommy makes them."

"What do you mean?"

"They're missing something. Maybe cranberries?"

"I don't think you put cranberries in waffles," said Rob doubtfully. (Did you?)

"Mommy does."

"No, she doesn't," said Zoe, who had slunk down the stairs in that feline way of hers and into the kitchen without any of them seeing her. Her hair was sleep-tangled but her skin and eyes were luminous. The unfairness of youth. Any day now Zoe was going to wake up to find that she'd turned into a full-fledged beauty. The thought of that made Rob's stomach twist, so he tried hard to think of the way Zoe used to dance along to *Yo Gabba Gabba!* and how she still slept with her very first stuffed animal, a blue elephant named Marvin. He said, "Morning, Zoe. Hungry?"

Zoe stretched and yawned prettily and said, "Not yet. I'll just have orange juice."

Rob was reaching for the orange juice and trying to keep an eye on the next batch of waffles when his phone buzzed. Deirdre, again? (Bad.) Eliza? (Better.)

"Oooh," said Judith. "Christine Cabot is calling you." (Worse.) "Shall I answer?"

"*No,*" said Rob. He felt dehydrated. The inside of his head felt like it was covered in peach fuzz. He downed the orange juice he'd just poured for Zoe and, when Zoe frowned, he reached into the cupboard for another glass.

"Then *you* probably should," said Judith.

Rob let the call go to voice mail. "I'll call her back."

Judith eyed him from over the rim of her mug. "Don't let the grass grow under your feet, Robbie. I know she's feeling very anxious."

"That's a funny thing to say," said Evie. "By the way, these waffles are actually delicious. I was wrong before."

"Which part is funny?" asked Judith.

"The grass growing part."

Rob could have hugged Evie for liking the waffles and giving him an injection of confidence at just the right time. "It's an expression," he said. "It means, don't waste time." He detached the second batch of waffles and loaded up Zoe's plate. Eliza would be proud: he was feeding their teenager!

Eliza. His heart hurt.

He'd better call back Christine Cabot. He said, "Going up to the office!" to the three females in his kitchen. Judith was deep into the first and only section of *The Barton Examiner,* and Zoe was tapping on her phone, her food untouched. Only Evie answered: "Okay, Daddy! When you come back, can I have another waffle?"

On the way up the stairs, Rob dusted off some memories of an Eastern Philosophy class he'd taken at Brown. They'd learned all sorts of things in that class—Confucianism, Taoism, Shinto—but the tenet that stuck with him was the most basic, the most unremarkable, the most applicable of all of these, and it came from the great Buddha himself. *Do not dwell in the past, do not dream of the future, concentrate the mind on the present moment.* At certain times in his life—when Zoe was born early, that time he navigated the Hinckley through pea-soup fog—he had leaned on those words, and he leaned on them again now. Yes! That was the answer to it all, that's what he would do: he would live in the moment.

In his office he braced himself, and dialed.

"Rob!" said Christine Cabot. "I'm so glad you called me back! I assume you got my message?" She sounded preternaturally happy—almost exultant. Maybe she'd also taken an Ambien and clocked a solid ten hours of sleep. Maybe Rob should take an Ambien. He might, tonight, if his mother would share.

"Nope," he said. "No, I didn't. I missed your call, so I called you right back."

His eyes scanned the office and fell upon the stack of papers from Phineas Tarbox, the papers that Eliza hadn't (wouldn't) sign. She was going to leave him, that was why she wouldn't sign the papers? He'd wondered about that before, but now he was certain.

"I've been trying to reach you, Rob. I left you messages last evening."

"I'm sorry," said Rob. "My mother's been visiting, we've had some things with the girls going on, and Eliza has had to go back up to help her dad . . ." Also, Mrs. Cabot, I got drunk and got improperly kissed at The Wharf Rat last night.

"Right," she said. "Your mother has told me about Eliza's dad and I'm very sorry to hear about it." Being sorry, he noticed, didn't stop Mrs. Cabot from skipping merrily ahead to her next thought. "But anyway, I called you because I've got to tell you about something I found, for the house. Something wonderful."

Rob said, "Yes?" Though on the inside he was screaming *No! No! No!* A client finding something for the house at this stage was rarely a good thing. Scratch that. It was *never* a good thing. Just ask Mo Francis. Ask any architect! A gentle thudding along the edges of his rib cage prevented him from speaking.

"Floor tile!" said Mrs. Cabot.

Deep breath. Deeper.

Mrs. Cabot said, "Anyone there? Are we still connected, Rob?"

"Now, Mrs. Cabot—you know you've already picked out the floors." He waited for affirmation, but none came, so he went on. "Hand-scraped hardwood everywhere but the kitchen, then tumbled crystal white for the kitchen. Those are the floors that we've ordered. Those are the floors that should be here any day now."

Rob stared hard out the third-floor window. The Cavanaughs' peonies had stopped blooming, and then drooped, and then they'd been summarily deadheaded. A stunning display of tiger lilies had taken their place.

"I know I picked out floors already, Robbie. But *this* tile," she said. "This tile is absolutely gorgeous, this tile is the most beautiful thing I've ever seen. I went with my dear friend Marianne Foley—you know Marianne, your mother and I are on the hospital board with her—to an architectural restoration place up in Vermont. Well, Marianne was looking for a particular kind of faucet, and I wasn't looking for a blessed thing, but they had just gotten this tile in, and I fell in love with it. I fell absolutely in love."

Rob considered interrupting this monologue, but he chose instead to lean his weary head against the windowpane and let the words wash over him. The tile had come from a historic castle in the north of England, and this fact spoke directly—*directly!*—to Mrs. Cabot's English roots.

"It's gorgeous," Mrs. Cabot said again. "Thick."

Rob swallowed and whispered, "Thick?"

"Gorgeous and thick. I bought it all! Everything they had. I want to install it throughout, if there's enough of it, kitchen, living room, everywhere. I'm not sure if there is enough, but it seemed to me like quite a lot of tile."

Rob summoned an inner reserve of patience and said, "How thick?"

"How thick?"

"Mrs. Cabot? Do you have the tile in front of you?"

"Not all of it, of course. They're delivering it directly to the site."

Oh, God.

"Any of it? Do you have any of it?"

"I do, I took a square with me, to show Jonathan. Not that he cares a nickel about any of this. Do you know that last week he—"

"I'm sorry to interrupt," said Rob. "But this is important. I need you to find a measuring tape, and I need you to measure the thickness of the tile you have. Not the length or the width, but the thickness. Do you understand?"

"Certainly," said Mrs. Cabot. "I know perfectly well what thickness means. Just hang on a minute, Robbie, let's see . . . looks like one and—"

well, let me see here, the tape measure just slipped. Okay, I've got it again. It looks like one and three-quarter inches."

Was it too early to start drinking? Another deep breath. "Okay," he said. "Here's the thing. I'm sure the tile you have there is beautiful, and I appreciate the connection to your roots, the English castle and all that, and I like an English castle as much as the next guy, but I have to tell you that one and three-quarter inches is not a standard thickness, not for floors. A standard thickness for floors is a half inch."

"And?"

"And. And the doors have been framed, and the windows too, all to the specifications of half-inch-thick floors. If we change that now, we need to change a lot of things. We basically need to restructure the first floor. We need our structural engineer back. We need to raise the doorframes to accommodate the extra inch and a quarter." He summoned his best diplomatic voice, honed from a brief, long-ago, and ultimately unsuccessful stint on the Brown debate team, and said, "I urge you, Mrs. Cabot, to consider sticking with the floors you already chose."

This time there was no pause; Mrs. Cabot launched in, missilelike, on her target. "Let me get something straight here, Robert." It was not lost on Rob that she had suddenly switched to his full name, typically employed only by his mother when, during his teenage years, he had gotten up to some trouble with the boys from school. "Are you telling me that it is *impossible* to use this tile, or that it is merely *difficult*?"

Rob's mind said, "Impossible," but his mouth was out of sync with his mind. "Difficult," said his mouth. "Nothing is impossible, with enough time and money." The second those words hit the air he regretted them. A fly landed on the window in front of him and stopped, the way flies do— it seemed to be studying him, perhaps offering him solace. Rob leaned in and studied the fly's furry legs, its oversized red eyes.

What an indulgence, what a colossal waste of money, to order one type of floor and then to arbitrarily choose another instead. What would Charlie Sargent say if he heard his son-in-law at work in this way? He'd probably have some enigmatic Down East way of telling Eliza she'd married an asshole, and he would be right.

"Wonderful," said Mrs. Cabot. "I've got plenty of both."

"But you don't, actually. You don't have plenty of time if you want to be in by Thanksgiving."

"So, then, I suppose we'd both better get up there when the tile arrives, hadn't we? Thursday morning, half past nine."

"Thursday morning," said Rob wearily. "Half past nine."

As soon as he disconnected the call a sense of panic seized him, and he hurried down the flight of stairs and into his bedroom. But he knew, even before he got up close to his dresser, that it was gone. He slapped the pockets of his shorts, felt their insides frantically, although he knew that if it wasn't on his dresser it wasn't anywhere. It was gone, baby, gone. *Vanished.* The ten-baht. His lucky coin.

26

Eliza

Eliza was ten minutes into a reluctant run. It was the middle of the afternoon, which was a terrible time for running, and the sun was high and bright and unrelenting, but she hadn't wanted to go until she knew for sure her father was asleep. She ran around the Point, and tried to take her mind off her legs' complaints. She thought she might end her run at the wharf, see if it was almost time for the boats to come in. She understood that her conversation with Russell from the night at The Wheelhouse remained incomplete and that as the person who'd lost her lunch in the scrub grass she was responsible for finishing it, just as she was responsible for apologizing to Rob, without using Evie as the intermediary. If he'd ever answer the phone.

Eliza ran straight down Main Street to get to the wharf. As she was approaching The Cup she saw a figure near a battered Subaru parked across from the café. The figure was leaning on the car with her head in her crossed-over arms.

"Mary?" called Eliza, recognizing her. "Mary!" And Mary looked up. "What are you doing?" Eliza thought about saying, *What are you doing, girlfriend?* but that was just the sort of thing that made Zoe wince and cringe with humiliation, so she stopped herself.

"Hey," said Mary, raising her head. She looked tired and defeated. She hit one fist on the hood of the car and said, "I have an appointment in Ellsworth, but my car won't start." Her voice had that trying-not-to-cry sound. "I'd open the hood, but I don't even know what I'm looking for."

"I wouldn't know either," said Eliza. She put her hands on her hips and studied the car. "I'm useless with cars." She was panting like a dog. "That sounds like such a girl thing to say, but it's absolutely true. Do you have Triple A or anything?"

Mary looked confused. "I don't think so."

"I do," said Eliza. "I definitely do. I think I can use it on a car that isn't mine. I just need my card, for the number. When's your appointment?"

"Four fifteen."

Eliza looked at her running watch and switched modes until the real time showed. It was three thirty.

"Never mind Triple A," said Eliza. "You won't make it if we have to wait for someone to come out. I'll drive you. Let me just run home and get my car."

"But—you're running," said Mary. "You're busy."

"Are you kidding?" said Eliza. "I was looking for a reason to stop. I hate running. I have such a cramp." To prove this, she raised one arm over her head and bent to the side. "I can never remember if you're supposed to lean toward the cramp or away from it."

"Toward, I think." Mary was starting to look a little less stricken.

"You're right. I was doing the opposite. Anyway. I would be delighted to take you to Ellsworth for your appointment. My dad sleeps a lot in the afternoons, and I can put Val on call."

"Really?"

"Really. Stay here, don't move. I'll be back in a flash."

———

"This is a nice car," said Mary as they started on the winding road out of Little Harbor.

"I guess so," said Eliza. "I'm not a car person, you could put me in this or my dad's pickup and I'd hardly know the difference." That was a slight exaggeration, of course: Rob's car was an Audi A8 and cost nearly one hundred thousand dollars, all in. Nobody could mistake it for a pickup truck.

To hide what an idiot she felt like for suggesting that you could, Eliza kept talking: "This is my husband's. I had to leave him the kid-friendly Pilot, the one with all of the Dorito crumbs, at home." She glanced at Mary and said, "I'm totally kidding. I don't let them eat Doritos. Much. I think those things are laced with heroin—they are so addictive. Right?"

"Right," said Mary, and she seemed to give a little shudder. Then she said, "This car is so *clean.*"

"My husband is not particular about everything," said Eliza. "But he is particular about his boat, and he is particular about his car. I'm just trying to do right by it, while I have it. It's *killing* him to be driving my Pilot around at home. But he needs it, with the kids. Do you have the address of where we're going?"

Mary nodded.

"After I press this button you just say the address and the GPS will pick it up . . . ready? *Go.*"

Mary said the address. She looked serious and slightly embarrassed, which was exactly how Eliza felt every time she spoke out loud to the GPS.

"Well done," said Eliza. "So is this an appointment for . . . ?" She nodded significantly toward Mary's stomach.

"Yeah," said Mary. "It's my first actual prenatal checkup."

"Good," said Eliza. "That's good, prenatal care. Very important." She paused. "Does that mean you—"

"I don't know," said Mary. "I'm not sure. But I have some time. In case I decide to . . ." She paused.

"I see," said Eliza.

They passed houses with broken lobster traps awaiting repair sitting out front, and they passed a house with an old skiff in the front yard with two kids playing in it. Then they passed a couple of brand-new, impressive houses: summer homes. Eliza looked at the area through the eyes of a tourist. Of course people came from all over. It really was a wonderful place to visit. The ice-cold Atlantic, the buttery lobster rolls, the blueberry crisp. *Great place to visit, but I wouldn't want to live there!* Wasn't that how the old saying went?

She saw Phineas Tarbox's face suddenly in her mind's eye; she saw Rob sitting up and saying firmly, "The guardian will be my mother." Her hands tightened on the steering wheel.

They passed the old sardine cannery, now closed, and a couple of antique shops attached to houses, and a sign for pottery pointing toward Machias. Eventually they passed the high school.

"High school," sighed Eliza.

"Yeah," said Mary.

"Goodbye and good riddance," said Eliza, and Mary made a small sound that sounded like affirmation. Eliza continued, "Do people in high school still go out to the Point and drink beer on the rocks?"

"I guess," said Mary. There was a wistful tone to her voice that sort of made Eliza want to cry.

"I used to like that part," said Eliza. "Among other things." She divided her high school time into two sections: before she was with Russell, and after. "But the rest of it—"

"Yeah," said Mary again.

"The good thing is, it only lasts four years."

"Right."

After that the speed limit increased and there was nothing much to look at but trees and the occasional side road leading to a house. Eliza pointed out to Mary where two of her high school friends had lived, and Mary absorbed the information politely, and after a while she said, "What would you do?"

Eliza was startled by the question. "What would I do about what?" Though of course as soon as the words were out it was obvious.

"If you were me."

Eliza cleared her throat and kept her eyes on the road. "If I were you, right now, in your situation?"

"Yes," said Mary fiercely. "Right now, what would you do if you were me, right now. Nobody will tell me. I just need somebody to *tell me what to do.*"

"Well," said Eliza carefully. "That depends on a lot of things."

"I figured you would say something like that."

Eliza felt like Mary had slapped her. "What do you mean?"

"I mean, something vague. Because you would never be dumb enough to get yourself in this position. You don't know."

Eliza glanced quickly at Mary and then back again. They were passing Jordan's. Eliza said, "Those are the best root beer floats in the entire universe."

Mary said, "I agree," and after that they were both silent for a while, until Mary said, "I'm sorry. That was rude, what I said."

"That's okay." Eliza stood on the edge of her thoughts and walked back and forth across them for a while. "I understand why you feel that way."

"So what does it depend on?"

"Well, most important, where's the father in all of this?"

She thought about what Russell said at the bar: *They think he's pulling some shit. That guy's no good.*

Mary said, "I haven't told him. So he isn't anywhere in this, yet."

There was a long pause. They were on the outskirts of Ellsworth now: the big city. As it were. Eliza waited for Mary to speak, and eventually she said, very quietly, "He gets in these moods—"

Eliza sucked in her breath and felt a thump in her stomach. She asked, "What kind of moods?"

"Just these—*black moods.* Where nothing is right. You turn right here, and then left into the parking lot." She nodded her head toward the window, and Eliza followed the instructions and then slid into a parking spot. At the same time the GPS announced, "You have reached your destination!"

FAMILY PLANNING, said the sign. PRENATAL CARE. Eliza turned to face Mary, who was looking steadily to the side, out her window.

Eliza reminded herself to tread carefully, reminded herself that this girl was not her daughter, that she had no true right to give advice, and said, "Let me ask you this," said Eliza. "Why are you with him?"

Mary shrugged and made a funny little motion with her mouth, curling her lip up. "I guess I'm not sure where else to be."

Eliza couldn't believe how swiftly the wave of anger rose up in her, quick as a licking flame. "That's a terrible answer. Mary, that's an awful reason."

Mary put her knuckles to her mouth and bit them and nodded.

"I'm sorry if that sounded harsh," said Eliza, in a softer tone. "But it's true."

Mary nodded again.

This girl was only *four years older than Zoe, only seven years older than Evie*! Eliza owed it to her to ask the next question, just as she'd expect someone Zoe or Evie might confide in in a similar situation to ask them. (God, please, seriously, absolutely forbid Zoe or Evie being in a similar situation.) She asked, "Has he ever hurt you?"

"*No.* No." But Mary paused before she said it, she definitely paused. *Black moods.*

Eliza pressed on, still looking straight ahead, in case that helped Mary answer more honestly. "Do you think he could?"

Mary shrugged. "I don't know."

"But you don't know that he couldn't." Eliza tightened her grip on the steering wheel even though the car wasn't moving. She watched the white fill in her knuckles.

No answer.

Now she turned toward her. "Mary. You don't know that he couldn't, is that right?"

Mary met Eliza's gaze, unblinking. "I guess not."

"Then you have to leave him. Now, Mary. Right away. I mean it. You can't be with someone you don't trust. You can't have a *baby* with someone you don't trust."

"I'll be late," said Mary. She opened the car door and climbed out.

Eliza said, "Wait!"

Mary waited, the door open, her hand on the Audi's outside door handle. Her hair hung over her face, and if Eliza had been Mary's mother she would have walked around the car and tucked her hair behind her ear, and then she would have squeezed her shoulders and told her it was all going to be okay.

Was it, though?

Eliza sighed and said, "I wish I could decide everything for you, Mary. But I can't."

"Yeah. I know." Something changed in Mary's face: a resoluteness seemed to come over it. An *adultness*, if that was a word. She pressed her lips together.

"But I can tell you—" said Eliza. She stopped, unsure what to say next.

Mary looked up from underneath her hair, and the resoluteness gave way to a hopefulness that made Eliza feel disconcerted and inadequate. "What?"

Eliza cleared her throat. "I can tell you that there are a lot of different ways to be okay." Mary didn't say anything, but her gaze was steady, her hand still on the door handle. "All right? You don't have to say anything. Just nod if that makes sense."

Mary nodded.

"Also, you're wrong, Mary. I do know. I know." Mary turned back toward her. "I do. I've been where you are now, at almost the same age."

Mary looked stricken. "And what did you do?"

Eliza sighed and folded her hands on the steering wheel. "Well, I don't have a nineteen-year-old kid, if that tells you anything." Mary narrowed her eyes at Eliza and then she nodded slowly and started to back away. Eliza said, "I'll wait here, until you're finished with your appointment."

"Thank you," Mary said. "Thanks."

When Mary was gone, Eliza pushed the seat back and stretched her legs in front of her. Rob would have a fit if he knew she was driving around in his billion-dollar car after running and before showering. She should be sitting on an old towel, like a dog. She'd wipe down the seat when she got back to Little Harbor.

She opened the Audi's sunroof and lifted her face to the glorious summer sun. She tried to keep herself from allowing the ghosts of the past to linger. Rob would also have a fit if he knew she was imagining Zoe seventeen and pregnant. She'd try to stop.

Zoe, whose biggest problem to date was how many people had liked her last Instagram post. Zoe, whose twelve-year molars were not even in yet, even though she was thirteen.

Why was it so easy to get yourself in trouble, if you were a girl?

And why was *that* the expression, *getting yourself in trouble*? Like it took only one person, like it took only the girl. What kind of a world was this? Eliza wanted to punch the world square in the mouth. Stupid freaking world.

27

BARTON, MASSACHUSETTS

Rob

Rob had been up with the lark—before the lark, even. Now he was driving down Main Street on his way to pick up bagels for the girls, who were sleeping like a couple of suntanned logs. When he'd checked on his daughters and seen how innocent and vulnerable they'd looked sleeping he'd felt a surge of tenderness for them. Zoe had turned off her iPhone before going to sleep, just the way she was supposed to, and Evie was hugging her giant rabbit like it was a life raft and she a noble drowning girl on the brink of rescue. He'd wanted to do something nice for them. Something parently, something like what Eliza might think to do if she were here. All he could come up with was fresh bagels from the shop downtown. Later that morning, he had to go up to Naples to check out the new floor tile that Mrs. Cabot had chosen, and Judith had a hair appointment she'd made months ago and *simply couldn't cancel.* He thought he'd ask the girls to stay home alone rather than make the trip. Bagels might help soothe the desertion.

Eliza might not approve of the desertion—they left the girls alone to go out in town, but she still called a sitter when they ventured beyond Barton. But he couldn't very well ask Deirdre for help; she might get the wrong idea. Besides, the girls would be fine. He'd be very strict. No swimming. Limited screen time. Three chores each that had to be completed before his return. He'd pay Zoe to babysit Evie, and then, because Evie hated the idea of being babysat by her own sister, he'd pay Evie to obey Zoe. But he wouldn't tell Zoe about the arrangement with Evie. It was the perfect backroom deal, shady and clever. And there would be the bagels.

Eliza, of course, would do the bagels better. She'd know each of the girls' favorite kinds and whether they liked them toasted and what they liked on them. But Rob didn't know any of that. To make up for his ignorance he'd get one of every kind, plus two big tubs of cream cheese, one plain, one flavored. Strawberry.

Wait, what if they both liked the same type of bagel, and he was perceived to be playing favorites by getting only one of that kind? He'd better get two in every flavor. Zoe was so *sensitive* these days.

It was exhausting, being a single parent. And he felt such a constant ache for Eliza; he wished there were more he could do for her, and for Charlie.

He was so occupied and distracted by his deep and bagely thoughts that he blew through the pedestrian crosswalk on Main Street, completely missing the woman and the black Lab waiting to cross. Pretty much every citizen of Barton had a black Lab—it could have been part of the town's charter—and he hadn't gotten a close enough look at the woman to see if he knew her or not. She could have been one of Eliza's friends, who'd recognize Eliza's car and slide the story into the Barton gossip wheel: Robert Barnes Almost Ran Over My Dog.

He'd better take it easy, or all sorts of things would start getting back to Eliza.

This is how a life went down, it was a fact: one mistake, which might seem innocuous, followed by another, followed by another, until before you knew it you were running down black Labs and their owners in pedestrian crosswalks and kissing your wife's friends in dive bars. Most likely Bernie Madoff himself had started off with a single ethical failing, something small and relatively harmless. And from there, well, it was easy to slide. The moral slope was so very, very slippery.

Rob continued down Main until a red light stopped him in front of Barton's Catholic church, St. Matthew's. Rob had been raised Protestant, sporadically attending Trinity Church in the Back Bay, but as an architect he appreciated a good, simple house of worship. St. Matthew's was an eighteenth-century New England church, white, center-steepled, a large gold cross above the narthex. Classic. The landscaping was simple and elegant, well cared for, with a mix of annuals and perennials—daylilies, snapdragons, a neat line of coleus—bordered by a low and tasteful stone wall.

Rob loved a good New England stone wall; he loved the history behind them, which he'd learned about in architecture school. First exposed during frost heaves after rapid deforestation, the stones were cleared from farmland during the early, arduous days of New England farming, often dumped on the edges of the farms. After such an unceremonious dumping, there was real artistry behind the eventual rebuilding. Rob admired people who could look at a pile of rubble and see something beautiful. Mo Francis put up a stone wall anywhere his clients would allow him to, and some places they didn't.

Rob sat for a moment—there were no other cars on the road—thinking about the landscaping at Cabot Lodge. He would suggest that Mrs. Cabot ask the landscaper to include some daylilies; they really would pop against the blue of the lake. Just then, he saw a familiar figure emerge from the side door of the church and hurry toward the parking lot. The figure, a woman, had her head down as though she didn't want anyone to see her, but even from a little bit of a distance he recognized the set of the narrow shoulders, the legs.

Deirdre!

Rob's palms, beginning to sweat, started to slide on the steering wheel. He checked the rearview mirror: no cars coming down Main. He pulled over to the side of the road. He didn't even know Deirdre was Catholic. And even if he'd known that he wouldn't have thought her devout enough to attend church on, of all things, a Thursday morning. Then Rob looked at the sign in front of the church. Beneath the list of Mass times was this: DAILY CONFESSION, 6:30 WEEKDAY MORNINGS.

Deirdre had been confessing!

Confessing her *sins*.

Confessing Rob.

Rob was a sin.

Now he felt worse than ever. Sure, Deirdre had been the one to kiss him. He'd been weakened by his fight with Eliza. *You don't work with your hands.* And, admittedly, by the worry he felt over Eliza spending time in her hometown, with her high school boyfriend. And by the strains of building Cabot Lodge. And, of course, by the many, many beers. But *he* had been the one who'd brought up the Colemans' holiday party, *he'd* been the one to stir the pot. And so, in a sense, what had happened had been his fault. And now Deirdre was sneaking out of St. Matthew's at six forty-five in the morning after telling a priest about it. Not only had he driven Deirdre to that, but he'd hurt Eliza.

Did it help, confessing? Was regret like the stomach bug, when you ached and ached until finally you disgorged your last two meals and then you felt better almost instantly?

He got out of the car and loped across the street until he was close enough to Deirdre to call her name. She turned, and when she saw him she frowned. She was dressed conservatively, in tan pants and a blouse with a little ruffled sweater on top. She said, "What are you doing here?"

"Bagels," he said. She nodded, as though that explained everything. "Hey," he continued. "I thought we should talk."

"I tried to call you yesterday. You didn't pick up."

"I got—busy," he said.

"Uh-huh." She squinted at him. She wasn't wearing any makeup, the way she had been at The Wharf Rat, and she looked somehow both older and younger than she had that night. "What . . . what do you want to talk about?"

"Well. What happened, I guess."

Deirdre cleared her throat and flicked her eyes at him. "What happened is that you kissed me."

"Um," said Rob. "Come again?"

"You kissed me, Rob," said Deirdre.

"*What?* No, I didn't. You kissed me."

"Did not."

"Then why are you at confession, if you don't think you did anything wrong?"

"How do you know I was at confession?"

He jerked his head toward the sign at the front of the church.

"Then how do you know what I was confessing? Maybe I have other sins, Rob. Maybe I have lots of sins." She pulled her sweater closer around her. "Anyway. It's not like we—" She lowered her voice and glanced around. "It's not like we *had sex.*"

"God, *no!*" said Rob. "It was a silly kiss, nothing."

Deirdre chewed on a thumbnail. "Well, you don't have to look like the idea of having sex with me is abhorrent to you." She gestured downward, to her tanned, toned body.

"It's not. I mean, it *is,* because I'm *married.*"

"You looked like I suggested eating slugs."

"I didn't."

"You did. Are you going to tell Eliza?"

In a nearby tree, a bird chirped in a manner that was probably flute-like and summer-morning beautiful but in Rob's addled mind sounded aggressive. "Nooooo. Are *you* going to tell Eliza?"

"No." She crossed her arms carefully in front of her.

Another bird joined in, then another. (Show-offs.) There was no equivocation in Deirdre's answer.

He thought about Charlie's tumor. Recurrence rate of nearly one hundred percent, even if treated. Pressing down on the part of his brain responsible for vision. The fact that Charlie wouldn't consider any treatment was killing Eliza: as a former med student, as a daughter, as a person who truly believed that you should give up on something only when you'd exhausted all of your options. "No," he repeated. "I feel bad enough to think that I hurt her. I don't see any reason to burden her with the hurt. For nothing."

Deirdre nodded slowly and then said, "You'd better hurry up, they always sell out of cinnamon raisin early."

"Huh?"

Deirdre sighed—it was the exasperated sigh women had been direct-ing at men since time began. "Cinnamon raisin," she repeated. "Zoe's favorite."

"Right," said Rob. "I know. Of course I know what her favorite is." (In fact, he had thought it was sesame.) "And Evie's is plain."

"Used to be plain," she corrected. "Now it's everything."

Was there no solace for the dad who was trying his best?

"Before I go," said Rob.

Deirdre said, "Yes?" a little too eagerly, in a way that caused a twinge in his heart.

"I was just wondering if you found my lucky coin. If it fell out when we—" He decided not to pursue the verb after all. "If it fell out in your car."

"You have a lucky coin?"

"Yes," he said defensively. How little Deirdre knew about him, after all! "It's a ten-baht. From Thailand. From my dad, from when I was a kid."

"Oh," she said, and her face softened. "No, sorry. I didn't see it."

"Okay," he said. "Well, bye, Deirdre."

"Bye, Rob."

She started back toward her car and he toward his, then Deirdre called after him, so he turned back. "Don't worry, Rob," she said. "I meant what I said. I'm not going to go all *Fatal Attraction* on you. I'm not going to boil your bunny!"

"I didn't think you were," he said. Then, after a beat: "We don't even have a bunny."

Deirdre turned toward the parking lot and pointed her key at the Tahoe, pressing the unlock button until the car beeped.

"One more thing," said Rob, and she turned toward him with a hope-ful expression that made him cringe. He hurried his words out, lest she get the wrong idea. "Did it help?" he asked.

"What?"

"Confessing. Did it help? Do you feel better?"

She looked at him for a long time, and finally she said, "No. I don't feel better. I feel like the worst friend in the world, and like a terrible wife. I feel like shit."

———

Two and a half hours later, at Cabot Lodge, Rob held, in his sullied hands, a square of the reclaimed tile from the English castle that Mrs. Cabot had discovered in Vermont.

The tile *was* gorgeous; he agreed with Mrs. Cabot.

"It comes from an eighteenth-century English castle up in the north of the country," Mrs. Cabot said. "Let me see, I wrote down the name of the castle somewhere, I'm just looking—" She plunged her hand into her giant Louis Vuitton bag and rummaged around. "I can't find it anywhere! It was right here, I'm sure, on a little sticky note, before I left the house."

"That's okay," said Rob. "You can tell me later."

Neither Ruggman nor the structural engineer seemed as put off by the prospect of accommodating the extra inch and a quarter as Rob thought they would be. Then again, Ruggman's thick and craggy face didn't lend itself easily to emotional nakedness: he could have been cursing both Rob and Christine Cabot and they'd never know it.

Ruggman grunted twice as he turned the tile over and over in his giant paws, and then he and the structural engineer set to work immediately on their tasks, conferring like a couple of political operatives, Ruggman punching numbers into his cell phone and the two of them walking back and forth along the rich brown mud that would one day be the back lawn of Cabot Lodge.

"Mark said he thought we wouldn't be too delayed by this," said Mrs. Cabot.

Guardedly, Rob said, "Hmm." He didn't agree. Was Ruggman committing the ultimate sin, was he telling the client what she *wanted* to hear rather than what she *needed* to hear? It was possible. It was likely. They all did it sometimes. He'd been doing it for months.

Mrs. Cabot smiled and issued an extended sigh. "Mark is really great," she said. "Don't you think so, Robbie? Very salt-of-the-earth."

Ruggman had his back to Mrs. Cabot and Rob, and he was on the phone; it was impossible to read his expression.

"Very," said Rob. "Definitely."

"I'm going to feel like Lady Grantham, living with this tile!" said Mrs. Cabot. "I can't believe I found this."

Rob didn't answer; he was looking out at the way the land sloped toward the lake. He could see two children on the dock that belonged to the house next door. That reminded him of his own two children; he should call to check in. He turned toward Mrs. Cabot, looking for a way to extricate himself.

"Do you watch *Downton Abbey?*" Mrs. Cabot asked.

"What? No. No, I don't. Eliza does, I think. Yes, she definitely does. Is that the one with the accents?"

"It is," said Mrs. Cabot. She didn't look like herself today; she looked almost, for lack of a better word, *happy.* "Actually, I guess it's not Lady Grantham I'd feel like, because she lives in a different house, a smaller house, and I'm not sure if that house would have tiles or not. I would be one of the Crawleys."

Some of that slope would be filled in once the construction on the massive patio began. Rob allowed himself to imagine the patio, the heat lamps, the Thanksgiving appetizers laid out on the Cabots' outdoor tables, which, along with all of the furniture, had been ordered and signed for and duly delivered into storage until the high-end cushions were ready to receive the bottoms of Christine Cabot, her progeny, and her progeny's progeny.

Rob didn't have the outdoor plans on him, but it seemed to him, just eyeballing it, that the edge of the patio would be closer to the lake than it should be. He was chewing on this concern when Christine Cabot moved closer to him.

Another pearl of wisdom from Mo Francis: *Trust your gut. If you think something is wrong, it probably is.*

He swallowed it down. Mo Francis hadn't *always* been right.

"You were always such a good boy, Robbie," said Mrs. Cabot. "I remember when your father first moved to Thailand and your mother was a wreck, you were such a comfort to her. *Such* a comfort."

Rob remembered it differently; he remembered that a bottle of top-shelf gin had been more of a comfort to Judith than he himself had been, but he thought he'd let that go.

"You know, Robbie," said Mrs. Cabot, "I do have a friend who'd like to build a house of a similar caliber up here."

Rob perked up. Mrs. Cabot had mentioned this mythical friend before, but she'd never actually produced a name or given Rob a contact number. She'd just dangled the fact of her existence in front of him like a lure. He knew from Ruggman that there were a few choice waterfront parcels for sale, and he knew from Ruggman's assistant, Sharon, whose sister worked at Sebago Properties, the firm that had the listings, that there had been lots of lookers but no offers.

"Nadine Edwards," she said. Rob thought, *Finally, a name!* He filed it away in his mental cabinet; he'd google the heck out of her later.

28

Deirdre

Deirdre was driving to the post office to mail the invitations to the gala. Lots of people went electronic these days, even for high-end events, but Deirdre did not believe that an email—no matter how elegantly put together—could carry the same weight as an actual hold-in-your-hand invitation. She believed in old-fashioned, cream-colored heavy paper with a proper font—Adagio or Belluccia—that you could magnetize to your refrigerator or affix to your kitchen bulletin board; something you'd walk by several times a day and that would cause you to feel the little flutter of excitement that reminded you that you had a Big Event to look forward to.

Deirdre parked her Tahoe on Main Street, not far from the post office, and was carefully removing the bag of invitations from the passenger seat when she heard her name. *Ugh.* There was no mistaking Sheila Rackley's voice, high and quivering, like a violin with a loose string. She waved quickly and continued toward the post office, but Sheila caught up and turned in front of her like a traffic cop, forcing Deirdre to choose between stopping or ramming right into her. Deirdre stopped.

"What've you got there?" Sheila asked breathlessly. She was wearing exercise clothes and sneakers, and she jogged in place a little bit, probably for show.

"Invitations. To the gala."

"Oooooooh. I hope there's one in there for me!"

"Of course there is," said Deirdre reluctantly. "You're on the decorating committee. I'm not going to not invite you."

"It's been on my calendar forever," said Sheila. She made a motion like she was writing something in the air above Deirdre's head.

Deirdre said, "Great. Well . . . ," and tried to step around Sheila, but Sheila mirrored her movement, like the two of them were learning a complicated dance together, and kept talking. "Why'd you pick East Africa, anyway? I never asked you that." She squinted at Deirdre. "Did you go there for study abroad or something?"

No, Deirdre had done a semester abroad in Florence, where she'd studied a lot of Chianti.

The truth was, Deirdre wasn't one hundred percent sure why she had chosen East Africa. Plenty of areas of the world were war-torn, ravaged, intolerably destitute. She could have chosen India or Bangladesh or, for heaven's sake, Iraq or Afghanistan.

Maybe because the names of the countries, when spoken one after another, were like a kind of poetry.

Burundi, Djibouti, Eritrea.

Ethiopia, Kenya, Rwanda.

Somalia, South Sudan, Tanzania, Uganda.

And also because the kids in the EANY posters seized her heart and wouldn't let go.

Not that she could explain any of this to Sheila Rackley.

Sheila had pulled her phone out of her bag and was texting while she was talking to Deirdre. The woman was *intolerable*. Why had Deirdre put her on the decorating committee? Could she even decorate?

"Kristi's been keeping Sofia busy!" said Sheila, eyes fixed on her screen. *Tap tap tap.*

"I guess so," said Deirdre. The morning was bright and sunny; she kept her sunglasses noncommittally over her eyes, although Sheila had used hers to push back her hair, revealing harsh brown roots at the base of her scalp.

"I don't know how you can stand so much time away from Sofia in the *summer.* I couldn't do it." Deirdre looked to the right and to the left of Sheila; Sheila's children were nowhere in evidence.

"Oh, brother, Sheila."

"*What?*"

"Grow up. We're not seventeen. This isn't study hall. Stop trying to stir the pot." She massaged the invitations.

"I was just *making conversation!*"

"Uh-huh," said Deirdre.

"I was!" Sheila's phone buzzed, and she glanced down at it.

"Excuse me, Sheila." Deirdre moved past Sheila and up the walk that led to the post office, where she was finally going to get her beautiful gala invitations in the mail.

29

Eliza

"Buy you a coffee?" said Eliza.

Russell glanced up at her, then back down, and concentrated on the knot he was using to tie the skiff to the float at the end of the wharf. A cleat hitch. Russell said, "I don't drink coffee in the afternoon, keeps me up past my bedtime. You know that."

"I'm not even a lobsterman and I can't drink coffee past noon."

"You make a hell of a sternman, though."

"Don't even," said Eliza. She looked at the sky, which was cerulean, with scattered puffs of clouds. Eliza didn't know which kinds of clouds they were, but she bet Zoe, the budding scientist, would know. "A beer, then?"

He laughed kindly. "You sure that's a good idea, Eliza?"

The vomiting, the scrub grass, the ride of shame home in Russell's pickup. She said, "I'm sorry, about all of that. I'm really sorry. What a rookie move."

He straightened and said, "That's all right. I've seen people drink too much before. I've seen *you* drink too much before." He had: summer before senior year, the night they camped out on Turtle Island, and other times besides. Russell gave her the full force of his smile. Other fisher-men were standing around in little knots or heading back to their trucks. A couple of them glanced over at Eliza and waved: Elton Cobb, Merton Young. She no longer felt like a stranger out here; she was turning back into a daughter. She was going native.

She tried not to remember how Russell's hand had felt holding hers under the table at The Wheelhouse the other night.

She thought of what she'd said to Rob: *You draw pictures of things for other people to make with their hands.* What a mean-spirited thing to say. She'd had to call back four times before he'd talk to her, before he'd accept her apology. And even though he had, it was still, and would be forever, a thing she'd said: she couldn't unsay it.

"I'll behave myself," she promised. "You have a beer, and I'll have a decaf. We'll go to The Cup, since they have both."

––––––

The day before, when Eliza and Mary had returned to Mary's car, Eliza had used her AAA account to call for service, and after fifty-five minutes a tow truck from a garage in Gouldsboro had come out and jumped the battery. Mary's car had started right up. Now the only acknowledgment between them was a quick, shy smile on Mary's part and a (she hoped) cryptic answering nod from Eliza.

After they had their drinks, Eliza sat down, and then Russell sat down, and then the Thing They Would Never Talk About pulled out a chair and sat at the table too. Invited or not, it was there. *Fine,* thought Eliza. She'd waffled on the decaf and then ordered a Sauvignon Blanc, liquid courage with a side of flowery peach, and she took a minute to feel the effects of the inappropriately large sip she started with. Then she thought, *Let's do this.*

"You know when I said the other night that I don't think about it?"

Russell nodded. She loved that she didn't have to explain herself more than that.

"That's not true," she said. "I do think about it." She took another giant sip to try to tamp out the burning feeling in her heart.

Russell waited, his gaze on hers.

I don't have a nineteen-year-old kid, if that tells you anything, she'd said to Mary.

"I think about it. I've never stopped thinking about it. When Zoe was born, I thought about it constantly. When she was born early I thought it was punishment for what I did back then."

"Eliza—"

"No, wait, let me finish. I thought I deserved it. She was so tiny. So fragile and vulnerable! Like a shedder."

Russell smiled.

"Those first few days of her life all I could think was, 'If there's something wrong with this baby it's all my fault.'"

Russell's hand, on the table, twitched—it looked almost like he wanted to cover hers with his own. She put her hands in her lap, because she was afraid they might want that too. She went on: "That's one reason I dropped out of med school, I think it was sort of a penance. Like I didn't deserve it all, like I had to pay the price." She lowered her gaze back to the table and asked, "Do you? Think about it?"

Russell took a long sip of his beer and didn't answer.

"I didn't, for a while," he said. "I got over it, and I met Beatrice."

"Beatrice Prince," said Eliza. She added softly, "Good riddance to bad rubbish."

Russell ignored that. He was much classier than Eliza was, all things considered. He said, "But she didn't want to have kids, and that's what really killed me. Because you know I did want that, Eliza. I always wanted that. A family."

She felt like someone had taken a pair of pliers to part of her heart and twisted. "Do you wish—do you wish we had done things differently?"

"Yeah," he said. No hesitation.

"Really?"

"Of course I do, Eliza, you knew that back then, you knew that's how I wanted to do it, keep the baby, get married."

Eliza tried on the next words for size. "Do you think we made a mistake?"

"Yeah." He took a long pull of his beer and set the bottle down, tracing the bottle with his fingers. "I always thought it was a mistake. But you didn't ask me. You just went."

"You knew I was going. I told you."

"You told me. You didn't ask me."

"You knew, and you let me go off alone. Why'd you let me go off like that, to Bangor? Without you? Why'd you let me go at all?" The inside of Val's Civic, the antiseptic smell of the room, the kind face of the doctor leaning over her, Val brushing her hair out of her eyes after it was all over.

"I was mad," Russell said. "I was so mad at you, Eliza." He twisted his hands together and stretched them in front of him, cracking his knuckles.

Eliza thought of all kinds of things then. She thought of the day she and Rob brought Zoe home from the hospital, and how they set her car seat in the center of the dining room table and stared at her, awed by her perfect little features, cowed by the responsibility now pressing down on their shoulders. She thought of Evie's first day of kindergarten and how she wore ribbons on the end of her braids. She thought of the way Judith had said, "Who gets married in the *winter*?" when she and Rob had planned a December wedding. But it had been gorgeous, the bridesmaids had fur muffs, the ballroom of the Ritz was decorated like an ice castle, and the Christmas decorations were up in the Public Garden.

"But even after—you never once tried to get me to stay, not once that whole time, not ever. You never tried to get me to come back."

Her first two months at Brown, Eliza felt like a gorilla in a land of gazelles. Everyone around her was so assured in the world, so confident. Eliza reread her mother's letter a dozen times a week, wearing the paper down so that it felt like suede.

Russell's hands were steady around his beer bottle now. "You think you would have been happy here?"

"I don't know," she said. Her eyes roamed the café, caught on the menu board. "Yes. Maybe."

Russell snorted. "It's not that I let you go or made you go or anything else. You went. You did what you needed to do. You never thought you belonged here. You wouldn't have been happy."

"I might have been," she said. "My mother was happy here. My mother was the happiest person I've ever known."

Russell nodded and said, "Okay, Eliza. Okay."

"Russell," she said, thinking of what she'd heard from Val, about Beatrice Prince taking Russell's money, thinking of the almost-broken reverse gear.

"What?" His voice cracked a little bit.

"Do you need money?"

The corner of his eye twitched. "Do I *what*?"

"Do you need money? Because—" She lowered her voice, like she was offering him drugs or human organs. "I can help you out, if you need help."

"Are you goddamn kidding me?"

She felt the same shame she'd felt at The Wheelhouse, trying to refuse the sternman pay. She whispered, "No."

"I don't need charity from you, Eliza."

"I didn't say charity."

"You said money."

"It's not the same."

"Yes it is."

"Of course it's not. It's a friend helping out a friend."

"Why is it—"

"*What?*"

"I mean, how'd you turn from what you were into—" He paused.

"Into what?"

"Into a person who thinks money fixes everything?"

Were they really doing this? They were. Fine. "It fixes a lot, Russell."

He stood and put his beer bottle on the table, hard, so she jumped. "Bullshit."

"Don't be an idiot, Russell. Of course it does." She felt her voice growing sharp. "Of course money fixes things. That's the *point* of fucking *money*. To make things easier. And better. It's not noble to pretend it doesn't. It's just *stupid*."

"Well, then, I guess I'm stupid. That's what you think really, isn't it?"

"That's not what I meant. You know it's not."

"Didn't go to college, I guess you think I can't understand the basics. I've been running my own boat for *years* now, Eliza. Years."

"I know you have. I'm sorry, Russell, of course you have. I just thought—"

"Thanks for the beer, Eliza. I'm going to get going now. I have an early day tomorrow."

"Just like that?" she said. Her throat was burning. She still had half a glass of wine left.

"Just like that."

Eliza sipped the wine slowly, giving Russell time to leave. Then she left a ten-dollar tip on the table for Mary *because money did help, of course it fucking helped,* and walked slowly back toward her father's house. At the last second she changed course and veered back to the wharf. There were a few guys milling around, a couple of trucks left, but nobody paid her any mind.

She sat down and breathed in as deeply as she could: it was the complicated, briny, utterly alive smell that meant she was home. Something inside her loosened and she began to cry, for her mother, for her father, who couldn't drive, couldn't haul traps, couldn't see right. For the little baby who had never been born, who would never row a skiff from the dock to a mooring, would never giggle when he touched a piece of bait for the first time.

She wiped savagely at her face and thought, *What if this is where I was supposed to be all along?*

Lesson Number Four: When you're choosing a cantaloupe, go by smell, not by feel. A ripe cantaloupe smells like a cantaloupe. An unripe cantaloupe smells like nothing at all. If you're planting tomatoes mix a little limestone into the soil. And there's so much more I wanted to tell you. I wanted to tell you about love and sex and how to shape your eyebrows and how to learn to drink coffee and choose a lipstick and what to do when you make a mistake and how to cook chicken cutlets the way your father likes them and not to be scared of childbirth and dozens, maybe hundreds, of things like that, but the truth is I'm running out of time

Her mother had died before she finished the letter. No more lessons. Not even a period at the end of the last sentence. That was the ending: no ending at all.

Her phone buzzed, giving her a start. A text from Evie.

I GOT THE PART! I GOT IT. FERN, IN *CHARLOTTE'S WEB.*

30

Deirdre

Deirdre was serving lunch to the decorating committee in forty-five minutes, and she was in a tizzy.

Judith Barnes had told Deirdre that there were always unanticipated disasters in the final few weeks before a big event, and, since Judith Barnes could raise tens of thousands of dollars with her eyes closed, her ears plugged, and a set of Crest Whitestrips on her teeth, Deirdre took her at her word. It was Judith who'd told Deirdre that the decorating committee could be one of the trickiest fund-raising committees to manage—they seemed innocuous, but, oh boy, did they ever have opinions.

At the moment, though, all was on track. She had most of the silent-auction items on deck. The RSVPs were coming in, and soon it would be time to finalize the seating arrangements, which were promising to be more complicated than the seating arrangements at her wedding fifteen years ago at the Wadsworth Atheneum Museum of Art in Hartford.

But she was almost there.

She had chosen the dress she would wear to the gala: an Ulla Johnson corded Japanese satin blouson dress in marigold. The Cleo dress, it was called. Not everyone could pull off marigold, but, with her natural skin tone plus the extra sun she'd gotten over the past couple of weeks, Deirdre could. (Sheila would never be able to pull off marigold.) Deirdre thought that the dress color would serve as a nice homage to Africa. She wouldn't do anything more obvious than that. Well, maybe some ruby earrings and a touch of green around her neck.

Though the gala was still weeks away, she had secured a mani-pedi appointment for the day before at Nails! Nails! Nails! and a hair appointment with Shonda, her stylist at Luxe, in downtown Barton, for the morning of. Shonda had been known to nail a killer updo, though with the ruffle collar of the Cleo Deirdre thought wearing her hair down and ironed silk-straight might be the way to go. Or maybe soft curls would be better. Not that the EANY kids would or should care how Deirdre wore her hair to the gala. Get over yourself, Deirdre. Keep your mind on the task at hand.

But her mind kept returning to seeing Rob outside of St. Matthew's.

"It was nothing," Rob had said, about their encounter, first in the bar, and after in the Tahoe.

She disagreed.

It was only kissing, but it wasn't *nothing*. Deirdre believed in being honest. It had happened, and calling it nothing didn't change the situation, just like putting glasses on a dog and naming the dog Professor Sparkles didn't make the dog any smarter.

She was getting a headache. It was a guilt headache.

Lunch!

Emily Boyd was on Phase 1 of the Fast Metabolism Diet: fruits, whole grains, lean proteins. Gabby Gardner was doing Whole30: no grains, all proteins, most fruits. Sheila could eat only protein, no fruits or veggies. Just one day a week, to keep her "plan on track." But that day happened to be today.

Holy moly.

At least Deirdre didn't have to serve wine with lunch. Nobody was drinking during the week anymore; half the women out on the last Ladies' Night had only had seltzer. They were all "saving their drinks" for the night of the gala.

What was she supposed to serve for lunch? Bread and water, like a prison matron? No, of course not, *don't be an idiot, Deirdre*. Nobody on the decorating committee would touch bread.

Her headache got a little bit worse.

This was normally something she would have called Eliza about—Eliza never dieted; her metabolism was naturally speedy—and she and Eliza would have snickered and felt nobly superior while Eliza worked her way through a package of Junior Mints and Deirdre ate salt-and-pepper potato chips straight from the bag.

But she couldn't call Eliza, not now, not after the *encounter*.

The day after the encounter, while Kristi Osgood took Sofia to the club, Deirdre had arranged for a mobile detailing of the Tahoe. The guy came right to her house with all sorts of equipment, and she sat in her office, peering out the window at him, working out her complicated feelings.

She kept thinking of Lady Macbeth, consumed by guilt and handwashing. She'd seen a production of *Macbeth* on a trip with her parents to

Stratford-on-Avon the summer between high school and college, and the image had really stuck.

Out, damned spot!

When the mobile car detailing guy rang the doorbell to present Deirdre with the bill he said, "I prettied her up as much as I could. But really that thing was already friggin' pristine."

"Not really," Deirdre had said, remembering her hand on the back of Rob's neck. "There was a lot of, um, invisible grime. I hope you got it all."

Out, damned spot!

Lunch! Think about the lunch.

In the end, she put an array of beautiful salad fixings in her favorite wooden bowls and laid them out along the sideboard in the dining room. She added two pounds of poached salmon she'd picked up from Whole Foods. Then, on further consideration, a bowl of hard-boiled eggs. Peeled or unpeeled? She wavered, then peeled half. To each woman, her own salad. She left fruit out of the equation altogether. Fruit was too fraught.

She was bringing into the dining room some of the materials that EANY had promised to send in time for the gala—giant blown-up photographs of the children in their dirt-floor school, a super-close-up of a beautiful Malawi girl with intricately braided hair, pierced ears, and giant crooked teeth—when her phone buzzed.

Eliza.

Out, damned spot!

She hovered her finger over the answer button. To answer or not to answer, that was the question. Obviously, a different Shakespeare play, but relevant nonetheless.

She answered.

"Hey," said Eliza. "I'm sorry if you're busy, with the gala. I just needed an ear."

"I have an ear!" said Deirdre. In her mind she rubbed away the damned spot. "In fact I have two."

"It's just—I don't know what to do. I want to bring my dad to Boston for treatment. He won't even entertain the idea. He's totally against it. I thought if I stayed here for a while I could convince him, but. He hasn't budged."

"Oh, Eliza." This was what real problems looked like—this, not some messy, drunken, college-like hookup in a bar. "Oh, *Eliza*. I'm so sorry."

"I think I should come home for a while, give him some space. I'm driving him crazy. And I need to see the girls."

A river of panic coursed through Deirdre. Talking to Eliza on the phone when she was safely four hours to the north was one thing; seeing her in person was quite another.

Her brain was thinking that *of course* Eliza should come home and see her girls, but then all of a sudden her mouth was saying, "Oh, Eliza. Your girls are fine. I promise you. I think your dad needs you more than the girls do right now."

Out, out, out damned spot.

"You think so?" Eliza's voice wobbled, and Deirdre's heart wrenched.

"I do."

"No, you're right. I should stay here. He does need me, even if he won't admit it. I wish they could come up here. But I know Rob is swamped with Cabot Lodge, he can't leave . . ."

Deirdre took a deep breath, swallowed her guilt and her remorse, and said, "I could bring them up to you." She would do it. She would sacrifice the gala preparations, and she would bring the girls to Eliza. This would be her penance.

"Oh no. No, Deirdre. Thank you, but I know how much you have going on. I know this is the crucial time for the gala."

Deirdre considered the salad bowls. She said, "Maybe you should see if your mother-in-law can bring them up to you?"

Out.

"I don't know—"

Damned.

"Do you think Judith would do it? Really?"

Spot!

"I bet she would. And, honestly, Eliza, don't you want the girls to see your dad now? Before, well—"

"Before it's too late," Eliza filled in.

"Well, yes."

"You're right. I'll ask her," Eliza said, suddenly and firmly. "What else are mothers-in-law for, right? You have to be able to ask for help when you need it. Whatever our differences have been in the past. Or the present."

"Exactly," said Deirdre. "*Exactly.* But you know if she can't do it, I will."

"I'm going to call Judith now," said Eliza. "I needed this talk, Deirdre. Thank you. You're such a good friend."

Out, damned spot.

As soon as she'd disconnected from Eliza, the doorbell rang: there they were, live and in person, the three members of the decorating committee. "Hello!" Deirdre said, employing her gracious-hostess voice. "Hello, hello, come in!"

Once they were inside, the dining room seemed too small for the posters, the food, the people. Deirdre watched Sheila considering the posters. She tipped her head to one side and then to the other, as though this were the Met and she a discerning patron.

"What, Sheila?" asked Deirdre. She heard an edge in her own voice.

"It's just—nothing," said Sheila.

"*What?*"

Sheila sighed. "It's just. Do you think we could get a different poster?"

"Why would we do that?"

"Maybe one where the children aren't . . . so *thin*. I mean, it's fine for them to look hungry, but too hungry? It might turn people off."

"Of course they're hungry," Deirdre snapped. "In fact they're starving. Literally."

And Sheila rolled her eyes at Gabby Gardner; Deirdre could practically hear her say it: *There goes Deirdre again. Overreacting.*

"I'll be right back," said Deirdre. She clenched her hands into fists. "I just need to grab some seltzer—"

"I am so goddamn tired of salad," she heard Sheila Rackley say cheerfully when she was out of the room. Then, *sotto voce,* "Do you think this salmon is wild?"

31

Mary

Andi and Daphne stood together in the doorway, looking at Mary like a set of proud parents. They were dressed up in flowered summer sundresses—

not identical, but very similar—and Andi was wearing an unfamiliar rosy-pink lip gloss.

"You sure?" said Andi for the nine hundred and forty-eighth time.

"Positive," said Mary. "Go ahead, I got this." Daphne's parents were up from Connecticut and Andi and Daphne were having dinner with them at Fathom in Bar Harbor. Mary hadn't been to Fathom, she probably would never go to Fathom, but she'd looked up the menu on her phone and seen items like *Drunk Shrimp* and *Massaged Kale Salad* and cocktails called *Bluette* and *Dirty Pearl.* She wasn't sure why kale would get a massage (Mary would kill for a massage herself), but she knew that a menu like this was right up Daphne and Andi's alley. They ate that stuff up, literally. They had to leave before the café's closing time to get to Bar Harbor for a seven-thirty reservation, so Mary would be in charge of emptying the canisters of milk on the sideboard, locking up the cash register, turning off the lights, and so on.

She'd never closed the café by herself before, but Mary was looking forward to her new responsibilities. If things went well, maybe she'd be asked to close up again, then again, and perhaps soon she'd get a promotion, maybe even a raise. Surely Andi and Daphne would like to enjoy their summer evenings away from the café sometimes; if you made it through winter in Maine, the saying went, you deserved summer. Actually, it was the other way around: If you can't stand winter, you don't deserve summer. But close enough.

"Have so much fun," said Mary now. They really did look very pretty, dressed up like that. One of them, she couldn't tell which, was wearing a light perfume that smelled like lilacs. Maybe they were both wearing the same perfume. Must be nice to be able to share things that way, with your partner. Your wife. Must be nice to be in love like that, in a flowered dress, on your way to Bar Harbor for dinner.

"Fun is relative in this situation," said Andi. "Daph's dad still refers to us as 'the gays.'"

"No he doesn't," said Daphne. She rolled her eyes.

"Not us as in *us,*" Andi told Mary. "I mean us as in *the community.* Like he'll say, 'Did you see that the gays got that marriage thing through the Supreme Court?'"

"He's come a long way, though," said Daphne. "You have to admit that."

"Do I?" asked Andi. Then, back to Mary, "And Daph's mom just puts

her lips together and looks into the middle distance and you can tell she's trying hard to think about her book club." She pressed her own lips together in imitation. "She prefers to think of us as roommates who are just sharing the rent until we can figure out what we really want to do with our lives."

"Okay, Andi, that's enough," said Daphne. "We can't all come from enlightened West Coast families." (Andi had grown up in Portland, Oregon.) But Daphne was laughing, and Mary saw her put her hand on Andi's waist as they exited, and Mary thought, *Isn't that what love is supposed to look like?*

There were only four customers in the café at that moment, sitting together at table seven, two tailored yachting couples with cardigans and summer tans, and while Mary watched over them and fiddled behind the counter she felt all of her usual worries swirling around in her mind. When was she going to tell Josh? When her belly swelled to the point where they couldn't ignore it? When she needed money for an abortion?

I don't have a nineteen-year-old kid, if that tells you anything, Eliza had said.

Would Josh even *have* money to help pay for an abortion? He was a terrible lobsterman, really hopeless, and things never seemed to get better for him. Maybe he had some money from the drugs, but she didn't like to think about that—or the little baggie collecting dust at the back of her closet.

Mary herself had some money saved from her paychecks, of course. But every time she thought about calling the clinic in Bangor to make an appointment, every time she pulled the number up on her phone and got ready to hit the call button, something stopped her. And every time she thought about telling Josh, she remembered the look in his eyes that night when she'd worn the yellow dress, and then how swiftly he'd turned from easygoing to angry at The Wheelhouse, and the same something (or maybe a different something) stopped her.

Anyway, she still had two weeks and five days to decide.

The customers were all drinking wine, three Chardonnays, one Cabernet. If they ordered another round, of course, Mary would have to serve them, even though, technically, she was underage. She hoped that they did order another round.

One couple owned a home on the Point and one couple was visiting;

Mary could tell this from the way one of the men said things like, "We contribute a handsome sum to the Lobster Festival every year, though of course keeping the local flavor is really the thing."

Mary wanted to tell him that *we* did not do anything, that it was *us against them* in this town, in case he hadn't noticed, that if he couldn't stand the winter he didn't deserve the summer, but then he caught her looking at him and flashed a smile that really did look friendly and sincere and she figured that he was probably just a guy doing his best, like most people. And in fact it was true: the summer people did contribute a lot to the Lobster Festival. Daphne was on the committee.

Mary tried to imagine what it might be like to be these people, sitting with their wine, fresh off their sailboat, taking a small and relaxing break before heading back to their gigantic summerhouses, where they'd drink more wine before putting on silk pajamas and climbing into oversized beds.

Silk pajamas seemed, to Mary, like the height of luxury.

However. Mary should be keeping busy, not judging the customers. The customers could say whatever they liked, as long as they paid their bill and (hopefully) left a tip on the table or in the tip jar on the counter.

Mary spent some time organizing the milk and cream and sugars and wiping up the cinnamon that had spilled out of the container, and then she stood, surveying the café the way a farmer might survey his fields, with a certain pride of ownership and the satisfaction of a job well done. A sensation came over her that was so pleasant she didn't recognize it. Then she realized that for the first time since she'd taken that pregnancy test the future stretched out before her in a way that didn't look like something she had to be afraid of. She touched her stomach. She walked over to table seven and asked the customers if they needed anything.

"All set, doll!" said the man who'd been doing the talking. *Doll.* Ugh. Still, she wouldn't mind a tip, so she smiled and retreated behind the counter, where she pulled out her phone and typed *How big is a baby at eleven weeks.*

A quarter of an ounce. She tried to equate that to coffee beans, to whipped cream. It would take so very little of each to get to a quarter ounce. She read on. A tongue, a palate, nipples, hair follicles. Fingers and toes beginning to form. Fingers and toes! Already?

The two couples got up to leave and she saw one of the men reach into his wallet for a few bills to leave on the table. She called out, "Bye now! Have a good night!" and busied herself behind the counter so she didn't look like she was watching for a tip.

When the door closed behind them, and when the café was silent and really truly Mary's for the first time, Mary touched her stomach again and pictured the baby, her baby, the little bunch of coffee beans with real fingers and real toes. She felt again the twinge of joy, the possibility of a future start to form inside of her. She imagined putting the baby in a carrier and walking down to the water, her body curled protectively around him. Or her! Either one, either one would be fine. *There there,* she said to the imaginary baby, when the wind off the harbor picked up. *Mama's got you.* Where was Josh in this picture? He was nowhere. She couldn't in a million years imagine living with a baby in Josh's house, the television blaring, the car shows always in the background. But it was just as hard—or maybe harder—to imagine living in her own house, with Vivienne's hair products scattered around, the counters covered over with Vivienne's clutter. Where would she even put the baby? Her own bedroom was tiny, and the whole house had only the two bedrooms.

It was almost official closing time; in five minutes, Mary would turn the sign from OPEN to CLOSED, then count the money in the cash register and record it in the ledger as Daphne had shown her. She'd lock the register and put the key in the secret spot that only the three of them knew about.

Mary was crouched down, peering into the second fridge, the mini, where they kept the smaller containers of half-and-half, when she heard the bell on the door ding. *Shit.* She should have turned the sign first. She started to call out, "We're closed!" in her best customer service voice as she rose but then she saw that it was Josh who had come in and the words lodged themselves somewhere deep in her throat.

Josh, swaying a little bit as he moved, drunk, his eyes lined with red. Or maybe it was more than drinking, maybe it was drugs, the ones he'd hidden in her closet, or something else, worse: heroin, cocaine. She didn't even know enough to know what to look for.

"Hey, babe," he said. Even these two simple words slurred. *Shit shit shit.*

Andi and Daphne would not like this. "We're closing," she said. "Josh, I'm not supposed to have anyone in here. I'm closing up."

Mary didn't feel good about the way Josh was looking at her, squinting, like whatever he'd drunk or taken or shot up made it impossible for him to open his eyes all the way. "Closing, huh?"

What she should have said next was, "Andi's coming right back, and then we're closing." She realized that after: Andi, who drove to Ellsworth for CrossFit four mornings a week, was tougher than Daphne and that might be enough to get Josh to go. But what she said instead was, "Yeah. I'm in charge tonight, Andi and Daphne went to Bar Harbor."

Stupid, stupid, stupid Mary.

His body language changed then; he grew in front of her. Or maybe she was shrinking. She stood up as straight as she could and pressed her fingers into the countertop, hard, so that the area around the knuckles turned a bright white.

Josh came up to the counter and leaned against it, chewing his lip and looking up at the menu like he was an ordinary customer who was trying to decide between an ordinary latte and an ordinary mocha on an ordinary day.

"So you're alone, huh?" He had a weird little smile on his face.

"Yes," said Mary.

He was still looking at the menu and smiling the little smile when he said, "Just talked to your mom."

"My *mom*?" Mary's heart dropped to the floor.

"Your mom, that's right. I went around to your house looking for you. She was just home from work so we got to talking and wouldn't you know it came out that she knew about something that I didn't."

"What's that?" asked Mary, and her heart was thudding hard against her rib cage. She really, really did not like Josh's little smile. She wanted it to go away, she wanted *him* to go away, but she didn't know how to make that happen.

"About the *baby*," said Josh, and when he said *baby* he hit his fist so hard against the counter that Mary jumped.

She was breathing hard now too; it was like her body had split off from her mind and was doing its own thing.

Josh's voice got library-quiet and she shrank back from the counter. His eyes didn't focus on her when he said, "When were you gonna tell me?"

To compensate, she tried to speak more loudly, but her voice wouldn't go the way she wanted it to. It wouldn't work at all. She said, "I was, uh—"

"When were you gonna *tell* me? *Huh?*" He was no longer quiet. Again the fist slammed down. She remembered that she hadn't locked up the cash register yet and she made a move toward it, stroking the key in her apron pocket, and Josh followed her around the counter.

Then his voice got soft again and he reached out and touched her shoulder and said, "I can't believe it, Mary, you and me are having a baby."

"Josh."

"But mostly I can't believe that you didn't tell me. Big news like that." He was squeezing her shoulder now, just a little bit at first, and then a little bit more, and then hard enough that it really hurt, and then enough that it really, really hurt. She tried to wiggle out from under his grasp but she couldn't, he had her too tight, his face was close to hers and she could smell his beery breath. She could see the red vessels in the whites of his eyes.

Then the bell on the door dinged again—Mary still hadn't turned the sign to the CLOSED side. *Please please please* she said to herself as she was turning around. Mary wasn't a religious person and she'd never been taken to church as a child and she didn't really know how to pray, so imagine her surprise when she saw an angel step through the door.

"Well now, look who it is," said Josh. "It's Charlie goddamn Sargent."

"Hey," said Charlie, nodding at the two of them. "I just came in looking to see if you had any of those lobster cookies, Mary."

"No cookies," said Josh. "Sorry." He shrugged. "All out. We're closing. Isn't that right, Mary? It's closing time."

"You okay here, Mary?" asked Charlie, looking back and forth between the two of them. Josh had removed his hand from her shoulder and she reached up and rubbed the spot he'd been squeezing—geez, it *hurt*. She bet a bruise was forming, a big one.

"She's okay," said Josh. "She's great. We're discussing some happy news we just got, that's all."

Charlie coughed; the cough was obviously manufactured to buy a moment. That seemed suddenly ridiculously thoughtful to Mary, that fake little cough, and she felt her eyes fill. Charlie said, "I didn't ask you, Josh. I asked Mary here."

"Closing time, Charlie," said Josh. "We're all closed up here for the night." He smiled, and Mary remembered how she used to think that smile was a sign of Josh's charm. It seemed like another person who'd fallen for that. Well, it *was* another person: a younger, more innocent, less pregnant person.

"Thanks for your input, Josh, but I'm not leaving here until I hear from Mary herself. If it's all the same to you."

"It's not," said Josh. He came around from behind the counter and Mary saw that the two men were pretty evenly matched in height. "It's not all the same to me at all."

Charlie ignored that. "So I'm just going to ask again: You okay here, Mary?"

Right then it seemed like the world switched to slow motion from the regular speed it had been running on, giving Mary time to think and consider before she answered. Mary looked at Charlie Sargent and saw the gray stubble around his chin and the anchor tattoo on his forearm. She noticed how strong he was; his forearm was thick and muscled and biceps made hills in his upper arms. She saw the way he was looking at her—it was the way she imagined that a good father would look at his teenage daughter when he was trying to help her work out something confusing about the world. The unexpected kindness of that look from a man she barely knew was almost too much to take: here was an almost stranger, a good man, who wasn't going to leave her alone if she needed him, who was asking if she was all right.

"I'm not sure," she said finally, and Charlie stepped a little closer to Josh. Mary's shoulder throbbed, and she touched it, and her head was throbbing too, and there was blood rushing into her ears, and then she said, "I mean, no. No, everything is not okay."

She heard Josh's sharp intake of breath. She thought of the lady in the clinic with her list of questions; she thought of the posters on the wall of the clinic's bathroom. *Silence hides violence.* She could be one of those women in the blink of an eye, the twist of an arm behind a back. Anyone could. She cleared her throat and said, "Everything is not okay, and I don't feel safe."

"Got it," said Charlie calmly. Mary didn't meet Josh's eyes, but she heard that under his breath he said, *What the fuck, Mary?* "Josh," Charlie said. "I want you to get the hell out of here."

Josh said, "Mare?" and she almost wavered then because his little-boy voice was back, the one that made Mary feel like she could take care of him, but then she touched her stomach and thought *eleven weeks* and *palate* and *hair follicles.*

"I'm not going anywhere," said Josh. "Last time I checked, Charlie, you didn't own this place."

Mary stared at the anchor tattoo on Charlie's forearm.

"Doesn't matter what I own or don't own," said Charlie. "Matters what I told you to do."

"She's with me," said Josh. *"Motherfucker."*

Josh started toward Charlie then and Mary saw him raise his hand, his fist closed, and she thought, *That's it. He's going to kill Charlie Sargent and then he's going to kill me.* Weirdly, she even had time to think: *How am I going to tell Eliza that her father is dead because of me?*

But Charlie was faster. And he punched Josh on the side of the face so hard that Mary heard a crunch and Josh fell back against table three, his elbows hitting the table, his feet sliding out from underneath. Two of the chairs clattered over and Josh struggled to get up. He had one hand on his chin, and Mary's first stupid thought was to run for ice. Her second thought was that Charlie was leaning over Josh to help him up.

But although he was leaning over him, he wasn't helping. He was talking to him *almost softly,* sort of gently, and he was saying, "I want you to get the hell out of this café and after that I want you to get the hell out of this town. We know you been messing with people's traps, we know all about that, and now that I see how you're treating Mary here. . . . You can take a day or two to tie up your affairs, or whatever else you need to do, and then I want you to go, and I don't want you to come back. We don't ever want to see your face around this harbor again. We don't need you here and we don't want you here. You hear me?" Then Charlie stopped and looked at Mary and said, "Unless I made some sort of mistake. Mary?"

Mary touched her stomach and thought, *Little fingers, little toes.* She said, "No. No mistake."

Josh had by then pulled himself to his feet and there was a stream of blood coming from his nose and maybe his mouth too but it was hard to tell. He made a noise that sounded almost like a growl and then he stomped his foot—*he stomped his foot, like a child!*—and he left the café; it was clear to Mary and probably to Charlie that he would have slammed the door if it hadn't been the kind of quietly self-closing door that didn't allow itself to be slammed. But he did punch the glass on the way out.

There was a moment after Josh was gone that Mary stared at Charlie and Charlie stared back at Mary and the only sound was the refrigerator and Mary's breathing and Charlie's too. Then whatever adrenaline had been shooting through Mary left all at once and she felt weak enough that she had to grip the counter again.

"Now, sit down," said Charlie. He lowered himself heavily into a chair at table three. His cheeks had gone saggy and he tipped his head forward and closed his eyes.

"Are you okay?" asked Mary.

"Just a little dizzy." He squeezed his eyes shut. "It'll pass. Sit with me."

Mary said, "There's blood on the floor, I have to clean it up."

"Later."

"I don't want it to dry."

Mary wet one of the bamboo cloths and got down on her hands and knees and wiped up the blood—there was a trail, from table three to the door—and then she crumpled up the cloth and stuffed it into her pocket. This one time she wasn't going to put it in to be washed. When she was done Charlie pulled out a chair for her at table three and said, "We'll sit for a minute, and then I'll see you to your car, and then you can go on home and forget that bastard. If you're okay with all of that."

"I'm okay with all of that," said Mary. She couldn't meet Charlie Sargent in the eye. She also couldn't tell him that the guy he'd just sent out of town was the father of the little bunch of coffee beans currently growing inside of her. And then, without even a speck of warning, she *was* telling him. She didn't break down; she didn't apologize or hesitate or dress the fact in some fancy language. She just said, very calmly, "I'm pregnant, and Josh is the father." Then she kept going: she told him about the paper bag in her closet at home that Josh had put there, and she told him about how she kept hoping her mother would turn into some other kind of mother but never did, and about how she couldn't imagine living with Vivienne forever, especially with a baby. She even swallowed hard and told him about how her teacher said she was really good at math and could do something with it someday but now, well.

Charlie took all of this in, nodding, and finally he said, "Oh, Mary," very gravely and gently, and she felt like those two words were an embrace. A long minute passed after that, and Mary realized that she felt better after having said all of that out loud, but because she didn't know what do with that feeling she said, "Were you really looking for lobster cookies?"

"Yes," said Charlie. Then, "No. Just went out for some air. But when I saw the lights on and saw Josh in here I figured I'd better take a closer look. The sign on the door said OPEN, so . . ." That made Mary remember she still hadn't turned the sign to CLOSED; she rose to do that, and then she went behind the counter and opened a fresh package of lobster cookies—she'd pay the cash register before she left for the night—and put two on a plate and brought them back to the table. Her legs were shaky and her breathing was still a little bit unsteady and she felt the way you do the first day back to school after a week home with the flu. When she bit into her cookie she realized how hungry she was. She hadn't eaten properly that day at all. Tomorrow: fruits and vegetables, everything that was good for the baby.

Charlie said, "I'd say you're better off without him. But what would you say?"

What would Mary say? Two days ago, even yesterday, she would have said that she was terrified to be with Josh, but also terrified to be without him. Now something had changed—a subtle shift in the atmosphere when she started imagining a pale yellow nursery, walking with the baby by the wharf. "I'd say yes," she said. "But I didn't plan to tell you any of that. I don't know what happened, I just—I don't know, it just came out." She squinted. "Are you going to tell anyone?" She didn't want Andi and Daphne to know—she didn't want anyone to know. But now she'd told Eliza Sargent *and* Charlie Sargent, and Vivienne knew, and Josh knew, and probably Alyssa Michaud had guessed too.

Charlie made a motion like a zipper closing up his lips. "It's your business, Mary, not mine. I don't go telling other people's business. Never have, and I'm not going to start now."

"Thank you," whispered Mary. Mary's phone buzzed: a text. Daphne. She'd forgotten she was supposed to let her know when everything was done at the café. The text said **ALL CLOSED UP? EVERYTHING OKAY?**

Debatable.

Mary put the phone down. She should lock up and go home, but she didn't really want to. The café felt warm and comfortable and she didn't want to leave it and go out into the fog of the summer evening, the uncertainty of her house, her mother, her room. So she searched for a way to keep the conversation going. Even with that in mind, she wasn't sure, later, where she got the courage to say what she said next. Charlie was almost done with his cookie, just the tail was left. She ate hers the other way, leaving the head for the end. She said, "I just told you the biggest secret of my life. Now you have to tell me something, so that we're even."

Charlie raised his eyebrows at her, saying nothing.

"Something that nobody else knows about you. It can be small, like your favorite ice-cream flavor. Or it can be big, like—well, I don't know. Something big."

"Oh, hey now," said Charlie. Mary couldn't tell if he was annoyed or pleased. "That's one hell of a question. You'll have to give me a minute on that one." Mary nibbled on her cookie and waited; she could still hear the little bubbling noises the refrigerator made every so often.

Finally he said, "Okay, Mary, are you ready for this one?"

She nodded.

"Now, you are absolutely not to tell anyone this, ever, okay? You have to promise. I don't want this getting out, getting around. Town like this. You know how it is."

"Okay. I promise." Mary breathed in deeply. She felt like she was holding a whole universe inside her lungs.

Charlie leaned close to Mary like he was going to whisper, although when he spoke he did so at a regular volume. And then he said the most astonishing thing. He said, "That accident I had on the boat, beginning of the summer?"

Mary could hardly breathe. "Yes?"

"That wasn't an accident."

Another text: **MARY? EVERYTHING OKAY? DIDN'T HEAR BACK?** This time she said, "Sorry," to Charlie Sargent, "I just have to—" And she texted back, **ABSOLUTELY**.

Mary looked at Charlie Sargent and her heart was throbbing in her chest, a little bird beating its wings, and she said, "Tell me."

32

One month earlier . . .

LITTLE HARBOR, MAINE

Charlie

This is it, thought Charlie Sargent. The last everything. The last cup of coffee, the last time rinsing the mug and leaving it to dry, the last time starting the truck, switching off the kitchen lights, blowing on his hands while the truck warmed up—because even though it was summer now it was still damn cold in the hours before sunrise when only the fishermen were out.

Of course he felt good today, of all days. (*You feel well,* Eliza would tell him. *Not good. You* are *good, but you* feel *well.*) He never really understood that. You got your point across, who cared how you did it. But Eliza sometimes came at him for his grammar. He had to accept that about her, it was just the way she was, got it from her mother, like she got everything else, her curly black hair, her freckles, her long legs, the way she squinted in bright sunlight and the way one of her feet was a half size bigger than the other. Sometimes if he looked at her too quickly now he could believe that Joanie was still alive.

If Eliza was there she would, after she fixed his grammar, laugh in that way she had, the way that made you want to laugh with her, and say something about how wasn't that always how it went, your hair behaved itself on the day you were going to get it cut.

Not that Eliza's hair ever behaved itself. Just like her mother's—just like Joanie's.

Last time pulling in at the wharf, turning off the truck, tucking the key under the passenger-side mat. Same damn spot every other lobsterman put the key to the truck—not so much a hiding place as it was an announcement. *Look at me. I belong here. And this is how we do things.*

"Thought you got yourself a sternman," said Josh Young, who was preparing to steam out at the same time. They climbed into their skiffs right near each other. "That guy from Ellsworth, you had him hauling with you. He quit on you?"

"Fired him."

"Yuh," said Josh, looking Charlie up and down. "I bet you did."

"That guy from Ellsworth was useless," said Charlie. He nodded and untied his skiff from the wharf, pushed off. Last time talking to Josh Young; no loss there. Over his shoulder he couldn't resist saying, "I do better on my own, you know how it is."

Josh grunted like he did know, but he didn't. That guy couldn't do a thing on his own, wouldn't dare go out for half a day without a sternman.

Last time rowing the skiff to the boat, mooring it, starting the boat's engine, heading out. The *Joanie B,* skeg-built, forty feet long, serviceable but not fancy, suitable for offshore later in the season.

Not this season, though.

Charlie Sargent knew every inch of this boat, knew it better than he knew any other forty-foot stretch in the universe. He knew the way the ignition stuck in really cold weather, and the way you had to jiggle the key real gently to get it going again. He knew the grooves marked in the floor of the wheelhouse from all those hours—days and weeks and months and years—of standing in the same spot. He knew the way you had to turn real easy when the wind was coming from the southwest because if you didn't the bow would fight back against you.

Last time steering around the buoys in the harbor, last sunrise, the sky filling up pink and orange with whites and blues right around the edges. Charlie Sargent was no poet and he wasn't a religious man but sometimes when he was out there on his boat with the wind lashing him and the colors of the sunrise spread out around him he felt a thump deep in his heart that made him want to be a little bit of both.

He turned the VHF on, tested it, turned it off again. A little farther out now, then a little more. But not too far. He came to a few of his own buoys, killed the engine, considering. Haul them, reset them, and send them back down? Didn't seem like there was much point in that. But to leave the work undone, that wasn't in his nature. That wasn't how Charlie Sargent operated.

Just a couple strings, maybe, just the ones right here. He wouldn't go beyond this area, though he had traps set all over. That would take all day and by then he'd lose his nerve, when there was no sense in that now:

already the thing was decided. Plus, he hadn't brought himself any lunch. Charlie's buoys were red and black and bright blue, he'd had those colors since he was a boy of sixteen, setting out in the old rattrap boat his father had let him use.

He reached over the starboard side with his gaff and his hook, grabbed the pot warp, pulled the line from the water to run it through the hauling block and into the hydraulic hauler. The line coiled itself on the deck below the hauler. The line strained, and the trap broke the surface. He broke that trap over the rail—okay, maybe that bastard Josh was right, maybe he could have used a sternman just then, because he was breathing heavy and his hands were shaking. He wasn't as strong as he used to be. Then the trailer traps, one after another, just three in this string, thank God, because it was a real struggle now to get them over.

But even so he did what he was supposed to do, what he'd been doing right along, since he was a boy of five, learning at his father's knee, and he unloaded the traps. Disappointing haul on this string. Not a keeper in the bunch. The first trap was empty, the second held a couple of crabs, and the third had three lobsters. One was too small, he could tell just by eyeballing—didn't even need his gauge. Two had undersides berried with eggs. Those had to go. He grabbed his V-notch and marked them, then tossed them over. "Off you go," he said. "Go out there and make your babies."

What was that little song Joanie used to sing to Eliza? *One baby two babies three babies four, you're the only one for me, it's you that I adore.*

Never made much sense to Charlie, but that didn't matter. Joanie could be reading a grocery list or a report from the traffic court in *The Ellsworth American* and Charlie would be all ears, drinking it up, like it was the sound of angels singing. Charlie had loved Joanie like that, with all of himself. To the ends of the earth and back. Not that he was given to talking that way. But he could think that way, sure. He could think it.

That was done, then. The sun was up, the sky a clear blue now with just traces of white around the edges. Not too foggy today, that was good. He looked around the *Joanie B* to see that everything was in order. He didn't like to think he'd leave anything sloppy behind for anyone else to deal with.

Something around his ankles, to make sure the job was done properly. He should have thought of that.

He remembered in eighty-five when that poor kid went over. Lucas Spaulding. Charlie had been a little bit younger than Lucas's dad, and Lucas was no more than eight or nine, just starting to learn the ways of it, out with his father and his uncle one morning. August, the height of a really good season, the traps practically hauling themselves. Right up to the guidelines they were that summer. That was the summer Charlie bought Joanie a new car, Eliza was six. It was a week before the Lobster Festival, the town about as lively as it ever got. And poor Lucas. Standing in the wrong place at the wrong time, the line looped around his ankles when the trap went over, so he went over with it. By the time they pulled him up his face was dead blue and his heart had clearly stopped beating. Better that way, almost, people said; if he'd come to, his brain would have been right ruined.

Jesus, he hadn't thought about Lucas Spaulding in ages. They canceled the Lobster Festival that year, and a bunch of summer people from the Point got all up in arms about that. Not that they could say anything *out loud,* so they whispered behind closed doors. But word got out. It always did.

He leaned over the stern and felt the water. Cold as all anything. *Jesus.* Well, he'd need something tight around his ankles, else it wouldn't work. He'd have something in the wheelhouse. Hell, he'd use one of his own traps if he had to. Wouldn't that be a kicker.

He remembered Lucas Spaulding's funeral, fishermen coming from as far away as Vinalhaven and Stonington. Charlie remembered the way Lucas's mother was sedated so bad she could hardly sit up in the pew, had to be propped there by one of her sisters. There were plenty of Spauldings to go around, back then, generations of them, but after that the whole group of them up and moved to Augusta. Away from the water. Landlocked themselves. Charlie didn't blame them a bit, he'd have done the same thing in their situation.

Now he hung over the stern even more, getting his arm wet all the way up to the elbow. It was practically numb already. How long would it take, to feel nothing?

And then, hell, his balance must have been off, everything was off, that goddamn dizziness. Because next thing he knew he'd flipped himself off the back of the stern, slamming his head on the transom on the way. And Jesus it was cold in that water, it was goddamn *freezing.*

He was expecting the cold. But the part he wasn't expecting was what happened next. Because even though Charlie Sargent knew exactly what he wanted, even though he knew exactly what he had set out to do that day, even though he was *already on his way to doing it,* at some point instinct took over. Same instinct (he would think later) that makes the choking woman push against the hands around her neck, the burning man try to snuff himself out. The instinct to undo what was being done.

When that took over, that's when Charlie brought his hands to the rail of the boat, found enough strength (from where? If he was a praying man he would have said it came from God himself) to pull himself up, up, then gracelessly back into the boat, where he lay on the deck, a heaving, shivering mass. Shaking so hard he thought his heart might stop from the force of it. One of his arms hurting like anything.

And a gash on his head—he felt for it with hands that were close to numb. Shit. Blood.

He pulled himself to his knees and the pain nearly blinded him, nearly knocked him right back down again. But he had to get to the VHF, all the way in the wheelhouse, so he forced himself to stumble there, where he took up the radio and switched it on. It defaulted to channel sixteen, same as always, dependable as the tides. He pressed the microphone button. He imagined for a second the kid getting the call in Southwest Harbor, some baby-faced twenty-year-old, barely out of training, uniform maybe a little too big on his skinny body.

More than fifty years on the water and Charlie Sargent had never needed to make a call like this. But now, the head. All that blood. No way he could drive like this. He choked out the words: "Mayday-mayday-mayday. This is Charlie Sargent, on the *Joanie B.*"

He'd never made the call, but he knew the protocol. *State the nature of your distress* was the next step.

Oh boy. Oh shit. The sun was now fully up, shining in his eyes like an insult. The nature of his distress? Too much distress to state, that was damn sure. "I have an injury to my head and I'm alone on the boat," he said finally. "I'll be listening on channel sixteen. This is Charlie Sargent on the *Joanie B,* over and out."

And in the end his body overrode his mind—he clung, after all, to life.

33

Eliza

Well, of *course* Judith knew somebody from some-committee-or-other who was staying for three weeks out on the Point and had an extra bedroom for Judith. *An* extra bedroom! The house had something like twelve bedrooms. Or eight bedrooms and twelve bathrooms. Eliza could never remember: the house was legend. This was the woman Judith had mentioned to her earlier in the summer, Gail Byron, no relation.

Eliza didn't even waste time being surprised about the coincidence; since she'd known Rob, she'd learned the basic tenet that money shrank the world and made it small and familiar. The opposite was also true: a lack of it made the world big and scary.

She was so excited to see the girls that she felt like somebody had blended her insides in a Vitamix. She sat on the front steps and waited until she saw Judith's silver BMW pull around the bend in the road and into the driveway.

Did Judith's BMW look natural pulling into Charlie Sargent's driveway? No, not even a little bit. That car looked about as natural on this side of Little Harbor as a banded Gila monster might look spreading out a beach towel in Santa Monica.

"My goodness," said Judith when she emerged from the driver's seat. "Isn't this just *charming*." She smiled. "I never realized, Eliza, how *picturesque* your hometown is."

Eliza squinted at Judith: Was she poking fun?

Judith smiled even more; she smiled so wide the lines around her eyes that had been dermatologically removed were almost visible.

No, Judith was trying. Judith was trying, and Eliza was a terrible daughter-in-law, trying to find fault where there was none.

Maybe this had been a bad idea, this visit. She was too shaken up and confused to be a good hostess or a good mother. She wouldn't be able to hide her father's deteriorating condition from her eagle-eyed girls. He'd exhaust himself, trying to pretend that everything was the same as it had always been.

Then Evie got out of the car and hugged Eliza so hard Eliza almost fell over, and Zoe got out of the car and gave Eliza an embrace that was about as enthusiastic and outwardly loving as Zoe's embraces got. Zoe wasn't looking at her phone—she wasn't even *holding* her phone—and her girls looked both so much the same and so totally different than they had the last time Eliza had seen them that her eyes got damp.

This was not a bad idea, this visit. This was a wonderful idea.

"Thank you, Judith," she said genuinely. "Thank you for doing this."

Judith waved a hand, and Eliza supposed that was her way of saying *You're welcome.*

"Where's Grandpa?" asked Evie immediately.

"He's upstairs, he's lying down," said Eliza.

Evie looked doubtful. "Grandpa doesn't lie down during the day," she said suspiciously.

Eliza's heart lurched and galloped. The girls knew *brain cancer,* but they didn't know *the very worst, mostly highly aggressive form of brain cancer.* "Sometimes he does," she said. "He was up late last night, he just got a little tired." They all knew Charlie Sargent was never up late. Nine o'clock was late, to Charlie!

"Well!" said Judith heartily. "Why don't I get the girls' stuff out of the car, and I'll let you all visit while I head to my accommodation. If you can just point me in the right direction, Eliza."

———

Zoe and Evie were in Little Harbor for three glorious days. One night they had dinner at The Lobster Trap, Charlie included. Zoe ate a lobster roll and Evie ordered steamed clams. Eliza ordered just a salad because she predicted correctly that Evie would never finish the clams. Judith had a lobster cake and the house specialty, a lobster Bloody Mary. Then a second. A third after that. Charlie ate next to nothing, but he ordered a burger he meant to eat, and that was something. One night, Eliza made chicken cutlets for everybody except for Evie, who ate yogurt. They played eleven games of Uno, fourteen games of War. They played five rounds of the Game of Life on Zoe's iPhone. Zoe checked her Instagram feed a total of thirty-one times, liked one hundred and seven photos, commented on seventeen. She posted three times herself, garnering seventy-five likes (her new record) on her photo of the lobster boats in the harbor with a spectacular blood-orange sunset behind them. Evie took one shower, reluctantly, and Zoe took four; Eliza had to rap on the door three of the four times to remind her that the hot water tank in this house was much smaller than it was at home. Evie mentioned one time that she was missing *Charlotte's Web* practice, but that it didn't matter, and Zoe made passing reference to a slumber party at Hannah Coogan's but then admitted that she really didn't care if she went or not. Charlie slept a lot and when he was awake he sat in his recliner and the girls sat next to each other on the sofa and watched him. When he wanted to talk they talked, and when he wanted to remain silent they remained silent, and overall they made Eliza proud.

There was one thing, though. It gave Eliza chills when she thought about it later, and forever after.

On the second evening Zoe was upstairs ("reading," she said, but Eliza knew that meant "texting") and Evie was in the living room with Charlie. Eliza was fiddling around in the kitchen, wiping down the refrigerator shelves, making a grocery list, when Evie came in.

"Grandpa just said the funniest thing," said Evie. Eliza realized later that she must have missed a clue in Evie's voice, a quaver. Maybe a hint of terror on her face.

"Oh yeah?" Eliza glanced up quickly, then back down at her shopping list. Eggs, definitely. Milk, maybe. "What'd he say?"

"He asked me if I could see the purple birds that were knitting little sweaters."

Eliza felt herself go all hot and then cold and then hot again. A hallucination, because of the tumor. Not uncommon. "Well, that's interesting," said Eliza carefully. "Birds can't knit."

"No," said Evie. "I don't think they can usually knit."

"What'd you say?" asked Eliza. She moved toward the living room, but not too fast, to keep from panicking Evie.

"I said I couldn't see them," said Evie. "And then he closed his eyes, and then I came in here." Her lip wobbled a little bit, the way it used to when she was a toddler.

Charlie was asleep, his head tipped back, his breathing slightly ragged.

"Okay," said Eliza brightly, falsely, returning to the kitchen. "I think Grandpa was just being silly, playing a little game with you."

"That's not Grandpa's kind of silly," said Evie accurately.

Eliza tried to steady her own voice, and she reached over and pulled Evie close to her, smoothing her hair. "No," she said. "No, it's not."

On the final evening, Judith and Gail Byron wanted to take the girls to dinner at the yacht club on the Point. Eliza, who had never, in her whole life, eaten at the yacht club on the Point, felt something within her shift uncomfortably at the suggestion.

"Of *course* you're welcome too," said Judith. "You and your father."

Eliza tried not to laugh in Judith's face at that, but it was difficult; the image was riotous. Sick or not, Charlie Sargent would rather eat a fistful of sandy lobster shells than put on a collared shirt (which he might or might not own) to eat at the yacht club with the summer people. He'd do The Lobster Trap, because of the girls, but he'd draw a hard line at the yacht club. Eliza was trying not to be rude, so she demurred politely and said Charlie was tired. She told her daughters to put on sundresses and she sent them on their way.

It was arranged that Eliza would pick up the girls when dinner was over so Judith didn't have to drive them back. (This was Eliza's idea, to prevent Judith from tipsily piloting her BMW down the Point's winding road.) As she drove to the club, she lowered the window and breathed in the truly excellent summer air. There really was something about it—it was as if the fog that rolled in almost every night had its very own texture. You breathed it in, of course, but you also absorbed it through your very pores, and somehow you felt cleaner for it. It was a magical time of night, a bit past twilight but not quite dark, and she could see figures on the porch of one of the big summerhouses; she could practically hear the ice tinkling in the glasses and smell the limes from the gin and tonics.

She got to the club early and stood silently near a small window that looked into the dining room where the girls were finishing dinner with Judith and Gail Byron. The table was clear of dishes; the women were drinking coffee, and Evie and Zoe had glasses in front of them with what looked like the dregs of Shirley Temples. Each girl still had a napkin on her lap and Evie was telling a story that involved lots of gesticulating.

Everybody at the table had a head tipped back in what looked like genuine laughter. From the get-go, from the time she'd said her first word (*pajamas*—three syllables!) at eighteen months, Evie had known how to tell a story.

But there was something else that made Eliza's heart stagger and wobble along in that particular way. Standing there in the dark, an outsider in the literal sense of the word, practically trampling on the hydrangea bushes that circled the building, she had to wait for a moment to figure it out.

Yes, here it was.

Her children were utterly comfortable and at ease at that table, in Eliza's own hometown, in a place she'd never been as a guest and wouldn't have known what to do if she had been. Her children knew which fork to use for shrimp cocktail! While deep down Eliza was still the scrappy kid she'd been at their ages: riding around on lobster boats, baiting traps, biting her nails, refusing to comb her hair, dirty hands, dirty feet, dirty mouth. Her children were wise and funny and tender and they'd probably end up teaching Eliza way more than she'd ever be able to teach them. Which was comforting, but also really, really vexing.

The next day, as Eliza helped Judith and the girls pack their things into the BMW, Judith said, "I wish you could have talked Rob out of his decision."

Eliza said, "Huh?" Then she corrected herself and said, "Excuse me?"

"He said it was both of you, but I'm sure he was at the helm. So to speak."

"I'm sorry, Judith, I—"

"The money," said Judith, her voice lightly tinted with exasperation. "As I told him, I planned to head right into some investments that make the bulk of it inaccessible. Which I have since done. And I just hope it was the right decision for all of you." She raised one eyebrow at Eliza. She had always heard that this was a genetic talent. Eliza couldn't remember if her mother had it. If so, she hadn't passed it on: Eliza couldn't do it.

Eliza said, "I'm confused."

"*Oh*," said Judith, and she put the eyebrow back down again and considered Eliza. "Oh, I'm sorry, I thought Rob said the two of you had decided together—"

"Decided what together?"

"My goodness, will you look at the time? Say goodbye to your mother, girls, we've got a drive ahead of us, and I want to get on the road."

And just like that, Eliza was hugged and kissed and left standing all alone in the driveway of her father's house.

34

Eliza

Later that day, when Eliza was talking on the phone to Rob, confirming that the girls had made it home safely, she remembered Judith's cryptic comments about money. "She said that she hoped it was the right decision? What did she mean by that?"

Rob cleared his throat, and said, in a way that caused Eliza to shift uncomfortably in the straight-backed kitchen chair in which she sat, "I don't know if we have time to go into that right now."

"I've got plenty of time." Her father had gone upstairs. He was tired again, always tired.

What had Eliza been doing in April, when Charlie was diagnosed? Worrying herself silly over Phineas Tarbox, avoiding signing those stupid papers, shuttling the girls to and from their activities, planning her *herb garden*? Drinking margaritas at Don Pepe's with the ladies on Tuesdays? What was she doing in the weeks, maybe months, before that, when the tumor was first forming, the nefarious collection of cells banding together, intent on their evil mission? *We will get you, Charlie Sargent. You don't know we're here, but we know. We know, and we're coming, and we're not going away.*

She'd taken the keys to his truck. She'd bring him some supper in a while, see if he felt like eating a little bit, but until then she had nothing to do. She said, "Do you have somewhere to be?"

Rob made a whistling sound, a quick exhalation, which signaled to Eliza that his nerves were on edge, and then he started talking. He told Eliza about the changes he'd experienced right around his fortieth birthday in the spring, about his newborn desire to support his family solely on his income, about his personal declaration of independence from a martini-infused, pre-*Pippin* Judith one night in Boston. He told Eliza about Judith's reaction, and about what Judith had told him regarding the money that usually went to Eliza and Rob—that if he was sure, if he was really, *really* certain, Judith was going to put it in an investment that her financial adviser, Bucky, recommended very highly, and which would make the money completely inaccessible until Judith's death. He ended by saying, "I should have told you, Eliza."

"Should have *told* me? What do you mean, *told me*? Never mind that you should have told me, shouldn't we have decided this together?"

Rob hesitated, and then he said, "I wanted to surprise you. I know it's always bothered you, how much we take from my mother."

She let the weight of that settle around her: that was true. "Well, of course it's bothered me," she said. "You know that. But don't we *need* it?"

"As soon as Cabot Lodge is done and I get the next job—"

"Then, what? As soon as that, what?" She felt a rising sense of panic.

"We'll be fine."

"We will?" She realized then the extent of her ignorance about their finances. How much would Rob make from Cabot Lodge, and how much from the next job? How much, exactly, did they get from Judith each month? She didn't know. Stupid, stupid of her: she didn't know.

"For a while."

"And then what?"

"And then I'll get another job after that, and make more money from that job too. Like . . . well, like a regular person. Like a person without a safety net."

Eliza was quiet, and Rob hurried to fill the space her silence left. "I *will* get another job, Eliza. Mrs. Cabot has all of these friends, and they all want houses, and you know how they are, those ladies, each one will want one bigger than the last one. Cabot Lodge will look like a cottage compared to what's coming. I just have to nail this job first. I have to nail Cabot Lodge, and then I'll be golden."

At another time, in another conversation, Eliza might have said, *Nail Cabot Lodge. No pun intended, right?* But now, in the present circumstances, she whispered the next part, like it was a secret: "But Rob. Our life is *really expensive.*"

As soon as she said that Eliza sensed a reordering of the conversation, and when Rob spoke she heard a tightening in his voice. "You know what? I'm surprised, Eliza. I thought you'd be on board with this. I thought you'd be . . . proud."

"If you thought I'd be on board," she said, "if you thought I'd be proud, why'd you keep it a secret?"

"I told you! I wanted to surprise you!"

Eliza felt a dread, long latent but still familiar, rise in her throat. How were they going to pay the girls' school tuition? The club fees, the mooring fees for the Hinckley? Even the electric and gas bills for a house the size of theirs, the grocery bills, the upkeep on the pool—Judith's money paid for *so much* of their existence. "Well, mission accomplished," she said, more nastily than she wanted to. "I'm surprised."

One great shame that would chase Eliza for a long, long time was not any of those words but the feeling underneath the words: that even with cancer clawing its way through her dad's brain, and with the past beating on her head like an anvil, and with regret gnawing at her insides, the idea of returning to a place where lack of money was a constant worry, a constant potential source of embarrassment, sat somewhere between dismaying and horrifying.

Rob: "You always said you didn't care about the money. But from the way you're reacting I can see that you cared, Eliza. You care now."

"Not in the way you think."

"But in some way."

"Yeah," she said finally. "In some way." He had her: it was true. She'd come so far from that girl in her freshman dorm room, counting out how many packages of ramen noodles she had left, pretending she bought her jeans from the vintage clothing store on Federal Hill because it was trendy, not because she needed to, saying no thank you to a night out because she didn't have even the dollars for dollar-draft night. Not allowing herself to think about the student loans piling up on top of each other.

She didn't want to go back; she didn't want to be that girl again.

"Well, I'm sorry I disappointed you."

And then, for the second time that summer, and also for the second time in the entire time she'd known him, Rob hung up on Eliza.

For some minutes after that Eliza wallowed pretty comfortably in her pool of self-righteousness. Rob should have told her, they should have talked about it before he went to Judith. It wasn't right that he hadn't, it wasn't fair!

She tried to banish the girl with the noodles, the motherless child with the tangled hair and the lobster traps and the chicken cutlets bought in a twelve-pack on sale at Dave's Shop 'n' Save, the girl who'd absorbed everything around her at Brown, always sitting back carefully, cautiously, in case someone noticed her and called her out for what she was: a fraud.

But the girl wouldn't go away. No matter what Eliza did or how she turned the situation over in her mind, the girl wouldn't go away.

———

Twenty-two minutes later, not that Eliza was watching the clock, Rob called back. "Don't hang up on me," she said, and to her own ear her voice sounded high and tight and not like hers at all. "Ever again. That's not what we do, that's not how we are!"

"I'm sorry, Eliza," he said. "You're right, you are. I never should have made that decision without you. We should have talked to my mother together."

Eliza swallowed hard, and said, "I wish we had."

After Brown, that same girl, grown into a woman, always watching before doing, always trying to understand, to learn, so that she wouldn't make any shameful mistakes that would reveal her. Those college loans had been such a burden on her, driving her nearly into the ground, and the two years of medical school on top of that. Judith's lifting of that weight, an easy gesture for her, merely a tiny fraction of her wealth, had felt like the lifting of a hundred bricks from Eliza's shoulders. She'd liked being able to offer money, to her dad, even to Russell; she'd liked the feeling of being able to say, "Go ahead, get this treatment, fix that boat, buy that drink, that dinner, whatever you want, I can pay for it."

She couldn't explain all of that to Rob, not right then, not over the phone—she wasn't even sure she could completely explain it to herself.

Then Rob said something surprising. He said, "Eliza. We talk all the time about how hard it was for you growing up without a mother."

She felt herself start to bristle. Of course she talked about it! Her mother's death was the defining event of her life: it had made her who she was, and it had also made her who she wasn't. She said, "But—"

"*No,*" said Rob. "Don't talk, Eliza. Don't interrupt. Just listen. Listen to me."

Meekly, chastened, she said, "Okay, I'm listening."

"We talk all the time about how hard it was for you growing up without a mother," Rob repeated, and Eliza remained silent. "But we hardly ever talk about what it was like for me, growing up without a dad."

He paused, and the weight of what he was saying covered Eliza like a lead vest. Rob went on. "Nobody showed me how to work hard, how to be a good provider. I'm trying to figure it out on my own here. The only thing I ever learned from my parents about money was that it was something to fight about. A bargaining chip, in a shitty, shitty game." Rob was right. He never talked about his dad; *they* never talked about his dad. She had always figured that because of the difference in their circumstances— her mother had been an angel, and she died, and hadn't wanted to, and Rob's father had been a bastard, and had left, and *had* wanted to—she was allowed to feel more pain than he was. After all, Robert Barnes I had deserted the family, had taken up with another woman, had begun a whole new life on the other side of the world. But now Eliza saw that that was such a grossly entitled way to look at things. Robert Barnes I chose Thailand and Malai, but he also *didn't choose* his son and his first wife; he chose *not-Rob* over Rob. Eliza's heart ached for Rob: suddenly, almost violently. She said, "You're right, we don't. It's not fair. I'm sorry."

There was a long silence. Finally Rob said, "Thank you, Eliza." His voice cracked on her name. Then, to his credit, and with the perennial optimism she'd always loved about him, he tried again. "At least one of Mrs. Cabot's friends will come through, I'm sure of it. There's one woman, Nadine Edwards, she's practically committed already."

Eliza could still hear a wobble in Rob's voice, and the molecules rearranged themselves again and she softened further. Here he was, her husband, a guy just trying, like everyone else. She blinked at the kitchen wall, where she could see the faint marks that measured her yearly growth from the time she could stand until her mother had died—they'd let the habit drop after that. The doorbell rang, but Eliza didn't want to risk dropping the cell connection by walking to the front door—the signal was much stronger in the kitchen—so she ignored it. It must be Val; she'd call her later, or, if she felt like it, Val would come in without an invitation. "Of course," said Eliza. "Of *course* they'll come through. Of course it will be okay. You're a talented architect."

"Even though I just draw the pictures?"

She took a deep breath and made herself acknowledge how much she'd hurt him with those words, how fraught they'd been, and how she'd known they were harmful when she'd said them, and how she'd said them anyway. "*Especially* because you draw the pictures, Rob. Especially. Without the pictures, there'd be nothing to build, right?"

A sigh of relief traveled over the cellular waves, binding them together in a way they hadn't seemed bound in a long time: because of Charlie's illness, because of Eliza's long absences over the course of the summer, because life was hard and marriage was complicated and there was really no such thing as smooth sailing.

"Rob?"

"Yeah?" His voice sounded rough. She took several seconds before she spoke again.

"I think it's a really good idea," she said finally. "We *should* be independent. I agree with you. It's the right thing."

"Thank you. Thank you, Eliza. I won't let us down."

"Anyway," said Eliza. "I guess if something crazy happens and Cabot Lodge blows up—"

"Don't even say that."

"I don't mean *literally,* like goes up in flames—"

"Even so."

"I mean, if things don't go the way you're expecting, which I understand is a Very Big If, I guess we can always sell the Hinckley."

"Don't say that either. Take it back."

"I'm kidding," she said. "Of course."

"Still." His voice was strained. He was such a believer in jinxes and superstitions: he always picked up pennies, never walked under ladders, didn't allow open umbrellas inside. It was one of the first things she'd found endearing about him. Forget about black cats: he'd cross three streets to avoid one. And, of course, there was the irreplaceable ten-baht. "Take it back," he said, and then, more gently, "Please."

"Okay," she said, "I take it back."

Then Rob said, "Eliza—" and before he could say more three things happened. The doorbell rang again. She heard the front door open and Russell's voice call out, "Hello? Anybody home?"

And, at almost exactly the same time, from upstairs, an awful noise, a clunk, and then a sort of awful roll, which could only mean one thing, and that was that Charlie Sargent had hit the floor.

35

LITTLE HARBOR, MAINE

Mary

"Mary! Mary, over here!" A familiar voice, one of those out-of-context voices that took a few seconds to recognize. Mary had her hand on the door handle of A Cut Above, but she turned when she heard her name and saw her twelfth-grade math teacher making her way down the sidewalk. Ms. Berry was holding a leash, and attached to the leash was a German shepherd: this must be the famous William. "Mary!" said Ms. Berry. She and William were both panting a little bit by the time they got to her.

Mary said hello, and then she crouched down to pet William. She had always wanted a dog, but Vivienne wouldn't allow it; she was fake-allergic.

"I'm glad I ran into you, Mary. I've been thinking about you."

"You have?"

"I have. I've been wondering what you're doing with yourself." Mary waited, figuring that Ms. Berry would go on. She did. "You have such a good math head on your shoulders. I was disappointed to learn that you hadn't applied to Orono."

"Oh," said Mary. The University of Maine, Orono campus. "Well. Things got complicated."

Ms. Berry had a broad face that was more tan now than it had been during the school year. When she smiled, you could see that one of her bottom teeth crossed a little bit over another one. Her hair was frizzy—frizzier probably because of the heat. She had kind watery blue eyes and a soft voice. Beside her, William whined gently, and she held two fingers up to him, and he quieted immediately.

"Of course, it's fine to take some time off—in fact, I believe it's sort of trendy these days—but too much time off and you might forget how to think." She looked shrewdly at Mary, and Mary got the feeling that Ms. Berry was looking through her, all the way into the center of her uterus.

"Right," said Mary.

"My advice is to keep up with your studies, even informally. There are math sites all over the internet that can keep you fresh. Send me an email, why don't you, and I'll send you back a list."

"Okay," said Mary. "Sure, okay, I will." She patted William one last time.

Math. Here was the math Mary had recently done. Google told her that the cost of raising a child was approximately $245,340 from birth until age eighteen. Mary made twelve dollars an hour at The Cup, in cash, which was very generous, considering that minimum wage was $7.50. Still, she'd have to work twenty thousand four hundred and forty-five hours in the next eighteen years to make that much, which was one thousand one hundred and thirty-five hours per year, which was twenty-one and eight-tenths hours per week. And that was just to pay for the baby, not for Mary herself, not for somebody to watch the baby while she made the money to pay for the baby. If she ever wanted to live anywhere but her mother's house (and of course she did) she'd have to pay for that too. Then she had looked up the cost of child care, which ranged between eight and twenty dollars per hour for an infant.

Mary was a whiz at math, always had been, but these numbers just didn't add up.

Almost twelve weeks. At twelve weeks the baby would be the size of a lime; soon, the baby would feel it if she poked her own tummy, very gently. When Mary opened the door to A Cut Above she didn't see Vivienne. Two of Vivienne's coworkers, Megan and Chelsea, were huddled over the computer. There was a girl she didn't know sweeping. In another chair, in Vivienne's station, a woman with foil-wrapped hair sat looking down at a celebrity magazine.

"Giiiiiirl!" said Chelsea. "Your mom didn't tell us you were coming by!"

Mary shrugged. "I didn't tell her."

Megan slid around from behind the counter and hugged Mary. When she was done hugging she lifted a lock of her hair and said, "I *knew* it! You came in to try the balayage, didn't you?" Balayage was some sort of special highlights Vivienne was always going on about. "Finally. I've been waiting for you to say the word. Let me do it, okay? You have to let me do it."

Chelsea was looking at Mary and squinting. "You should totally try it, Mary, you'll love it."

"Totally," said Megan. "*Totally*. A little golden brown right through here . . ." She reached out and stroked Mary's hair. "You'll think it's going to darken you but I'm not even kidding, it will lighten you right up—"

"I'm not here to get my hair done," said Mary, as kindly as she could.

"Oh," said Chelsea.

"*Oh*," said Megan. "Okay." They both looked completely crestfallen, but in short order they went back to what they had been doing on the computer, going over the next day's appointments. At that point the woman with the foil highlights turned around and Mary saw that it was Vivienne's friend Sam. At the same time Mary recognized Sam, Sam recognized Mary.

"Mary!" said Sam with genuine enthusiasm. Sam was the only one of her mother's friends Mary really liked talking to. Sam and Vivienne had been inseparable in high school, and since then Sam had gone about things the expected, acceptable way—she'd waited to get married until she was twenty-seven, and she'd gotten pregnant after, and now she had an adorable five-year-old boy named Stephen and a two-year-old girl named Penelope, who was called Penny for short. Sam worked as an intensive care nurse at Maine Coast Memorial and part-time as a home health aide for the elderly. Before Mary started at The Cup she had sometimes babysat for Stephen and Penny.

"Your mom's in the back," Sam said. "Sorting out orders or something." Mary nodded. Ordering the products and tracking the sales were part of Vivienne's job, her least favorite part. "She's been after me forever to do something with my hair, so here I am," said Sam.

"You too?"

"Yup." Sam frowned in the mirror. "I told her I don't have time for any upkeep, so that's what I'm worried about."

Sam indicated that Mary should sit in the chair next to her, and she closed the magazine and leaned forward to put it on the table that held Vivienne's combs and scissors and hair straightener and curling wand and all the mysterious bottles and potions that helped Vivienne work her magic. When she was younger, Mary used to love to come in and pretend to use the products and twirl around on the chairs. Now, though, she didn't feel like twirling or using the products. She just felt like sitting.

"How's Penny?" asked Mary, once she was settled. "How's Stephen?"

Sam had asked Mary to babysit for Stephen and Penny twice early in the summer, but once she was working and the second time she had plans with Josh. Now that she thought about it, she hadn't always loved babysitting. There was that time, for example, when Penny, who was supposed to be napping, screamed in her crib for twenty-five solid minutes while Stephen made a tic-tac-toe board in red crayon on the kitchen floor and Mary ran between the two of them, not sure who to tend to first. Sam had said not to worry if Penny had trouble settling down for her nap, but this seemed beyond having trouble settling down.

Mary had been at her wit's end, but when Sam got home from work she had simply popped Penny's pacifier back in her mouth (Mary had tried that, but Penny had spit it heartily out each time) and had Stephen sit for two minutes in a straight-backed kitchen chair while she sprayed cleaner on the kitchen floor. The crayon had come right off, and Stephen had accepted his punishment uncomplainingly, even stoically. Sam hadn't even seemed aggravated with Mary for letting things get into such a state.

How did mothers *know* these things? How did they do it? How was *Mary* going to be able to do it?

Sam used her forefinger to make the universal symbol for *nutso*. "It's the usual at my house," she said. Sam's husband worked construction. They lived in a pretty little house that was within walking distance to downtown Ellsworth, and Sam even found time to make gourmet cupcakes that she sold to a bakery on Main Street. Sam was the opposite of Vivienne in almost every way. Sometimes Mary wondered how it was that they were still friends. ("Habit," Vivienne had said once when Mary asked.)

"How's the hospital?"

Under the black robe that the customers at A Cut Above put on while they got their hair cut and colored it looked like Sam was still wearing her navy-blue scrubs. She was definitely wearing her nursing clogs, which were also navy blue but had lighter blue flowers all over them. Sam always told Mary she'd make a good nurse. She was calm in a crisis, Sam said, with a good head on her shoulders. Of course, that was before that day with the crayons and the crying.

"Not the best day," said Sam. "We lost a patient." Sam had little purple half-moons under her eyes, and her skin looked pale.

"Oh! I'm sorry," said Mary. She couldn't imagine what that was like, being around sickness and death all the time. She'd never seen a dead person before; she'd definitely never seen anyone *die*. She thought Sam was wrong: she'd make a terrible nurse.

"That's okay," said Sam. "She was old, and really frail. And then pneumonia got her." She shrugged. "She was ready. Just yesterday, she told me she was ready. Her kids knew she was ready. Her husband's been gone for three and a half years. If you ask me, the body hangs on way past the point it should sometimes."

"Yeah," said Mary.

"It always takes something out of you, though, you know. Watching a life end."

Mary was quiet; she didn't know what to say to that, but she tried to look sympathetic and understanding.

"I tell my husband all the time that when it's my turn to go he'd better slip me something nice and peaceful and sit there with me. Not that that's legal in Maine, not even for doctors to do it, but I could tell you stories and stories about how it should be. Man, I could tell you stories." She rubbed her eyes and studied herself in the mirror and said, "Boy, who's a downer today? I'm sorry, Mare. I'll try and shake it."

"You don't have to," said Mary. "I don't mind." She thought about the conversation with Charlie in The Cup, the night he'd saved her from Josh, about the accident on his boat not being an accident at all. She thought about the way he'd told her, his fingers tapping on the table in a sort of rhythm. Not panicked. In fact, he'd been calm, like he was telling a story about someone else, someone he didn't know very well. He'd apologized to her too, just as Sam had now, and Mary had said the same thing to him: *I don't mind.* She didn't; she hadn't. She thought of it as a sort of honor.

Now, in the salon, she picked up the magazine and flipped through it. There was a whole section on summer reads. The photo showed a few books with beachy covers and women staring out into perfect blue-green oceans. Unrealistic, if you lived in Maine, where the water was too cold to swim in and most of the beaches were rocky and uninviting. People came from forever away to summer here anyway. They lapped up the lobster meat and the blueberries and the glimpses of the ocean through the native firs.

Sam said, "I wonder if these highlights are going to make me look as good as nine hours of straight sleep would." She pulled the skin under her eyes down with two fingers and made a face. Then she turned to Mary and said, "So, listen. Your mom told me, about you." She looked significantly toward Mary's stomach.

Inside, Mary fumed. The news wasn't Vivienne's to tell. Mary stared hard at the counter with the hairbrushes and the scissors.

"You okay, kid?" Sam's voice sounded the way it did when Penny had a fever and Sam was trying to get her to take some Tylenol. Mary felt like Sam was stroking her forehead with her voice.

"Yeah," she said. "I'm okay."

Sam leaned toward her and lowered her voice. "You sure you're doing things the way you want to? Anyone pressure you to make choices that weren't your own?"

"Nobody's pressuring me," said Mary. "I'm sure."

"And the father—?"

"Gone," said Mary. "Left town." Mary had heard that Josh had moved out without paying July's rent, which he was late on anyway. He'd packed up most of his belongings—he'd taken the flat-screen TV, his landlord had said—and he'd disappeared. His boat was gone from the harbor, and his buoys were nowhere to be seen.

"That's what I thought." Sam nodded firmly. "That's what Vivienne said. And that's—what, a good thing? A bad thing?"

"A good thing," repeated Mary. She didn't tell Sam anything else. She didn't tell her that sometimes she woke up in the middle of the night, startled by an image of Josh with his hand on her shoulder. She didn't tell Sam that sometimes she thought about what might have happened if Charlie Sargent hadn't come by at just the right time, and she didn't tell Sam about the posters in the clinic that showed the pregnant woman with the bruises on her arms. She didn't tell Sam about the brown paper bag in her closet that Josh had never come back for, and her middle-of-the-night fear that Josh would come looking for her, looking for the baby, looking for the paper bag, and that there'd be nobody around to help her.

Well, she'd do whatever it took. Whatever that might be. She was capable of things people didn't even realize. *She was capable of a lot.*

Sam said, "Mary?" and Mary had the feeling that Sam was going to get into things a little deeper, that she had *real questions* for Mary, but then

Vivienne came out and said, "Hey, look who's here!" She was wiping her hands on the apron she wore for hair coloring, and she was sucking on a mint. "Come here, baby girl. Did you finally come in to try some of that balayage?"

Mary sighed. "I don't need balayage, Mom."

"Then what do you need?" Vivienne peered at Mary's face. "Brow wax? Just a little off the top of the left one—"

"*No.*"

Then the rage and hurt and resentment and—*yes!*—the fear bubbled to the surface, and while what Mary said next surprised her, it also made her feel good, and satisfied, and self-righteous. She said, "I need a mom."

All eyes were on Vivienne and Mary: Sam's and Megan's and Chelsea's.

Mary felt like something had loosened inside of her, and words came out all in a rush. "I'm all alone with this! I don't have any help and I don't have any money and I'm scared to death and I just want you to help me. I don't want you to wax my eyebrows or cut my hair or my nails, I just want you to be a *mom,* and I just want someone to tell me everything is going to be okay even if it's not. I need to hear everything is going to be okay. Okay? *I just need a mom.*"

"Oh, for Christ's sake, Mary, don't be so *dramatic.*" Vivienne's eyes were flashing. "You have a mom. You have a mom right here. I'm sorry if I'm a shitty mom, but I'm the one you got stuck with. And guess what? I wish I could promise you everything is going to be okay, but I can't, because I may be a lot of things but I'm not a liar. And being a single mom is no picnic. I should know."

Suddenly the silence in the shop was so aggressive that you could have heard a bobby pin drop.

Later that night, when Vivienne got home, long after Mary did, she knocked on Mary's bedroom door. Mary didn't answer, pretending to be asleep. When she opened the door—Mary would have locked it, but the lock had been broken forever and then some—Mary lay very still. She could feel Vivienne standing in the doorway for a long, long time, and then Mary heard her whisper, *I'm sorry, Mare,* and she stood there even after that, but Mary didn't move, because she was sad and she was mad and she was scared and one stupid sorry wasn't enough.

She willed Vivienne to leave, but instead Vivienne sat on the edge of the bed and she brushed Mary's hair back from her forehead. Mary could tell Vivienne had been drinking because she could smell some kind of sweet liquor on her breath and when she started talking her words were a little slurry. She said, "I'm sorry, Mary. I'm sorry I didn't do better. I wanted to do better. I wish I had done better. I never wanted to be all alone doing this, never. It's hard, honey, it's really, really hard. It's not what I wanted for you, that's all. It's not what I ever wanted for you."

Then she started to cry softly, and a tear landed right on Mary's cheek and Mary had to try really hard not to wipe it away. She fought the urge, and she fought it some more, until finally she felt Vivienne's weight shift off the bed and she heard the door open and then close again.

The next morning, at home, Mary lay on her bed and touched her stomach. If the baby could feel a *gentle poke,* then couldn't it feel—ugh. She couldn't let herself finish the thought. Thirteen weeks and six days, that was the deadline.

Eliza had done it, and look her now, *look at her now.*

She called the number in Bangor. She wrote the date and the time on the wall calendar in her room. August 3rd, ten o'clock in the morning. She'd be eighteen that day; she wouldn't need any forms, she wouldn't need anyone's permission. But she'd have to get a ride. She'd have to take the day off from work.

36

LITTLE HARBOR, MAINE

Eliza

It was only once they were talking to the ER doc, a middle-aged Korean woman with long, tapered fingers and a calm, kind manner and a name tag that read DR. KWANG that Charlie mentioned the odd, not unpleasant, déjà-vu-like feeling that he'd experienced right before he'd fallen from the bed. Not quite a smell, but almost; not a memory, but sort of.

"An aura," said Eliza and Dr. Kwang at the same time, and Dr. Kwang

explained to Charlie, "An aura sometimes precedes a seizure, and sei-
zures appear in approximately sixty percent of patients with occipital
glioblastoma multiforme." When Charlie looked at Dr. Kwang blankly
Eliza said, "That's what your tumor is called, remember, Dad?"

"Fancy name for a tumor," said Charlie.

Dr. Kwang looked at Charlie's chart and frowned, and then she looked
at Eliza, and then Eliza asked if she could speak with her privately for a
moment, and in the hallway Eliza told her everything, quickly, efficiently,
the way she'd learned to speak back in med school. Dr. Kwang's expression was inscrutable; she nodded, and they went back into the room,
where Charlie was waiting.

Dr. Kwang cleared her throat and met Charlie's eyes directly and said,
"You understand, Mr. Sargent, that without treatment your condition will
continue to deteriorate, most likely rapidly. I'll write you a prescription
for antiseizure medication, but that won't have any effect on the growth
of the tumor itself."

Charlie nodded and didn't look at Eliza. "Yes," he said. "I do understand that." Eliza watched again as the doctor wrote *Comfort care
measures only* on the chart, and then she wrote out a prescription for
antiseizure medication, and she handed it to Eliza with a look of genuine
compassion in her eyes, and then she shook Charlie's hand and said,
"Best of luck, Mr. Sargent."

Eliza had heard one of the nurses talking about a three-car accident
on the road to Bar Harbor, and in the waiting room she'd seen one weepy
child who'd sprained her ankle slipping from a rock near Otter Cliff and a
man who had presented with classic food poisoning symptoms. She knew
Dr. Kwang was busy and that she had to move on, but even so she wished
the doctor could stay there until Eliza had the chance to pull her aside
once more and say, *Please. Fix him. Whatever it takes.*

She led her father back to the waiting room, where Russell was sitting
on a gray chair and thumbing through a *People* magazine, and for the
first time she noticed that he was wearing very un-Russell-like clothes, a
collared shirt and jeans that looked almost new.

They stopped at the pharmacy to fill the prescription for antiseizure
meds, and then, soon enough, they were on their way back to Little Harbor, Eliza driving, Russell beside her, and Charlie stretched out in the
backseat of Rob's Audi, his eyes closed.

They rode for a long, long time in silence, and after a while Eliza said, "Thank you for coming with me, Russell," and he said, "Of course," and after that they were silent again and Eliza thought about how with strangers or casual acquaintances you always felt like you had to keep the conversation moving with useless chatter, but with someone you'd once known very, very well—even if that was a long time ago—you could just be quiet, and that was okay.

Back home, Eliza woke Charlie gently and with Russell's help she got him upstairs and into his bed. He closed his eyes again almost immediately, and Russell and Eliza tiptoed down the stairs, and somehow it was only then that Eliza remembered to ask Russell what he'd been doing at Charlie's house in the first place. Was he there to continue their recent argument?

"Oh," said Russell. "That, yeah. Forgot all about it." He looked uneasy.

"What?" said Eliza.

"Some of the guys were talking about maybe splitting up Charlie's traps to haul them. But we need Marine Patrol to sign off on that, so I wanted to ask him."

Maybe that was what made it seem more dire than anything had, and she felt her face crumple, and she said, "I'm scared, Russell. I'm really scared."

"I know," he said. "I know."

Eliza didn't mean to lean against him, but she had to lean against something, and he was there. He put his arms around her and that felt like a gift, to have someone to cry against. She cried, and she sniffled, and she gulped, and she stayed there longer than maybe was strictly appropriate because it felt so nice just to lean on someone, just to be held.

"I'm sorry," she said, finally pulling away.

"That's okay."

"You look nice. You have a date?" She had been sort of joking, because she wasn't sure who in Little Harbor would be available for Russell to date, but Russell nodded seriously and said, "Maybe."

She sniffled and realized there was a wet spot on his shirt now. She said, "You do? A *date*? Who with?"

"Don't worry about it." He smiled. "Nobody you know."

She squinted at him. "Summer person?"

He shrugged.

"Not a local. Right?"

He shrugged again.

"Make sure you dry off your shirt first."

"I will."

"I hope it's a summer person. I hope she's stinking rich, and I hope you marry her and she pays to fix that reverse gear on your boat."

He laughed. "Don't worry about my reverse gear. I'll worry about that."

"Actually, if she's stinking rich, you won't have to haul anymore."

"Right," he snorted, and put his hands in his pockets and rocked back on his heels and they stared at each other for a long moment and just like that the years passed between them and the electric jolts from earlier in the summer turned into something else, nostalgia, history; they crossed all of the lines, slid into the past. Then Russell cleared his throat and said, "Listen, I'll come by tomorrow, talk to your dad then, okay? About the traps. If he's feeling like it. You let me know."

Eliza's throat clotted with the words she could have said. She didn't say, *I'm sorry for all the things that happened.* She didn't say, *I'm sorry for all the things that didn't happen.* She didn't say, *I'm sorry for the stupid things I said at the café.* She didn't even say, *I'm sorry I cried on your shirt.* This was because she was a native: she knew to show her emotions through actions instead of words, so she grasped Russell's hand and she squeezed it and he squeezed back. And even though she knew she'd see him again it felt solid and right, like the perfect goodbye.

"I hope you have a nice date, Russell," she said. "I mean it. And thank you, for today."

"Anytime, Liza. You know that." She held the door open for him and he gave a little wave after he went through it and then he sauntered off, taking a little bit of her heart with him. But not the most important part. And anyway, the heart is a renewable resource. Even people who didn't go to medical school know that.

37

Rob

Zoe and Evie did not want to drive up to Long Lake with Rob, but Christine Cabot had requested an in-person, on-site meeting, and Rob put his parental foot down, insisting that the girls go with him.

"We just got back from Maine!" they said. "We've been in the car *so much!*" They could stay alone, they said; they'd be nice to each other, they'd stay off their screens. They'd play board games! That usually got Eliza, the promise of playing board games. Eliza ate that stuff up. But Rob wanted the girls with him. The last time he'd left them alone for the whole day, the time he'd gone to look at the new floor tiles, he'd come home to find a dollop of peanut butter on the living room rug, popcorn kernels in the bathtub, and Zoe napping with the door to her room closed while Evie sat in a chair by the pool, getting lavishly sunburned and reading a young adult novel that very likely contained teenage sex. They were not to be trusted.

"We can stay with Deirdre!" Zoe said. "She won't mind, I know she won't."

"Deirdre never minds," inserted Evie unhelpfully.

"Nope," said Rob, shifting uncomfortably. "I've already decided. Let's go, ladies." He opened the car door. "If it helps, I can guarantee that there will be ice cream involved at some point during the day."

———

In the category of pleasant surprises, the girls got along famously both on the car ride and once they arrived at Cabot Lodge, and, admittedly, Rob felt some stirrings of pride when he pulled up in front of the lot and was able to show them what he'd been working on all spring and summer. If he burst an ulcer before all was said and done, at least they'd have a visual of the cause.

When Rob introduced them to Mrs. Cabot they shook her hand solemnly and firmly and inserted *please*s and *thank you*s in all the right places. His heart swelled: his daughters were doing their best for him. They were trying. And because they were trying, he didn't complain when they began to walk around in the mud pit that a recent rainfall had been kind enough to create from the bare soil.

Ruggman was late—Ruggman was never late!—so while they were waiting Rob took a stab at polite conversation. He mentioned to Mrs. Cabot that her friend Nadine Edwards had contacted him and that he was going to send her some preliminary sketches in the next couple of weeks. They walked through the house and noted the progress made in the installation of the floor tiles. Mrs. Cabot told a funny story about her son, Jonathan Junior, and even though Rob knew Jonathan Junior was a complete cokehead and a liar and a thief he laughed agreeably.

"*I* don't mind waiting," said Christine Cabot. "Jonathan's out on the boat all day. I have nowhere to be. Apparently it's a gorgeous day for a sail, although honestly I've never learned to read the wind."

Rob set his teeth together. It *was* a perfect day for a sail: southwest breeze of fifteen knots, seas of a foot and a half, temperature resting comfortably right around seventy-eight. He thought of *A Family Affair* and his heart ached.

When the girls got cranky he told Mrs. Cabot he'd be back and he took them for lunch at a restaurant on the other side of the lake. He invited Mrs. Cabot to accompany them, but she pulled an exquisitely wrapped sandwich from her elegant handbag and declared that she was going to take it down to the dock to get a taste of al fresco dining in her new home.

At the restaurant they sat on the deck, at a table inadequately shielded from the sun by a striped umbrella, and Rob thought about the bottle of sunscreen he'd forgotten to pack, which led him to think about all the sunscreen he'd forgotten to apply to the girls since Eliza had been gone. He stared out at the glass-smooth lake and thought about the vast number of sunburns for which he was personally responsible.

He watched Zoe and Evie work their way through their lunches. Zoe was eating a Caesar salad with blackened haddock, which he knew would make Eliza happy, and Evie had ordered a peanut butter and jelly sandwich, which he knew wouldn't. Rob had the lobster stew. He studied the cocktail menu. There was something called the Sebago Perfecto: Patrón Silver tequila, Grand Marnier orange liqueur, sweet-and-sour mix, and lime. It looked like something Deirdre Palmer and the other ladies at the club would drink, which made him think about Eliza, which made him think about Charlie, which made his heart seize with sorrow. When the waitress came to check on them, he ordered a beer.

"That lady is nice," said Zoe.

"The waitress?"

"No, the lady at the house."

"Mrs. Cabot."

"Right. She gave us candy."

"She did? When?"

"When you were talking to the guy."

"Oh," said Rob.

"Peppermint Patties," confirmed Evie. "My favorite."

Then he said, "Did she seem happy?"

Evie squinted at him and pulled off a small section of her sandwich, squeezing it until the jelly squirted out. Rob thought about stopping her but didn't, and he and Zoe both watched, a little entranced, as Evie repeated the performance until the entire sandwich had been torn into pieces. Then Evie said, "She seemed regular. Is regular happy?"

"It is for a grown-up," said Zoe philosophically.

They were all silent for a moment, soaking in the sun or the atmosphere or their own grim thoughts. After a time, Zoe said, "When is Mommy coming home?"

"Soon." He noted that she said *Mommy,* not *Mom,* when normally she said *Mom* all the time now. Eliza had told him once that she'd be devastated when Zoe stopped saying *Mommy;* Eliza herself had lost her mom before she'd gotten to that point.

"Soon?" said Evie.

He remembered that when his children were small they had no real concept of time—you could say that something was happening tomorrow and they'd forget all about it by the time tomorrow came, or they could dredge up a three-week-old promise and want it fulfilled as though it had just been made.

"How soon?" asked Zoe.

"Very soon," said Rob. "She'll be home for your play, Evie."

"For good?"

"I'm not sure. Maybe."

Evie sighed and said, "Brain cancer is bad, right?"

Rob cleared his throat and opted for honesty. He said, "It's not good."

"Is he going to die?"

Rob considered his younger daughter, her little snub nose, her wide brown eyes, her smooth skin. He'd always believed the truth was better than the not-truth. He said, "Yes." And then he amended it: "We're all going to die someday."

"But is he going to die *soon*?"

Rob looked out over the lake: the *Songo River Queen II* was making her slow and mighty voyage. Off to the right he could see a giant water trampoline with bodies bouncing off it. Traffic moved by on the Causeway, and a red pontoon passed out of sight. "He might. We really don't know."

Evie took a drink of her Shirley Temple and said, "Is Mommy really sad?"

"She is." Rob nodded. "Yes, she is."

"Of course she is, dummy," said Zoe. "Aren't you going to be sad when Daddy dies?"

Evie squinted at him and put a French fry in her mouth. She chewed it thoughtfully and said, "Definitely. I'm going to be *heartbroken* when Daddy dies."

"Okay," said Rob uneasily. "Maybe we change the subject to something happier?"

"I don't see why," said Evie. She shielded her eyes and regarded the lake. "If what's happening is sad."

She was wise beyond her years, that one. Wise beyond her years.

"Are you sad?" Evie asked. "About Grandpa?"

"Of course I am," Rob said. He thought about the first time he'd gone up to Little Harbor with Eliza, and how Charlie had taken them both out on the *Joanie B*. He'd felt like a pansy, the way he'd first reacted to the smell of the bait, but if Charlie thought the same thing he didn't let on.

"I remember when he came to my class for show-and-tell," said Zoe.

"He did that for me too," said Evie. "Lots of times. With the two lobster traps, wooden and metal."

Then the waitress brought Rob's beer, and Rob's phone began to ring.

"Mrs. Cabot," he said to the girls, glancing at the screen. "Hurry and finish up your lunch." He drank half his beer in one gulp.

"I see her!" said Zoe delightedly. "Mrs. Cabot! We can see Cabot Lodge from here, right, Daddy? At least the dock."

Rob hadn't noticed this. Because of the way his chair was angled he'd been fixing his gaze on the western side of the lake, but Zoe's seat faced the eastern side. He pivoted in his chair and, yes, there it was. The dock extending into the lake like a finger. A figure at the end. He squinted. Was the figure holding a phone?

"That's funny," said Zoe, "that she's calling you. When we can see her. She must really want to talk."

———

"Rob. We got a problem."

Rob had barely stopped the car when Ruggman approached.

Rob reached first for levity. "Don't hold back, Ruggman," he said. "Don't waste time with all the niceties, all the small talk." He laughed; Ruggman didn't.

"No, Rob, I'm serious. We got a real problem." Ruggman cleared his throat. Ruggman was always clearing his throat, and his throat never sounded clear.

"Just since I left for lunch?"

"Just since you left for lunch."

Rob took a deep breath and felt a chunk of lobster threaten to rise up in revolt. "Tell me."

"Landscaper was here, getting the final sizes for the patio and the walkways. He says that where you want to put the patio we gotta get state approval."

"We *what*?"

"He said that because of the slope of the land, they're gonna have to fill in, adjust the grade, and anytime you do that around here you need state approval."

"But the building inspector—he didn't . . ." Rob wanted to finish the sentence but he felt like there was a small animal trapped in his throat, something wild and furry, and he couldn't talk around it.

"I'm gonna anticipate your next question," said Ruggman then. "Forty-five to ninety days, to get the state approval. Usually closer to ninety."

"*Ninety* days! Shit, Ruggman, that takes us to—"

"Mid-October. Maybe later."

"Mid-October."

So that meant they couldn't sod in September, like they had planned. They couldn't do the front walkway either. The trucks carrying the blue-stone for the patio would ride roughshod right over everything. They'd have to wait. They'd have to wait on the walkout for the lower level, too, because they couldn't do the stone retaining wall before they'd filled in the slope. Shit. Shit. *Shit.*

"How'd we not know this, Ruggman? How'd we miss it?"

"*We* didn't miss anything," said Ruggman. "It's not my job to do the due diligence on this stuff. It's yours."

38

Mary

Thirteen weeks. A peach. Vocal cords. This baby could put its thumb in its mouth.

———

"Here," said Daphne, handing Mary a package from the bakery in Ellsworth. "I way over-ordered the lobster cookies today, take them home to your mom." She squinted at Mary and tilted her head sideways. Two vertical lines appeared between her eyebrows when she did that. "You okay, honey?"

"Fine," said Mary. "Why?"

"I don't know," said Daphne. "You look . . ."

Mary waited, not offering anything. Over the course of the summer she'd learned that sometimes the less you offered the better off you were.

"You look tired, I guess," Daphne continued. "But more than tired, or, I don't know, a different kind of tired." She squinted some more. "You look like you're tired from the inside out."

Mary dipped her head. Tired from the inside out was exactly how she felt: Daphne was hitting close to home.

While she was chewing gently on these thoughts Daphne was saying, "Missing Josh, are you?"

Daphne wasn't so close to home anymore.

Mary shook her head. "Not really."

"When's he coming back?"

"Not sure." *Never.* "I'm fine," she told Daphne. "I just had trouble sleeping last night." In fact, she had slept great the night before; she'd slept like a rock. She'd slept like a . . . well, like a baby. She took the package of cookies from Daphne. "Thank you," she said. "My mom will love them."

When she got into her car outside The Cup, Mary sat for a minute and considered the cookies. Vivienne would eat them, sure, but she'd complain the whole time about how she shouldn't be eating them, and she'd be dramatic about it, and she'd make Mary wish she'd never brought them home. Vivienne sometimes had a way of turning a nice gesture on its head.

Mary started the car and turned away from the road that led her home. She knew someone who loved these cookies, someone who wouldn't feel bad about eating them and who wouldn't make Mary feel bad about bringing them. Also, she was hoping Eliza would be home. She planned to ask her for one more ride, a ride to Bangor on August 3rd, at ten o'clock in the morning. She was supposed to arrive at nine thirty to check in. They'd have to leave by eight. It was a lot to ask. But there was nobody else.

———

Mary almost turned around at the last minute—it was weird, maybe, dropping in on Charlie Sargent like this—but what the heck. The man had brain cancer. He was dying. He had six months, maybe a year to live, that's what he'd told her at The Cup. And it had almost been much less than that, if he hadn't called the Coast Guard. He'd told her that too. The least Mary could do was bring him some cookies.

Mary had a clear view of the living room through the front window and she could see Charlie there, in his recliner. There was one lamp on, right beside him, and the front porch light was on too, like maybe he was expecting a visitor. His truck was in the driveway but there was no sign of the Audi that Eliza drove. There was a flicker of blue light that meant the TV was on.

Mary rapped softly on the door. She didn't want to make a sick man get out of his chair, but she didn't want to barge in without an invitation either. After a good long time, Charlie opened the door. When he saw Mary there with the cookies he smiled and said, "Mary!" like he was really glad to see her, and that made her feel good.

"Here," she said, holding the cookies up. "These were extra. I thought you might want them. I know how much you like them."

"I do," he said. "I sure do."

He stepped back and motioned for her to enter.

Charlie Sargent didn't look so much like a knight in shining armor now, he looked pale and weak and thin. Charlie was more stooped than he had been just ten days ago, and his eyes looked almost colorless, like some of the light had leaked out of them. He looked exhausted both from the inside out and from the outside in.

Mary suddenly felt shy and out of place. "Where's, um," she said, looking around.

"My pain-in-the-ass daughter?" He smiled again. "I sent her to Ellsworth. Told her to catch a movie. Don't know if she'll do it, but I told her to. Sent Val with her."

Mary laughed uncertainly, and Charlie said, "I'm kidding, about the pain in the ass."

"Okay," said Mary. "I know."

"Sort of. I love her, you know, but sometimes there's only so much concern one person can take."

Mary nodded. Even Mary understood that. Ever since that night after her visit to A Cut Above, the night Vivienne had cried onto Mary's cheek, when she was home with her mother, just doing something dumb like putting an ice-cream bowl in the dishwasher or searching through the On Demand movies on the cable, she sometimes caught Vivienne *staring* at her in such an uncomfortable way. A few times Mary even saw Vivienne's eyes *fill up with tears*. It made Mary want to chew glass and spit it out at the world. "I know what you mean," she said. Then she noticed that she was still holding the cookies and that she was still standing on the doormat. "Here," she said. "Why don't I put these in the kitchen. I have to be home soon anyway." (She didn't.)

"You can do that, sure, that'd be great. But after, if you have a few minutes, how about you just sit here with me." Charlie moved slowly back toward his recliner. "Maybe we talk or maybe we don't talk, either way is okay with me. But the company would be nice. Would that be okay?"

There was something pleading and kind in Charlie Sargent's eyes when he said that, and a little of the color reentered them. He moved aside so she could pass into the kitchen.

"That would be okay," she said. She had sort of been dreading going home to an empty house anyway—Vivienne was going out with the girls after work. "I wouldn't mind that at all. I'd like that."

Charlie settled himself in his chair and said, "It's just that, sometimes you send everybody away and then you look around and wonder why you're so lonely. You ever do that?"

She nodded. Did she ever. She brought the cookies into the kitchen, which was toward the back of the house and looked out over a small, untended garden. When she returned she took a seat on the edge of the couch and then, after a moment, sat all the way back. She looked around the room. It was simple and spare, with none of the ornate clutter and figurines that Vivienne favored. There was a single photograph resting on the table next to the couch—a beautiful woman who looked just like Eliza with her arms around a little girl. Eliza and her mother, clearly. Hanging on the wall behind the recliner was a photograph of what Mary guessed to be Eliza and her family: besides Eliza there was a man with thick white-blond hair and two little girls, maybe ten and eight.

Charlie closed his eyes, and Mary thought he might have gone to sleep, so she just sat there, looking at her hands and occasionally up at the TV. She didn't mind sitting there. It was peaceful in the living room; there was a clock ticking somewhere. The television was on but the volume was turned down low: it was some cop show that Mary didn't recognize, and a man and woman were speaking urgently to each other. While Mary watched, the woman started crying. The TV was much smaller than Josh's TV. Then, after a few moments, Charlie started talking, although his eyes remained closed.

"Tell me some gossip," Charlie finally said. "Who's loading up now?"

"Oh," said Mary. "Oh, I'm sorry, I don't really know." Loading up meant hauling a lot. With Josh gone she didn't keep track of the hauling—the people who came into The Cup weren't talking about it, that was for sure. If she tried she could maybe scare up some summer-person gossip, but she didn't think that was what Charlie was after. "I'm sorry," she said again.

"It's all right." He lifted a hand and let it fall back down to the recliner;

his eyes were still closed. "Doesn't really matter to me anymore anyway." He didn't say that in a self-pitying way, the way Vivienne might have said something like that; it was just a fact. Then he said, "How's that baby you're growing? You taking good care, now?"

"I am," she said. She tried not to think about August 3rd, ten o'clock in the morning.

"Good," said Charlie. "Good."

Mary put a hand on her belly, where it was starting to jut out a little bit. She'd always been very thin—too thin—so to her it seemed very noticeable, this addition to her shape. She'd taken to wearing loose shirts, and she put her apron on the second she walked into work. She thought of the peach-sized bundle of nerves and cells, veins and organs, with the big alien head.

And then the next thing she knew she was blubbering like *she herself* was the baby. She swiped her arm across her nose and hiccuped, but she couldn't stop, she just kept crying.

Charlie Sargent turned his head toward her and sat up a little bit and said, "Oh, now, Mary. Hey, now." He made a motion like he wanted to comfort her, leaning toward her. She didn't want him to bother himself getting out of the chair, so she shook her head and tried to talk. But she found she couldn't; she just blubbered on.

"I didn't mean to upset you," he said. He rested his head back in the chair, like he was giving her privacy to collect herself.

"I know," she managed. "I know you didn't mean to upset me. I'm sorry." She snorted ungracefully.

"Nothing you have to be sorry about in front of me." She nodded, grateful, and then he said, "There's Kleenex in the kitchen. Bring the whole box, why don't you."

She knew that because she'd seen the tissues when she'd gone to put the lobster cookies down. Charlie's kitchen was small and extremely tidy. There was a dish drainer with two plates drying in it. It sort of made her heart break, those two plates in the drainer, they seemed so lonely and brave. In the center of the table was a vase of cut flowers. A dish towel hung from the oven handles, its corners lined up with each other. When she came back from the kitchen his eyes were closed again and she thought about tiptoeing out the door, but then he said, "You okay? Can I do something for you?"

She thought, *For* me? He was the sick one. She said, "No. Thank you." She waited a minute and then common sense and manners kicked in. She said, "Can I do anything for *you?*"

She expected him to give her the same answers she'd given him but instead he said, "You know what you can do for me?"

"What?" she said. "I can do something for you, I can do whatever." I mean, *brain cancer*. The least she could do was help the man out.

"Just—just sit there for a little bit, will you? Just sit right there where you were sitting and talk to me."

Mary sat. "That's what you want me to do? That's all?"

"That's all. Make yourself comfortable."

Mary sat all the way back on the couch. Then she took off her shoes and tucked her legs underneath her. Charlie opened one eye and smiled and said, "That's more like it. Now, just talk."

She hesitated. "About anything in particular?"

"Nope, just whatever's on your mind. I like the sound of your voice. It relaxes me, makes me feel peaceful."

So Mary talked. She told him all sorts of things, things she'd never told anyone. She told him how sometimes she woke up in the night and the future felt like a big dark hole she might actually fall into. She told him that when she imagined the baby, imagined caring for it and loving it and having it love her back, sometimes she felt terrified and she broke out in a sweat. She told him sometimes she got scared Little Harbor was the only place she'd ever see in her life. She felt herself gearing up to cry again and pulled another tissue out of the box and got it ready.

She told him that she didn't know how to be a good mother.

Charlie said, "Course you do. You'll know how when the time comes, anyway, if you don't know it now."

"I don't," she said. "Nobody ever showed me how."

He sat with that for a moment and then he said, "My wife, Joanie, was the best mother you ever saw, and her mother didn't exactly show her."

"So, how'd she know what to do?"

"She learned by doing. Boy, the way she loved Eliza, it was something else. When she died, I wondered how I'd ever do right by Eliza without her."

"But you did."

"Lots of times I figured it would have been better if I'd been the one who died."

"Oh," said Mary. "Don't say that, please don't say that. You don't mean that."

"It wasn't fair to Eliza, to lose a mom like that. Just when she needed her the most. But she's been okay. She's tough, Eliza. A fighter."

Then Mary told him about Vivienne's friend Sam. "She's a good mother, I watch her all the time. She works hard, she's a nurse, and then sometimes after she's done being a nurse she works other shifts taking care of really sick people in their homes."

"That's a real hero," Charlie said. "Someone like that. Where's she do that kind of work, now?"

"Ellsworth."

He nodded and then sat very still for a moment, so still that once again she thought he was asleep.

"The people she takes care of are dying," said Mary. "And then she goes home and she's with her kids, and—I don't know. I just like watching her with them. It makes everything seem, I don't know how to say it. It makes everything seem possible, I guess."

Right after she said it she wished she hadn't. Dying people! What an idiot she was, to say that to a sick man. She said, "I'm sorry, about that one part."

"What one part is that?"

"The—" She hesitated. "The dying part."

He let out a parched little laugh. "'S okay," he said. "You're not talking 'bout anything I'm not thinking about."

"Still," she said.

"Sometimes I get so scared about what's coming, Mary, that I shake in my bed."

"That's awful," she whispered. "I'm sorry."

"But worse than that is when people pretend nothing's happening."

"That makes sense," she said. "That would be worse."

"The cancer, it's in my brain. A tumor."

"I know. You told me. I'm so sorry."

"Got some fancy name to it, I can't ever remember it half the time, glio-something or other. It was the size of a walnut, when they found it. Now—well, who knows. Who knows what size it is."

She nodded and felt her eyes fill up again. She said, "Does it hurt?"

"Some headaches, that's about the worst of it. From the pressure, Eliza told me, I don't know, I guess there's no pain receptors in the brain. I didn't know that. Did you know that?"

"No," said Mary. "I sure didn't." Then she said, "I just talked so much about myself. I feel awful about that, when you're—"

"That's what I wanted," Charlie said. "That's exactly what I asked for."

"Okay. But . . . now do you want to talk? And I'll listen."

He didn't answer right away and then he sat in silence for some minutes and she could hear the clock ticking. The television had changed, a news show now. With his eyes closed Charlie said, "Would you mind if I talked to you about Joanie, about Eliza's mother?"

"No, of course not," said Mary. "I wish you would. I really wish you would."

He smiled. "First time I saw her, I was coming in from hauling, and she was sitting there on the wharf, swinging her legs back and forth, and I thought I was looking at a fairy-tale princess."

"She was beautiful," said Mary. "I can see in the photograph."

"Inside too," Charlie said. "Corny as that may sound. Beautiful inside and out." He opened one eye and said, "I loved her so much, you know. She was all of it to me, all of it. And then when Eliza was born the two of them were all of it."

"A love like that," said Mary. "I bet there's people who never get to feel that way, lots of people." What Charlie was describing was so far from the uncertainty she'd felt around Josh, and later the fear, that they didn't even belong in the same category. They didn't even belong in the same *conversation.*

"Eliza, she's upset with me that I'm not fighting this thing, this tumor. But what I saw Joanie go through, fighting something that was just going to beat her in the end—boy, Mary, I don't want any part of that. I don't want to go down like that."

"I understand," said Mary. "I don't blame you."

"You don't?" He opened his eyes.

"I don't."

He sighed deeply. "Thank you, Mary. Thank you for saying that. I need one person to say that to me."

"You're welcome." She felt the weight of that responsibility settle across her shoulders, but it felt right and satisfying, like the heft of a heavy blanket.

"They say that when you're dying your world gets real small. They say you shrink it down to the people who are really important to you, that that's what you're supposed to do, that that's what's natural."

Mary didn't know what to say to that. She wished Sam were there; Sam would know what to say. Sam probably had conversations like these all the time. She waited to see if Charlie would keep talking, and he did. "The thing about it is that I know someday soon I'm going to see Joanie again."

"You will," said Mary fiercely.

"And we'll both be whole and neither one of us will be sick. I don't worry about Eliza without me. Eliza's tough as nails and she's got her family. I know she'll be okay."

"You talk like you're dying tomorrow or something," Mary said. "I'm sure you're not."

He laughed that parched little laugh again. "Probably not tomorrow, you're right."

"Probably not the next day either."

"Well," he said. "Probably not."

Then Charlie closed his eyes again and he didn't open them when he said, "You're going to do just fine, Mary, you and that baby of yours. I know it."

"You do?"

"I feel it in my bones."

"And how are your bones, usually? Pretty accurate?"

"Pretty accurate."

After that it seemed like Charlie was fading in and out of sleep and Mary put her shoes back on and got ready to leave. Was she supposed to do something, though? Bring him water, put him to bed? When was Eliza coming back?

Once he opened his eyes and looked right at her and said again, "I know I'm going to see Joanie again. I just know it."

"You will," said Mary. "Of course you will." She hesitated next to his chair and she said, "Can I do anything for you? Can I bring you something?"

"No," he said. "I'm good here, I'm peaceful. But if I ever did need something you'd help me, right?"

"Sure," she said. "I'm around."

Now he opened both eyes and looked right at her and said, very earnestly, "Can you lean close to me for just a minute, before you go? So I can say something?"

Mary did as he asked, putting her ear close to Charlie's mouth, and he whispered something, and she listened, and it took her a minute to process it, but after she did, she said, "I have to think about it."

PART THREE

August

39

Rob

On the first day of August, Rob met Christine Cabot in the Oak Room at the Copley Plaza: his choice, but he knew that Christine Cabot approved. The place conferred a sense of history and class that Christine Cabot would appreciate. The room was quiet and paneled in dark wood and it would be a very difficult place to make a scene, if one were inclined toward scenes.

Mrs. Cabot was already seated when Rob arrived, which put him immediately on uncertain ground. *He* wanted to choose the table, have the upper hand. He wanted to choose the drinks. Mrs. Cabot had already ordered two Mount Gay and tonics. Before lunch.

They nibbled on a handful of the pretzels, nuts, and spicy sesame sticks that the Oak Room had been serving since Rob was a small child, picking the pretzels out one by one while his mother drank with her friends.

When Rob had taken a few sips of his drink, and when he had squeezed the lime with vigor and fear, he cleared his throat and said, "Listen, Mrs. Cabot. About Thanksgiving."

She didn't answer, but she cocked her head in a way that said she was listening.

Closing his eyes he whispered, "I don't think the outside is going to be ready by Thanksgiving." Pause, then onward. "I don't think the lower-level walkout is going to be accessible from the outside either."

Rob had prepared himself for all sorts of reactions: quiet rage, barely controlled rage, louder rage, the ragiest rage. But he had not prepared himself for what actually happened; he hadn't prepared himself for

Mrs. Cabot's level gaze, and for the four words issuing from her glossy lips: "That settles it, then." She signaled the hovering waiter—his name tag read MILTON—for the check. He must have been close to Christine Cabot's vintage; he probably came of age working in the Oak Room, but he moved with surprising agility toward the bar and returned with the black check holder before Rob had a chance to gather his thoughts and answer.

"That settles what?"

"Mark and I met about this earlier in the week."

"Mark?"

"Mark Ruggman."

"Ruggman?" Thinking about Ruggman with a first name was like thinking about Jesus with a last name. "You met with Ruggman without me?" There was air-conditioning blasting from the creaky vents, but Rob felt hot all over, as though he'd been dipped in a lobster pot.

"I did. I met with Mark, and he walked me through the problem with the patio, and he told me about the permit. And we decided, *together,* that we could finish the project. On time. Without the permit."

"We meaning—"

"We meaning Mark Ruggman. And myself."

"Without me."

"Without you."

"But Ruggman told me he wasn't willing to go ahead without the—"

Mrs. Cabot placed a platinum card on top of the check, and Milton tottered off with it.

"We discussed it, and he came around to my view. He was really quite reasonable about it. I'm going to rent a little place up there, an adorable little cabin, and stay there through the fall, so I can visit the site, make sure things are on track."

Without Mrs. Cabot, Rob was sunk. Finished. Not only did Rob need the rest of the money from this job, he needed Mrs. Cabot to recommend him to her friends.

"*I* can visit the site, Mrs. Cabot! We're so close. The primer coat is on. The towel racks are in the bathrooms. The carpets are in upstairs. I can rent a cabin!" There was a pain in his chest he'd never felt before. Cardiac arrest?

"Oh, Rob." Christine Cabot shook her head. "You can't rent a cabin."

"Of course I can." He reached for his cell phone. "I'll rent a cabin right now. I'll rent two cabins!"

"Surely you see that that isn't the answer. You've been—how shall I say this—*distracted* since the building really got under way. You've been pulled in many different directions. I'm sure you understand that your work has suffered as a result. But that isn't the biggest problem here."

To his horror and dismay, Rob hiccuped. Milton, who could probably hear about as well as an elderly spaniel, turned from another table and regarded the two of them. "It's not?"

"No. The bigger problem is—well, I'm not sure you were ever the right man for the job in the first place. Mark and I have been talking about it, that maybe it was simply a lack of experience that led to some of these problems."

Ruggman had thrown him under the bus. Ruggman had seen the bus coming, and he'd picked Rob up and thrown him right under it. Goddammit.

"Rob," Christine Cabot went on, and her voice took on a plaintive twinge. "This has been my dream for two years now. My project. My focus. I was just about to get to the fun stuff. Picking towels, choosing sheets, getting ready for the best Thanksgiving my family has ever seen. I was *just about* to start all of that, and then I was told that I might not be able to. I've dreamed about my grandkids frolicking on the lawn. And then I was told that there might not be any lawn!" There were real tears in her eyes. "It was a grandmother's wish, a perfect holiday with the family. I'm sure you can see how disappointing it was to me, to hear that it might not happen."

Rob said, "Mrs. Cabot—" but his voice broke.

Mrs. Cabot signed the check and handed it to Milton. "I'm sorry," she said. "But it's been decided."

"What will you tell people? Who ask about me?"

"I'll tell them the truth," she said.

"Which is?"

"Which is that we loved the design and had trouble with the execution."

She paused and removed her cardigan, revealing sun-spotted shoulders that were surprisingly toned for a woman of her age. "Thank you for the drink, Robbie," she said.

"I didn't buy you the drink," said Rob.

"Nevertheless. Thank you."

Rob wanted to remain in his chair. He wanted to throw the snack mix across the bar, and stamp his feet like the little boy he'd once been. He remembered a long-ago tantrum in this very room, appeased by his mother, held at the shoulder by her firm hand. He remembered the scent of his mother's perfume. He wanted to cry on Milton's shoulder. He wanted to belly up to the bar and drink six more cocktails.

But good manners prevailed, as they had since Rob was a tot in a swim diaper, and a gentleman stood when a lady stood, so he got to his feet and accepted the dry kiss Mrs. Cabot planted on his cheek, and he tried not to let on that he was shaking like a dog in a thunderstorm, and he tried not to sound bitter and regretful and desperate—though he was all three—when he said, "If you change your mind, Mrs. Cabot, you know where to find me."

40

LITTLE HARBOR, MAINE

Eliza

"Evie found us a Plott hound named Jelly Roll," said Eliza. She and Val were walking Sternman near the harbor, past the wharf, near the outskirts of town. The boats were still out. Every now and then Sternman lifted his face to the wind like he could read a message on it.

"What's a Plott hound?" asked Val.

"That's what I asked." Eliza read the text aloud: **A LARGE SCENT HOUND BRED FOR HUNTING BOAR.**

"Good heavens," said Val. "Those kids of yours are something else, Eliza."

"I'm pretty sure the wild boar population in Barton is under control, though. So I'm going to tell her no."

They turned back when they got to where Main Street veered off, and headed around toward Val's house. Sternman looked tired but determined, his tongue out, his tail wagging occasionally.

"Can I ask you something, Eliza?"

"Of course. Anything."

"Did you get everything all sorted out? With Russell?"

Eliza blushed, and ducked her head so Val couldn't see her blushing, and then she said, "Yeah."

"Good." Sternman stopped to do his business, and Val whipped out a plastic bag from her pocket. "Those girls of yours, that husband, you're about as lucky as anyone ever gets, you know."

"I know," said Eliza. "I am, I know. But I've done a shitty job of showing it, this summer." She watched Val tie up the bag. Val made a groaning noise when she stood up, and that reminded Eliza that Val, along with everyone else, was aging. If Joanie were still alive she'd be nearly sixty, just like Val.

When Val had finished working with the bag she said to Eliza, "No, honey. Of *course not*. With what you've been dealing with, with Charlie—you've done the best you could, as good as anyone would have. Better than most."

Eliza shook her head, intent, like a child, on proving herself right. Then she said, "Val? You know that letter you gave me from my mom when I was sixteen?"

"Yuh." Val had a strange look on her face, something indecipherable.

"I wish I had the rest of the lessons, all of them. I need all ten."

"Oh, Eliza, you don't need any more lessons. Look at you. You've figured everything else out on your own."

"I haven't," said Eliza. "I haven't at all. I've been gone, I've missed so much, I've said terrible things to Rob—" She paused. It was more than the things she'd said, really. Things said in a fight could be forgiven. She went on, trying to get at the root of it. "It's not just that. I've been doing this weird thing where I'm sort of, I don't know, keeping myself apart from him. Like I've not completely bought into our life together, like I'm letting myself be an outsider." She didn't mention Phineas Tarbox, but he was there, with his minty breath, his smooth brow.

Val made an odd noise, like a goat coughing. "But."

"What?"

"Nothing. I didn't say anything." Val bent to fiddle with Sternman's collar, which didn't appear to need any kind of adjusting.

"Yes you did. You said, *But.*"

A long moment passed and stretched between them and then Val stood up again and considered Eliza.

"There aren't any more lessons," said Val. "But there's more to the letter."

That was weird: Eliza's ears were playing some kind of trick on her.

"For a second," said Eliza, "I thought you said there was *more* to the *letter.*"

"That's what I said." Val looked straight ahead, her gaze almost presidential in its dignity, its seriousness of purpose. "There's more to the letter."

41

Deirdre

Mrs. Palmer said she would buy the flowers herself.

Not really, of course. But during her penultimate meeting with Bree Dawson, the event manager at the club, Deirdre couldn't help but channel a little Virginia Woolf; *Mrs. Dalloway* had been one of her favorite books in Modern British Lit at Penn.

"Almost there!" said Bree. She was young, in her late twenties probably, and head-to-toe gorgeous, with a tousled, short, choppy haircut that only those women blessed with perfect cheekbones can pull off. Deirdre tried to listen to her instead of looking at the hair; she tried to tamp down her envy and think instead about the EANY children, who sometimes had no hair at all. "You must be *so* excited," Bree added. There was less than a month to go until the gala, and all of the pieces were sliding into place.

"I am excited," Deirdre told Bree. "I am."

In reality Deirdre would *not* buy the flowers herself. (What was she, crazy? She couldn't buy all of those flowers herself, how on earth would she transport them, keep them fresh?) No. The flowers would be brought up from Lotus Designs, in Boston, and the sometimes overzealous decorating committee would use them to put together the centerpieces, and also a few larger arrangements that would be placed strategically around the ballroom. Deirdre would have to remind them to exercise restraint and caution; she wanted the centerpieces to be tasteful, not to scream excessiveness and waste—excessiveness and waste, of course, represented the opposite of the EANY mission.

Come to think of it, she should probably oversee the putting together of the centerpieces her very own self. She made a note.

"Okay," said Bree, glancing down at her clipboard. "Let's go over everything." They sat at a cocktail table near the bar and covered the menu: the passed appetizers, the cold-appetizer station, the sit-down dinner, the specialty cocktail, the liquors, the wine and beer. They walked through the foyer between the grand ballroom and the outside deck where the long tables holding the auction items would be set up. Deirdre produced her list of auction items, and they went through them one by one. They went over the seating arrangements.

She felt her phone vibrate. Kristi had taken Sofia into Boston for the day; they were going to go on the Swan Boats and get ice cream and maybe do a little shopping on Newbury Street. It was the kind of outing Deirdre would have liked to have with her own daughter, but Judith had told her that the last few weeks before the gala were when the proverbial blank could hit the fan, and that she should stay local. (She'd said it like that, *blank*.) "Stay on your toes!" Judith had said. "I'm here if you need me." Deirdre didn't know what she'd do without Judith. She wished it were possible to adopt someone else's mother-in-law as your own. She wondered if Eliza might lend Judith out on a semipermanent basis.

"Excuse me," she said now to Bree, who was running one hand through her gorgeous hair and making a note on her clipboard with the other. Deirdre dug in her bag for her phone. Sheila Rackley. **WANT TO HAVE LUNCH AT THE CLUB?**

She rolled her eyes, hesitated, and texted back, **ALREADY HERE. I'LL GET A TABLE.**

When she and Bree had completed their business, Deirdre asked for a table on the outside patio. The day was stunning, not a trace of humidity, and the sun was shining as though it were getting paid by the hour to do so.

While she waited for Sheila to arrive she checked her phone again, to see if Kristi had texted any photos of her and Sofia on Newbury Street. Kristi hadn't, so Deirdre checked Sofia's Instagram account. Nothing. Then Sofia's *fake* Instagram account. Still nothing. Well, she'd just have to use her good old-fashioned imagination.

When Sheila arrived she ordered a burger, rare, no bun, and Deirdre ordered a Cobb salad. Then Sheila ordered a bottle of Piper-Heidsieck. Champagne. *Good* champagne!

"I thought you weren't drinking," said Deirdre. She hoped that this lunch was going on Sheila's club tab and not hers.

"I'm making an exception," said Sheila.

"For what occasion?"

"For the occasion of a beautiful summer day and lunch with my friend."

That sounded suspicious. There was something else at play here, Deirdre just didn't know what it was.

After the champagne arrived and the fresh young server had opened it and poured it into two flutes and they'd each had a quarter glass Sheila leaned forward and said, "So. Public service announcement. I'd check in on Sofia if I were you."

"Why?"

"Kids are sending stuff around. Body parts."

The champagne had gone straight to Deirdre's head; she was picturing severed limbs in cardboard boxes. "You mean, actual body parts?"

"*No,*" said Sheila. "Duh. On their phones. *Photos.*" She gestured toward her chest and then vaguely beneath the table. "I'd check Sofia's phone."

"Really?" *Ugh.* "Well, I'm not worried about Sofia doing anything like that."

"That's what every parent says," said Sheila. "Until they discover that their kid *is* doing it, was doing it the whole time."

Deirdre was pondering the shoddy state of the world and the dangers of social media when she saw a familiar figure striding across the deck.

"Rob!" she called. The champagne made her wave extra vigorously. He started toward them, saw Sheila, stopped, probably realized that looked suspicious, started toward them again.

"Hey," he said. She watched Rob take in the champagne, the glasses, and say, "Celebrating something?"

"Not really," said Deirdre. She tried not to let her eyes meet Rob's.

"Just life," said Sheila. "Why not?"

"I see," said Rob, nodding. He looked agitated; he kept shifting his weight from one foot to the other. Was he okay? "Great. Celebrating life. No Sofia? No Jackie?"

"She's in Boston," said Deirdre. "With Kristi. And Sheila's kids are—where are your kids, again, Sheila?"

"Camp," said Sheila firmly. "All day. Thank God for Little Sailors!"

Rob nodded again and said, "Actually, I'm thinking of going for a sail."

"Alone?" asked Deirdre.

"Nah," said Rob. "I'll scare up a crew." His eyes scanned the patio.

Sheila's phone buzzed and she glanced at it and said, "I'm so sorry, you two, I have to take this, I'll be quick." Because cell phone usage was frowned upon on the patio and in the dining room—you could do some covert handbag texting, but you couldn't really talk—Sheila hightailed it toward the indoor bathrooms, leaving Deirdre and Rob together.

"You okay?" asked Deirdre. "You look—upset."

Rob pressed his lips together and said, "I don't want to talk about it."

"Okay. You want to sit down?" She motioned toward Sheila's seat. "I can ask for another flute."

"No," said Rob. "Thanks. I'm going to head out."

"Wait," said Deirdre. "Hang on. When you get home, you should check Zoe's phone. I've heard there's been some texting. Of . . ." She scanned the patio and lowered her voice. *"Body parts."*

"I don't know what you mean," Rob said. He looked genuinely per-plexed: worried and yet approachable, like a shar-pei puppy. "What kind of body parts?"

"Well," said Deirdre. "I don't think they're talking about feet and elbows, if that helps."

Rob understood then. He said, *"What?"*

"I know," said Deirdre. "They're thirteen. They make bad decisions. Their brains aren't fused!"

"They aren't?"

"*No!* They won't be fused for years."

"Yikes."

"And, come on, it's *Zoe and Sofia* we're talking about here, they're pretty innocent. Sometimes I still catch Sofia playing with her American Girl dolls. But even so. Worth checking." She lowered her voice and added, "It probably all started with Jackie Rackley."

She wanted Rob to snort-laugh and say, "Probably," but he didn't. He just shifted his weight again and said, "Does Eliza know about this?"

"I don't think so. I just found out myself."

"Okay," said Rob. "I don't like the sound of it. I'm going to go home and check it out, right now."

"Check Zoe's texts," said Deirdre. "And her Instagram. And her Finsta. Just in case."

Rob said, "Her what? What was that last thing you said?"

"Her Finsta."

"I feel like you're speaking another language." He looked *so* bewildered.

"Just ask Zoe. She'll explain it."

"Okay. Okay, I will. Nice to see you. You guys enjoy your lunch."

"Thanks. But listen, Rob?"

He turned back. "Yeah?"

"Do you think we could talk about—I mean, do you have a second to—"

Then Sheila was back and Rob gave a quick shake of his head, and he waved at both of them and was gone.

"He looks stressed," said Sheila, shaking out her napkin, putting it back on her lap.

"He probably is," said Deirdre. "He has a lot going on."

"I heard," Sheila said, leaning in.

"What do you mean? You heard what?" Deirdre's heart thumped. Had someone seen them at The Wharf Rat?

"Eliza's still in Maine, huh?"

Why was Sheila Rackley always trying to manufacture drama? It was exhausting.

"Not so much *still* as *again*," said Deirdre.

"What does that mean?"

"She's been back and forth. She's coming back for Evie's play."

"Will she be here for the gala?"

"Of course." Deirdre was not actually sure that Eliza would be, but she hoped, with a fervent childlike intensity, that she would be.

"Well, don't you think that's a long time to be gone?" Sheila poured herself more champagne and topped off Deirdre's glass. "I heard," she said, "that she might be staying up there. *For good.*"

In this case Deirdre thought it was okay to bend the rules of Eliza's privacy policy, not only to squash Sheila Rackley's ridiculous rumor like a bug but also to defend Eliza's completely defensible absence this summer, her completely defensible life. "Her father is dying, Sheila. He has a brain tumor. Eliza is the only person he has. He needs her."

Anybody else would be embarrassed about having misread the situation in such an egregious way, but Sheila kept right on going, like a train toward its station.

"That's terrible, but. Why isn't Rob there too, in that case?"

"Because he needs to be here. For work."

"It just seems strange. That's all I'm saying. I mean, didn't she almost marry a lobsterman? Wasn't she almost a lobsterman's wife?" Her eyes twinkled with the potential of it all.

That settled it. The surge of loyalty and tenderness Deirdre felt for Eliza at that moment eclipsed everything else: her envy of Eliza and Rob, her frustrations with Brock, the vestiges of her own bad deed. She downed the rest of her champagne in one giant gulp.

"Listen to me, Sheila. Rob and Eliza are the real deal. Better than Brock and I will ever be. Better than you and Mike will ever *ever* be."

Sheila raised her eyebrows and sat back. "Wow, Deirdre. That's kind of harsh."

"Well." Deirdre lifted her hands as if to indicate that the level of harshness was out of her control.

"After I've spent my summer working on *your* gala."

Deirdre gasped. Did she really. Had she actually. "*I've* spent my summer working on my gala! You've come to three meetings, tops. You missed two."

Sheila put her flute down hard. "I couldn't get a sitter for the other two."

Deirdre leaned toward Sheila and said, "Your kids are thirteen and eleven. You don't need a sitter to go to a ninety-minute meeting."

"Look who's talking. How many hours is Kristi Osgood working for you this summer?"

No, she did not. Sheila Rackley *did not just go there*. "That's different! I've been *consumed* with the gala this summer. I'm not just on a committee. I'm on all the committees. I *am* the committees. And Sofia is an *only child*. I can't leave her all by herself all summer. It is *so not the same*." Maybe, Deirdre admitted in the recesses of her mind, it was *a little bit the same*. But she would never, ever, say that to Sheila.

Sheila refilled the flutes.

At the table in the corner somebody spilled a glass of water, and that made Deirdre think about her very first date with Brock, when he knocked over his water and left an extra-large tip to make up for the mess. She felt something in her heart turn over once, then twice. She thought about how on that first date he'd had a recent haircut. It was too short on top, and Deirdre could see a little bit of his scalp, which looked pink and vulnerable and called to mind a half-sheared sheep. Maybe it was the champagne, but she felt a wave of tenderness for the old Brock, the old them.

"Should we talk about the centerpieces?" asked Sheila. Deirdre couldn't tell if Sheila was mollified or plotting or just plain drunk.

"I'm doing the centerpieces," said Deirdre. "On my own, like I've done most of the work for this gala."

"But—"

Deirdre waved over the server and said, "I think we're all done here, thank you so much. You can put this on the Rackleys' tab."

42

Eliza

The next part isn't a lesson at all. There's something about dying that makes you want to clear your conscience of anything you're ashamed of. And I'm ashamed of this.

Oh, Eliza. It got dark so early in the afternoon in the winter. Every day was the same after the same after the same, with your dad getting up before dawn and leaving the two of us alone. I'd lie here in bed sometimes and I'd hear his truck pull out of the driveway and I'd look at the clock and it would say four thirty and I'd think about all of the hours ahead of me that stacked up to one day and then the days that would stack up to a week and then a month and then a year.

When you were two and a half years old, I thought I didn't have it in me to be a good mother. I didn't think I could do right by you. I dropped you off with Val one afternoon when she was done working and I told her I was going into Ellsworth to do some shopping. But when I got to Ellsworth it looked so small and suddenly I felt it like a punch: This was it. This was all it was going to be, this was the big city to our tiny, tiny town. I thought I was doing you a favor, leaving you with someone who was more cut out for that life than I was. I didn't think I deserved you, didn't think I deserved your dad. He loved me so much, and I knew I didn't have a right to be loved like that.

So I kept driving. When in doubt, I used to tell you, choose brave. I didn't choose brave that day. I left. I drove all the way to Boston, and I used the last of the money I had tucked away to stay in a hotel. I wasn't happy to be there, though—I was tortured. Every day was an effort to get through. Every night I dreamed about you, and I dreamed about the wharf and the boats and the way the air smells in the evening, and the way the fog looks rolling in. Every morning I woke up and said, Today I will go back. And every day I didn't.

Six days went by like that and on the seventh day I went to a pay phone and I put in all of the coins I had and I called Val's house. I didn't think I was going to say anything, I just wanted to see if I could maybe hear you in the background, hear some of your babbling, the little sentences you were trying to string together. Then I was going to hang up.

I knew you'd be at Val's because it was hauling time. But when Val answered I heard you screaming in the background, not babbling. So right away I said, "It's me. Val, it's me." She put Charlie on the phone. He wasn't out hauling, he'd come in because you'd come on with a fever out of nowhere earlier that day and somebody had radioed out for him to come back. They were both in a panic, trying to quiet you, get you comfortable until the fever broke.

I got in my car and I drove as fast as I could and by the time I got there the fever had broken and you were sleeping on Val's couch and they were both sitting there, not touching, but sitting close, and watching over you.

They looked like two parents.

Your father has the biggest heart of anyone I've ever known, Eliza, a heart bigger than the universe. I was never worthy of him, not really. He forgave me for leaving, and he accepted me when I came back. We never talked about it again, never once, and he continued to love me and I did my best to love him. I tried my hardest to be as worthy as I could be, worthy of him, worthy of you. I'm so sorry I left you, Eliza. But I've never, ever been sorry I came back.

I thought when I fell in love with your dad I was like a character in a fairy tale, waiting on the wharf for the boats to come in, for the men to appear out of the fog. Then I found out that there's no such thing, no fairy tale. I guess that's Lesson Number Five. I love you, Eliza, I have always loved you. I know a lot more people will love you in your life but nobody will love you the way I have.

When Eliza looked up from the letter she was alone in Val's living room, except for Sternman, who was flat on his side, his front paw twitching, his big lips rising and falling with each breath.

"Val?" she called. "*Val?*" She hadn't heard the front door close; hadn't heard if Val had said anything to her before she'd gone. She searched the small kitchen, the dining room with the round maple table, the copper curtains that had hung there as long as Eliza could remember.

Of course she knew where Val would be. It was getting on toward the late afternoon, and the boats would be coming in. She'd be at the wharf.

"Come on, Sternman," she said. "Let's go, boy. Get up, we're going for a walk."

———

She was right. There was Val, back straight, facing the water. All of the boats were out except for the *Joanie B.* You could read a lot of different things into the sight of that boat, if you didn't know the backstory. You could read loneliness or comfortable solitude. You could think the captain of that boat had taken a vacation or that he'd fallen on hard times and couldn't afford fuel or that he'd come back early because he had to go to the dentist or that he'd had the haul of a lifetime over the last three weeks and had just, plain and simple, decided to sleep in and take a day off. So much of life was about knowing the backstory.

Eliza stood for a moment, watching Val watch the water. Sternman wagged his tail and whimpered low and long and pulled a little bit on the leash. When they got closer to Val, Eliza said, "How come you didn't give me the whole letter at once, Val?"

Val looked up at her, and Eliza saw that her eyes were wet.

"Sit down, sit down here." Val indicated the space next to her on the dock, but she was looking back at the harbor, toward the stand of pines. She wasn't looking in the direction of the *Joanie B.*

"No." Eliza's voice could have sliced wood, it was so sharp.

"Yes. Eliza Sargent Barnes, you sit down next to me right now, and that's an order."

Eliza sighed and did as she was told. Sternman settled beside her, his chin on his paws, looking out at the water along with Val and Eliza. Eliza said, "That's the last lesson? That there's no fairy tale? I can't believe that's the last lesson."

Val said, "I know it's easy to think that people who aren't here anymore were perfect—"

"*Don't,*" said Eliza. She had never talked to Val with an ounce of anger, not even when she was a teenager, not even during those moments every teenager has of being angry with everyone, angry with the world.

"No. Let me say it. Of course Joanie wasn't perfect, she was a human being like all the rest of us. She made her own mistakes, did selfish things sometimes, did thoughtless things sometimes, same as you and me do."

Eliza set her lips together. "I don't want to hear this."

"Want to hear it or not, it's true. Your mom wanted me to give you that whole letter when you were sixteen. You know what you were doing when you were sixteen?"

"No." Yes.

"You were so crazy in love with Russell your head was up in the clouds, Eliza, *way* up there."

"But still."

"You were breaking your daddy's heart."

Eliza's breath caught. "I *was*?"

"Of course you were."

Eliza laid her hand on Sternman's giant square head and held it there. Sternman closed his eyes and she rubbed behind his left ear, just the way he liked it. Part of her was trying to keep the memory down, but there it was. She remembered now.

She was sixteen, and Russell was waiting for her in his truck. Russell leaned on his horn the tiniest bit and Eliza, having brushed her hair fourteen times, brushed it once more.

"I'm going out," she would have called to her father. Where was he? In his recliner, the hauling done for the day.

He said, "Where?" He was just asking. As he had every right to. But she didn't want to talk to anybody but Russell, so she said, "Just *out!*" in a new voice, an awful voice. And when she passed by the living room she saw his face crumple in hurt and bewilderment—just for an instant, before he regained his usual inscrutable expression and waved her on like it didn't matter. He might even have said goodbye, not that she deserved it. He might have said, "Have a good time," or "Be careful," or some other mundane and fatherly thing, and she just left.

She could have stopped, could have done something to make it better. But she was sixteen, and she was in love, and Russell was waiting outside, and there was all of that newly discovered desire between them. She was the Mary to his Springsteen. She let the screen door slam and she didn't look back. And she knew that that was one of many times, not the only one.

This was what it meant to have children, this was coming for her one day, this was her future. You loved them and loved them and cared for them and they loved you back, unconditionally, absolutely, so much love you thought you might drown in it, until one day they slammed the screen door and they got into someone else's truck and they drove away. How could that not be the saddest thing in the world?

"Oh, Val," she said.

"Or eighteen. You know what you were doing when you were eighteen?"

Eliza took a deep, shuddery breath. She knew. "Leaving."

"Exactly right. You were leaving. We took that trip to Bangor together"—Eliza winced, remembering the then-brand-new Civic, the smell of the clinic, the pitted unloveliness of the parking lot, the kind look on the doctor's face—"and then you packed your bags for college, and you never looked back."

Eliza said, "Right."

"To add to that for you, or for Charlie, to remind either one of you that there was a time when Joanie wanted more—forget it. I never wanted to make someone else's burden heavier just so I could make mine a little lighter. So I kept the last part of the letter. And I'd make the same choice a hundred times in a row if you asked me to."

Eliza glanced to the side to see Val more clearly. A complicated expression was crossing her face, and she said, "Charlie worshipped your mom, Eliza. I never saw anything like it before or since. Never." Her voice broke off and she pressed the back of her hand to her mouth.

Eliza thought of how Val was leaning over Charlie that first day Eliza arrived early in the summer. She thought of the way Val had hidden the evidence of Charlie's illness because that's what he wanted, how she'd handed him the water, fed him, cared for him, taken him to the doctor, let him sleep. She imagined Val and Charlie, caring together for sick little Eliza.

Of course.

Of course! How could she not have realized this before? She took a deep breath, and she felt like she was unearthing a secret as old and reliable as the lobsters themselves when she said, "You love my dad. You love Charlie."

"Course I love him. I love you too."

"No, I mean you *love* him. You're in love with him."

"Eliza—"

"I know you are. I know you always have been."

Val was silent for a long time. A trio of seagulls circled overheard. Out on a channel marker, Eliza saw a cormorant perched, spreading out its wings to dry. At any other time she would have pointed out the cormorant, but now she was holding her breath, waiting.

Eliza had heard the story dozens of times, but now she could replay it, cast it in a different light. "When you met my mom that day, you weren't just waiting for the boats to come in, not all the boats. You were waiting for him. But he picked Joanie, he picked my mom."

A long time passed, and then eventually Val spoke. "Part of me didn't want her to come back. She was my best friend, Eliza, but when she left I thought, *Good.* Now I can have what was supposed to be mine. I would have loved you just as much as she did, I would have cared for you and for Charlie. I was here. I was ready. I'm sorry if that's an awful thing for me to say, Eliza, but it's true. It's the way it was."

Eliza moved closer to her and rested her head on Val's shoulder. Sternman, offended, sighed and rolled partially on his side. "That's not awful," said Eliza.

"Yes it is."

"It's not, because that's exactly what you did, you did care for me, when she was gone."

There was a low bank of fog out along the horizon. Eliza stared at it and waited a beat and then she said, "I have to go home for Evie's play, I promised her up and down. I have to leave tomorrow. I'll come right back after. Will you take care of him when I'm gone?"

"Of course I will."

They looked out at the water and Eliza said, "That's a long time."

"A long time for what?"

"To love someone who doesn't love you back the same way."

Val sighed, and her sigh was so deep that it seemed to contain decades of a life inside of it. "There are lots of different kinds of love, Eliza. You must know that by now."

43

Rob

Zoe was just back from science camp—she'd been dropped off by Hannah Coogan's mother—and was lying on her bed with her eyes closed.

"Zoe?" said Rob, and waited until she opened her eyes and regarded him. "Zoe, I need to see your phone."

"Why?"

Rob had fallen back on the oldest parenting line in the book, the one he'd sworn, when five-pound Zoe first entered the world, and later, for a terrifying two days, when she had a breathing tube taped inside her nostrils, he would never use: "Because I said so."

The family rule was that all electronics were ultimately in control of the adults. Zoe handed over her phone, and he said, "Thank you," in a manner that was very courtly, almost bowing, and left the room. Rob stood in the hallway and stared at the phone until he realized he didn't know any of Zoe's passwords. So he slunk back and held it back out to her and said, "Will you please pull up your Instagram account."

She did as she was told and handed the phone back. Zoe had two hundred and ninety-one followers on Instagram. Zoe didn't post that often, and when she did she posted carefully curated shots: a close-up of a hydrangea, a sunset, a photo of her and Sofia Palmer with their arms around each other, dressed up and filtered into perfection. A gorgeous shot of *A Family Affair* taken from the launch. One of the lobster boats from her trip to Little Harbor. *Wow*, thought Rob, *Zoe might actually have some talent here.* Each shot had about ninety likes and several encouraging comments. There was nothing untoward in any of it.

Rob took a deep breath and said, "Okay, so what was Deirdre talking about?"

"Deirdre?"

"I saw her at the club. Something about a secret account? With secret photos?"

Zoe smiled, and she looked younger. "Oh. That's not my Instagram account. That's my Finsta account."

"That's it," Rob said. "That's what she said."

"It's not secret, exactly."

"So what is it?"

"It's fake."

"I'm sorry?"

"Finsta. Fake Insta: Finsta."

Rob felt an unnamed pressure behind his forehead. He said, "Can you please explain this to me in a language that I understand?" (He hadn't expected to start saying things like that at age forty. How depressing.)

"Fake Instagram. *Finsta.*"

"Okay," he said. "Let's see it. Show me." He handed the phone back to her and she tapped and swiped at the screen and handed it back to him.

"Here she is," she said. She looked a little bit embarrassed. "Finsta Zoe."

Rob scrolled through. Finsta Zoe was totally different from Instagram Zoe. Finsta Zoe posted several times a day and had only twenty-two followers.

Finsta Zoe was carefree and silly. Finsta Zoe took photos of her grilled cheese sandwich, a hot chocolate mug loaded with whipped cream, a friend's border collie wrestling with a tennis ball. Finsta Zoe didn't use filters; Finsta Zoe posted selfies. Rob looked more carefully at the selfies. They were all appropriate, more goofy than anything. He stopped on one photo and turned the phone to face Zoe. "You look scared in this picture. You look scared and sort of sweet."

She shrugged and ducked her head. "So."

"I don't mean that in a bad way. You look like you looked when you were six. You also look like yourself."

"Well, *duh.* That's the point of a Finsta."

"May I sit down?" He nodded at Zoe's bed.

"Sure."

He sat and took another deep breath and handed the phone back to Zoe. "Let me just go through this one more time, to make sure I have it straight. Your real account is the fake you, and your fake account is the real you?"

"Sort of. Yeah. That's how it is."

"I think I get it." It was weird, but he got it. "Does everyone have one of these? All of your friends?"

"Yeah."

"Do *grown-ups* have these accounts?"

Zoe chortled pleasantly. "*No.* Of course not."

Rob rubbed at his temples. "I really need your mother to come home," he whispered.

"I do too," said Zoe. "I do too."

"Zoe?"

"Yes?"

"It's okay to cry, you know." Her eyes darted up to meet his. "About Grandpa being sick. It's okay to be sad, it's okay to cry."

She put the phone down and cracked the knuckles of each hand. Rob tried not to wince. He had trouble with the sound of cracking knuckles. She said, "Hashtag, I know."

"You do?"

She nodded. "Of course I know." She blinked at him, but her eyes were clear and dry. "I just don't want to."

"Okay, then," he said.

"Okay."

The conversation could have ended there, but Rob wasn't ready to leave the room yet. It felt precious and fleeting, this time with his oldest daughter, just the two of them, alone. His eyes scanned Zoe's room and fell on a metallic envelope on her nightstand. He pointed at it and said, "What's that?"

"Oh. Blood-testing kit. For science camp." She brightened. "Want me to test you? I have one that's not used yet. I tested Evie."

"You tested Evie?"

"Yeah, she's O negative. I'm B negative. I tested Mom in Little Harbor too. She's also B negative. So you'd have to be . . ." She picked up her phone and tapped on it a little bit and then said, "You could be A or B or O. You have a lot of options."

"Wow," said Rob. He was impressed. "How'd you know that?"

She shrugged again. "It's just formulas. If your mom is one type and your dad is one type there's only certain types you can be. That's just how it works. Go wash your hands, and dry them with a clean towel, and then come back."

Rob repaired to the girls' bathroom, then returned to Zoe's bedroom. He wasn't about to mess with Zoe's instructions: he followed them to the letter, even taking a clean towel from the linen closet to be sure.

"Now rub your hands together. Make sure they're warm."

Rob rubbed his hands together and made sure they were warm. Zoe said, "Hang on," and whipped her hair back into a ponytail. She looked like a miniature doctor. She opened the metallic envelope and set a card with four labeled circles on her nightstand. "This is an EldonCard," she said. She held up a small green cylinder. "This is a lancet," she said. "It's just going to be a little prick."

Zoe pressed the lancet into his middle finger and pulled it away, then squeezed his finger until a large drop of blood appeared. Rob looked away.

"You did this to Evie?"

"She didn't mind. It was in the name of science." Zoe glanced at him. Her lips were set in a thin straight line and her expression said, *I'm all business.* She said, "You okay?"

"Fine," said Rob. "Just don't love blood, that's all."

"Yours, or anyone's?"

"Either. Both." When Eliza had come home after beginning her cadaver dissection in med school he'd thrown up just hearing about it. He turned his face to the ceiling and closed his eyes.

"But blood is so *interesting,*" said Zoe. "It tells us so much. It's, like, the secret to everything." She held up a thin white stick and said, "This is an EldonStick. I'm squeezing a drop of blood onto each of the sticks and mixing them into the water drops on the card. See?"

Rob opened one eye and looked at the smears of blood in the circles on the card. He felt a little bit nauseous, but he also felt awestruck by his own daughter. He used to carry her on his shoulders! He used to feed her mashed carrots and bananas with a tiny spoon! He used to push her in a baby swing! And now she could figure out his blood type like it was no big deal. The world was a wonderful, wacky, confounding place.

Zoe tipped the card one way and then tipped it the other way. She moved her lips, counting, and finally she said, "Okay. Here you go. It should be dry." She squinted down the card and then looked back at the directions. "You're O negative," she said. "Just like Evie."

"Good to know," said Rob. "That's very good to know." Then he said, "You know something, Zoe?"

"What?" She collected the debris the blood-testing kit had amassed and swept it into the wastebasket.

"You're going to make a very good doctor someday. If that's what you decide to do."

"Thanks, Dad," she said. She smiled. "I hope so."

"Just so we're clear," he said. "I'm going to request to follow this . . . this *Finsta* account. Your mother is too. And if you don't accept us, or if you do and we don't like what we see, it's gone. The account, the real Instagram . . ."

"Rinsta," said Zoe.

Rob sighed. "Are you serious? Is it really called that?"

Zoe nodded.

"Okay, your Finsta, your Rinsta, your Zinsta, your phone, all of it. It's gone. Am I clear?"

"You're clear." Zoe held up the card and said, "Look! It's all dry." She placed a thin piece of plastic over the card and handed it to Rob. "You can keep it," she said. "As a souvenir."

44

LITTLE HARBOR, MAINE

Mary

"Um," said Mary, on the phone. "I'd like to cancel my appointment?"

At first it came out too much like a whisper, or a question, so she said it again, louder, more firmly: "I'd like to cancel my appointment."

The woman took Mary's name and her number and then she said, "Okay, then, you're all set." It was that easy.

All set. Just like that. *Don't you see?* Mary wanted to say. *Don't you understand what this means, this changes everything, everything about my life is going to change now.* But the woman wouldn't see, and why should she? She was just a voice on the other end of the line. She got calls like this every day, every hour. This was her job.

Mary lay on the bed for a while and tried to think about how she felt. She'd taken the day off from work, and now she didn't need it. She needed the money more. She could call Daphne and Andi, see if she could come in anyway. Maybe one of them wanted the afternoon off. Maybe they both did, maybe they wanted to go out for the evening, maybe she could close. She shuddered, thinking of the last time.

Mary swung her legs over the side of her bed. She opened the closet door. There was a knock on her bedroom door, and she jumped nearly out of her skin and slammed the closet door closed.

"Knock knock!" sang Vivienne, opening the door. She was wearing a birthday hat, striped, with a ridiculous purple pom pom on the tip. She was holding one for Mary too, and, in her other hand, a cake, supermarket bought, with two candles in it, a one and an eight. Luckily the candles weren't lit, because Vivienne's hair was dangling over them, almost in the frosting.

"Happy birthday, baby," she said, looking at Mary expectantly. "Happy, happy birthday."

45

BARTON, MASSACHUSETTS

Rob

"You sure you want to go out today?" asked the Marshall twin. "There's supposed to be some weather coming."

Eliza was going to drive home for Evie's play; Evie was at rehearsal and Zoe was at science camp, and he had the morning. Without Cabot Lodge, and without the houses of Mrs. Cabot's friends on the horizon, exactly the thing Eliza had predicted was going to happen. He was going to have to sell the Hinckley. Soon, before he lost his nerve. He was going to have to do it on the sly, without telling his mother. By the time she found out, the thing would be done.

He had to say goodbye.

"There's always weather," Rob told the Marshall twin. "And, yeah, I'm sure."

The launch pulled up alongside the Hinckley, and the Marshall twin let out one of his world-famous low whistles. "Sorry," he said. "I just can't get over this *boat.*"

"I know," said Rob. "Me either." He felt part of his soul shrivel up and die. This was what he got, for loving a material thing too much. This was what he got. He deserved to have to sell it.

"You going out alone, for real?"

Rob had promised Eliza that he'd never try to sail the Hinckley alone.

"For real," he said.

Rob unlocked the hatch. Down below, he turned on the battery switches. He let the diesel engine warm up, took the cover off the boom. He untied the mooring line and tossed it overboard. These were actions he'd performed hundreds of time—thousands, even, on different boats, throughout his life—but it seemed to him that he had never been so focused on each little task and the sensations surrounding them. There was the feel of the mooring line in his hand, and the sound of the engine coming to life. A lone gull overhead, unleashing on Rob and the ocean a large, ominous, bossy cry. There was the slapping of Rob's shoes as he ran to the helm to put the boat in gear and head it into the wind.

Rob put the boat on autopilot, set the throttle, studied the sky. He would put the mainsail up first. He attached the main halyard to the head of the sail, then headed back to the cockpit to raise the main. Two or three cranks of the winch and the main began to rise. No problem.

Okay, this part was a little more difficult on his own, he could admit that. He'd like to be in the cockpit, it would be helpful to have somebody else guiding the main. But. It was nothing he couldn't handle. He'd guide the main himself.

Now the main was up, and it was a glorious sight. It never failed to take his breath away. There was enough wind now, so he could turn the engine off. He trimmed the main.

"Easy day," he said aloud, though of course there was nobody there to hear him. Even the lone gull had taken off. Four knots.

Would this be his last time on the boat, before he put it up for sale? It might be. But even here, on the water, the peace Rob sought was elusive. It was his phone, his phone was teasing him; his phone wanted him to check his emails, check his texts.

Rob turned the phone off and tossed it down the companionway and into the cabin, where it bounced off the navy-blue cushions and landed on the floor.

He wanted the jib up too. He unfurled it, loaded the winch. Trimmed the jib. Up from four knots to six, and now the sight was even more magnificent, the two sails up, the wind out of the southeast. Cruising now. Rob had sailed lots of boats in his life but really there was nothing like *this* kind of sailing, like sailing a Hinckley, every part of the rigging placed exactly where you wanted it to be. Magic. Bliss.

An errant thought still nibbled at him, something he'd forgotten to do.

Now he had to undo the jib sheet, so he was shifting from port to starboard trying to get it done. This was maybe a *little* bit easier with someone else on board. Slightly easier.

It was while he was undoing the jib sheet that he remembered what it was he had forgotten: the VHF for the marine forecast—the very same radio, of course, that the fishermen in Little Harbor used for the same reason. Because no matter who you were or what kind of boat you had you were just as vulnerable to the whims of nature as the next guy. The ocean was the Great Equalizer. You could be aboard the *Titanic* or a lobster boat and disaster could find you either way.

He switched on the VHF.

Now he scanned the horizon, and he could see the storm clouds gathering at the edge. He should have seen these sooner, he should have been scanning the horizon the whole time, but instead he'd been looking down, thinking about Eliza, about Charlie, about Mrs. Cabot, his faltering business, the money.

Something made Rob think of John F. Kennedy Jr. and his ill-fated flight from New Jersey to Martha's Vineyard. This was big news for a lot of people, of course, but in particular for other pilots and for sailors, and the big question all of them had was not *why* (as it was with the general public) but *how*. An experienced pilot, a short and familiar trip: *How?*

These clouds were far enough away that Rob figured he could outrun them, could sail back to the harbor, back to his mooring.

Of course, he had the option to take down the sails, furl the main, motor back. On another day, in another summer, perhaps he would have done exactly that. That was the more cautious of the choices, and Rob was a smart and experienced enough sailor to know when caution was called for. But on this day, in this summer, the one day he'd had the boat out in weeks, he didn't choose caution.

He'd been four when his father started taking him out on his boat. His father's departure for Thailand, his leap from Judith's arms into Malai's, and the shambolic aftermath of that leap, was still four years in the future. Rob had been too young, too unsullied and innocent and naive, to realize that his father might eventually leave them. He hadn't known fathers *could* leave. Who'd ever consider such a thing? Fathers were real and solid and present; they were teachers, they were gods. Like Charlie was to Eliza.

Eliza! He'd promised her he wouldn't go out on the boat alone. But he'd also promised Mrs. Cabot he'd get her in before Thanksgiving. He'd promised himself he wouldn't need his mother's money. When he and Eliza had stood up in front of two hundred and fifty people in Trinity Church in the Back Bay he'd promised God and everyone he'd never kiss another woman, and then he'd allowed himself to be kissed by Deirdre Palmer.

Fuck cautious. He'd keep the sails up.

He remembered sitting at his father's knee and learning about the way the wind filled the sails. He remembered their first overnight sailing trip, to Rockport, Maine, just the two of them. He remembered waking in the bunk to smell breakfast cooking: the most delicious bacon and eggs Rob had ever eaten in his life.

Rob pulled his life jacket from the cockpit locker and put it on. As he zipped it, his mind went again to JFK Jr. and the question: Not *why*, but *how*?

The answer was, of course, in the backstory. All answers were in the backstory. The sister-in-law delayed at work, the flight pushed back, and back again, so that they were flying in darkness instead of daylight. It became impossible to tell the sky from the water.

The wind picked up; the storm clouds were moving fast. They were directly above, and Rob could see his error. He should have doused the mainsail when he had a chance, when all was still calm. He should pull it down now.

The wind pressure on the sail was now so great that the boat was beginning to heel. Rob wrestled with the sail, but alone he was no match for the wind. And, anyway, he should be at the wheel; he should have another guy, maybe two, with him, so they could pull the sail.

Rob's breath was coming fast now, and he braced himself against the wind.

It was then that the autopilot's compass lost its memory. Rob, still struggling with the sail, had no say in what direction the boat was headed, because it steered itself wildly back and forth, the autopilot searching for a course. It was as though the devil himself had taken the wheel. And maybe he had.

Now the question was whether or not to leave the sail and run back and take the wheel himself. An unfair choice: between bad and worse.

The grease from the bacon that long-ago morning in Rockport, his father's hand on his shoulder, the sensation of being utterly cared for. The certainty that all things were in their place, that all was right with the world.

That was what he wanted for his kids, for Eliza, for their lives. He wanted to give them that sense of order, of being loved unconditionally—his three females, with all of their flaws and foibles and beautiful hair and delightful quirks and confounding social media habits. He wanted to deserve being loved back the same way. And if he'd failed them in the past, he wouldn't fail in the future.

That's what he was thinking when he was thrown to the deck with a force as strong as a gunshot, and the world went black.

46

LITTLE HARBOR, MAINE

Eliza

Eliza didn't want to leave her father, but she had promised Evie ninety-three different ways that she'd be home for *Charlotte's Web,* and home she would be. Besides, Val was there. She'd stay the night with Charlie, if he'd let her. Eliza had washed and replaced the sheets for her own twin bed in case.

As she drove out of Little Harbor, and through Ellsworth, and past the lakes and ponds along Route One, she put the words in her mother's letter on repeat: *I'm so sorry I left you, Eliza. But I've never, ever been sorry I came back.*

Not only that, but this: *Then I found out that there's no such thing, no fairy tale. I guess that's Lesson Number Five.*

And, finally, this: *I know a lot more people will love you in your life but nobody will love you the way I have.*

Her mother, who Eliza had always thought was perfect, had not been. Her mother's happiness, which Eliza had accepted as an absolute truth, had been fragile. She, Eliza, as a little girl of two, had been deserted, and then reclaimed. She didn't know what to do with these new pieces of information, but she couldn't let them go either, so she just kept turning them around and around in her mind, breaking them into jigsaw puzzle pieces, trying to fit them back together again.

She was crossing the Wiscasset bridge, more than two hours into her journey, when her cell phone rang. The screen showed her father's number. Her nerves were already on edge because she hated driving over bridges, but now the too-familiar ball of panic and dread rose in her throat. This was it. He was having another seizure, or worse. She swallowed around the dread and scraped out her question in place of a greeting: "What's wrong, Dad?"

"Nothing's wrong. Guy can't call his daughter?"

"Do you need to go to a doctor? Are you in pain?" She kept her eyes straight ahead, her peripheral vision snagging on the steel-gray water, tinted here and there with azure, with turquoise. "Have you been taking your AEDs?"

"Don't know what that means."

"Your anti-epileptic drugs, Dad. Your seizure meds." Deep breath, and she was over the bridge.

"I took the pill, just as I was supposed to. My head's fine," said Charlie. And: "Why would I want to go to a doctor now, after all of this time not going?"

"Maybe you changed your mind."

"Nope."

"Does something else hurt?"

"Not a thing."

"So why'd you call?"

"I just wanted to hear your voice, Eliza, something wrong with that?"

"Of course not." Except that it was wildly out of character.

"Your voice sounds just like your mom's did, you know that?"

The ball of panic and dread took on weight and rolled back and forth somewhere deep inside Eliza. "Dad. You're scaring me. Do you want to come stay in Barton for a little while? I'll turn right back around and get you. I'm only two hours away, I have plenty of time. I can set up the guest room for you, I promise you'll be comfortable, you can see the girls, see the play tomorrow . . ." She pulled over into the first parking lot she saw and prepared to reverse her journey. Sprague's Lobster, with the requisite picnic tables, the signs for lobster rolls and clam fritters, the tourists.

"I just saw the girls. I wanted to say goodbye, that's all. I was sleeping when you left. Getting lazy, I guess." He forced out a little laugh that made her want to cry.

"Dad. Not *lazy*. Obviously. You're sick. Your body is fighting itself, you need to sleep. Let me come back for you."

"No. I just missed saying goodbye to you, is all. Wanted another shot at it."

Eliza pulled back out into the traffic. She said, "You said goodbye, last night, remember? When I was packing up. I said I'd leave early in the morning, I wanted you to sleep in."

"That's right. Yuh. Must've forgot."

Eliza blinked and concentrated on the road, on the car in front of her. The car had Maryland plates and she could just make out the words TREASURE THE CHESAPEAKE before her watering eyes started to make them blur. *No, stop it, Eliza, no crying.* She just had to get used to the new reality of having a sick parent, that was all. This could drag on for months, a year, more. She couldn't panic over every short phone call, she couldn't read disaster into every tone of voice. She'd drive herself crazy. She'd definitely drive Charlie crazy. What she needed was a plan to get through each day. So her plan for now was that she'd go home for Evie's play, and then the very next day she'd come back, and she'd be the best caretaker the world had ever known, and she wouldn't give up on trying to get her dad to Zachary Curry, and no matter what she wouldn't leave her dad's side.

"Sorry," he said now. "Didn't mean to worry you."

"That's okay, Dad."

She thought about what Val had told her; she thought about herself at sixteen, running out the door, into Russell's truck, not looking back, leaving her father alone in the living rom. At eighteen, packing for college, salivating at the thought of starting fresh. At twenty-five, thirty, thirty-two, thirty-five, setting up a whole different kind of life while all along Charlie continued his: up every morning, out on the boat, each day so similar to the one that had just passed and the one that would follow, just like her mother said in the letter. She thought about how Charlie had carried that burden around with him forever, the knowledge that there had been times when he hadn't been enough for his wife or his daughter.

"Daddy?" she said after some time. She tried to keep her voice steady. "I'm sorry."

"For what?" The way Charlie's voice was gruff and vulnerable at the same time tore a little hole in Eliza's heart.

Stop and go, stop and go, the car with the Maryland plates couldn't make up its mind.

"For being a jerk," she said. "When I was sixteen. Running around with Russell Perkins, thinking only about myself. Leaving you alone all the time."

"Eliza, when you were sixteen you were an angel. The best I could have asked for."

"There's no way that was true."

"That's how I remember it, and how I always will."

"I'm still sorry."

"You don't need to be sorry for a thing. Not a thing, Eliza. Not ever. Goodbye now."

There was more she wanted to say. But what? Sorry that I failed you? Sorry that I made you feel like you weren't enough for me either? Sorry that you won't let me help you now, when I might be able to?

No. It wasn't possible. It was all unsayable. So instead she said this: "Bye, Daddy. I love you. I'll see you in a couple of days."

Outside of Wiscasset the traffic eased suddenly, and Eliza felt the liberation of unrestricted movement; it felt like a breath of fresh air after leaving a stifling room.

47

Mary

Late in the afternoon on the 3rd of August, two days after she turned eighteen, Mary Brown knocked on the door of Charlie Sargent's house. She didn't hear an answer, and her first thought was, *Okay, maybe it's done already,* so she let herself in. Then she heard his voice.

"That you, Mary?"

"Yup." She sounded small and frightened.

"Come on up, if you don't mind. Come right on up to the bedroom." He sounded pretty chipper, considering.

Mary walked up the stairs. There were two bedrooms at the top, one on either side of the staircase, and she followed his voice to find the right one. Charlie Sargent was on his bed, propped up by pillows so that he was sitting with his legs straight out in front of him. His hair was wet and neatly parted and combed over to the side, and he wore a long-sleeved plaid shirt that looked new, or at least recently ironed, and a pair of blue jeans. It took Mary a minute to figure out why he looked so different from how he usually looked and then she realized that he wasn't wearing one of his usual ball caps. Almost all of the lobstermen wore ball caps, almost all the time.

She had expected this to be a somber occasion, but Charlie smiled at her, a big, open smile, and she realized she was smiling back.

"You have what I'm looking for, Mary Brown?"

"Yes." She pulled the baggie out of her pocket.

"Orange!" he said. "Aren't they sort of cheerful."

"Um. Yeah. So, I did some research. Sixty milligrams each. Which means between three and four to get to two hundred, which is the amount you want. So I guess four?" She tried not to let her voice crack when she talked but it cracked anyway. *When in doubt, choose brave. Choose brave choose brave choose brave.*

Charlie nodded. "Sounds right." Then he said, "I hope it was no trouble, bringing these to me. I never did want to cause anyone trouble."

"I know you didn't. Don't worry."

Mary saw then that next to Charlie on the bed were the photos she had seen downstairs the last time she'd been here: Eliza and her mother, and the photograph of Eliza's family. It was seeing the photographs that made this all seem real, and suddenly her hands were slick with sweat and her face was warm and her eyes were wet.

"Are you scared?" she whispered.

"Nah," he said. "Not anymore, not like I was last time we talked. My head was hurting something awful this week, but all of a sudden it's not hurting anymore."

"Okay," she said. "Good. I'd be scared."

"I bet you wouldn't."

"I bet I would."

When in doubt, choose brave.

"Now, Mary. Here's what I want you to do. I want you to put the pills down but don't hand them to me. And then I want you to leave. After a little bit, maybe an hour, I want you to call Val and ask her to come by the house. Just tell her I asked you to, that's all. There's a note with her name on it in the kitchen. Never been much of a writer, but I did my best. She'll find it, you don't need to worry about that. There's one for Eliza too. Val'll take care of talking to Eliza, so you don't need to worry about that either. I know Eliza, she's going to make a lot of bother about it, but my note explains that this is exactly how I wanted it, and you're not going to be involved."

"Got it," Mary said. She didn't know exactly what she had expected, but definitely not for it all to be so . . . so *businesslike*. So organized. On the nightstand was a glass of water with two fresh ice cubes in it. She did as she was told, putting the bag of pills on the nightstand.

"The most important thing is you get out of here, okay? No reason you should be around for any of it."

"But then . . . but then you'll be all alone."

"I'm not going to be alone at all. I'm going to see Joanie again. Soon I'm going to be less alone than I've been in twenty-five years."

Well, that did it. She couldn't talk any longer, she was crying.

"Don't cry, Mary. Hell, *I'm* not crying."

"Okay," she said, nodding and wiping at her mouth. "Can I—do I, uh, say goodbye?"

"Hell yes, Mary. Come and give me a hug."

"That's okay, for me to do that?"

"I'm not so fragile, not yet. Could do with a hug."

When the hug was over Charlie's voice got softer and he said, "You're my angel, Mary, and I thank you for what you've done for me."

"It's okay," she whispered, because *You're welcome* seemed too formal, and also too casual.

"Now it's time you were getting out of here."

"Yes," she nodded. "Right. I will."

Downstairs Mary opened the front door and then closed it again, so if Charlie was listening he'd hear the sound of that. But she didn't leave.

48

Eliza

Evie's play took place in the auditorium of the high school attached to the girls' private day school. Eliza drove Rob, Zoe, and herself to the play. Rob couldn't drive. His arm was bound up in a sling, and he was jacked up on prescription painkillers—he said he felt pleasantly fuzzy some of the time, but when the medicine started to wear off he just felt glum. He looked glum. His arm hurt, and his pride hurt, and even more than his arm and his pride, his heart hurt. His heart hurt the most.

Judith said she'd meet them at the play—she'd been running lines with Evie for weeks, and she wanted to see how the whole thing turned out.

("The spider dies," Zoe had said in reply. "That's how it turns out.")

Eliza couldn't help looking around the auditorium and wondering how, without Cabot Lodge, without Judith's money, without the prospect of more work for Rob, they'd ever be able to keep the girls in that school. Maybe she could get a job, but she was basically just a medical school dropout, trained only in quitting, mothering, and hauling traps. The lobster population in the waters near Barton was minimal, not enough to support a family of four accustomed to living at a certain level.

Eliza sat between Zoe and Rob, and Judith sat on Rob's other side. Rob immediately got caught talking to another parent, a dad who was obviously only thirty percent okay with missing work to attend an amateur theater production. He kept looking at his phone. Judith's eyes were searching the auditorium, probably wondering if they sold cocktails in the lobby like they did at the Ethel Barrymore on Broadway. Zoe was tapping away on her iPhone. Eliza reached over and slid the phone gently from Zoe's hands and into her own bag.

"Hey!" said Zoe.

Eliza shrugged unapologetically and tilted her head toward the stage, where the curtain remained closed but of course could open at any moment. Zoe made slits out of her eyes and regarded her mother. Eliza regarded her right back and remembered when Zoe was a chubby, bald lump of pudding who dissolved into laughter anytime Eliza bent over her crib. Ancient history.

Then, as though she were reading her mother's mind, Zoe allowed herself the freedom of a smile, a *real* smile, as wide and bright and forgiving as sunshine itself, and she looked suddenly the same way she'd looked at age six, the year she'd started losing teeth. She also looked, oddly, like Mary on the day Eliza had driven her to her appointment in Ellsworth and Mary had gotten out of the car and smiled at Eliza. *Was* that odd? It was, but also maybe it wasn't. The two were not so far apart in age. And maybe all of the girls in the world were just different versions of all of the other girls in the world, with their universal femaleness, female problems and wisdom, challenges and triumphs, female perspectives. The great, universal sisterhood.

Eliza turned her eyes back to the curtain, which was a deep, delicious red, darker than cooked lobsters, more like the color of rubies and also of the lipstick Eliza remembered her mother wearing when she got dressed up. She felt little pinpricks of tears, and she blinked them back aggressively: this was neither the time nor the place to wax nostalgic. Eliza remembered the massive fund-raising that had gone into restoring this auditorium two years ago, and she took a moment to appreciate the golden proscenium arch, the better-than-Broadway seats, the plush carpet, the teardrops of lights suspended from the ceiling.

Then the curtain opened to reveal a white picket fence, a tilting farmhouse and barn, and everything else went out of Eliza's mind. When Evie said her first line, from offstage—*Where's Papa going with that ax?*—Zoe nudged her and she nudged Zoe and Rob took her hand with his un-injured one and squeezed and Eliza could see that Judith was beaming.

The play went on, Act One, Act Two, the farm, the pig, the spider, the county fair.

Normally Eliza would have known every line to this play, from practicing with Evie; she would have been reciting in her head along with the actors. But her dad's illness had forced her to forgo many of the *normally*s, and as it turned out her memories of the story were hazy. Each scene contained a delightful revelation. When she stole another glance at Judith she thought she saw her lips moving along with Evie's. Eliza was a little envious, but it was also sort of nice, to see Judith doing that. *Fair enough,* thought Eliza. *Let her have this.*

Then the funniest thing happened. Evie was saying one of her lines—an innocuous line: *Scrub Wilbur up real good, Aunt Edith. He's got to win that blue ribbon tomorrow*—and there was something about the set of her jaw and the way she moved her hands that looked so much like Charlie that it seemed not just like a coincidence but like an actual homage, and again the pinpricks of tears threatened.

Eliza looked up at the gilded, gorgeous ceiling, and suddenly she felt like the luckiest person in the universe. She felt almost dizzy with the awareness of her luck, and also with the awareness that what she was feeling was more profound than luck. It was as if her soul and the souls of those around her were knitted together into a sum that was bigger than its parts: she and Rob and the girls and Judith and Charlie and, sure, throw Mary in there, throw in Val. (Not Christine Cabot, though—she wasn't invited.) And how could Eliza ever have thought for a second that she didn't belong here, that her place wasn't *right here?*

Charlotte wrote the word *humble* in the web at the fair; Wilbur got the bronze medal; Fern rode the Ferris wheel with Henry Fussy; the circle of life, inevitably, heartbreakingly, claimed Charlotte.

One of the narrators had the saddest line of all:

Of the hundreds of people that had visited the fair, nobody knew that a gray spider had played the most important part of all. No one was with her when she died.

That did it. Waterworks. Eliza thought she was being subtle enough, reaching into her bag for a tissue, but then she saw that Zoe was watching her in alarm, and she heard her whisper, "What's wrong?"

"Nothing," Eliza whispered back. "Good play, that's all. So much emotion." She swiped at her eyes with the tissue. *No one was with her when she died.*

She expected Zoe to roll her eyes and shift an inch away—tears *plus* the word *emotion* from her *mother,* of all people, *in public*—but she surprised Eliza by grabbing the hand Rob wasn't holding and squeezing it tight, and Eliza noticed that Zoe's fingers were now nearly as long as her own.

Then it was time for the bows, and Eliza knew Evie wouldn't be able to pick her family out of the audience—the stage lights were that good, they'd raised extra for that during the renovations—but she waved and beamed anyway, and she watched Evie's face, guileless and proud, searching, searching.

49

LITTLE HARBOR, MAINE

Mary

Mary waited downstairs in the living room for ten minutes. Then she waited ten more minutes, and then she tiptoed back up the stairs. She pushed open the bedroom door, afraid of what she was going to find.

But all she saw was Charlie Sargent sleeping in his bed. He'd taken the photo of Joanie from beside him and had put it on his chest and he was holding on to it.

After a time, Charlie's breathing became irregular; there would be long pauses where he wasn't breathing, and Mary would think, *This is it.* And then he would draw a long breath. And then the same thing would happen again. That same thing happened many times in a row. Charlie's mouth had fallen open, but his eyes remained closed. After a while, Mary pulled up a chair from the corner of the room and sat next to Charlie and held his hand. Once there was a really long pause between breaths, and Mary thought, *This is definitely it.* Then there was another breath. And then finally there came a breath that didn't have anything after it although she waited and then she stood and moved the chair back and pressed the back of her free hand to her mouth and let out one sob— just one.

The strangest part, the part that Mary hadn't anticipated, was how quickly Charlie Sargent's body changed after that. It was pinkish, regular body colored, and then not five minutes later the pink was gone and his skin had turned a waxy yellow color all over. And that's how Mary knew that it was done.

She touched her belly and wondered if somehow the baby knew something about what was happening.

Leaving Charlie's house, Mary wasn't looking around her to notice who might be seeing her or what was going on in the small road. She didn't notice the clouds scudding by or the way the wind changed, sending the scent of the harbor right up through Charlie Sargent's bedroom window. She just got in her car, and she gathered herself, and she put both of her hands on her belly for a moment before she put them on the steering wheel, and when she was ready she drove.

50

LITTLE HARBOR, MAINE

Eliza

Rob and the girls took a room at Little Harbor's only bed-and-breakfast for Charlie's funeral. The bed-and-breakfast was on the Point, and while it was booked solid most of the summer the innkeepers opened a room they didn't usually offer to guests and gave it to the Barnes family.

After Charlie's body had been taken away by the funeral director from Ellsworth, Val had gone into the house and cleaned it and washed and changed the sheets. Eliza told her over the phone that she didn't need to do that—she'd pay a cleaning service, Eliza said, she'd arrange for it all on the drive up.

"No," said Val fiercely. "No, Eliza, I want to. Let me."

The night before the funeral they were all sleeping, but Eliza couldn't. She climbed out of bed and crept down the stairs and outside and drove to her father's house, passing the beautiful homes on the Point, dark and quiet in the night.

She considered Charlie's house from the outside: it was so small, so unassuming, you wouldn't have given it a second look if you'd been driving past. And yet what full lives had begun and ended there. In fact, the little house seemed to know that; it seemed, in the pale light offered by the moon, to draw its very own rhythmic, settled breaths.

Eliza took her own shuddering breath and pushed open the door.

She flicked on the front hall light. She turned toward the living room, half expecting to see her father in the recliner, and it was like someone had punched her directly in the heart when he wasn't. She inhaled carefully, and took in a scent of Pine Sol that called to mind her high school cafeteria.

Her foot slipped on something, an envelope with her name on it.

Dear Eliza,

Okay, here goes.

You know how gossip spreads whether it's true or not especially in this town. I know how people talk here, and I know that what they're talking about right now is some pills that were next to your dad on the nightstand when he died. I know people are talking about where he got them and if he meant to take as many as he did.

I know where he got the pills because I gave them to him. And I know that he meant to take them because he asked me for them.

Your dad helped me with something earlier in the summer. It's a long story but basically I was in real trouble, and I was scared, and your dad made sure I was okay. He saved me.

The most important thing I want to tell you, Eliza, is that when your dad died I was with him. He didn't ask me to stay with him. But it didn't feel right to leave him alone and so I stayed and I'm glad I did. I didn't know what to expect. I've never seen anyone die before. But when your dad died he wasn't scared or sad or uncertain. He was peaceful. He believed he was going to see your mom again and he was happy about that. I would say he was almost excited, or anyway relieved. He had pictures of you and your family all around him. He took the pills, and he went to sleep, and he didn't wake up. That was it. And he wasn't alone for any of it, I promise. I didn't leave until it was over.

Your dad loved you so much. I'm telling you that because he seemed like the kind of man who might have some trouble saying it out loud. But he did, he lit up every time he talked about you. My dad is someone who was never around and I know the difference between lucky and not. I know that you are lucky and I hope that you know it too.

I know what I did is against the law in Maine. I know I could get in a lot of trouble for writing this down if anyone but you reads it. I know I could go to jail. I don't think you will tell anyone else but I guess I don't know that for sure so I'm just trusting you. I'm not writing to say I'm sorry, because I'm not. I would do it again. I know how sick he was and I know he didn't want to get sicker. Your dad was a hero to me. He gave me hope when I didn't have any. He was an angel. He's more of an angel now, I'm sure of it.

Eliza read the letter three times in a row until she had committed it to memory and then she tore it up into very small pieces and she put the little torn-up pieces in her pocket and then she got into her car and she drove to where her family was. Her grief was unbearable, a weight pressing down from high above and settling on her shoulders, in her gut, in her soul, but she knew she had to bear it, and so she knew that she would.

51

Eliza

"Turn on the hauler, Mommy," instructed Evie. "Let's catch some lobsters."

"I can't, sweetie, it's a Sunday."

They had buried Charlie—the whole town had buried Charlie, there hadn't been a funeral like that since, well, since forever. Then they'd had an early dinner at The Lobster Trap, and then they'd all gotten restless, so Eliza had suggested that she take the girls out on Charlie's boat. Rob stayed back out of necessity—the sling—and Judith by choice, but the girls were eager.

"Ohhh." Evie looked interested. "I forgot about that. What would happen if you did anyway?"

"Well, if I got caught, I'd lose my license."

"You don't have a license."

"Even worse."

"Who would catch you?"

"Marine Patrol."

"What will happen to Grandpa's traps?" asked Zoe.

"We'll take them up," said Eliza.

"Who will?"

"I will."

"When?"

"Soon."

"Who will help you? Daddy?"

This made Eliza smile. "No, sweetie, not with his arm hurt."

"Maybe Grandmother."

Eliza laughed. "Maybe. But probably not."

"Do you need someone strong?"

"Yes."

"Deirdre's strong," suggested Zoe.

"She is."

"But I don't know if she's the right kind of strong. Can *I* help you?" That was Evie. "I'm the right kind of strong."

"No you aren't," said Zoe.

"I think you're both the right kind of strong," said Eliza.

"Can I help too?" asked Zoe.

"Sure."

"Are you crying, Mommy?" asked Evie.

"No."

"Why not? Aren't you really sad?"

"I am really sad. Sometimes people get so sad they can't even cry."

"Are you that kind of sad?"

"I think I am."

"Are you *heartbroken?*"

"That's a good way to put it."

Evie leaned against her and said, "Me too." Then she said, "Can't we just haul *one*? Nobody's looking, I promise. Just one. Just to see what's in there. We can put it right back down, I just want to look."

For a split second Eliza thought about it. But the rules were far too ingrained in her; she couldn't break them.

"I can't," she told Evie. "It's the law. The law is sacred out here."

"*Sacred,*" said Zoe. "Regarded with reverence. Secured against violation or infringement."

"Wow," said Evie.

Zoe shrugged modestly. "It was a vocab word last year."

"Also, it's dangerous, just me out here with the two of you, you could get hurt or worse if you got caught in the trap lines. It's not worth the risk."

"So how will you take them up, without Daddy?"

"I have a friend who can help me."

Zoe said, "Grandpa told me once that you can't touch someone else's traps, but is it okay since he was your dad?"

"Sort of," said Eliza. "If I had to I could get a special pass. But I don't have to because Grandpa left me a note, to give me permission."

"He did?"

"Yup."

"Was that the last thing he ever wrote?"

"I think so." There had been a note for Val, and a note for Eliza. Eliza didn't know what Val's note said. Her own, in her father's distinctively sloppy scrawl, said, *You and your mom were everything to me. I've been as blessed as any man out there. This is how I wanted it.*

You could know someone, but you didn't always *know* them. You didn't always know the depths of their soul. You didn't always know they had such simple poetry inside of them.

She thought about the description of Charlie and Val in her mother's letter, standing over a sick little Eliza. *They looked like two parents.*

And then she'd said to Val, *That's a long time.*

A long time for what?

To love someone who doesn't love you back the same way.

But who was to say for sure that he hadn't? Charlie had been alone for years and years and years, after Eliza had gone. And Val had been alone too. Unless they weren't alone. The heart, with its four chambers and its endless and unknowable and un-mappable sub-chambers—who was to say, really, about any of it.

Her father had let her think for so long that her mother had been perfect: he gave that to her, a gift, when she'd needed it the most. By being who Charlie Sargent was, and also by being who he wasn't, he'd let her go, he'd let her fly, he'd let her soar, gliding like a cormorant. And look where Eliza, lucky, lucky person, wife and mother and daughter and friend, had landed.

Her mother had been right about a lot, but she'd been wrong about one thing: there was such a thing as a fairy tale, if you looked at the story the right way.

She thought of how her father had looked in the coffin, like himself and yet not, familiar and *other* at the same time. She thought of Zoe and Evie as babies—their pure skin and bright eyes, their pockets of perfect fat. From here to there, from that to this—it was hard not to wonder what the point of it all was.

Eliza motored out to the closest set of her father's buoys and regarded them. Maybe the fishermen had it right all along, going out into the vast sea every day, voyaging, coming back home, doing it again and again, making a life out of that. Maybe the journey was the whole point.

Well, no use losing it now—it was hard to drive a boat when you were crying. A gull circled and then disappeared. The water was smooth as glass, no chop. At peace. The next day, or the day after that, she'd ask Russell to come out with her and help her. She'd give away the traps, as Charlie had requested, but she'd keep one and bring it back to Barton. She'd put it in the side yard and plant flowers in it and around it. She wondered if the yacht club would let her put the *Joanie B* on *A Family Affair*'s mooring, just for now. Just until winter.

Probably not.

Definitely not.

It was getting on toward sunset, and yellows and oranges were tiptoeing into the blue of the sky. Soon the whole sky would be flaming.

"I think I see Grandpa up there," said Evie. "Looking at us."

"No you don't," said Zoe. "That's impossible."

Eliza said, *"Zoe"* warningly, and Zoe clamped her lips closed.

Evie put her arm around Eliza's waist and leaned into her, and that was not unexpected nor unusual, and then Zoe did the same, and that was both unexpected and unusual, so Eliza cut the motor and stayed as still as she could, not wanting to destroy the moment. Then came a sob, and another, and another, and Zoe was crying—not even trying to hide it, or play it cool, she was just crying, and crying, and crying, messy, unpretty crying, an eruption of gulps and tears. Eliza let go of Evie for a moment and wrapped both of her arms around Zoe and held her as tightly as she had when she was a baby, and when she was a little girl, and she thought, *Finally.*

When Zoe had calmed herself Eliza drove the boat back to the mooring, where they all climbed into Charlie's old skiff. Eliza let each of the girls take a turn rowing and then she took over and rowed them back to the dock, where she could see two figures waiting. Judith and Rob, still in their funeral clothes. The juxtaposition was startling—Judith! At the *wharf*! Waiting for a *skiff*!—but at the same time it bolstered Eliza. The universe could tilt, two worlds could collide, and there was a good chance neither one would fracture.

"There she is," said Rob, when they got close enough. "The captain's daughter, and the captain's daughter's daughters. What a sight for sore eyes, the three of you."

52

BARTON, MASSACHUSETTS

Rob

"Rob," said Deirdre, coming toward him. "Rob, Rob, Rob." She laid a hand briefly on his forearm.

"Deirdre!" he said. Deirdre seemed to be emitting a glow. It was probably the light from the tiki torches surrounding the patio, of course. Tiki torches could make anyone glow. Rob was happy to check in with himself and realize that he was admiring Deirdre from a distance, as a casual observer. That was all. He was looking at her like she was a piece of art, something to be seen but not closely interacted with. He moved his head to indicate the patio, the beautifully set tables, the silent-auction tables, the blissful, pretty, moneyed people in early stages of inebriation. "It's perfect. It's everything you wanted. Are you happy?"

Deirdre was a little tipsy—in control, but tipsy. She sighed. "I am," she said. "I'm as happy as I get." She furrowed her brow and whispered, "Any news on the boat?"

"Oh, *that*." Rob waved his good arm, spilling a bit of his cocktail as he did. "They're still working on it," he said. He couldn't keep his voice from splitting. "Anyway. It's just an object, right? It's just a thing."

"'Ships at a distance have every man's wish on board,'" said Deirdre.

Rob said, "Pardon me?" Maybe Deirdre was drunker than she appeared to be.

"Zora Neale Hurston. *Their Eyes Were Watching God*."

"I see," said Rob, who didn't.

"Have you bid on anything yet?"

Rob didn't want to say, "My financial situation is precarious at the moment," so he just said, "No. Not yet," and made a face that he hoped indicated that he simply hadn't had a chance. Eliza was deep in conversation with Judith at a small bar table and had been for quite some time. What in the world could they be talking about?

"You can set it up on your phone, you know. If you haven't already.

There are instructions over at the table, on those small white cards. That way you'll know if someone outbids you and you can place another bid."

"Cool," said Rob noncommittally. Just what he needed: an opportunity to spend money he didn't have.

"Your mother is going for the African safari."

"Wow."

"She's, like, *really* going for it."

"I'm not sure I can picture my mother on a safari."

"Oh, I can," said Deirdre. "I definitely can."

They both glanced over at Judith and Eliza; indeed, Judith had taken her phone out of her evening bag and was examining it. Eliza was clutching a cocktail napkin. She looked like she'd just finished crying or was about to begin. Rob wanted to go over to her, to make sure that she was okay. He wanted to place his hand on the tender part of her heart, to protect her from any more sadness.

But of course you couldn't really protect people from sadness, you could only be there for them once it hit.

Deirdre cleared her throat and the pressure on Rob's arm increased. "There's something I've been wanting to talk to you about."

"Uh," he said. "Is it about—" He lowered his voice and looked furtively around to see who might be observing them or, worse, listening. He didn't see Brock anywhere. Gaggles of Barton women and groups (what was the masculine form of *gaggles*?) of Barton men were milling about, and among them were various unfamiliar faces: imports from Boston or Nantucket or the Vineyard, corporate sponsors, Judith's nearest and dearest. He saw his dentist, Dr. Choo, and Zoe's husband-and-wife orthodontist team, the Drs. Smith. Nobody seemed to be paying any attention to Deirdre and him. He continued, "Is this about That Night?"

Deirdre nodded.

"Okay," he said. "Shoot." The African Sunrise was going down easy. His arm, which often throbbed by the end of the day, was merely thrumming pleasantly. "Go for it."

"Okay." Deirdre took a deep breath and looked down, fixing her eyes on the tile. She said, "I'd like to say I regret that night." Her next sentence came out in a rush, like the words were running over each other to get out. "But I don't regret it even though I know I should." Then she looked up, closed her eyes, and sucked in her breath sharply; she looked like Evie did immediately after saying something like, "I spilled chocolate milk on the couch" or "Your iPhone fell in the toilet."

"Oh," he said. He squinted at Deirdre and started to feel a little bit nervous. He glanced over again at Judith and Eliza: they were laughing. Now his arm was throbbing. He might have to go for something stronger than an African Sunrise on the next round.

He saw one of the gala minions watching them; she was quivering importantly, waiting to talk to Deirdre. He made a motion to indicate the minion but Deirdre ignored him and said, "Listen, Rob. I don't know about you, but I've had a few times lately where I've almost told Eliza what happened that night."

Rob's heart jumped from his chest and landed somewhere near his ears, and when it was done jumping, he said—very quietly, almost in a whisper—"I know what you mean."

"But I didn't."

"I didn't either."

"And here's why. It would seem, in the telling, like it was so much more than it was. At a time when Eliza is—well, she's fragile. I've never seen Eliza so fragile. And who wouldn't be? I don't want to lay anything else on her just so *I* can feel better. Especially when the thing was, it was a stupid mistake, that I turned a conversation into anything physical. It was nothing."

"It was *less* than nothing!" Rob agreed heartily, and he thought he saw a trace of hurt flicker in Deirdre's eyes and then disappear. "I mean, in the big scheme of things," he hurried to say.

"Right," she said. A long moment slid between them. The minion gave up, sighed, and left. Deirdre said, "Just one more thing, Rob, then I have to go check in with the chef."

"Is it the coin? Did you find the coin?"

She furrowed her brow. "The what?"

"My ten-baht."

"Oh." Her face softened. "From your dad."

"Yeah." His voice was rough.

"No, I didn't. I'm sorry."

"That's okay. I don't really *need* it. I just—"

"You want it. It's from your dad. I get it." She closed her eyes and said, "For such a long time I thought of you, Robert Barnes II, as the one who got away."

Rob was at once flattered, perplexed, and a little afraid. "But how could I be the one who got away? I've only known you since the kids were born."

"I know," she said. "I *know*. That's what's funny about it. But it's how I felt. You're decent, and you're kind, and the way you listened to me that night at The Wharf Rat—I just hadn't been *listened to* in so long. So I wanted to say thank you for that."

"You're welcome," said Rob.

"And, as far as anything *physical* goes . . ." She hesitated.

Rob cringed. "Deirdre, we really don't need to—"

"No, let me finish," she said. "This is important. You had a lot to drink that night."

If a cringe could get deeper, that's what Rob's did.

"You didn't . . . how should I say this? You didn't have your usual faculties about you. And I, well, this is embarrassing, but I took advantage of you."

"You did?" asked Rob.

"I did. I offered you a ride home, you remember."

"I don't remember. All I remember is that we were in the bar, and then we were in the Tahoe kissing."

"Right. Only kissing! But even that—you tried to stop me, Rob. I ignored you. Then you got out of my car and drove your own car home."

"You did? I *did*?"

"And then when I saw you outside St. Matthew's, I let you think you were equally to blame. It was terrible of me."

"No," said Rob. "I *was* equally to blame. It takes two to make a mistake like that."

"The funny thing is, the past few weeks things have been better than great between Brock and me." Deirdre looked shy and sort of sweet, like someone had taken her sharp edges and filed them down to a rounder, softer version. "It's like what happened between us made me realize that I should put my energy into *that*, into my own marriage, instead of, well, you know, envying someone else's. And once I started trying harder, Brock did too."

"That's great," said Rob. "Deirdre, I'm really happy to hear that."

"I mean, the sex has been *fantastic*—"

Rob held up his hand and said, "Okay, okay, we don't need to—"

"You're right," said Deirdre with a private smile. "We don't need to. But it's like what happened between you and me fixed whatever was wrong. And you're not the one who got away anymore. You're just—you're just you. You're just Rob."

"I'm glad," said Rob, "about Brock. I'm glad I'm just Rob."

"So thank you."

"Well," said Rob. He'd been attending social functions since before he could button his own suit coat. He came from a world where *manners trumped everything*. If there was one thing he knew how to do it was how to respond to gratitude. "You're welcome," he said, and meant it. "You're very welcome, Deirdre."

53

Eliza

"You won't believe it," Deirdre told Eliza when they greeted each other. "One of the corporate sponsors who *wasn't even going to come* called this morning to say that they were coming. With guests! We had to redo three of the front tables. I'm out of my mind." But Deirdre didn't look out of her mind. She looked blissful and in control. She was the happiest version of Deirdre that Eliza had seen in a long, long time.

Everything had come together beautifully. Eliza was in awe. At each end of the long room separating the grand ballroom from the patio were two bars, and in between the bars were two long tables holding the silent-auction items. One of the most popular items was a donation from a new jeweler that had just moved to town: twenty-five "mystery boxes." A clutch of women were holding up each box and shaking it in turn. The whole idea of shaking twenty-five mystery boxes of jewelry made Eliza feel exhausted, but the women were getting super into it.

In the grand ballroom were twenty-five tables set for ten, with the simplest, classiest centerpieces Eliza had ever seen: tall thin vases filled with sand, each holding a single bloodred desert rose. There was a large screen set up at the front of the room, which for now was blank. Eliza saw Catherine Cooper and Sheila Rackley deliberating over something near one of the bars, so she went directly to the opposite one. Eliza was still getting her Barton legs back; she felt like a newborn colt, unbalanced one moment, sure of herself the next.

Eliza ordered the signature cocktail of the evening: an African Sunrise, served in a highball glass. She found a small round bar table to sit at, from which she surveyed the scene. Glittery dresses. Tanned legs, tanned arms, manicures, pedicures. Perfume. Professionally straightened hair, professionally loosely curled hair, gold bracelets, silver watches. More money in Claire Foster's earrings—pear-shaped diamonds, a famously extravagant "push present" from her husband after the birth of their third son—than some men in Little Harbor had invested in their boats or their houses.

When a familiar voice said, "Excuse me, is this seat taken?" Eliza turned around: her mother-in-law.

"I bought two tables," Judith said. "Early on. Stocked them with my richest friends; I promised Deirdre they'd drive the silent-auction prices to the sky. And they will."

"Wow," said Eliza. "Two tables! That was really nice of you."

Judith shrugged and said, "Nice, schmice. I love a good gala. People get drunk and they're wicked and generous all at the same time. It's the perfect storm." She felt at her neck for her diamond-wrapped pearl pendant. "Of course," she went on, "I did have a seat for Christine Cabot. She's been known to spend at these events. But . . ."

"I know," said Eliza. "I know." Christine effing Cabot.

"We're not speaking, just at the moment," said Judith. "Christine and I."

"I'm not speaking to Christine Cabot at the moment either," said Eliza, and Judith surprised her by laughing genuinely.

Judith wore an asymmetrical peplum dress in white. Daring, for a woman of sixty-five, some might say, especially the white. But Judith made it work: she was like the Susan Lucci of—well, everything. Just when you thought she was done for she came back stronger and more alive than ever, with more extravagant hair. Judith settled herself in the chair opposite Eliza and arranged herself so she had a view of the glittering crowd. She took a long sip of her African Sunrise. "This goes down easy," she said.

"It does. I wonder what's in it?"

"Ethiopian coffee, grapefruit vodka, sparkling water, simple syrup."

How *did* Judith know so much? She knew everything!

Judith leaned toward Eliza and said, "How are you doing, Eliza? Now that you've been home for a while. I know how it goes with these things, you're so caught up in the details, the arrangements, that it takes a while for your feelings to settle. And of course it was all such a shock. And even when it isn't, mourning takes a long time. There are so many ups and downs along the way. Of course you remember that, from when your mother died."

"I do." The early, dark February days, the iron sky low over Little Harbor, the lobster boats and the traps pulled out of the water: it all seemed like one long, desolate winter's dream.

"I once heard it described as walking upstairs with a yo-yo."

"That sounds about right."

"There's just no way to rush it. Because life is long, Eliza. It goes on and on and on, and if we're lucky we can recover from sorrow, and we can even reinvent ourselves. I understand reinvention, you know. I get why Robbie's trying to do what he's trying to do about the money."

"You do?"

Judith nodded, and her hair didn't move. "Living with money is a complicated business. You haven't learned how to do it yet. It takes years."

Eliza said, "I've had years."

"It takes more years, longer. Believe me, I know. It took me *so long* to get used to the kind of money that's in this family."

"It did?"

"Sure it did. Of *course* it did. I grew up *decidedly* middle class. In New Jersey. When I met Rob's father he introduced me to a world that I hardly knew had existed before."

Eliza said, "*Middle class*? How did I not know that? I knew you were from New Jersey. But I always thought it was rich-person's New Jersey."

"I don't talk about it much. But it was not rich-person's New Jersey. And it was lovely. Right along the shore, the beaches were something else. The boardwalk. Bruce Springsteen land, as it came to be known. My childhood was idyllic."

"I love Bruce Springsteen," breathed Eliza. She thought about The

Wheelhouse, the jukebox, the men coming in off the boats. She thought, *"My Hometown,"* and her heart constricted a little bit.

"Come to think of it," said Judith now, "Rob's the only real native among us, when it comes to the money, the only one truly born into it. So he is the only one entirely comfortable with it. Which is why it's so funny that he—oh, why talk about it. That's all between the two of you now."

There was a brief, hopeful moment when Eliza thought Judith was going to reveal her stance on Rob's financial misjudgment to be some sort of a joke—Eliza thought she might say, *Of* course *I'm here if you need me. And so is my money!*

But Judith didn't say that. Judith lifted her empty highball glass and said, "Another one?"

Eliza wasn't sure she was ready to be drunk under the table by her own mother-in-law. "Maybe in a minute," said Eliza. "I need to get some food first."

The menu, both the sit-down dinner and the passed hors d'oeuvres, was a mix of East African–inspired cuisine and good old New England fare. Deirdre had arranged for a top chef from Boston to oversee the staff at the club.

"Let's try the lobster mac-and-cheese bites. I hear the meat is fresh off the boat," said Judith. Eliza searched her mother-in-law's face for signs of irony, but Judith's expression was sphinxlike.

"Okay," Eliza said, even though sometimes the thought of eating lobster seemed cannibalistic, like she was eating one of her own children.

As they waited for another waiter to come by with food they considered each other.

"Eliza, are you crying?"

"I know," Eliza said. "I shouldn't, I'll ruin my makeup. I never wear this much eyeliner, I never should have—"

"Don't worry about the makeup," said Judith. "That's my advice to you and to girls and women everywhere: never worry about the makeup." She said that with a face full of Estée Lauder, but at least she said it. Judith handed Eliza a cocktail napkin with a Malawi flag printed on it.

Eliza closed her eyes and tried to see down the long tunnel that was the future, that was life going on and on and on, with its smooth patches and its bumpy patches and its messiness and chaos and beauty; she could even, she thought, see a time when she might feel okay about her father, when she might start to feel quite normal. Not yet, maybe not for a long time. But someday.

She opened her eyes and took another sip of African Sunrise. Almost empty. There was a waiter heading their way, palming a tray of fresh drinks.

"Lovely," breathed Judith. She removed two glasses and set them down on the table. "Since the very first time Rob brought you home I've been intimidated by you, Eliza."

Eliza choked on her next sip. She said, "Excuse me? *You* were intimidated by *me?*"

"Of course."

"Why?"

"Because, well, you're *intimidating.*"

"Me?"

"You're so smart, and, pardon the expression, but you really pulled yourself up by your bootstraps, and you work hard, and you know your way around a lobster boat and a scalpel, and you're an amazing mother . . ."

"Wow," said Eliza. The liquor made her bold and she said, "I thought I was the consolation prize. I thought you always wanted Rob to marry Kitty Sutherland. All these years, I thought you thought Rob married down."

"Kitty Sutherland is a moron with a twentieth of your personality. Kitty Sutherland would have been the consolation prize. Rob married *up,* my dear girl. Rob married up."

Judith tipped her glass toward Eliza, and Eliza tipped hers toward Judith, and they clinked lightly, though the sound was swallowed by the background noise, by the party for the East African children.

Maybe it was the cocktail making its way through her veins, or maybe it was the fact that Judith's white dress gave her a faintly religious air, but Eliza was beginning to feel something wash over her that might have been absolution.

The next morning, first thing when she woke up, she was going to find those papers from Phineas Tarbox's office, and she was going to sign the heck out of them.

"There but for," said Judith, taking a sip of the African Sunrise. Despite the white dress, the coiffed hair, the glittering rings and necklace, Eliza could see in her a teenager, long-legged and lighthearted, buoyant and free, her whole life ahead of her, running along a twilit beach on the Jersey Shore.

Eliza had never heard the quote shortened that way—that was nervy of Judith, like a lot of things about Judith were nervy: her hair and her clothing and her eyebrows and her attitude. But Eliza liked Judith's version. It fit. It made for a good ending.

Epilogue

Two weeks after Deirdre's gala, which netted sixty-two thousand dollars for East Africa Needs You, at approximately eight thirty one evening, Robert Barnes II got a call from one Nadine Edwards, who had just returned to Boston after spending the summer on the Vineyard.

She had received Rob's preliminary sketches for the home she was thinking of building in Naples, Maine. She was *smitten*. She simply *adored* lake culture; she thought it was quaint and genuine after so many summers of her life spent on the ocean. She thought pontoons were a fabulous and welcome change from yachts; she thought her grandchildren would leap at the chance to own a water trampoline they could access from the dock; her son was simply *dying* to do some serious hiking off the Kancamagus Highway. She was over the moon about the sketches. She couldn't wait to get started. Could he get her in by, say . . .

"No promises," said Rob. "I'm sorry."

"No promises," agreed Nadine Edwards, sounding only a little bit disappointed. "But maybe if you could just say that, at the *latest*—"

"I would love to work with you, Mrs. Edwards," said Rob, politely but firmly. "I'm so happy you liked the sketches. But I won't be able to say until the work is well under way when it might be complete."

Nadine was sorry Rob had had such a difficult time with Christine Cabot—Rob, Nadine was happy to share, was not the first person who had had a difficult time with Christine Cabot. Christine Cabot had fired her dog groomer, her hairdresser, her dry cleaner. Her landscaper, twice. Her driver. "She'd fire her kids if she could," confided Nadine. "I think she did fire one of them." ("I bet it was Jonathan Junior, the cokehead," said Eliza to Rob, later.) "I mean," continued Nadine, "I love her to pieces, but she is absolutely impossible to deal with. And I would love to hire you to build my house, Rob."

Rob considered this proposition. He felt a few things. He felt an instant solidarity with Nadine Edwards. He felt an urge to look immediately for GCs who had no relation to Mark Ruggman. He felt a touch of heartburn, from the scrumptious seafood risotto Eliza had made for dinner that night. And he felt something else, something blooming inside of him, something that at first was difficult to identify. But after a moment it became obvious: it was the certainty of his own good fortune.

———

Andi and Daphne were determined to keep The Cup open through the whole of the winter even though there were days when they had not a single customer. Three days after the start of the new year, Mary was sitting at table twelve at The Cup with Andi, who was teaching her to do the bookkeeping, when she felt a dull ache that radiated around her belly. It went away, and then it came back again, more insistently, a seizing, aching pain deep inside. "Um," she said. "Andi?" She gasped.

"Oh, *shit,*" said Andi. "Holy shit, Mary, is it happening?"

Mary nodded and whispered, "I think so. I mean, I don't know. But I think so?"

Twelve hours later, in the obstetrics wing of Maine Coast Memorial in Ellsworth, in a room with pale green walls, Mary gave birth to Patrick Charles Brown. ("I would have named him Charlie," said Mary. "But come *on,* I can't do that to him. Charlie Brown.") Patrick weighed six pounds and two ounces and his blood type was O positive and his eyes were indigo and he had a set of lungs on him like you wouldn't believe—the nurses said they thought his screams could be heard in Bangor and beyond.

Mary's body recovered quickly from the birth, the way teenage bodies do, and she was back to her old slip of a self in no time at all. ("Not fair," said Vivienne, but she was making googly eyes at Patrick while she said it.)

Daphne and Andi permitted Mary to bring Patrick Charles to The Cup during the slow midwinter days, and, if all went well, they were going to allow the same thing when things picked up.

"It'll get better, come summer," said Daphne a minimum of four times a day.

"No question," agreed Andi.

Trap Day came in April, and the boats filled the harbor once again.

Then Memorial Day arrived, and the summer people started to come back, and then it was June, and then the season was in full swing.

"I told you it would happen," said Daphne.

"*I* told *you*," said Andi.

Patrick grew too big to stay in his little car seat, so Daphne bought a Pack 'n Play for him and Andi stocked it with toys and he played in there making his lovely little baby noises and giving the customers something to smile at. Often the customers thought he was Andi and Daphne's baby, and Mary didn't mind that.

When Vivienne wasn't working at A Cut Above she came and took Patrick for walks by the harbor to look at the boats, or fed him little spoonfuls of the mushed-up organic food that Andi and Daphne insisted he eat. Vivienne remembered a surprising amount about babies and there were certain times when only she could quiet Patrick—she did a little rocking thing with him over one shoulder that was pure magic.

This is not to say things were not difficult for Mary sometimes. No matter how much help she had she was still a young, single mother who never had enough money and who always felt the great weight of responsibility pressing down on her slender shoulders and who sometimes got really scared about the future and who sometimes cried in the dark hours of the morning when Patrick had gone back to sleep and she hadn't. But she was managing.

Sometimes Mary jumped when the door to the café opened, especially if she was in charge on her own, remembering the time Josh had come in and Charlie Sargent had saved her.

Mary thought about Charlie Sargent a lot, at the most unexpected times, and in some way she felt that Patrick, although he was a fatherless boy with four mothers, had a real and true father guiding him along, and ushering Mary into this unexpected adulthood she'd found herself in. Mary Brown wasn't religious and she didn't believe in any god, but sometimes she directed into the universe a message of gratitude for all she'd been given, and that could have been considered a prayer.

And maybe—who knew?—someday the door would open and somebody would walk into the café who would smile at Mary and cause a particular thump in her chest, and her universe would tilt, but she had loads of time for that, and maybe she didn't need that at all. Anyway, for now she had everything she needed, and then some.

When Charlie Sargent had been gone for six months and Zoe and Evie were well settled into the school year and their activities and Rob was hard at work Eliza saw a flyer on a bulletin board at the Barton Public Library advertising for hospice volunteers. Cell phones were not permitted in the Barton Public Library, but Eliza took hers out anyway and surreptitiously snapped a photo of the flyer. The librarian behind the reference desk shot her a disapproving look, but Eliza just smiled and tucked her phone back into her bag.

It took Eliza over a month to make the call. Then, after she did, it took her six weeks to complete the mandatory thirty hours of training. By the time she had done so it was almost summer all over again and she was busy organizing the girls' camps and activities and making sure Rob had plenty of time to travel back and forth to the property in Naples, Maine, where he was in the middle of overseeing construction of Nadine Edwards's summer home, which was exactly five hundred square feet larger than Cabot Lodge, and whose patio placement required no filling in for the slope of the land.

So it wasn't until September that Eliza was able to dedicate the required five to eight hours a week to her hospice volunteer duties.

She held the hand of an eighty-four-year-old pancreatic cancer patient while the light went out of her eyes. She sat by the bedside of a seventy-eight-year-old man suffering from Parkinson's who could hardly swallow. She helped record the childhood memories of a sixty-one-year-old man whose liver transplant had failed and who wasn't eligible for another. She gave primary caregivers a break to run errands or cook dinner or even sit in a café with a book for half an hour and know that their loved ones were not alone.

Eliza wasn't the medical expert in any of these cases—she deferred to the hospice nurses, as her training had dictated, and she never mentioned her time in medical school. The deaths she saw in other people's homes were not the first she'd seen, of course, but she realized that she was seeing them now through a different lens, and that some were awful, and some were peaceful, and that the best two things people could have at the end of their lives were a say in how it all went down and somebody to be with them so that they were not alone, so that they were not afraid of the dark.

By then Deirdre was busy starting work on the next EANY gala. Even though Brock had eventually agreed that Deirdre could look into adopting an East African baby, Deirdre had decided that she could help more children by helping all the children. That's what she told the world, but privately she told Eliza that she didn't think she had it in her, to start from scratch again with the diapers, the middle-of-the-night wake-ups, the teething. She sort of felt (she whispered) like Brock had called her bluff.

"I don't know *how* you do it," said Deirdre every time she and Eliza got together, about the hospice work. "I don't know how you can be around all of that sadness when you don't need to."

"It just feels like the right place to be," said Eliza. It was hard to explain to anyone, so she didn't really try, but if she had to condense it into a single word she would have said that it felt like *homage.*

The Barnes's newish dog—found, of course, by Evie—was a brown-haired, crooked-eared mix named Jupiter whose scraggly little body contained so many different breeds it was really difficult to pick out even one. Jupiter was in training to be a hospice paws volunteer. He was enthusiastic and he was trying really hard, but he had a little work to do in the patience category before he was ready to take his act on the road. He'd get there, said the trainer. He obviously had the heart for it.

ACKNOWLEDGMENTS

Lindsay Mazotti, Molly Burnett, and Bob Truog, all physicians, were incredibly generous with their medical expertise. Dave Considine and Brad Mascott were equally so with their sailing and boating knowledge, as was Phil Bennett of the Hinckley yacht company. Cathy Burnett shared personal details of her husband Bob Burnett's battle with glioblastoma with me and I am grateful to her for that. Jennifer Thibodeau and Victoria Abbott from Maine Family Planning procured the proper medical advice and appointments for one of my characters. Lisa DeStefano of DeStefano Architects shared her professional expertise, as did Judy Anderson of Alexander Haas. Sue Santa Maria and Priscilla Hare put me up in their beautiful home in Owls Head, Maine, and fed me when I first started this book and needed a few days away. Kelly Doucette and Lisa Broten helped with legal matters in the story. The other member of the Newburyport Writers' Club, Katie Schickel, always offers invaluable friendship and a professional sounding board. The members of the Newburyport Mom Squad: you know who you are, and you rock. Besides being two of the best besties out there, Jennifer Truelove and Margaret Dunn are always ready to name a boat or a lighthouse, complete a metaphor, or share a laugh or a trip. In addition, Margaret offered just the right editorial insight at just the right time. Elise Willingham helped keep the household moving for much of the past year.

Phillip Torrey, who fishes out of Winter Harbor, Maine, answered so many of my questions about the world of lobster fishing with such delightful detail and enthusiasm that I feel ready to apply for a lobster fishing license myself. (Not really—don't worry, state of Maine.) I am grateful for Phillip's patience and expertise, and I admire the hard work he and all of the fishermen up and down the coast do day after day in all sorts of conditions. The book *How to Catch a Lobster in Down East Maine* by Christina Lemieux Oragano also shed a lot of light on the world.

Thank you to the team at Doubleday for their hard work all around. My editor, Melissa Danaczko, is brilliant, patient, forgiving, and always willing to push a little harder to make a book better. Every writer needs that. Margo Shickmanter, a talented editor in her own right, scooped up many dangling pieces of story line and kept the details in order, and Mark Lee and Lauren Hesse kept publicity and marketing moving in the right direction. My agent, Elisabeth Weed of The Book Group, is a formidable presence in the agenting world and at the same time a warm, supportive, and absolutely necessary part of my writing life. Thank you always to my in-laws, Cheryl Moore and the Destrampe family. I never thought I would thank my parents, John and Sara Mitchell, for moving me to Down East Maine my *senior year* in high school (I've almost gotten over it), but I can safely say that without that experience this book would not exist and so for that and many other reasons I thank them. My sister, Shannon Mitchell, is a tireless cheerleader and a generous and loving aunt. My daughters, Addie, Violet, and Josie, are endless sources of amusement— and sometimes bemusement—and also laundry, love, inspiration, and support. I began this book years ago, put it down for a good long while, and eventually came back to it. My husband Brian's belief in it and in me never wavered, and for that and pretty much everything else he does and is I count myself the luckiest of the lucky.

As I was finishing the final edits on this book my father-in-law, Frank Moore, lost his battle with lung cancer. I conceived this book and wrote most of it before he became ill, but now I see that some of the best qualities of Frank and some of the best qualities of the character of Charlie Sargent echo each other—hardworking men who loved their families and lived lives that might have looked quiet from the outside but brimmed over from the inside. I like to think of the spirits of both living on.

ABOUT THE AUTHOR

Meg Mitchell Moore is the author of the novels *The Admissions,*
The Arrivals, and *So Far Away.* She worked for several years as a
journalist for a variety of publications. She lives in Newburyport,
Massachusetts, with her husband and their three daughters.